# HAVE YOU MET NORA?

Also by Nicole Blades

*The Thunder Beneath Us*

Published by Kensington Publishing Corp.

# HAVE YOU MET NORA?

## NICOLE BLADES

KENSINGTON PUBLISHING CORP.

www.kensingtonbooks.com

DAFINA BOOKS are published by

Kensington Publishing Corp.
119 West 40th Street
New York, NY 10018

All Kensington titles, imprints, and distributed lines are available at special quantity discounts for bulk purchases for sales promotion, premiums, fund-raising, educational, or institutional use.

Special book excerpts or customized printings can also be created to fit specific needs. For details, write or phone the office of the Kensington Sales Manager: Kensington Publishing Corp., 119 West 40th Street, New York, NY 10018. Attn. Sales Department. Phone: 1-800-221-2647.

Dafina and the Dafina logo Reg. U.S. Pat. & TM Off.

eISBN-13: 978-1-4967-0462-7
eISBN-10: 1-4967-0462-2
First Kensington Electronic Edition: November 2017

ISBN-13: 978-1-4967-0461-0
ISBN-10: 1-4967-0461-4
First Kensington Trade Paperback Printing: November 2017

10 9 8 7 6 5 4 3 2

Printed in the United States of America

*For Scott,*
*my listener, my love*

# HAVE YOU
# MET NORA?

# CHAPTER 1

Nora opened her eyes and stared through the darkness at the ceiling. Three twenty-eight, she thought, before rolling up off her back a little and craning her neck to look just past Fisher's shoulders at the blue numbers on the clock by his nightstand. He was dead asleep, the rhythmic flow of his deep breathing like white noise. The numbers gleamed: 3:41 AM. Close enough, she thought, and returned to the ceiling. Although Nora had long been an early riser—she couldn't remember a time when she had slept later than the sun—this was different.

She eased the covers off and slid out from under Fisher's muscled arm, moving slow and steady toward the edge of the bed. She hopped down, landing with a soft thud, and then froze, shifting her eyes back to Fisher. No change. Not even a break in the beat. Nora grabbed her iPhone and padded along the hall. The moon, pushing through the floor-to-ceiling windows of the penthouse, provided more than enough light for Nora to find the handle to the mini champagne fridge that Fisher bought for her last year. Nora gave the half-drunk bottle of Armand de Brignac—a gift from a client—her deepest bow with prayer hands before grabbing it and shutting the fridge door with her foot. She pulled the orange stopper from the bottle, letting it drop to the floor, and started typing into her phone on her way to the bathroom at the far end of the penthouse. Nora waited until she was inside the empty, freestanding tub before taking her first, long swig from the bottle. She rested her phone on the ledge of the tub and pressed a button on a remote that sent the massive blinds skyward. Nora stayed there in the empty basin, soaking in the city's glow, and waited.

Her phone buzzed and vibrated against the acrylic. She took another sip before answering it.

"What the hell is wrong with you?" a croaky voice said.

Nora shook her head. "I'm just—"

"Nervous? You're just nervous, hon. It's pre-wedding jitters. You're fixin' to get married to that gorgeous, big-dicked, super-hot bastard in twenty-two—no, *twenty-one days* and you're feeling anxious. That's all. No Biggie Smalls."

"Jenna, I'm sitting in an empty tub, pounding old champagne *straight from the bottle,* and staring out the fucking window. Do you really think it's necessary to remind me that there are twenty-two days—"

"Technically it's twenty-one—"

"Jesus, fine, twenty-one days. It's twenty-one days before the wedding. I'm aware. My whole entire body is aware. We're all very aware."

"Deep breaths, sweetheart. You're freaking out. This is what freaking out looks like on all normal women," Jenna said. Her Southern twang, though soft, still tickled Nora. "You're just different. It's foreign territory for you."

Nora stopped mid-swig, her arm wobbling and then dropping with the weight of the bottle into her lap. "What does *that* mean?" she said, squinting her eyes and bracing her body.

"Nothing, just, I don't know. . . . I mean, you're always even and calm; it's preternatural," Jenna said. "No matter what's going on, you're on like perma-chill. It's automatic for you. No headless chicken stuff." A chuckle. "It's why we kept calling you I.Q. when we first met you. Ice Queen."

Jenna's full creaky cackle made Nora move the phone away from her ear and level it on the ledge of the tub. She could still hear Jenna from that distance, but pushed Speaker anyway and went back to drinking her champagne. Nora reclined, cradling the bottle into her chest. "Ice Queen? Seriously? And here I was thinking you were dazzled by my smarts."

"Oh, we were. Totally. By your smarts, for sure, and also your long legs, your frat-boy mouth, your perky tits, them Kelly Ripa arms, and your entire wardrobe, *espesh* the shoes. Plus, you speak fluent French—I mean, *fucking French*—and you're the first white girl I've ever met who can actually dance. Like, legit, Beyoncé backup dancer dance. Need I go on?"

"Yes, you need. Come on, I'm practically perfect," Nora said, the beginnings of a laugh tickling her throat.

"Practically?" Jenna said, yawning. "Okay, so we've thoroughly covered your Boss Bitch status. It's why Fish is locking you down so fast, while those eggs are still viable." Nora's expanding grin disappeared, replaced by a clenched jaw and gnashed teeth. "What I need clarity on is: Why are you dry-tub drinking again?"

"How did you know I'm in the tub?"

"Echoes, booby. Also, you said so earlier. Either way, I've got you pretty much figured out. You're not the QB on this play. What's the wedding planner's name again, Gloria? Glenda? Whatever. *She's* the quarterback. She's the one calling all the plays, and you're watching from the sidelines and it's driving you *bananz.*"

"First, are you talking sports at me?"

"A little," Jenna said through her teeth.

"You're still hooking up with that sports writer guy?"

"A little."

"Wait, isn't he the one who sent you the dick pic when you asked to see his new coffee table?"

"Well, it was pretty impressive . . . *the coffee table.*"

"Jesus, Jenna. What needs to happen to get you out of these dating app traps? Nothing but Dumpster fires on there."

"Hold up, I met Sports Guy the old-school way, my dear: at a bar, not on a dating app," Jenna said. "You kidding me? My filters are *tight*. He would've never made the cut."

"What about the one who called you from rehab on what was supposed to be your third date?"

"Oh, that whole thing was about me trying to be charitable. I'm from Texas. It's how we do."

"Father-God, you need prayer," Nora said, closing her eyes and leaning her head back in the tub.

"You sound like my sister's nanny, Bernadette. She says that all the time about those twins: *Fahdah-Gowd,*" Jenna said, mangling it. "She's from Trinidad, I think. No, St. Kitts. One of those islands. But you got that accent down solid. So many tricks in your little black hat, woman."

Nora sat up straight, her eyes popping open as if called by a siren. The empty champagne bottle clanked against the bathtub.

"Oh, God, did you just fall asleep on me?" Jenna said, chuckling.

"No, I didn't. . . . I should go, though."

"Thought we were fixin' to talk about wedding planner Glenda."

"It's Grace, and no, we weren't *fixin' tuh* do anything, Dolly-wood," Nora said. She placed the bottle on the floor and curled her knees up into herself, burying her forehead and trembling chin into them.

Jenna's tone got sharper and the grogginess dissipated. "First of all, Ms. Dolly Parton is from Tennessee. Secondly, you know the Texas comes out when I'm tired or drunk. And third, are you, like, mad at me because I forgot the wedding planner's name?"

Nora knew her voice could not be trusted right then, that it would likely betray her and reveal too much. She swallowed hard, and once more, and again. The vein by her left temple pulsated. It was long, bluish, and exposed itself when she was angry. Nora's mother said she got it from her deadbeat father. The vein, piercing green eyes, and a surname—Mackenzie— are the only things she inherited from the vanished man. Nora needed to push all that was rising up just behind her tongue back down to the underneath, the subterranean pit where these kinds of things were free to unfold, to fester, and to die.

"Are you serious right now?" Jenna said.

Nora extended an arm to the phone, her finger hovering over the button to end the call. Her mind flashed forward to her next steps, but nothing was clear or sensible. Then, as fast as it came, the tumult in her brain was gone. Her heartbeat quieted; she relaxed her muscles, took a deep breath to quell her knotted stomach, and fixed her face, like her mother always told her to do. The morph ended with a light clearing of her throat. "Sorry, J. I was reading a couple emails," she said, faking a yawn. The sound of Jenna's long exhale only made Nora's shoulders relax even more. "What were we talking about?"

"About how many sheep just jumped over the fence," Jenna said. "Go to bed, Nora—your real bed, the one with the man in it."

"Yeah, it's crazy late. Thanks for listening, Callaway." Nora rolled her eyes but maintained the brightness in her voice.

"It's what we do," Jenna said. "Good night, moon."

"G'night."

Fisher traced the length of Nora's body first with his eyes, then the back of his fingers. When he reached the top of her head again, he massaged her temple and brushed back her hair from her damp cheek. Nora, feigning sleep, tried to maintain a natural breathing pattern and keep her body still, especially her eyelids that twitched under the pressure of the tears pooling behind. Nora wanted to turn and look up at him, be awakened by him, and surrender to his lifting her out from the cold hollowness of the bathtub, carrying her back to their bed. But she couldn't; she wasn't *her* yet. She wasn't Nora Mackenzie.

His touch was warm, gentle. For no clear reason, in that moment, the touch reminded Nora of that of Dr. Bourdain's in the earliest days, back when he was still the husband half of the kindest couple—and her mother's employer—who saw something special, "a spark," in young Nora; back when he still looked at her as a girl, a child to guide and tutor, instead of a viable conquest to seduce.

"Babe," Fisher said. "Mack, wake up. What are you doing in here?" He lightly squeezed Nora's shoulders.

She flinched.

The ruse could not play on. Nora opened her eyes partway and rolled her head toward Fisher. He was wearing only underwear, and his brawny torso glistened in the moonlight spilling through the window. "Hey," Nora said. The phlegm and tears from moments ago added frog and gurgle to her voice, lending a layer of drowsiness and veracity to her hoax. "Wow. What time is it?"

"It's late," Fisher said. He stroked her hair once more. Her eyes fluttered as she tried to blink away the memory of Dr. Bourdain's revolting touch. She rubbed her brows with the back of her hand, wanting to scrub the gross sensation of the old man's spotted paw on her with the very same swipe.

Nora sat up in the tub and breathed in her fiancé. "Sorry. I didn't want to wake you. I came in here to"—her eyes fell on the empty champagne bottle by his feet. "It's Jenna. Boy drama, again. And let's just say it required time, tears, and, of course, champers." Nora gestured to the bottle with her pinky. She was grinning at him in her way—their way. A smile curled up the side of Fisher's face and he stepped into the other end of the tub, rolling out his legs as best he could, encasing Nora. Fisher was here, not *him,* she reminded herself, and settled back in the tenderness of his embrace.

"*Champers,* huh?" he said, his smile stretching up to his bright eyes.

"Of the finest grade," Nora said, nodding.

"Full bottle?"

"Halfway," Nora said.

Fisher pulled his legs, along with Nora, closer and leaned into her face, speaking barely above a whisper. "Tipsy?"

"Mmm. Halfway," she said, matching his hush. He dragged Nora onto his lap, making her straddle him. "What's next, Mr. Beaumont?" Nora said, leaving her lips pursed and arching her body into him.

Fisher took a deep breath and let it out slowly, looking up at his Nora, at her lips, her long neck, the bones along her collar, and then down the deep V of her top, at her hard nipples pressing through the thinness. He rested his forehead between her breasts, and Nora caressed the back of his head, patting the dark blond hair at the nape. There was something off, something tired, resigned about him. Nora slid back so she could better see his eyes. "You okay?"

"That's what I'm wondering. About you."

Nora stifled her eye roll. "What do you mean—about me? What *about* me?" She lifted herself all the way off of his legs.

"Easy," Fisher said, tilting his head and raising his palm. "All I'm saying is, this is the third or fourth time I've found you in here—drinking, upset, sad. Look, I know my mother can be a bit much and . . . old school—"

"Lady Eleanor? Why would you think anything's wrong there?"

"I don't know. I keep thinking I should have never told you that whole story with Rock's first girlfriend . . . her being Asian and my mother's completely wrongheaded reaction to that and—"

"Your mother has been perfectly lovely. Has been since day one."

"Right, but you're white, so that ugliness isn't an issue here." Fisher shook his head. "Anyway, I just don't like seeing you so uneasy and not knowing what I can do to fix it for you. Is the wedding planning getting to be too much?"

"The wedding planning is tied up in a bow handcrafted by Grace and Co. It's all completely handled." Nora shrugged. "There's really nothing for me to even do."

"So, it's the wedding itself?" He placed his hand on Nora's foot. "Are these flawless things feeling a bit of a chill?"

Nora looked at Fisher, at his beautiful, soft face set with sharp edges—his nose, his chin, his jaw. She let her eyes rest on his sweet grin and the laugh lines gently etched into his creamy complexion, taking in all the majesty of him, and she decided right then to open a gate, just a hair, and let a slip of truth spill out. "No, I want to marry you," Nora said. "It's just that it doesn't feel like that. It doesn't feel like it's me marrying you and you me. It's this bigger, grander thing set on a bigger, grander stage with the photographers trailing everywhere, the online stories, and all the speculation and talking about *every little detail*. Jesus, this town always needs to know everything about you, your family. It's just so public. I'm not into being public. You know that."

Fisher reached out to calm Nora's teetering head with a gentle stroke of her cheek. "Mack, I get it. I get it. It's a lot. But," he said with an easy shrug, "I'm a Beaumont. It's always going to be a lot. And I don't want to come across like an asshole here, but you're going to be a Beaumont, too, love; you need better skin. Like my father told me and his told him, and back and back centuries all the way to France: We can't show cracks. We can't have them seeing any cracks on us."

Nora's chuckle came out like a sneeze. She felt the snot edging out of her nose, but did nothing about it. She instantly regretted starting down this line with Fisher. Showing cracks and better skin and France—she didn't want to hear any more about it and was desperate to end the whole interaction. *You don't get it,* that's what she wanted to say, because he didn't. Instead, Nora nodded and smiled brightly at her fiancé. He squeezed the top of her arm, kissing her face and stepping out of the tub in one smooth movement.

"Come back to bed," he said, and tipped his head toward the door. He was standing with his hands resting on his trim middle and his body squared, the only thing missing, a red cape flapping behind him.

"In a bit. I want to just clean up," Nora said, nodding and smiling once more. "I smell like subway homeless." She paused, off his look. "The subway . . . it's this mode of transpo, kind of like a train, only underground . . . totally out of your scope."

"You'd be surprised by the kind of underground things in my scope," he said, smirking and shaking his head. "Just come to bed, smartass. I'll wait up—for a bit. But word to the wise: Leave the *champers* out here." Fisher turned and glided out of the room. The minute he cleared the door and his footsteps were at a proper distance, Nora popped out of the tub and made her swift way to the closet just outside the bathroom. She slid the door open as quiet as possible and stooped down to ease a flat box partway out from the lowest shelf. Nora peeled back the dusty quilt draped over it and slowly cracked open the topside of the box wide enough to slip her hand in. She still knew exactly where to go, how to navigate blindly through the clutter and grab it by its dog-eared corner. Nora went back to the bathroom, a photograph clutched close to her chest. She looked behind her, listening for any stirring from Fisher.

Silence.

Nora went straight to the farthest corner of the whistle-clean bathroom with all its white and height and steely, modern edges, and she squeezed her body tight into the space where the glass and wall met, her forehead pressed against the cool of it while she angled her face to look out the window and steady her mind. Nora only dragged this photo out when she was at the lowest point on her rope, deciding whether to let go or pull herself up again.

The picture was from that long-ago Christmas, one of the first in the Westmount mansion. In it, posed by the lavish, heavily decorated tree, stood a smiling young Nora, her mother, and the Bourdains. It was the photo Nora used to love, the one she had pinned to the corkboard above her frilly, pink-and-white-everything bed in her pink-and-white-everything bedroom in the Bourdains' basement. There were two bedrooms, a bathroom, and a cozy nook off the side of the small, basic kitchen down there. It was the basement, Nora knew, but no one in the house ever called it that. It was *the flat* according to the Bourdains, and *our place* to hear Nora's mother tell it. Warm and reasonably bright, it was a considerable step up from where Nora and her mother came. Although Nora's memory of their cramped, crappy beginnings was limited—they moved in with the Bourdains when she turned six—she could still recall, with a woeful precision, the moldy, dank stench soaked into the walls of their old *fall-apart-ment*.

Three years after that photograph was taken, it was folded into a tight square and shoved into the toe box of an ugly shoe Nora had long outgrown. The picture needed to be out of her sight, its specialness completely destroyed, after that one vile summer evening when Nora went to Dr. Bourdain's fourth-floor study with a message from her mother: "Will your company tomorrow require something more substantial than the trimmed sandwiches with the tea?"

Nora, then a freshly turned nine-year-old who rarely paid close attention to her mother's directives, jumbled it. She skipped over the longer words, boiling it down to what she felt was the crux: "Do you desire more for your company tomorrow?"

Dr. Bourdain, a man of great intellect and refinement, knew what the girl meant, but he didn't reply. Not right away. Instead, he let his eyes linger on Nora, on her lanky body, for too long. Instead, he asked Nora to go into the alcove off to his left and fetch a book shelved low on the built-ins. Instead, he sidled up behind her as she stooped, and brushed then pressed his pelvis on Nora's shoulder, on her head, sweeping her thick, wavy hair from one side to the next. She felt the sick twitching in his dress pants against her ear, her jaw. Nora froze, unable to process anything beyond the books' titles on their spines. She kept her eyes locked on them. And as the speed of his repulsive rubbing increased, Nora could only recite the titles in her mind on a slow loop.

*The Flowers of Evil. In Search of Lost Time. The Red and the Black. Notre-Dame de Paris. Remembrance of Things Past.*

Looking down at the photograph now, the creases dingy, worn, and cracked, Nora could still make out the top part of Dr. Bourdain's face behind the black ink splotch. She shook her head, disgusted at herself anew, thinking about the countless times she nearly tore the picture to crumbs or burned it or threw it down a sewer grate. But it was always *nearly, almost, not all the way,* because she knew that obliterating the picture did nothing to erase what happened. All of it—the scrape of his calloused palms along her inner thighs; the set-in stench of tobacco on his clothes; the low, persistent rumble in his heaving chest as he twitched and trembled behind her—it was never going away.

Nora swallowed hard and reached for her phone, still balancing on the narrow edge of the tub. She stared at the web page for a moment before squeezing her eyes shut and swallowing once more. She scrolled down to the bottom of the short post, the same one that had haunted her for the past eighteen hours, and quietly—barely moving her lips—read the last lines again: *Dr. Bourdain is survived by his loving wife, Elise, and adopted daughter, Nora (estranged). He was preceded in death by his parents, Jacques P. Bourdain and Odette V. Bourdain, as well as his brother, Anton J. Bourdain. In lieu of flowers, memorials may be sent to the Montreal Heart Institute.*

Nora's stomach lurched into her throat as she clutched the phone and photograph in each hand. After a long breath, she grabbed the champagne from the floor—the picture wrapped around the bottle's neck—as she stepped into the tub, took a long swig, and collapsed back into the sunken middle.

# CHAPTER 2

Still battling a headache and dry mouth from bathtub drinking the night before, Nora almost didn't show up at The Chestnut. But she knew that flaking was not an option, not with Jenna. She also knew that skipping out on their weekly lunch meet-up would only push her best friend deeper into wedding-jitters-something-ain't-right theorizing.

Wednesday afternoons were reserved for Snack Time with Jenna. The snacks were always mini dinners—full-cut steaks, whole pizzas, raw bar towers, burrito platters—and the food themes were always decided upon by Jenna at the start of the month. These were in no way meal replacements. ("Listen, from my G-cup tits to my size-eleven shoes, I'm a Real Bitch, and I eat real food," she explained, after Nora balked at her habit that first time.) The way it worked was: Jenna would have lunch with the other editors and publishing folks at noon sharp, clockwork, and then an afternoon snack with her best friend, Nora, somewhere "far enough from these Midtown monkeys, please," which usually meant Brooklyn.

Nora arrived at the restaurant early and glided over to the bar to order her drink, the one perfect for a Wednesday afternoon: a French 75. And there she stood surrounded by an assorted box of special artisanal Brooklyn hipsters, waiting between the silence and noise, staring out through the window. Although Nora could feel the many eyes on her, this long, corn-silk blond beauty poised like a ballerina about to take flight in a grand jeté, she actively ignored them, pushed them to the blurred periphery, and tried to look unconcerned about anyone or anything. This was a skill she honed in middle school, when stares and sneers were aimed at her almost hourly. She checked the clock on her phone. Jenna was late, which was not her style.

Nora met Jenna Callaway shortly after moving to New York City to launch her own reimagined life. They were both at an exclusive investment banking event—two of only five women there. Nora was shadowing Vincent Dunn, her ever-fabulous mentor and fashion fairy godfather.

"Did you get a load of that fucking giant gray tooth?" were the first words Jenna had said to Nora that night. She was in between sips of her short, iceless drink and gawking at a curvy woman hanging off the arm of a saggy, older man. "I can't stop looking at it. Every time she opens her mouth, I stare at it like it's going to tell me something about the future."

"She's a toothsayer," Nora said, surprised at how easy she slipped back into high school mode. She shook her head, slightly disappointed with herself.

That's when Jenna unleashed her laugh—a roar, really—and grabbed on to Nora's shoulder as she folded over, red-faced and hollering, "Oh, my God! *Toothsayer!* The best!" After more gasps and bellowing, she righted herself and looked into Nora's face. "Honey, you're the best. But you already knew that. We need to know each other forever. Let's go get a snack after this," Jenna told Nora.

Jenna was at the event with her editor, hoping to sway a young banker known as the Dog Star of Wall Street to publish his book with them. She was this hard-shelled Texan from old money and oil, with thick brown hair and broad shoulders, a full body, and a healthy cackle to match. Watching Jenna move through the investment banker room, slicing people's necks with one steely-eyed glance, Nora was instantly transported to Vermont and the Immaculate Heart School. Jenna's all-black ensemble morphed into the kick pleat tartan skirt, white shirt, vest with school crest, and gray socks pulled to the knee. Even with her curves barely encased in the uniform, Jenna would have still sweat confidence and cool, wearing Clark Kent–style glasses and a fashion-forward short, blunt bang to set off her severe blue eyes. All hard lines and sharp edges, she reminded Nora of her best friend from boarding school: Emily Beck, the very blond and very rich media heiress, who was the mean, raw, feared flip side to Nora's kind, sweet, and revered high school avatar. Like Emily, Jenna didn't leave space for the feelings of others.

In Nora's mind, Jenna was going to be fun and temporary. But she continued the night aligned with Nora's every step, pushing out more statements, no question marks, about their wonderful, freshly minted friendship and about what good things would happen next for the two of them.

The rigorous rattle of ice in the bartender's shaker broke Nora's thoughts and pulled her back into now: waiting for Jenna, still. Nora checked the time on her phone again, which in itself annoyed her. She didn't like to appear perturbed or pressed, so she slid the phone under the square napkin next to her drink. She swept her hair over her shoulder with full flair, allowing her to take a quick scan of the room with her head toss. Her eyes landed on the good-looking black man she had seen at The Chestnut a handful of times over the last few weeks. She noticed him each time. Couldn't help it. More than dapper or handsome, the man had a soaked-in cool and a captivating energy that rested on his shoulders. Nora would steal looks at him, in his bespoke suits and high-shine polished shoes, firmly shaking hands and slapping backs. She even marked how his beard, tinged with gray, was getting fuller and settling into his face, looking as if it always belonged right there. He would move through the tight backroom with an easy familiarity like he had lived there once before.

It was always his suits that plucked at her attention most. And this one Nora recognized instantly: blue pinstripe, wool, three-piece, Gucci, Fall 2017. She had placed her hand on the actual fabric years earlier on a stop-off in Florence en route to men's fashion week in Milan.

For the last four years, she had worked exclusively with the city's wealthiest young men—the new guard of founders, investors, owners, and actors—styling them, reinventing them, suiting them up for their best moments over and again; each of them trusting her word and infallible taste, and paying her just as handsomely as she dressed them.

It was how she got together with Fisher Charles Beaumont. Like anyone living in the Tri-State, Geneva, or London, Nora knew his name. She knew the lofty titles: heir, magnate, famous bachelor, and philanthropist, of course. When he breezed into her atelier alone, no assistants, no handlers, she noticed his eyes first—so bright and adoring. She drifted down to his wide grin and then moved along to the rest of him, studying each element of his spell. She had met him for the first time earlier that week and he was following through on the "see you soon" line he tossed off when they parted. Even with his undeniable swagger, he blushed when they shook hands this time, too. Nora always remembered that. And neither of them could keep a straight face with the sweet glances volleying between them like a worn tennis ball. By the time he asked her out on an official date on their second stylist appointment, Nora knew she was done, smitten, full but still going back for more. She tried to continue on as his stylist, personally pulling looks for him and even flying out to Givenchy headquarters in Paris once to get a pinstripe tuxedo from Riccardo Tisci's capsule collection of evening pieces for Fisher's special presentation in Geneva. After that, they both agreed to dissolve their work relationship.

"You're firing me, aren't you?" Fisher said, tilting his head up at Nora. He was lying in her lap as she finger-combed his hair.

She looked down at him and nodded. "I went to Paris . . . for a suit . . . for you. I don't do that. For *anyone*."

"But you did," he said, winking. "For me."

Nora playfully pressed her hand into his scalp. "Exactly. This is textbook nepotism. I can't have that kind of conflict of interest in my business. I take this shit seriously."

And she did. Nora knew the fabrics, the yarns and thread counts, and moreover, she understood the psychology of fashion, why these moneyed men chose that pant made of wool from a family-owned mill in Italy; that jacket, a careful blend of wool, viscose, and silk; and the burnished walnut leather of this pair of brogues. Her enviable stylist life had taken her around the globe so much that the sparkle and giddy of jetting off to Italy and Paris and Hong Kong had long since evaporated. Her interests moved over to Fisher, falling in love with him. It almost surprised Nora how quickly it became just work.

But seeing this particular suit on this particular man in The Chestnut, it was made fresh and new all over again; it crackled, popped, and glistened on him. Nora realized she broke her own hardened rule about staring at other people when the suit—and the grinning man wearing it—started walking toward her. Unlike so many other men who had approached Nora over the years, this one was unflustered. He seemed almost heedless of her beauty, immune to the piercing shimmer of her green eyes or the glow of her skin, and instead just rested his gaze upon her as if she were plain and regular. As far back as Nora could remember—before Fisher, before James, before Wyatt, or even Daniel, the son of the Bourdains' gardener, and all the other curious neighborhood boys who would routinely sneak Nora through backdoors under the thick dark of night and into the basements of their parents' Westmount mansions—getting a guy to fall for her was easy. She didn't need to plan or think it through, it would just happen, fast and fluent.

This felt different. Strange. Wrong. And Nora was nervous behind it. With each step the man and his suit took, the timbre of her thumping heart got clearer. She would be a married woman in less than a month's time—a married Beaumont woman, specifically—and that meant something more than taking a new surname. (She had already done that before.) But becoming Mrs. Fisher Charles Beaumont, well, that refinement would bring a greater shift, one that Nora had been wanting throughout all her other lives.

The Beaumonts of Manhattan were a known and venerable brand. Nora had heard the name for the first time shortly after she stepped off the bus at Port Authority. She read about their black-tie galas and deep-pocket fund-raising events in the Style section of the *Times,* learning more details about their beginnings with each printed story.

Wealthy and respected dating back to its storied French pedigree, the Beaumont family sailed stateside as the nineteenth century was nearing its end, settling in New York City and quickly expanding its fortune by adding luxury goods and cosmetics to its steady, if unglamorous, ball bearings empire. Nora was surprised to see the brand names of some of Mrs. Bourdain's European favorites—the plush leather handbags, expensive lipsticks and fragrances, and even her ever-elegant, flared-hem trench coat—on the list of the Beaumonts' major subsidiaries. (Of course, with that level of affluence, there is also an assured arm reaching into philanthropy, namely, The

Beaumont Medical Institute, the largest private funding organization for biomedical research and helmed by Fisher with his
two surviving younger brothers, Irish twins Rockford and Asher,
working below him.) For Nora, becoming a Beaumont meant
most likely giving up her own stylist business and being a full-
time woman of the house like his brothers' wives. But the other
end of the sword meant her life would be whiter and brighter
and better than anything she had ever dreamed. She would finally be inside of something, accepted, *permanently,* and even
if disaster (i.e., divorce) visited their union, she would always
have the name, the trademark that showed the world she was
validated.

"Hi," the man said. "I'm Julius." The name slipped from his
mouth, with all of its swagger and chill, and rested on his smooth,
brown bottom lip like some homegrown brand of warmed-up
honey. He extended his hand into the charged air between them.
Nora slid hers into his warm grip. It felt good.

"I'm Nora Mackenzie. Beaumont," she said, then stuttering,
"well, wait—n-not yet . . . the Beaumont part. Soon, that'll be
it." Nora closed her eyes and dipped her head as if she had bit-
ten her tongue—wishing she had.

Julius smiled. "I think I got it."

As their handshake lingered, Nora nestled into it, saying his
name in her head like a lyric on repeat. She let her eyes rest on
him, the pleasantness of his features and frame, digesting the
whole of him. The last time—the only time—she felt such a
forceful, frightening pull toward another person was four years
ago when she first met Fisher. It was foreign then, this feeling
of being drawn in, so intense and out of hand. More com-
pelling than a mere wish, it was a want, to be closer than close,
to crawl right under the other person's skin and live there with
them—happy, full, and settled. And what made it truly power-
ful was that Fisher felt the exact same way about Nora; he professed this on the fourth day of knowing her.

When she was with Fisher, Nora could loosen her knotted insides and let her thoughts breathe; she didn't have to keep track of the threads of her intricately woven story. She could tell him the truth (most of it) about her past (most of it) and her indecorous ways. She shared with him her "fast" days with the neighborhood boys before getting shipped off to Catholic boarding school; her reign as honor roll beauty queen while there; her reckless wandering through Manhattan shortly after graduating; even her confession about the sobering threesome she had with Vincent and his bronze god-like fit model back when she first landed the job with Dunn Design—and it was met with what was tantamount to a shrug. Fisher didn't care about any of it.

"Those things, those moments, the people, they don't define you," he said. "They're ghosts, Mackenzie. They can't haunt you if you don't give them that power. Leave them in their boxes and live your life."

Their love came fast, but it was also very real, in a way that was strange and pure at once. For Nora, this meant feeling at ease and like herself—or as much as that was possible considering her special case.

But then the proposal came.

It was part of the après-ski in St. Moritz; Nora didn't suspect a thing. She had reached for her wineglass on the table behind her and turned back around to find Fisher on bended knee, with mist in his eyes and a green ring box in hand. The heat from Nora's wine-warmed belly spread to her face. She felt the thump of that vein by her temple, convinced that the blue thing was lit up like a fluorescent sign in a storefront window. She was in love with Fisher; there was no doubt in any part of her body. But she hadn't processed that loving a Beaumont could lead to becoming a Beaumont. At the time, she wasn't sure that she was ready for the weight of it. What she did know with certainty right then was this: If Fisher had been a banker, real-estate starter-mogul, or successful generic businessman, the urge to shut down and walk away would have been overwhelming.

But he wasn't any of those things. He was Fisher Beaumont, and he was there at her feet waiting for a one-word, sparkling answer. And so Nora made a willful choice to bury her apprehension deep beneath her gut and cover it over with a beaming grin and a shriek, "Yes!"

Then, three months after the grand proposal, something had sprouted in that buried-over plot in the center of her—a weed with tough roots—and it was spreading fast through her and Fisher's rarefied space, leaving Nora desperate like an animal with the tip of its tail caught in a vicious leg-hold trap and considering whether to gnaw it off and try to move through the world without it.

The fact that Julius was still gripping her hand—or was she holding on to his?—brought Nora back to the strange electricity of the present moment at the bar. She wanted to let go, end the handshake, but somehow couldn't.

"Actually, I know who you are," Julius said, looking sheepish. He tossed a glance toward the bartender. "Asked about you."

"Is that right?" Nora's back straightened and she clenched her jaw.

"Yeah, that's right. I need to be your client."

"My client?" Nora smirked and raised her brow at Julius's natty tweed jacket. "From my view, you're doing pretty well on your own."

"I can be impressive, at times."

"So what do you need from me?"

"Your edge, your mastery."

"*Mastery?* We are talking about menswear here, right?"

"Right." Julius unleashed his wide, bright smile and nodded slowly. "Do you have a card?"

"No, I don't do cards."

His grin grew wider. "Carrier pigeon?"

Nora smiled back. "Listen, Julius, I . . . I'm sure you're a good guy, a nice guy, but I can't"—she leaned away from him— "I'm . . . I'm with someone."

"Right. Beaumont. Fisher Beaumont."

Instinctively, Nora covered her ring finger with her thumb. A futile move; her tremendous engagement ring—a vintage Cartier, four-carat diamond set in an emerald halo—wasn't even on her finger. The heirloom was being resized, but because of its history and preciousness, that process took some time. "We'll definitely have it for you well before the wedding, Mr. Beaumont," the family jeweler had said, although Nora was sitting directly in his eye line, while Fisher stood off to her left. To anyone watching, Nora appeared clearly disappointed, anxious for the ring's safe return. But it was the first time since St. Moritz that Nora would be without the massive ring, and inside she felt relieved to have it off her finger.

Julius's soft chuckle stirred in his throat. "I have to say"—the laugh folded into a snicker—"I find you, what you're doing, interesting. But now, looking at you up close, I'm downright amazed . . . and low-key surprised by ol' Fisher Beaumont." He raised his glass to his lips. "Guess you can't assume, huh?"

The look he gave Nora drilled right through her skin and made it prickle. She knew exactly what he meant. Her mouth filled with cotton wool and a twitch started in her stomach. It happened so fast; she felt off-balance as the heat from her ears spread across her face. She knew that tears would arrive next but couldn't string together a clear enough thought to save herself from them.

Julius's smile dropped and an oddly scornful expression took its place. He moved to touch Nora's elbow, but she rocked back and away from him. His face morphed again; this time the kindness and warmth reappeared. "See, now, I didn't intend to upset you. I say shit not always thinking it through. I apologize." His smile pushed through. "You all right?"

Nora formed her mouth to say "I'm fine," but those words—and any others—were tangled up in the cotton wool.

A sound broke through the uncomfortable silence: the rattle and buzz of her cell phone vibrating against the bar top. Nora snatched it up without looking at the screen. She held up her index finger near Julius's face.

"What the hell, Nora?" barked the voice through the phone. "Jenna?"

"Uh, *yeah,* it's me, calling you like it's goddamn 2004, because you're acting like texts are not a real thing."

"Oh, I'm here. Waiting for you."

"No, *I'm* here. At Holy Moly. Waiting for *you.*"

"I thought we were doing Chestnut. I'm at Chestnut."

"It's pizza-snack, Nora. They do pizza at fucking Chestnut? Look. I'm here. I'm waiting. Get here. It's Snack Time," Jenna said, and hung up.

Nora, more grateful for Jenna and all her sourness than ever before, used the phone call as a ripcord and raced out of The Chestnut with the silent phone still pressed up to her ear, refusing to look back at Julius—the risk of turning into a pillar of salt was much too high.

———————◆●◆———————

Jenna was waiting at the door of Holy Moly Pizza with her arms crossed and her face bent. Before Nora could plant both feet out of the cab door, Jenna started in on her.

"Thin ice, you hear me?" She unfolded her arms only to jab a finger near Nora.

"All right, all right. I'm here. Dial it down," Nora growled.

"You know how this goes, Nor. We do not fuck around with pizza-snack."

"Got it. Easy mistake."

"Is it, though?"

"Drop it," Nora snapped.

Jenna put her open hands in the air. "All right, sugarplum. It has been dropped like a bag of bees." She rubbed the top part of Nora's back. "There's just one small hiccup," Jenna said, holding the door open for Nora.

"You've only got thirty minutes, tops?"

"You know me well. Yeah, I've got to head to Williamsburg to meet your *favorite* comedian. Ugh. He's such a little pig. But then there's this." Jenna swung her arms out, gesturing at the table in front of them where two Asian women sat chatting and sipping from giant mugs.

"What am I looking at, Jenna?"

"*Them.* They're at our table."

"So . . ." Nora brought down the volume in her voice. "We'll sit somewhere else."

"No," Jenna said, raising her voice. "That's not how it works."

Nora rolled her eyes and took a breath to say something more (she wasn't really in the mood for the hangout anyway), but Jenna had already moved in toward the women at the table.

"Hey, y'all. Excuse me. This is actually our table." Jenna was practically leaning on the shoulder of the younger-looking friend.

She looked up at Jenna, smiled, and started, sweetly, "We *just* sat down here, like, a bit ago. Is it okay if we stay here? Our table is over there . . . and it's totally fine, but I can't see my dog from there. He's just right outside"—a delicate point of her finger at the storefront window—"so . . . do you mind?"

Jenna let out a long sigh. "Yeah."

"Thanks," she said, ending high like a question, and started to turn her attention back to her friend.

"No. You asked me, do I mind? That was my answer: Yeah,

I do. I mind. I reserved this table because I reserved *this* table."

The woman's head snapped over to her friend. "*Féi zhū shì èle,*" she said, decidedly not under her breath. The friend giggled. It was clear from the quick up-down glance they both gave Jenna that they had said something unkind.

"Talking about me in your language doesn't move the needle here, sugar. You're wasting everyone's time at this point."

"Are you serious right now?" the younger woman said.

"Yes," Jenna said. "Oh . . . that's my answer: Yes, I'm serious."

The two women, simmering and gagging on eye rolls and bitter cackles, slid out of the chairs, letting them scrape the floor loudly. The friend with the dog spat out one last secret insult: "*Yang gui zi.*" But as they turned to walk back to their designated table, Jenna unleashed her own string of contempt—in flawless Mandarin: "*Qù nǐ de! Guěn huí shí ba céng dìyù.*"

With their faces flushed in embarrassment, shock, and indignation, the two women slunk off to their table whispering and looking back at Jenna with mouths slightly curled in amazement.

"What in the *hell?*" Nora said, her own mouth wide.

"I've been speaking Mandarin since college, and I'm more than halfway through learning Japanese. It's called business strategy." Jenna shook her head and started scrolling through her email on her cell phone. "People rarely win when they assume," she said, not looking up from her screen. "My daddy taught me that."

Nora thought back to Julius; the look he gave her covered over everything in her brain like a thick quilt. She heard Jenna's voice in the distance until it crystallized, loud and shrill. "Uh, why do you insist on fucking up Snack Time with Jenna today? Order your pie or dainty slice or whatever already."

It was all too much for Nora right then. Things long buried were resurrecting: the obituary for Dr. Bourdain; the mean-girl moment about "our table" that brought Nora crashing back to the terror Emily would regularly unleash on their fellow classmates at Immaculate Heart while Nora sat by in silence, seething and secretly cringing; and the way Julius looked at her, steeped in conjecture, a look she faced for years in Montreal when yet again she was judged as not enough for either the black kids or the white. Even the itch beneath her skin and the insomnia was back along with the slippery grip on her emotions—uncertain when she'd break down in tears. Soon, if history were truly repeating itself, her natural blond glory would start falling out in clumps in the shower.

"*No,*" she said first; then shook her head hard. Nora jumped up from the prized table, nearly knocking the chair back, and bolted, leaving Jenna shouting her name behind her. She needed to get home to put these ghosts back in their rightful boxes.

# CHAPTER 3

*Montreal*
*Nora, age 9*

*Fix your face.* Nora could set her watch to those three words. Her mother said them nearly every time she looked over at her. It wasn't because Nora had some proclivity for sulking or an unpleasant resting scowl and needed regular reminders to adjust her hanging grimace. The mother's directive was steeped in something else, something more disheartening than basic berating. This mother believed that Nora—her only child—was destined for good fortune and greatness, but it all hinged on how beautiful she appeared to others, how gracious and pleasant, welcoming and willing. This mother, she wanted her daughter to always be seen as pretty, pure, and simply better. Nora was to be the preferred and obvious choice, far greater than all that surrounded her.

*Light, bright, right:* three more words that were baked into Nora's entire being. From her exceptionally green eyes and naturally blond-streaked hair to her tiny face, all fine and symmetrical and the color of the milkiest tea, Nora was an unmistakable beauty—an extraordinary one, as her mother tells it. But to Nora, none of it mattered. The fawning and fixation from her mother and strangers alike, it was all just words, wishes, and when it came down to it, a weight around Nora's neck.

"What did I tell you about staring out into the sun like that?" Nora's mother said, frowning. "Now, come over here and help with this. It's coming up on tea and I ain't even cut up the cucumber yet." She shook her head, annoyed, and returned to folding a basket of white clothes, separating out those shirts that would be ironed in the afternoon, during her late, late lunch. "And fix your face."

Nora did as told, resetting her expression, removing the scrunch from her brows, letting her jaw settle, and dimming her eyes, but not before rolling them—in full view of her mother.

She glanced down at Nora. "You act like life is so hard. But it's not. Not for you." She shook her head once more. "You don't know the first thing about hard life. People like you, a girl-child like you, you could never know." She jabbed a crumpled men's undershirt in Nora's face, her lips pursed, waiting for her daughter's good sense to take hold. "You know, when I was a little girl, back home in Bim," Nora's mother said, a tender smile creeping across her face, "I was all too happy when my Auntie Pearl asked me to help her do *anything*. Folding clothes, washing the wares, cleaning up fish heads, combing her hair—anything. I was there when she called on me. Just to spend time with her . . . and on a bright summer morning like this? You could tell me the sky was turning green, and I wouldn't care. I wasn't going nowhere. I was with my Tauntie Pearl."

"Dumb," Nora mumbled. Doing chores—particularly this chore of folding someone else's clothes—was boring and useless enough, she thought, without having to listen to these stories *from back home in Bim* with their little lessons tucked into the hem. And hearing her mother talk about green skies only made her crave escape even more. Nora stepped up on the tip of her bare toes, hoping to see past the broad clothesbasket and look through the laundry room's bay window. All she could make out was a clear strip of blue sky and a swatch of green—some ivy dangling from the rear stone walls.

"Rah-Rah, if you're going to help me fold, then fold." Her mother gestured at the undershirt—*his* shirt—still a jumble in Nora's small hands.

"I don't like this. You know I don't." Nora tossed the shirt back into the basket and folded her arms instead. "And I wish you'd stop calling me that, too. All of those names: *Rah-Rah, Tauntie, Doctuh B, Mistruss B.* It sounds old and corny and . . . ignorant." She pushed her chin out, closed her eyes, and waited for it: her mother's loud kiss of her teeth, a rough nudge in the small of her back—or worse, the pinch—and a few sharp words, letting her know that she was dismissed from laundry duty. Free to go nestle in the prickly lawn out back and gaze up at the cloudless sky.

After a long pause, Nora opened her right eye, then her left, and was startled by what she saw. Her mother was still standing next to her, neatly folding each white item. No heated glares, no slaps to the ear, no muttered threats. Just folding. Nora watched for a moment as her mother, with her crisply pressed uniform, continued to move slowly and evenly, plucking things from the basket. One crumpled pillowcase—to the iron pile it went. Two slinky women's trouser socks—matched, then rolled together as a pair and placed on top of a short stack of the doctor's cotton T-shirts. Nora stayed locked on the neat pile. Even though the shirts were freshly laundered, his scent— a distinct mix of salt, whisky, and dead leaves—lingered, making its way up Nora's nostrils. She felt the tops of her ears heating up and she clenched her jaw, fixing her stare on her mother's dark brown, chapped, dry hands, so dedicated to this ridiculous task. As the silence began to fill each corner of the narrow, white-tiled space, Nora could feel the heat from her ears spreading across her face. The long, bluish vein at her left temple started to quiver—or so it felt. Nora ran her two fingers the length of it, thinking of the countless times her mother had cursed the thing, this reminder of the white father Nora never met. And then she said it: "Your life isn't worth much, you know?"

Finally, her mother stopped moving, resting her hands gently on the edge of the wicker basket. Though the words were intended to hurt her mother, something—a stinging residue—lingered on Nora's lips.

The mother tilted her head toward her daughter and spoke slowly. "Now, you can hold your breath and stomp your feet all morning, Miss Nora. But you're nine, a child. You don't know the first thing about what anything is worth." She went back to folding. "Besides, my life—*our* life—is the best it can be, Rah-Rah. All thanks to Doctuh and Mistruss Bourdain. Them people are good to us; treat us decent. One day you'll see that. You'll see beyond all your selfish, spiteful ways. And you'll be grateful for this. But it might be too late."

Nora released her arms from the tight twist across her chest, but kept her fists clenched. "I hate this life," she said, and punched the side of her own leg.

"You're almost done here, Nora," her mother said, pointing at the near-empty clothesbasket. Rolled up at the bottom of it were an odd tube sock, a hand towel, and Dr. Bourdain's golf shirt.

Nora peered at the shirt and back at the side of her mother's plump brown face. Then, without a qualm tingling in any part of her, she spat into the basket. A line of dribble clung to the bottom of her lip.

"Child!" her mother snapped.

Before her mother could look her in the eye, Nora ran off, down the three narrow steps, through the kitchen, and out the back door. Nora's bare feet slapped the cool grass as she sprinted across it. The ground of the backyard, though covered with a grand, expertly manicured lawn, was uneven. Nora felt as though she would tumble at any moment, but didn't slow down to catch her balance. And turning back was not an option.

Everything behind her was broken, smashed to useless chips with sharp edges.

Dr. Bourdain's awful violations continued, growing more frequent and egregious with every year Nora added to her life. And after each sickening, secret visit to his study, she'd leave a larger broken-off piece of herself on his dark wood floor. Soon all she had left were her tucked-away wishes. Empty as they were, Nora still clung to them. She continued to close her eyes tight and blow out her birthday candles atop the chocolate banana layer cake—a homemade favorite—wishing for a return to the before, the one where Dr. Bourdain's only touch was a pat on her head as he walked by her on his way to his regular, adult life. The before where Mrs. Bourdain still watched her with warmth in her eyes instead of looking through her with barely veiled contempt; the one where she and her mother would sit shoulder to shoulder in the kitchen, their heads tossed back, holding their bellies filled with laughter and raw shelled peanuts, and whispering stories about the ways of *some white folks*. Nora also wished that somehow her mother would notice the missing fragments of her daughter and go off looking for them, gathering them up from under beds and behind bookshelves and beneath heavy rugs, and she would rinse the dust and dirt from them and slide the pieces back into place, making Nora whole again.

*Nora, age 13*

The wetness on her cheek woke Nora. She opened her eyes and wiped the drool from the side of her face. Lying flat on her stomach, Nora arched up, looking around the room, still groggy. Next to her hand was a splayed copy of *Girl, Interrupted* and a note on top of it:

> *Daughter,*
> *Gone down the road. Back home shortly. There is*
> *soup in the pot you can warm up in micro oven.*
> *Boil some ginger tea for your other troubles.*
>
> *Your Mother*

Nora always found it funny and a little sweet that her mother called the microwave, essentially, an extremely small oven. She had stopped correcting her about it long ago since the interpretation wasn't completely wrong. Nora stared at the note, focusing on the neatness of her mother's handwriting. Despite the persistent tremble that her mother had developed in her right hand and arm, the handwriting remained pristine. She read the note over and again, even squinted a couple times as her eyes moved from one word to the next, trying to find some hint, a deeper meaning spelled out beyond what was written. The mother's mystery trips—first by public transit, then later always by way of the Bourdains' driver Geoff—had grown frequent and her time spent away from the home stretched the limits of "be back shortly." Her mother's health was obviously failing, and she refused to give Nora anything resembling straight talk about her feeble state. As her mother's body continued to battle itself, all that she would offer Nora were assurances that God was good and so were the Bourdains. But Nora knew that both of these things were untrue.

She stayed fixed on the words for a few more seconds, then crumpled the note in her tight fist. Nora dropped her face into her pillow, squeezing her eyes shut and pressing her nose deeper into the fluffy padding. She forced her head into the pillow more, so much so she started seeing dark spots and shapes knocking around the insides of her eyelids like Ping-Pong balls, and her breathing was muffled. Nora finally broke the seal, turning her head to the side. Her vision was blurry and her breath quick. She let her eyes float around her, taking in the fog of the room, before rolling over and sitting up at the side of her bed.

It was her thirteenth birthday, but she felt nothing. The day could have been any other. Nora started to regret that she insisted on nixing her birthday cake and special lunch in the sunroom tradition with her mother. It was a hasty decision built on the flimsy idea that thirteen was not special. Though it meant she crossed over, an official teenager, to Nora thirteen was just more of the same. Thirteen was not worth celebrating, especially since Nora's same and only wish for the last four years was to travel through time and go back to her world before nine. Turning nine was the start of all things dirty and awful. She stared at her feet—the bright blue, forbidden nail polish chipped and faded—and wiggled her toes. She slipped her new Ralph Lauren white sweater—one of the early birthday gifts from Mrs. Bourdain (or Elise, as she insisted Nora start calling her)—over herself and headed upstairs to the kitchen. Part of her hoped that she would discover the poorly hidden ingredients to her chocolate banana birthday cake. No luck. Just spotless and sanitized everything gleaming back at her. She glanced at the rooster clock by the elaborate coffee maker: 10:43 AM. The only reason her mother allowed her to sleep this late—birthday be damned—was because she lied the night before and said that her period was starting. The same story spared her from Dr. Bourdain the week prior.

Nora pulled a mug from the cabinet and poured some of the freshly steeped ginger tea from a saucepan on the stove. The homemade brew, her mother's panacea, was still warm. She sipped the biting mix despite the taste, despite not really having cramps, and scanned the span of the kitchen once more.

The Bourdains were out of the country at a cardiothoracic surgeons' conference in Berlin, so Nora did what she always had when she was fortunate enough to be home alone: went straight to the Bourdains' bedroom.

She pushed open their door. The creaking sound, loud as usual, made her pause. She shook her head. *No one's home.* Nora continued through the broad hallway, gliding past the large reading chairs, stopping when she reached the bulk of the bedroom. Everything was bright, drenched in late-morning light. Even the monochrome gray bed linens seemed illuminated. She did a quick sweep of the room—the matching night tables, each with books stacked neatly on the same edge; the sharp folds of the long, silk, French-pleat drapes pulled wide open; the antique family portrait on the farthest wall flanked by framed silhouettes—until her eyes finally rested on the gaping bathroom door. Nora figured one of the Russian women who help clean the house probably left the door that way, the wrong way; she knew her mother was much too careful for those kinds of simple slip-ups.

Although the Bourdains' master bathroom had always been a lure, Nora hadn't been in it in over a year. When she was younger, and the couple was out and her mother was otherwise occupied, Nora would find her way into their bedroom, splitting the stolen time between the bathroom, poking around Mrs. Bourdain's vanity—a cosmetics gold mine—and the woman's large, elegant dressing room. There Nora would slip her feet in and out of the many pairs of shoes all arranged by hue, neatly propped up along slanted shelves.

The adjacent, smaller walk-in closet belonging to Dr. Bourdain held almost zero interest for Nora. Mrs. Bourdain's version had three-way, floor-length mirrors, recessed lights, and fancy chairs—specifically the stiff, slim wingback and the elaborate chaise lounge with gold gilt upholstery—into which

Nora liked nestling. Dr. Bourdain's had none of this. Instead, his closet was all grays and blacks and navy blues, with a few strips of crisp white tucked into the duskiness. There was one section of his corner of things that Nora actually found captivating: the narrow armoire just outside of Dr. Bourdain's closet that housed his collection of ancient fountain pens and antique miniature travel clocks. Nora would be sure to polish away any smudge marks her sweaty fingers left behind by gently brushing each of the intricate clock faces against her shirt.

But Nora closed the door on the doctor's armoire for good one week before her ninth birthday when, in haste, she left out one of the small clocks. It fell and broke. "My oldest, most delicate one, cobalt blue and lemon yellow with the double enamel." Nora always remembered his exact description of it, exactly how he said it to her in a fevered whisper when he called her to his study to discuss it the following Sunday. Nora's mother was at church, her morning off, and his wife was at a charity luncheon. He told Nora that he wouldn't mention it to her mother and that it was best to leave the misstep between them. It was the first—and least vile—of their "secrets" that he ordered her to keep.

Standing there now in the lion's den, a half cup of cool, golden tea in her hand and an indecipherable stinging in the center of her stomach, Nora decided to open the armoire again; this time taking a pen and a small clock—the shiniest one. She shoved them both in her sleeve, eased the armoire's door closed, and walked out.

Back in her basement room, Nora stashed the items from her sleeve under her pillow and moved on to opening the next birthday gift from Mrs. Bourdain. The note on the perfect-wrap box said: *Pretty for pretty,* in curly script and signed, *With love, Elise.* It was a leather cosmetic bag filled with makeup in copycat shades and colors to her beauty essentials

upstairs and a polished compact mirror with OUR NORA en-
graved on the back.

Mrs. Bourdain's return to benevolence baffled Nora. About
two years earlier, nearing her eleventh birthday, Nora had noticed a distinct change in her. She went from kindhearted to
cool, and the transformation was swift, like a heat switch flicked
from on to off overnight. That year the Bourdains hosted a party
for forty people at their home. With little time or planning, Mrs.
Bourdain still insisted on the rather impromptu gathering and
that it be held on Nora's birthday—a Wednesday. The party required an all-hands maneuver that left Nora's mother working
alongside a cast of hired servers, butlers, and caterers, and
without her usual time to prepare for her daughter's birthday
celebration, not even the cake. The only birthday gift from
Elise that year was a shapeless, dour dress—"a frock," her
mother called it, making a sour face each time—given to her in
a pretty box early that morning.

"You don't have to wear that frock, chile," Nora's mother
told her quietly when they returned to their basement quarters.
"You did right in tellin' she thanks and with a smile 'pun yuh
face. That's all yuh could do, darlin'."

That plan changed when Elise told Nora's mother that the
party would require an extra set of hands to serve water.

"We can let Nora do it. See? Problem solved," Mrs. Bourdain said to Nora's mother, and floated her manicured fingers
in Nora's direction. "And it would be very nice if she could
wear the dress I bought her."

On her twelfth birthday, there was no party. The Bourdains
left for a "quick getaway" to Martha's Vineyard that morning,
returning early the next week. And Mrs. Bourdain was sure to
leave another frumpy dress in a beautifully wrapped box for
Nora on the kitchen counter.

Nora was relieved that there were no wrapped boxes holding frocks this time around, but found it odd all the same.

What made thirteen the year that Mrs. Bourdain returned to giving her nice and thoughtful things again? She pulled out one of the lipsticks in a slender, black shiny casing and pursed her lips in the small mirror, gliding the color along. It was a deep red, like fresh blood. Nora puckered up and smiled and posed and then back to puckering and smiling again. She stared at her mouth in the mirror before turning the compact over and studying the inscription again. Nora wiped away the lip color—and her smile—with the pads of her fingers and slammed the opened mirror against the wall next to her bed. She let the tiny shards sprinkle onto her quilt. A sharp splinter landed on the top of her leg. Nora pinched the glass between her fingers and ran it up along her thigh, digging it into her flesh as she dragged her nightshirt up to her floral underwear. She stayed watching the deep scratch redden and bleed until the sound of the mowers outside interrupted her.

Nora hopped up and dusted the quilt, pushing the broken mirror bits to the side where the bed met the wall. She rubbed off the blood as best she could, slipped a bulky hoodie over herself, and raced upstairs to peek out the back kitchen window. She kept leaning and dodging and skulking, hoping for a Daniel sighting. Actually, she was counting on it.

Daniel was the son of Mr. Park, the Korean gardener who had tended to the Bourdains' lawn for as long as Nora could remember. Mr. Park was polite with the Bourdains, of course, and fairly civil with Nora's mother. Over the years, Nora had overheard Mr. Park and her mother talking about the same two things: the weather, specifically rain, and the price of tulips, her mother's favorite cut flowers. Her mother would always refer to him as Mr. Park, while he only ever called Nora's mother by her first name, Mona. Never Ms. Gittens or Miss Mona, at the very least. Still, of all the different service staff who had breezed in and out of the Bourdains' home since

Nora's mother worked there, the Park family was the only one whom Nora could really tolerate. It had little to do with Mr. Park's gardening expertise or his wife's gentle smiles or how patient she seemed waiting for her husband, back in the earlier days, sitting in their parked van out front sucking on tangerines. Her fondness for the family had everything to do with their youngest son, Daniel. He helped his father with business over the past two summers, until last year when he was accepted to the prestigious Pre-Med Summer Program for high schoolers at McGill University.

Daniel was tall, lean, and had a creamy complexion with intricately chiseled features. At fifteen years old, he was handsome, not merely cute. His high, hard cheekbones would devour his eyes when he smiled. Nora especially liked how his impeccable hands were usually tucked into his pockets, making his shoulders edge up toward his chin. Daniel liked to read, another pleasing thing about him. He often had a soft book wedged into the back pocket of his jeans or rolled up and somehow squeezed into the front of his hoodie. Nora enjoyed spying on him as he read under a tree or draped himself across the back of the Parks' work van, his classic aviator-style sunglasses perched on the straight ridge of his nose. Even damp and dingy from the day's work, he looked magnificent. She would replay the slow, syrupy moments during her steamy shower late at night. Nora could close her eyes and instantly see him gingerly licking his index finger before using the dewy tip to turn the page. Or she'd have a tight close-up of his mouth as he nibbled on his red pillowy bottom lip.

As much as she liked watching him from a distance over the summers, it took Nora almost three months to stir up the nerve to move beyond their usual charming exchanges made up of waves, glances, and smiles, and finally talk to him. She had asked him what he was reading and he turned the book's cover over to face her, danced it around a bit. *The Remains of the Day*.

"It's this Japanese author, Kazuo Ishiguro," Daniel started, quietly. He stepped out from the shade of the back door canopy and closer to Nora. "The whole book is like the main guy's diary. Stevens. He's an English butler, and he's totally in love with the housekeeper—" He stopped and looked behind him into the house as if someone had called out to him from the kitchen. Then he bit the corner of his lip, tugged at it gently with his teeth. "He's, like, so proper and so focused on dignity—but he takes it too far. He never tells anyone what he really thinks or feels. It just becomes regret. Like, heavy-duty regret. And sadness. Anyway . . ." He trailed off and smacked the soft book on his leg a few times. Nora remembered how greedily she watched his mouth, waiting for more words to slip out. Instead he licked his lips and smiled.

Nora kept peering through the scatter of workers out on the back lawn—the usual rotation of brown men from different regions of South America who Mr. Park had working for him. Looking at the men's shapes and stances, Nora tried to figure out if one of them was Daniel. He was supposed to stop by to return a medical book he had borrowed from Dr. Bourdain (as she overheard Mr. Park tell her mother the week prior). Nora really wanted to be home when he showed up.

But she saw no sign of him.

Nora was heading back to the basement when a light knock on the door came. She smiled before even turning around and opening the door. It was Daniel.

"Hey."

"Hey."

"You're here," he said, and moved closer to Nora, leaning into the doorjamb.

"Shouldn't I be?"

"When I stopped by earlier to drop off Dr. B's book, it looked like your mom was heading out. Thought you were, too." Daniel shook his head. He had grown his hair out. Nora liked that. It was messy, thick, wavy, and brown, not black like at the start of the summer. "So, I took a chance and—"

"And I'm here."

Their smiles stretched wider.

"Oh, wait . . ." Daniel took a small step toward her standing in the open door and tilted his head. "Happy Birthday!" There was a small tug in his brow. "It's today, right?"

"Nah, next month." Nora's face remained stiff through the lie.

"I could have sworn you said *May.*" He shook his head again. "Sorry about that. That was kind of lame."

"No, don't . . . I'm not big on birthdays. It's fine. It doesn't mean any—"

"Did you cut yourself?" he said, his face scrunched as he looked down at the blood spot printing through Nora's night-shirt.

"Yeah, I guess . . . maybe when I was in the kitchen. It-it's nothing." Nora tugged at the end of the thin nightgown peeking out from beneath her large sweatshirt. "What are you reading now?" She used her chin to point at the rolled-up book jammed into the back pocket of his jeans.

"This? Oh, this one is hardcore." He pulled the book out, handed it to her, and took a seat on the top step closest to Nora's foot.

"*Lord of the Flies?*" Nora slid down and sat next to him in the doorway. "Didn't you read this in English, like, a couple years ago? We did, last year."

"Yeah, it's a reread." He reached over and slipped the book out of Nora's hands and thumbed the pages. "I'm working my way through a list: the hundred best novels of all time." He rolled up the book again and leaned over to slide it back into his pocket, his body lightly pressed against Nora. A warm tingle swam up from her stomach to the top of her throat.

"What's next?" Her knee brushed his. More buzz and fluttering through her body.

"Not sure. I'm not going in order. At first I was going to at-tack the list from the bottom up, of course skipping the books I've already read . . . unless it's a really good one, like *Lord of the Flies* or *Animal Farm*; then I would read it again. But that felt, I don't know, boring. So I decided to go in a more random order." He chuckled and glanced at Nora. "I mean, like, crazy random."

"What, do you pick a number from a hat?"

"Almost. After I finish a book—or I'm super close to the end—when I wake up in the morning, before I even open my eyes, I think of a number. Whatever number pops into my head, I read that one from the list. It's stupid . . ."

"It's not."

"It kind of is," he said, chuckling. "We all have our things, right?"

She watched the corners of his mouth curl up. He may have blushed, too, Nora couldn't be sure and she didn't want to stare any more than she had already.

"Think *Lolita* is next. No death and destruction," he said. "Bring on the apples and sex."

Nora looked at him.

"Shit. That came out wrong," he said, and cupped his hand over his eyes. "Sorry."

Nora laughed. "No judgment here, perv-o."

"Maybe you can read it with me. I'll send you a copy." He was looking right at her. "We could email each other notes on the book." Daniel licked his lips. Nora tried not to notice how inviting it all was. She casually turned away from him and let her breath out, slowly.

She pointed to one of the workers on the lawn. "Hey, is that a new guy you have working for you?"

"Not me, my dad. No one works for me," he said. "That's Tobias. He's actually a student—or he was. He's the son of one of my parents' church friends who needed some *guidance*.

Supposed to help out a couple days a week or something. They've kind of taken him in."

"That's cool of your parents."

Daniel nodded. "Yeah, they like to help out. Not Bourdain-level stuff, but they do what they can." He shook his head. "I'm sorry. I didn't mean it like—shit. My foot is really wedged in my mouth today."

Nora shrugged, and the two stared out at the men working.

Daniel looked over at Nora, but only through a quick side glance, and bit his lip before breaking the quiet. "Did you find out anything?"

She shook her head.

"I'm sure it's fine. She's fine."

"I don't know . . . I mean, I want to believe that all the way, but everything with my mother just seems so off. I told you about the hand tremor thing. . . . It's worse. Like, way worse. And she's tired all the time. Even when she wakes up from ten hours or whatever of sleep, like, a lot of sleep, she's still exhausted. She's just not herself."

"Have *they* let on that anything's wrong?"

"No, not really. Well, except she keeps asking me to call her *Elise*. Since 'we're family—practically.' All these years later, *now* we're family?"

"*Practically.*"

"Right." Nora snorted, rolling her eyes. "Practically."

"What about Dr. B—what's he think?"

Nora's whole expression curdled, her lip twitched, but she forced herself to stay locked on Tobias, watching him root around the large, twin shrubs near the deck.

"You want to come inside?" She stood up.

He paused for a moment, looking up at Nora. "Is that okay?"

"Why wouldn't it be?" Nora extended a hand to him, her palm up. Then she wiggled her fingers. "Coming?"

Daniel nodded and took the help up. "Why do I feel like I'm about to step into some trouble?" He was balancing himself on the edge of the top stair, leaning in closely toward Nora and smiling. She could feel the warmth of his breath along the side of her neck. She turned her head, slightly, so they didn't bump into each other and clumsily knock him off his ledge. From this angle, Nora could only see half of him—half of his flushed, remarkable face—and her eyes moved down and stayed for a moment on his mouth, the etched laugh line, his glossy bottom lip. *He must have just licked them,* Nora thought, as the flutter around her heart returned.

Nora led him into the laundry room, not looking back his way for several steps, not until she heard the soft click of the back door closing. She turned to catch Daniel looking around at the white of the room, unsure but curious as he walked over to her.

"You've never been in here?" Nora lifted herself up onto the washing machine to sit; her feet dangled and knocked against its front-load door.

Daniel chuckled. "No, never once, not even to wash my hands at that sink."

"You're here now." Nora stopped kicking her heels against the machine. It was quiet inside, only the chirping birds and intermittent whirl of the landscaping tools interrupting their hush.

"I guess I am." He pushed his hands into his front pockets so deep that his shoulders moved up to his ears.

"It's maybe my favorite room in this house."

"Seriously?"

Nora nodded. "I know. Random, right?" Daniel inched over to Nora and the washing machine. No longer taking in the tiles and shelves of the room, he was looking directly at her. "I guess I like it because it's where things get clean and neat and new again. You could put the dirtiest, muddiest, grossest piece of whatever in here"—she touched the machine gently—"and after a quick spin, it's good again."

Daniel squared his jaw, licking his lips and nodding. "That's pretty poetic." His eyes drew a line from her hand resting on the washer, along her side, up to her face.

A flash of heat moved from Nora's ears down to her ankles. It tickled and she smiled, but Daniel didn't. His face was straight and serious, but not steely. He walked in closer, stopping next to the machine. He was within her arm's reach. Nora stretched hers toward him, her palms up like before. She danced her fingers again. And he took her hand again. The kiss started soft. Soon Daniel's hand was sliding along the small of Nora's back, gripping her waist. Leaning forward, Nora's calf brushed the top of his worn jeans. She felt a scrape—the book in his back pocket—as he roughly pulled her into him. Daniel's lips tasted exactly as she wanted them to. His breath was hot and a little sweet.

They separated and Daniel's eyes finally opened as he pulled back, his hand still resting on Nora's neck and jaw. He looked at her, taking her in. Nora wanted another kiss. A longer, deeper one—if that were possible. She wanted to wrap her legs around his waist and pull him hard into her. Slide his shirt over his head. Unbutton the top of his jeans, forcing the zipper down halfway. Arch her back gracefully as he made his way down her neck and the wide line between her breasts. And do all the things she had seen women do on the daytime stories her mother loved to watch.

Daniel stroked the back of Nora's head. He gently massaged her scalp with his fingers. "Is this safe?"

Nora giggled. "As in, what, you might get crushed by the washing machine?"

He smirked. "I mean, is it safe to be doing this—here?"

Nora shrugged and tried to drop her head into his chest, but

Daniel leaned back a little farther. "I'm serious. What if some-one sees?"

Nora looked up. "No one's here. You know they're gone this week, and my mother's out. She's been gone all day, actu-ally. So there's, like, literally no one here."

Daniel's expression turned uneasy. He slowly drew his hands back. His intention started to take shape, clear enough for Nora to see it. Her grin dissolved. "What are you worried about; who's going to see us?" She pulled away from him, but kept her eyes locked on his. Leaning back, waiting for Daniel to say the words she could already hear in her head, Nora winced. The moment was familiar. Unlike the others, though, Daniel kept his head up and looked her in the eyes.

"Nora, it's . . . it's not me. My parents, they're old school. They wouldn't be okay with you and me—It's how they were raised, you know? They're stuck in the old way. And they really respect Dr. Bourdain and his wife." He ran his hand through his hair, pushing the tousled heap over to one side. "They pride themselves on doing a good job here and being proper and I . . . I wouldn't want to do anything to mess that up." He dropped his head and dragged his hands through his hair again. "You know I'm not like that, Nora. It's not about me."

"And it's not about me either, *right?*" Nora's grimace was pulled so tight across her face it pinched the corners of her eyes. She took a deep breath and let her glare fall away from Daniel, staring past his feet until the white of the room swal-lowed him up and he was a blur. "It's fine, Daniel. Don't worry about it." She fanned her hands by his face.

"Come on, Nora. Don't do that. Don't act like a six-year-old. I'm talking to you in a real way here about, like, real things. They're my parents. Think about if your mother—"

"Nope, you don't get to say that to me. No." She shook her head hard and pulled her legs up on the washing machine to fold them under her. A fresh sting from the cut on her thigh rose up and she bit the inside of her cheek, trying to mask her wince. "It's fine, okay? You're fine. Don't worry about it."

Daniel stepped back and covered his mouth with his hand, rubbing his lips with the tips of his fingers. He let out a loud breath. "I don't want you to be . . . Just tell me you understand where I'm coming from. I'm not like that, Nora. You know me."

"I know that you really believe you're not like that. I can see it in your face. And I know that you really want me to believe it, too." Nora jumped off the machine. "But it doesn't matter what a person believes. It never does."

He took a step toward Nora. "Come on," he said, and put his hand out.

She slapped it softly. "Thanks for stopping by, Daniel. Good luck with the Harvard stuff, eh?" Nora reached for the large clothesbasket on the shelf nearest her and started sorting the small heap of colorful clothes.

"Nora," Daniel said, crestfallen and trying to catch her eyes with his.

"Hey, do me a favor?" she said sweetly, adding a grin. "Just close the door in good behind you." She turned back to the basket and continued separating her fresh, clean pieces from her mother's, listening for the sure click of the patio door. The minute the sound hit the air, Nora's ribs caved, pitching her forward into the yawn of the clothesbasket. She shook her head slowly as the tears dripped on a half-folded nightgown spilling out the side. The vein by her temple throbbed as Nora's breathing stepped up, getting louder and more fierce until that's all she could hear. She wrapped her fists around the clothesbasket, squeezing tighter and tighter as a growl burned from the center of her belly through her lungs and finally came booming out of her mouth in flames. Nora threw the basket over her head, wild, roaring to the skylights. It was enough. It was too much. The ground-in misery and rancor of her young life—one spent on the outside of every circle—seeped in, and Nora's thicker outer shell finally cracked all the way through.

She left the clothes strewn across the laundry room and returned to her basement bed. A piece of broken glass hidden in the folds of the sheets jammed into Nora's knee as she crawled to her pillow. She moved to pull it out, but stopped—stopped wincing, stopped crying, stopped gritting her teeth—and let the sliver remain.

# CHAPTER 4

Fisher reached over and placed the green ring box on the glass top between them. He sat back, staring down at the quaint thing as it glowed beneath the lights. After a long beat, he smiled first, then leaned in and looked over at Nora.

"Should we do this all over again, then?" he said, grinning even wider. "That is, if your answer is still the same."

Nora bit the small center of her bottom lip, a shaky dam to keep any hard truths from trickling out. She stayed quiet, gazing at the pretty box, barely moving, only a slight curl pulling at the corners of her mouth. As her silence stretched out, Fisher's smile began to droop and his brows inched toward each other. Catching himself, he chuckled and pulled away from the table, resting back in the patio chair. He picked up his beer bottle in a loose, three-fingered grip and brought it to his mouth for a slow sip. His usual ease returned as the pale ale flowed down his throat.

"You love the ring. You love me," he said, gesturing with the bottle. "I'm not ruffled by any of this." Fisher traced a lazy circle in the night air around Nora. "And I know the answer is still yes. The real question is, what's got you so out of sorts?"

Nora finally looked up from the ring box and over at Fisher.

Their twinkling patio lights made his face shimmery and almost translucent. She shrugged and shook her head before pushing out a tight smile. "There's nothing. It's nothing. I'm . . . I'm just tired. My sleep's been off." Nora moved her gaze over Fisher's shoulders. Looking right at him was asking too much. "It's normal stuff, you know . . . jitters."

"Jitters," he said. Another slow sip.

"Yeah, wedding jitters. Totally normal." Another light shrug.

"Right. But you're not totally normal and you're not a *jitters* person. You're Nora Mackenzie. So, what's really going on?"

Nora took a deep breath and considered what it might look like, the truth, standing between them raw under the stars. She imagined how Fisher's face might morph from sweet and calm and kind into something more pained and sickened; how his eyes would narrow, barely able to stay open, watching as she spilled every drop of her warped and mangled story onto the spotless glass. Would he push himself back in his chair, arching his body away from the rancid sewage that poured from her mouth across the table and dripped onto the limestone floor? Or maybe he would stay stoic, unable to process what she said and want nothing more than for her to stop talking and just leave. As horrible as the visions of this potential future were, Nora never felt so on the cusp of coming clean. Looking at him, sitting across from her, leaning into her, waiting on her next breath, Nora wanted to answer Fisher's question, she wanted to tell him *what was really going on,* convinced that she could actually do it. She bit the inside of her bottom lip once more, inhaled deeply once more, and set both of her sweaty palms flat on the table to steady herself. She wanted to speak it, let loose the words jumbled at the back of her throat, quickly before the tears could rush in and turn everything into a shapeless, soggy mess. She even opened her mouth, slightly, but still big enough for something to slip through and at least begin. But it didn't work. Nothing came. Not even her choppy breath skated over her lips. Nora glanced down at the ring box still sitting there perfectly centered, and allowed the tears to move freely.

"I . . . I am just so, so excited to be your wife," she said, moving her damp hands to clutch high on her chest. "I want it to happen tomorrow or tonight—*right now,* this minute we're in right now. Everything else . . . it all could fall off the edge of the terrace," Nora said, waving her hand toward the end of the long table. "I don't need it. It's you. That's it. That's what I want. You."

Fisher signaled with the slightest dip of his head that he was falling for this woman all over again. Nora reached for the box and pushed it over to him.

"Ask me once more," she said, her face bunched into a wet knot.

Fisher grabbed the box and left his empty beer bottle in its place. He stood up, never breaking his focus on Nora, and walked around the table to her side. When he dropped to his bent knee, his eyes bright and smile wide, Fisher paused and looked up at this blond beauty, tracing the outline of her warm, glowing face with his gaze. He took her left hand from her lap and brought it to his lips—the only time his glance left her. Nora didn't bother to hold anything in—she couldn't. The tears, the trembling heart, the vertigo, it was all happening outside of her control, set to their own rhythm.

Fisher popped open the ring box and angled it toward Nora, his smooth, lightly tanned face in full blush. He licked his lips and brushed two fingers over the dew left behind—a nervous tic. He let his grin fall away and, after a short breath, he started. "Nora Mackenzie. I'm in love with you," he said, nodding. "I love everything about you. Even the things that you don't like about you—*especially* those things you don't like. I do. I love all of it. I knew this was real from the moment we met. You were trying to pretend I didn't exist"—he paused for a chuckle and wink—"but you saw me, because I saw you. And I want to spend the rest of my life doing just that: seeing you. Loving you. Being right here for you." Fisher removed the ring from the box and steadied it on the very tip of Nora's finger. "My beautiful, wonderful, lovely Nora, will you do me the honor of being my wife?"

Nora lunged into his body, throwing her arms around his neck and burying her face there as she sobbed.

"Hey, hey, Mack," Fisher said softly, craning his neck to catch a view of her face. "Babe, what's happening here? This is not the first time you're hearing this." He gently shifted Nora's weight back into her chair and tried again to make eye contact with her. "These tears, this isn't joy—you're *crying,* and it's so much sadness. What's wrong? You can tell me. You know that; you can tell me what happened." He stood up and pulled Nora's limp body up with him. "First, let me just put this on you properly." He took her trembling hand and slid the ring over Nora's finger. "There. Where it should be."

Nora shook her head, her body swaying, as she barely stood up straight enough to receive the celebrated piece of fine jewelry. "I don't need it," she said, sniveling and trying to break from his embrace. "It's not for me. This, it's not me."

"Listen, hey, hey. Listen. This ring *is* for you. It's yours." *Thud.* Fisher slapped his chest. "I'm yours. I'm for you. I messed up on the sizing. That's on me. And those guys, they're specialists. They're old and precise. That's the only reason it took so long. But this ring is yours, okay? It's for you."

All Nora could offer was a stiff nod. And Fisher accepted it.

"Mack, is this"—he folded her into him and hugged tight—"is this about your mother? You said it was good this way, but I don't know. Maybe it's too close to the date, to her anniversary."

Nora's back locked up and her jaw clenched. Although a

day did not go by without her thinking about her mother at least once, she wasn't prepared for the woman's death to be brought to mind and space right then. She pressed her head into the middle of Fisher's chest, trying to force herself to pull back and look at him. Counting breaths wasn't working this time. She closed her eyes and like that, it started again: the names.

During her high school years, whenever it felt like the ground was shifting beneath her, Nora would calm her anxiety by reciting the names of her senior classmates, alphabetized.

*Jennifer Abbott, Katie Adams, Camryn Agnor, Grace Ah-Su, Lauren Atkinson.*

Even after she left the school abruptly, one month shy of graduating as the class valedictorian, Nora would still run through the same names—her private meditation. She held on to this practice like a sturdy, double-braided rope keeping her tethered to something rooted and real for years. Nora was well into her newest life as an independent, thick-skinned, scrappy stylist—albeit with a blurry origin story—thriving in New York City before she finally packed away the recital game along with all the other things she shoved into the deep margins.

*Jennifer Abbott, Katie Adams, Camryn Agnor, Grace Ah-Su, Lauren Atkinson.* "Bianca Amato," Nora said, under her breath. "I always forget about stupid Bianca Amato. Christ."

"Mack?" Fisher frowned and looked confused.

Nora shook her head hard and after a long, steady breath, met his eyes. "No, it's not . . . it's not her. My mother, she wouldn't want that. She wouldn't want me to hold on to that day—this morbid anniversary, carrying it hanging around my neck like some kind of—"

"Noose?"

Nora felt the fluttering return to her heart, but didn't allow it to distract her. "Yeah . . . like a noose. It's not her. That date, it doesn't mean anything. We said good-bye before. That day, it was just ashes. Not her."

"I'm sorry. I'm sorry you went through that—so young. You were a kid. I know how that feels. It's maybe the worst thing a kid can live through." He squeezed her shoulders. "But like I said before, Mack, this is one of those big days. It's a milestone, and you not having any family there, standing with you for this huge moment, it's going to affect you. Maybe that's what's happening now. The residual sadness, it's bubbling up to the surface like black tar. It's physically hurting me to see you like this. And what's fucked up is, it's too late to change anything. We're locked in. It's, what, eighteen days away? I can't—"

"Fisher, I don't *want* you to change anything. I agreed to this date. No one forced me. It's . . . I just want it to actually happen," Nora said, raising her voice. "I want to marry you and move ahead with our life together. But"—Nora slipped out of his arms and took a step back—"every time that I want something or I try to hold on to something, hold someone close, it gets taken away. It doesn't matter what I do to stop it from happening, it happens. And I'm left with nothing, just dust. I don't want that to happ—"

"Nora. Look, no one's taking me anywhere. I'm with you. No one is changing that. It's us. It's you and me, okay? Fish and Mack. Mack and Fish. Mack and Cheese and Fish," he said, unleashing a goofy grin and stepping closer to stroke under Nora's chin. "It's us, darling. Always." He moved in even closer, slow, angling his mouth to kiss hers, but Nora turned away.

"I'm sorry. I'm kind of a mess right now. I should—" She felt the vibration of his cell phone against her side.

"Ah—shit. I thought I left it in the kitchen."

"It's okay," she said, wiggling her way out of his caress. "Take the call. It's fine. I need to clean up anyway. I'm sure I look crazy."

"Never that," he said, and pulled the slim phone out of his front pocket. He slid it up next to his face, held it up by his ear with the lightest grip. "Yes, I'm here. Go ahead," he said into the phone, raising his index finger at Nora. She nodded and mouthed, *Go, go,* as she waved him away. This brand of interruption was so baked into Beaumont life that Nora had stopped taking offense long ago. "That's the goal. Correct. Rock is handling all the amendments and Asher's on top of the reprogramming effort, plus Liam is tying up the few loose ends on that." Fisher continued, pacing in his usual slow pattern. He made his way toward the far end of the terrace, his mellow voice trailing him. Nora stood watching, taking it in: his broad, built back; the carved shoulders printing through his shirt; his free hand clapped to the back of his neck. She wanted to rush up behind him, wrap her arms around his steely middle, spin him around to face his square jaw, and devour every sinewy line, every sculpted arch of him.

It was this view of Fisher that first drew her in. Only it was early evening, not night; they were at The Met for a lavish fund-raiser, not atop the terrace of their (his) Tribeca penthouse, and he was wearing a custom-made tuxedo, not an easy, white linen button-down and slim-cut, broken-in navy chinos. His caramel blond hair—a military undercut with perfect sides—was rigid and serious, not the softer, more disconnected cut he sports now with the playful, tousled quiff on top that looks like some woman just ran her hand through it. He was holding court, as he often does, not on a phone but live, in the company of other wealthy men with stiff backs holding even stiffer drinks. He was dashing—from the back view alone— and Nora was immediately curious. She ended up at the black-tie benefit as she always had back then: tagging along with Vincent Dunn, being ushered into certain rooms, welcomed by exclusive circles, no questions asked. And where Vincent didn't provide the entrée, Nora's charm served as her passport.

"It's the man who knows what he wants that gets what he wants," she said to the nodding circle of men congregating near Fisher; her finesse was turned up on high. "This is the truth in style, business, love."

She knew that finding her way around Fisher's rapt crowd of middle-aged white men named John would require some careful maneuvering. Nora didn't want to appear forlorn and fawning like the endless string of young, single (and quite often not-so-young or single) women who would do whatever they could to brush up against him, hoping to catch his attention and squeeze into the opening, a chance to stare into his very blue eyes. Nora wanted to stay cool, maintain her reserve and poise. She needed to keep her jacket on, as her mother would say. But she also wanted—*needed*—to glimpse what his front side had to offer. So strong was this need, Nora almost begged Vincent to make the introduction, under the guise of networking and growing the business, of course. It all sounded too limp in her own head, so she scrapped the ask, opting instead to stay put and continue watching the art of Fisher's back on the sly.

Like every other man or boy who had ever encountered her, Fisher noticed Nora the minute she entered the space. Between sips of his neat drink and after each rumble of overbearing laughter that rose from his posse of penguins, Fisher would turn his head to glance at her. Like clockwork or punctuation or blinking, it was repetitive and automatic and completely out of his control. Anyone watching the two of them would have been dizzy by the momentum of their human-style Newton's cradle: standing on opposite sides of the opulent room, unable to stop stealing looks at each other on the offbeat. Organic and fated at once, the back and forth went on for much of the night.

After getting distracted by Vincent's flagrant seduction of a fresh-faced, long-limbed Beverly Hills jock, Nora lost track of where Fisher went. She was about to tug Vincent's velvety

56 / NICOLE BLADES

coattails and check out for the night, when Fisher showed up; he stepped right in her path and introduced himself. Both Vincent and his new boy-ingénue fell silent and stared at them, mesmerized by the palpable current running between Nora and Fisher.

"I should have come over sooner," Fisher said, smiling down at her. He moved in close to Nora and leaned against a wall, his long, lithe top half almost stretching over her like a sheltering tree. "Playing it cool, I almost lost you."

Nora narrowed her eyes and pursed her lips, playfully. "Lost me? I didn't know I was yours to hold."

A grin spilled across his face. He licked his lips and followed that with the brush of his fingers along the glistening dampness left behind. "Ah, but you look like the kind of woman who is held by the world."

Somehow that did it. That line, doused in his special brand of magnetism, cracked Nora's polished, porcelain mask and left a slip of space open for Fisher to nestle in underneath her skin. She inhaled and let herself melt into the moment, enchanted, as they stayed fixed on one another, sinking in fully, unprepared and unwilling to move. Three days later he was walking into her studio under the flimsy guise of needing "a few suits," and two nights after that, they were on their first date, both incapable of living another day without each other.

---

Sensing her eyes on him, Fisher, still on his call, turned to Nora. He shook his head and put his hand out flat into the air, raising a shoulder—a recycled mea culpa wrapped up in a bow made of his dashing smile and good looks. Nora, using two hands this time, waved him off again. *Don't worry about it,* she said in a stage whisper. She tilted her head, motioning to the wall of folding glass doors behind her. Fisher gave her a hurried nod and went back to sending directives through the phone.

She stepped out of his view. The doors couldn't slide closed fast enough behind her before Nora made a dash, her long legs striding to the guest bathroom. Though they've never once entertained a guest, the bathroom was extravagant, well appointed to the tiniest detail, and tucked into the quietest corner of the penthouse. It was Nora's instant favorite; a retreat that reminded her of the bathroom of the hotel in which Vincent put her up while on her first solo business trip to Paris. She had only been working for him a half year after having just landed in New York a few months earlier—this pretend orphan with old money and a newish name. He told Nora that there was an upstanding quality emanating from her, something about her personality that felt familiar and warm and honest. Likable, he said finally. "Even if you're doing something awful, I think I'd still *like* you," Vincent said, somewhat incredulous during her second interview with him.

As she reached the bathroom's entrance, Nora was breathing fast and loud, tears clouding her eyes. She leaned over the sink, trying to catch her breath, but it only quickened. Nora squatted in the corner behind the door. She put her hand tightly over her mouth and cried.

It had become too much today. This week. Maybe it had been this way all month. All she could recognize was the feeling building, swirling in her gut. Today it felt like something the size of a grapefruit jabbing her insides and making her feel actual pain. Vomiting brought no relief, Nora knew. It was only two nights ago that she was on her knees with one hand clutching the side of the cold toilet bowl and the other holding her hastily pulled together ponytail, keeping her hair away from any parts of her mouth or brushing against her cheek. Even as she dangled her face over the same bowl now, Nora was thinking about her hair. Thinking about not letting any throw-up splatter on so much as a strand of her gorgeous golden pride: her shiny, lush mane of bouncing, moving hair.

Good hair, as her mother had called it. The same good hair that made the other black girls at St. Gabriel Elementary School choose to either envy her or pick on, as well as push, kick, and punch her.

"This too shall pass, Ra-Ra," her mother told her when Nora came home in tears yet another day. "They're children. Them can't understand that you're special. Children can be real cruel, but it will pass." She was rubbing an ice cube through a tangled section of Nora's head, trying to dislodge a thick wad of bubble gum someone had left behind. "You have good hair, child. Best thing about you. Those other black girls wish they had what you have . . . no picky knots rolled up at the nape of your neck, no scratchy broken-off ends. Beautiful, good hair. That's what all them want for themselves."

It took just fifteen months for Nora to learn how to use the "good" of her hair along with her green eyes. The older boys in the seventh and eighth grades learned how good Nora could be, too. "You don't look black," the boys would usually comment early into meeting Nora. And when she responded that she was "mixed," it would prompt queries about her white half—things that she had no real clue about since she never once met her father. But soon the boys would move on to other questions, like what kind of music she liked. "Everything," she'd say, desperate to end the quiz show. And the boys quickly became more interested in her pink plump lips, her advanced kissing techniques—Nora knew how to use her tongue, and her hands around their heated penises. And to them, deciphering the mystery of *what Nora was* quickly became insignificant.

She straightened out from hunching over the toilet and sat back on the floor, letting her eyes rest on her reflection in the full-length mirror. Strands of her golden hair floated around her streaked face. The light freckles that dotted the straight ridge of her slightly turned-up nose were illuminated, the tip of it red and wet. Her eyes—the whites of them, stinging and sore—were ringed in the black smudge of what was left of her mascara. The color and chaos of all of it lulled her. Nora stopped heaving, her mind quieted, and she returned to silently reciting the names.

*Jennifer Abbott, Katie Adams, Camryn Agnor, Grace Ah-Su, Bianca Amato, Lauren Atkinson . . .*

# CHAPTER 5

"Perfect weather, perfect people, Fisher by your side—it's a solid cure to those jitters," Jenna said, a little too loudly, through the phone. Her voice hung off the hand-painted wisteria branch twining across the wallpaper behind Nora. "Geneva is exactly what you need right now, hon."

Nora sat back in her narrow, coral-colored desk chair and looked around the room for a hint of what to say next. Her office was airy and favored by natural light courtesy of the tall, steel-framed window that ran almost the full length of the loft. The fresh-cut flowers in squat vases; the repurposed dining table with a raw-edge stone top used as a desk; the carefully selected club chairs and the French-styled settee; the crisp-white upholstery smartly blended with quiet colors—mint greens, pale blues, smoky grays—even the lamp shades and the custom garment racks: all of it was designed to make Nora's atelier feel familiar to her upper-crust patrons and look aspirational to her younger, newly minted clients.

"It doesn't work like that," was all Nora could gargle out after a too-long pause. She looked down at the cell phone resting on her stack of oversize, hardback fashion books and rolled her eyes at herself. These conversations with her best friend were draining her. "He asked me to come with him."

"Perfect!"

"No, he only asked because I was"—Nora took a beat—"not feeling well last night." She shuffled in her chair and slicked her hand along the side of her scraped-back, tight bun. "He was just being nice."

"Aw. I think Sweet Fish is maybe my favorite Fish."

"I don't think he meant it. Plus, this is a really quick-jump, all-hands kind of emergency trip. Some issue with this new steroid drug and some shady pharma company. Rock will be there, obviously, and Asher's flying in from London, no wife. When Fisher's with his brothers and wrapped up in the whole thing—all officious and direct and clipped—it's not my favorite Fish."

"First, officious is such a great word," Jenna said. "Next, are you kidding me? Watching a man be all business, barking orders, not asking just telling, demanding that shit get done right now, goddammit—that's like sex on a stick."

"Fisher is not the barking type." A smile inched across Nora's face as she glanced at the small, square photo framed on her desk—the only real slice of her private life set out in the open at her studio. It was a candid shot of her and Fisher bunched up together on a yacht bench, her arm slung around his neck, his face pressed against hers, their profiles in near silhouette, with a wash of cobalt, pastels, and flecks of gold behind them. It was their first trip together. Italy, the Amalfi Coast. A grand surprise for Nora, complete with blindfold, private jet, and directions to bring only her passport and an overnight bag. "Yeah, he's serious about the business—I don't blame him; it's a lot," Nora said. "But he's not an asshole. That's just not his style, you know?"

"Agree. He's a total diplomat . . . unless you're deceitful

and/or crooked. Then that statesman shit goes out the window and the Beaumont venom bubbles right on up to the surface," Jenna said, with a snort. "We've all seen him wearing *that* black hat, right? Or as I call that cautionary tale: 'The Spectacular and Hapless Fall of Jacob Winthrop the Fourth.' You know, I still want to get him to write that memoir. It would be fire wrapped in a hardcover."

"Jenna, I honestly do not want to talk about Jacob—"

"I know, I know. Not the point. But like I said, the book would not besmirch the Beaumont name. This is not the *New York Post* treatment. It's a book. We control the narrative."

"You know how horrible that whole scandal bullshit was on Fisher and his brothers and the board—and, Jesus, his mother. That woman is used to being in the paper because of some hospital wing dedication or their typical generous donations to things, not a frickin' *lawsuit*. She was mortified. They all were."

"Well, it never made it into court so—"

"Jenna, don't start."

"Okay, but let's be real, though: a threatened lawsuit is not adjudication, right? And, come on, the Beaumonts were never going to set foot in a courtroom anyway. But I hear where you're coming from. Those *gotcha* pics in the *Post* were not a good look. I can see why Fish and the fam were so pissed. But . . . *you* looked good in the background."

Nora pursed her lips and let the silence brew.

Jenna soon cleared her throat. "Anyway, I think going to Geneva would do you some good. It'll be just like our trip to Maldives—only no overwater suites, no lagoon, no yoga on the white powder sand, and no tans. Although, you were able to soak up that sun with such ease and rock that bronze goddess look. Me? These pale limbs are impenetrable. Someone needs to make like a perma-tan pill for my brand of white person."

Nora shifted in her seat again.

"The whole point is: I still think you should go with Fisher. Just head home now, throw some shit in a bag, and take the limo to the airport. That's what I'd do. Plus, there's also the Jesus factor."

"What Jesus factor?"

"You said that Jesus was flying out with Fisher, too, right? Well, you're probably more familiar with his earthly name: *Liam*. Liam is Jesus. With all that luscious rock god hair—even in that questionable man-bun he seems to favor—and then the crunchy beard, I mean, goddamn. *Super* fuckable."

"Oh, good Christ," Nora said, cringing and looking away from the phone.

"And I heard he has a flying bald eagle tattoo that runs along his collarbone and chest, like, right over his heart, and goes down his shoulder."

"Gross. Liam's basically a minor."

"He's over twenty-one, Nora. That's the line in the sand these days. And he's a Harrison; he's got dirty, raw, and reckless deep in his DNA," Jenna said, barely able to contain her cackle.

Nora closed her eyes and let her head fall back so she was staring, in full disgust, at her high ceiling. "He's a child. He's been Fisher's mentee for, like, years. Since he was in high school."

"But he's got all the grown-up boy parts."

"Can we end this call now?"

Jenna's laugh filled Nora's studio. "It's all good, clean fun. Sorta."

"I can't do this with you. This whole thirsty old woman thing you're into lately, I can't be a party to it."

"Sure you can. Corrupting young souls is the whole point of getting older. It's in the bylaws."

Where she would normally chuckle at her friend's crassness,

instead Nora went silent. Her usually comfortable chair was too small right then, too hard and practically poking at her back. She stood up from it with a start and tugged at her chiseled gold necklace. It was a rare piece composed of a series of layered interwoven rings—one of many gifts from Fisher—and, despite all of its magnificence, it was choking her.

Nora moved quickly over to the window and pressed her forehead on the cool of it. This is what she used to do back at Immaculate Heart whenever she woke suddenly in the dead of night, gagging on her memories. She would pad over to the small window in her dorm room, press her head against it, angling her face to the right, just past where the sugar maple tree–lined, gravel path was, trying to see if this time, this night Caswell Coop was visible through the thick darkness. The Coop—or Hen House, as it was typically called—was the converted stable where the Convent of the Immaculate Heart nuns once raised chickens. Once the old building transformed to a school, The Coop served as the art gallery, displaying the homespun talents of the students. Nora had spent countless hours staring out at it, envisioning what her life might look like had it been molded better—in the hands of a ceramic artist instead of the Bourdains—and painted with different colors.

"Nor?" Jenna said. "Honey, did I lose you?"

"No," she said, raising her voice to cover the distance.

"What's going on over there? Are you at the window? Bring me with you, girl!" Jenna giggled, but it sounded nervous and artificial in Nora's ears. She let the forced laugh run its course and then dropped her voice. "Seriously. You okay, hon?"

"Yeah, of course." Nora straightened her shoulders and readjusted her deep-cut white blouse, tucking it farther into her jeans. She fixed her necklace and slicked her hand along her side part. "I'm good. Totally. Just had to pull a file. I have a big client meet today." She walked back over to the cell phone on her desk. "Another reason why I can't go jetting off to

Geneva, running behind Fisher. I've got shit to do. And the wedding planner emailed this morning. She's sending somebody over to get paperwork going for the married name change." Nora pulled at her necklace once more, sat back down in her seat, and forced out a loud sigh close to the phone. "So, yeah . . . busy, busy."

"Are you hyphenating?"

"No." Nora knew she sounded terse, but didn't care.

"Well, *all right* . . . hyphenation not optimal. Guess going double-barreled is out, too?"

Nothing.

"Got it," Jenna said in a heavy whisper. "Moving on . . . Do you want to do dinner tonight? You only have a few weeks left as a single girl—correction, an *affianced* lady. I say take your lovable maid of honor out and get her drunk enough to sing 'Single Ladies' at karaoke—complete with Beyoncé hand dance moves."

"You're doing the moves now, aren't you?"

"Yep!"

Nora laughed, finally. "All right. Where to?" she said, still smiling.

"Ugh. I have to meet that chef and his agent at his new restaurant. I already know the food will be awful. I'm going to be starving after. Let's do nine-ish at Chestnut. His place is just over the bridge."

Nora's grin vanished and she sat up straight in her seat. "I can't go back there. I . . . I am . . . going to be way uptown later today. Basically Harlem, so I can't get back down to Brooklyn to meet you."

"I could send Mr. Wally to get you."

"Don't," Nora said, sharply. "I don't want that—" She quickly brought back her smile, pulling it tight over her face. A trick she learned from being around Mrs. Bourdain: Anything sounds like sugar when squeezed through a toothy smile. "It doesn't make sense to do all that. We could just meet some-where else for dinner. I'll text you options." The strained smile was starting to make her jaw sore.

As one of the youngest editorial directors of a Penguin Random House imprint, Jenna was overly concerned about ap-pearing too flighty, too unreliable, and effectively, too young for the job. Mr. Wally, a slight but stately black man in his early sixties from Barbados, was Jenna's driver. He knew every shortcut that ever was in the city—even mapping some new ones all his own. If Jenna needed to jet over to meet one of NYC's elite chefs/musicians/comedians/artists-turned-memoirists or she had to get back to the office, not on time but thirty minutes *early,* for a meeting, Mr. Wally knew the way. He had been driving Jenna exclusively for three years. She said that she liked how his mellow singsong accent soothed her ever-frayed nerves. Plus, she said, his close-cropped silver hair reminded her of the Uncle Ben's character from the rice box. "I just trust him with everything," she said, when Nora questioned why she had given the elderly man keys to her Chelsea apartment. But Nora didn't like him—more, she didn't like how she felt around him. She didn't like how she'd catch him spying on her through the rearview. It wouldn't be straight on; instead, he'd sneak looks through the side of his eyes and always unsmiling and steeped in something suspicious and bitter. He didn't do this every time, and Nora couldn't be sure she wasn't reading too far into all of it. But it had happened often enough that Nora avoided riding along with Jenna whenever possible.

"I gotta go," Jenna said. "We're prepping for an auction. I'm actually a little giddy about it, too. Catch you later . . . unless you're in Geneva." Jenna sent an air kiss—*mwah*—through the phone and she was gone.

Nora sat quite still, looking at the silent phone. When she fi-nally moved to pick it up, she noticed her hand trembled. It was slight, but real. She held her next breath, hoping to steady her hand as she tapped and scrolled to Dr. Bourdain's book-marked obituary. This time she studied the picture at the top of the web page. She homed in on the details of his face, taking in his lipless mouth, his eyes, and the wrinkles around both. He looked different: older, a little sad. His hair was nearly all gray and cropped close to his head. The lines by his eyes were etched deep, almost carved in, and his eyebrows were thicker, bushier, and more unruly. He wore the same tortoise-shell glasses—or something very similar to the ones he always wore when Nora was a girl. She remembered every facet of those glasses (or specs, as he called them). When he started making Nora "visit" with him in his study, he would remove them the minute she entered the room and gently rest them on his desk before directing her to the alcove with a dart of his eyes. And when he was finished rubbing himself on her and it was time to move on to the next phase in his nasty production, he'd scoop up those eyeglasses from his desk as he ushered Nora over to the slim daybed in a corner of his office, where he set them, al-ways, on the small round table by Nora's head. He would make her lie back so he had easier access inside of her—first with his crooked fingers like branches, then years later, his raw penis. Nora would turn her head in the direction of the glasses and stare at them, just waiting for it to be over. And when it was, he'd pick up those glasses and gently position them on his face again. That was her prompt, Nora's cue to leave his study with-out a single word or even a glance back at him.

The loud jangle of keys snapped Nora's attention. In her rush to look immediately casual and cool, as if nothing were snatching the breath clean out of her lungs, she dropped her phone and knocked over a vase, spilling water over everything, her desk, books, phone, lap.

It was Oli Chung, one of Nora's assistants. "Sorry! Didn't mean to startle," she said, removing her giant earmuff-like headphones and covering her mouth in one smooth motion. "Ohmigod. I'm *so* sorry, Nora. Here, let me clean that up. I'm so, so sorry."

Nora leapt to her feet. "No, no. Don't you dare," she said, shaking her head and hand. "This is all me. I can clean up my own mess." She righted the vase, jamming the flowers back in dry, and moved what didn't get wet off to the side.

"Let me at least get some paper towels." Before Nora could move to stop her, Oli shuffled off to the back room—the storage closet-slash-kitchen and prep space where clients never go. "I was so wrapped up in this podcast, you know?" Oli shouted back from deep in the closet. "It was about . . . hang on."

Nora looked at her phone and knew it was a goner. It was dripping with water and stray leaves and petals. She clenched her fists and pounded them on the desk. Like every horrible thing that had seeped into her once-simple life, this too was the Bourdains' fault. She was sure of it. It's always them, destroying things, blighting them, and rendering them critically damaged, warped, and useless. Had she not been reading his wretched obituary; had she not been dragged back in time, blinded by graphic flashes of his sickening ways; had she been focused on now and not then, there would be none of this soaked mess. Or any of the other ones, Nora thought, shaking her head.

Oli trotted back with a roll of paper towels and a crispy-dry sponge. She still had her bags slung across her slim body and her headphones around her neck. "So this pod," she said, lunging toward the edge of Nora's desk to catch the waterfall. "It's that true crime series—*Slay*. You've heard about this, right?" Oli nodded on Nora's behalf. "They follow one case over thirteen weeks; one delicious episode at a time, and I . . . am . . . *obsessed*." She paused on sopping up the water and stood looking at Nora.

Olivia Chung is Nora's ardent and loyal No. 2. She came to work for Nora just days after the two met in a cramped bathroom at a Fashion Week event three years ago. Nora had dipped into the loo to check her hair; it was unreasonably humid for September and she was . . . concerned. There she found Oli crouched in the only functioning stall with the door half-open, bawling. The sick sound pouring from this small body rolled up into a tight ball made Nora push the stall door the rest of the way open. Oli barely looked up, unconcerned about being so exposed, and kept crying. Her face was smeared with wet makeup. Her shoulders jerked as the rest of her trembled against the clammy bathroom floor. She stayed there trying to tuck her head deeper into her neck and bend her neck into her convulsing chest past where it was physically capable of going. She was trying to disappear; fold into herself until there was nothing left. Nora knew this because on that one horrible day in June, she had wanted her body to do the same thing, to tuck itself into itself, squeeze all of its matter into the tiniest space until it was rendered invisible.

Seeing the young woman, a stranger, so uncontrollably sad and broken by the world pulled Nora back into the black hole of when her mother died. Cancer. At first the disease was just rare and that's all they could process, but then it turned merciless and cruel.

"It's called mucinous cystic neoplasm," Dr. Bourdain had said, his voice low and dour. "And unfortunately, it developed into pancreatic cancer." He and his wife, both with severe sadness drawn over their faces, sat across from Nora in the still-spotless kitchen—her mother's sacred province—trying to explain to her what was happening, prepare her for what she would see at the hospital. All Nora heard was that her mother was dying, and fast.

"Just breathe," Nora had said to Oli, when she sunk deeper

into her wailing and started to cough and gasp. "Breathe," she'd said, squatting down beside Oli and gripping her shoulders.

Oli could only shake her head. "*IcantIcantIcant,*" she sputtered. "I can't breathe. Not like this. Not . . . without her." She had just been dumped by her girlfriend of eighteen months. Speaking that truth, saying the words, putting her lost love's name into the stale air was too much for Oli. She fell into Nora, a sobbing, shivering, sweaty heap. Nora pulled her, this shattered stranger, closer, crushing her own precious couture jacket—dismissing its high-end specialness—and she cried with Oli, stroking the sides of her night-black hair piled atop her head like a dark mountain. She stayed rocking her as Oli's baying unwound, settling into sniffles, and her breathing caught a smoother rhythm. She stayed with her, waiting, like she wished someone had done for her back on that wretched summer's day when the world Nora knew crumbled into dust. She stayed with her until they were both ready to stand and return to life, pieced back together—if only for that night. The two women walked out of the stall, leaning on each other and with a tacit promise to leave their sorrow whole and untouched on the damp floor behind them and to cover their splintered hearts with layers of the finest fabrics and the most fabulous accessories their trained eye could find.

Nora looked at the water spread all over her desk now and at Oli trying to sop it up. "You really don't have to clean up after me," Nora said. She reached for the paper towel roll, but Oli arched it away from her.

"Nonsense," she said. "I'm on this. Plus, you gotta listen to my whole thing about this podcast." Oli returned to wiping up the water in her precise way. "So this guy, Edmund Thackeray—which is the most British and *brillz* name at the same bloody time—he's a former MI6 intelligence officer who for

years had this cover as a biomedical sciences professor at Ox-
ford. Already I'm seeing a young Harrison Ford or maybe
Christian Bale playing this part in the movie. No—younger!
And Asian! Daniel Henney. Yes, that damn Daniel Henney is
perfect. And for the movie, instead of retired, we'd make him
very active in the spy game. Who could direct that, though?"

"Wait, are we on a tangent of another tangent?" Nora said,
and twisted her face in faux confusion.

Oli laughed and shook her head, trying to toggle her brain
back to her original thoughts. "But, come on. That damn
Daniel Henney is such a good tangent to be on."

"Point taken." Nora scooped up her fried phone, rolling it
in her palm as she sat back in her seat. She thought about *her*
Daniel from long ago. He was a really good tangent to be on,
too, she wanted to say, but didn't. Instead she added the sentiment to the others on the long list of things she couldn't say.
Not out loud. Not in this version of her life. But with Oli the
temptation to say "me too" was particularly high. Like when
she told Nora that her surname was actually Hogan. Chung is
her Chinese-Jamaican mother's maiden name. Hogan belonged
to her Irish-American father, who died before his memory could
find a place in her heart.

*Me too.*

When she talked about being an only child who fiercely
loved her hardworking mother, but still found herself on an
unrelenting search for a father.

*Me too.*

And each time feeling betrayed and shattered when this
search led her straight into nothing.

*Me too.*

When she talked about how frustrating it was to grow up
living in that very thin middle between being Us and Them,
and winding up on the outside of circles anyway.

*Me too.*

Or when, with anger and hurt swirling in her throat, she talked about the irritating, incessant question: *Where are you from?* And followed that with an explanation of what microaggressions are—in terms Nora, *the ally,* might understand.

Nora understood. It had been over a decade in this new skin, but she understood. She remembered.

"What about this spy guy and the podcast?" Nora said. Guiding Oli back to the center of the conversation was one of Nora's regular tasks.

"Oh, yeah, yeah." She draped her dark curtain of hair across her left shoulder and took a deep breath. "All right, so this Thackeray goes back under for a last mission investigating the Alton Brothers' energy company and ties to the Russian mafia."

"Alton Brothers . . . wait, this story is sounding familiar."

"Let me get there," Oli said, holding the saturated sponge up near her beaming face. "So Thackeray meets this other British agent—Barnes—for coffee in North London to talk their hush-hush. Two days later, Barnes turns up dead."

Nora began a slow nod, forming her lips to speak.

"Poisoned!" she chirped, before Nora had a chance to say anything. Oli was pleased by the startled look on her boss's face, it didn't matter that it was probably owing to her screeching. She took her points however they came. "Big bad dose of radioactive polonium-210, which is—"

"Highly lethal. I know," Nora said, her mouth sailing open and eyebrows pitched high on her forehead. "Actually, Fisher was talking about this case last month. They have a compound just like it at the research lab."

"Beaumont Medical is dabbling in polonium-210? *Whut?*"

"They're not dabbling in it," Nora snapped. "It's a different element. There's no radioactive piece to it."

"Is it still poisonous and mad dangerous?"

"Yeah, but you can't use it for anything nuclear."

"Sounds pretty close to it. That's crazy. Is the lab owned by the Alton Brothers?"

"No." Nora swatted at Oli's words hanging in the air. "Of course not. It's part of The Beaumont Medical Institute. It's all Beaumont, with some shareholders, obviously."

"Right. Obviously," Oli said, her face flushed. "I didn't mean to imply—"

"It's fine. I know you didn't mean . . . Anyway"—Nora grabbed a paper towel and wiped off the ruined book jackets—"so who poisoned Barnes? *Thackeray?*"

"That's why I'm so obsessed with this podcast!" The gleam returned to Oli's face. "Thackeray got pinned with it, but now—twist! Fingers are pointing directly at the British government, who may have been in cahoots with the silent Alton brother, the estranged baby brother, or was he adopted? Both maybe? That's a pretty gnarly deal, right: adopted *and* estranged?"

Nora's modest grin fell away, replaced by a clenched jaw and folded lips.

Oli noticed the minute her mood shifted. She had become acutely aware of Nora's wild swings, especially in these months leading up to the wedding. "Hey, do you want me to see if Mateo can run this out to the Apple store"—she slid Nora's phone toward the newly dried section of the desk and picked it up—"maybe get you a new one? He's due here in, like, fifteen minutes and he's got returns to do anyway."

Nora shook herself out of her temporary fog. "It's okay. I'll do it later." She swallowed hard, her heartbeat quickened in her ears. "Actually, I'll just run out now." She snatched the phone from Oli's hands, gripping it as if it were a safety bar on a ride.

"Oh, for sure. Now is always better than later." Oli started fidgeting with her sternum piercing—a nervous habit—as

Nora breezed by her on the way to the door. "It'll be fine. Don't worry. It can be fixed." Oli raised her chin, motioning toward the useless, slim brick pressed into Nora's palm.

"Me too," Nora said, barely above a whisper, and glided through the propped-open white door.

# CHAPTER 6

The whirling sound from the sleek blender lulled Nora as she stared, unfocused, at its fancy, illuminated base on her kitchen counter. Only when she pressed the Off button did she hear the front door: the end of the bell's melody first, then a loud series of knocks.

She didn't bother checking the video monitor, instead spending those few seconds slicking her hand up through her hair and adjusting the necklace along the deep plunge of her blouse. Nora touched the handle and pressed her eyelids together tight before opening them along with the door.

"Mateo," she said, half breathless and smiling. "I had the blender going. I didn't hear a thing. I apologize."

"No problem," Mateo said. "Doorman sent me right up. Said you were expecting me, so I figured you were somewhere in there. Plus, Oli said you went straight home." He craned his neck past her shoulder into the dim foyer.

"Oh, gosh—sorry." Nora shook her head and dragged the door open wider. "Come in, come in." She spanned her arm out and in stepped Mateo Ignacio de la Vega. Great-grandson of the late, renowned New York artist Rafael Ignacio "Iggy" de la Vega, Mateo brings his sharp sense of style to Nora's company as her trusted accessories editor.

"There we go. I was wondering, because . . ." he said, trailing off and adding a dramatic raise of his brow as he walked in. Though he's worked for Nora for less than a year, their relationship is somehow new and familiar at once. Part sweet: he is like her witty, little brother and astute apprentice. And part sour: Nora often considered him a rival-in-the-making just resting under her wing, waiting for his felicitous moment to pounce and gobble her up whole. He'd watch her closely, how she worked, the way she'd handle even the most demanding client with unending grace and patience. Early on, he'd always have a list of questions to ask Nora "real, real quick," but she noticed that he soon put that curiosity on mute, opting instead to make mental notes and quietly find his own answers. Though it didn't worry Nora—she knew her value here—it did give her pause. She kept an eye on him, kept him close, and made sure she always knew what he knew; a lesson she had learned the hard way at boarding school.

Growing up under the broad shade cast by the Iggy de la Vega prestige, Mateo moved through the world scrappy, hungry, and ready to prove that he was worth more than a surname. He told Nora as much during their first meeting; a protracted semi-interview that started with coffee late morning and spanned the whole day, ending with drinks that night. Oli joined them near last call to add her stamp of approval, which came easily after she bonded with Mateo over being raised by Caribbean parents (his mother is Puerto Rican) and, by extension, the correct pronunciation of *plantain*. Nora could only listen in and smile, a forged look of wonder painted on her face.

"I was about to make a frozen drinky-poo . . . well, after I down this thing," Nora said, gesturing at the sludge in the blender. "Green gross: It's what's for dinner."

Mateo shook his head and leaned back on the counter, his nose pointed to the sky. "I don't know how you do it. For real. Some things are not meant to be liquid."

"Got to fit into that wedding dress." Nora poured the foamy green mud into a waiting cold cup. She tilted it in Mateo's direction and raised her brows.

"Hard pass," he said, and put a palm up between their faces. "Like, super hard."

Nora closed her eyes and took a long, deep sip. She slammed the stainless-steel cup on the counter and wiped the mossy residue from her lips with the back of her hand. "If I told you it's actually not that bad—"

"Yeah, no. I'd say that's bullshit."

"You'd be right." She had the beginnings of a natural chuckle rumbling in her lungs, but it quickly dissipated. The sadness settled back onto her face like a shaken snow globe returned to the shelf. *Get it together.* She looked up to meet Mateo's eyes, dark and shining at the same time.

Nora knew that if she were to give him even the slightest signal, Mateo would happily slide up in her sheets. She saw how he looked at her on the sly—she felt it, actually—and, regrettably, it was all too familiar. Although he was straight as an arrow, it was often assumed that Mateo was gay. It was a stale hypothesis tied to his profession that he never bothered to confirm or deny. He saw it as an asset, a unique edge, like being a Trojan horse, and would use this winning card stashed in his back pocket whenever it served him. If it meant models (and lesser women) stripping naked in front of him in fashion closets, fine. Or men openly flirting with him and having to find creative ways to politely turn them down, also fine.

Mateo shifted in place, breaking through the thick silence, and reached into his jacket pocket. He pulled out a white plastic spoon and jammed it in his mouth.

"Still doing that, huh?"

He nodded, keeping his eyes locked on her.

"But you smoke *so good,*" she said with an amplified whimper. "It looks so cool the way you smoke, Matts. When you hold the stick in between your lips, dangling just off the side—I bet the girls love that. My thing is that first big exhale you do after lighting up, and that huge, dirty-white plume floats everywhere and you're kind of winking a little like a young Johnny Depp."

Mateo opened his mouth wide with exaggerated outrage. "You're so corrupt! Seriously, I want to quit this time, but I'm not down with the patch. And you already know my general beef with gum. So"—he slipped the spoon out and held it near his lips—"sublimation. That's what I'm rockin' with."

"Oral fixation without the weight gain. Got it." Nora moved the cup with her half-drunk glop to the sink to clean it. She skipped the dishwashing gloves and used more soap than was needed. Her engagement ring swung around her finger, covered in thick suds. A flash image of letting it drop and go down the drain jumped to the front of Nora's mind. She shook her head to clear the thought.

Off her look, Mateo piped in. "I was doing toothpicks at first, but I landed on spoons and kept it rollin'. It's kind of unique, you know?"

"Yeah, for sure. You definitely stand out in a crowd with a white plastic spoon falling out the side of your mouth."

"Oh, you got jokes?"

The chuckle found its way back and out into the air. "So, did you want a cocktail? I'm feeling some kind of frozen peach champagne goodness. Or there's beer . . . by the spoonful."

"*Har-har.* Nah, I'm good. I've gotta head way uptown for something."

"For something or some*one?*" she said, bending down and

peering into her champagne fridge. When she returned to Mateo and the blender, Nora's smile had spread clear across her face.

"That's good," he said, matching her grin.

"What—this year?" Nora danced the bottle around. "Yeah, I opened it last night."

"Nah, I mean it's good that you're smiling and joking and stuff. You've been mad serious lately. I guess the wedding business got intense. Which I don't get." He looked around the sparkling kitchen, deliberate and with added drama. "You're about to marry into a dream, and you're super stressed out. Does not match, man."

Nora poured even more champagne into the blender cup and looked at him blankly. "It's not that simple, Mateo."

"It never is, though, right?" He rolled the spoon around his mouth and smirked.

She exhaled loudly, resting the bottle hard on the counter. "There's just a lot I need to work out and the wedding only adds more to the plate." She was surprised at how much she said already, how freely she was speaking, and continued anyway. "I have choices to make, real decisions with real implications, and I can't say I'm sure what's the right way to go."

"Look"—Mateo leaned in closer to her; his face focused and eyes dense—"people seem to believe, especially in the most dire situations, that there are only two options available. They think that they should either do this or do that. The poor fools never once consider that there's a third option: They can do nothing. And then be pleasantly surprised when it all works out in the end."

Do nothing. It was so simple it was almost absurd.

Nora looked at him, at the lopsided grin edging up the right side of his face with the plastic spoon jutting out the other end, and she tried to process all that Mateo had just said. There were times when he would prove to be a true twenty-three-year-old, cavalier, beautiful boy with a modest trust fund waiting in the wings. Doing a line of coke off model Bianca Munro's freshly tattooed sternum at the *Vogue* after-after-party, for instance. But then other times, like right now, Mateo felt wise, as though informed by something outside of his realm, beyond his years.

*Do nothing,* Nora said to herself once more, nodding this time. She felt her shoulders slide away from her ears. Her back straightened and she cocked her head at Mateo, still standing close and smiling at her. He looked as if he were standing taller, too; his already broad chest puffed out. He removed the spoon, tucking it in his pocket. She was seeing him. Nora didn't always see him—not as a person. Mateo was often more of a symbol, a bookmark to the pages she thought were turned over and long behind her. He was a proxy for those Montreal boys: rich and wrapped warm in privilege, good-looking always, and good-natured until they figured out they didn't have to be. Those hand jobs, blow jobs, and gropes of exposed young tits were theirs for the taking. Cajoling, begging, floating out empty promises, none of these things needed to be in order for these young burgeoning men to land "full pen" sex, not with girls like Nora; girls who were never given the chance to know the free and absolute kindness of strangers.

"That's actually good advice, Matts." Nora looked down at the half-filled blender, smiling. "I kind of feel better already. All thanks to *nothing,* right?"

"Yeah, you look it."

"Thanks *a lot,*" Nora said through her teeth, and flipped her middle finger at him.

"Ah, man. You know what I mean." He swatted at her. "And you know you look good, Nora. I'm sayin' that you already look less stressed. Like, the lines in your forehead disappeared right quick."

"*What?!* I have lines in my forehead?" Nora said, taking exaggerated umbrage and pretending to paw at her reflection in the chrome toaster.

"You and the jokes." Mateo shook his head, chuckling. "Anyway, boss, I gotta bounce. I'm heading uptown for—"

"Something, yes, we established this. You sure I can't fix you a drink for the road? Fisher has a flask or fifteen around here that you can hold."

"Thanks, but nah. I want to be sober for this," he said. Nora raised a brow. "Uh, ma'am, I *can* be sober at parties, okay? This isn't even a party. A friend, she's part of a theater group and they're putting on this amazing one-act musical uptown. It's supposed to be like the next *Hamilton*. I don't know . . . I just want to support her. And I want to go in fresh and clean, you know? No opiates, no lubricants, just me, whole."

The light on him shifted again, and Nora tilted her head again, seeing him again. "That's sweet."

He shrugged and looked down at his shoes. "I try sometimes."

"She'll notice." Nora stepped over to him and opened her arms. "All right, get out of here. Hug me before we both start crying or some shit."

"There she is! And now I know you're legit feeling better," he said, squeezing Nora tight.

"So . . ." Nora started talking into his shoulder. "Are you just happy to see me or is that an iPhone in your—"

"Oh, shit. I almost forgot." Mateo pulled away and reached into his pocket. "Here." He handed Nora the slim phone. "Brand new. It's all powered up, but you'll have to handle grabbing all your shit from the cloud."

She ran her hand over the spotless face of it. "Seriously. Thanks for doing this. I was all set to go on my own, but then I just started thinking about stuff and got overwhelmed and came home—"

"To make cocktails. I get it. Life be rough sometimes."

"Jesus, I know, right? Just ridiculous." She rolled her eyes at herself. "But, really. Thank you. This is not part of your job."

"Sure it is. It's my job, it's Oli's job, it's the whole team. We work at Nora Mackenzie, LLC. Which means we work for Nora Mackenzie, which also means we work at taking care of Nora Mackenzie. You're our General of the Army, five-star, special grade, homie," Mateo said, raising a stiff hand to his head and saluting her.

"Oh, in the World War of Fashion or . . . ?"

"*Cállate,*" he said, making a fist at Nora. "Yo, you want to ditch that stale cocktail business and roll with me uptown?"

"Please . . . I'm way too old to be hanging with you young'uns."

Mateo threw his head back and flung his hands in the air with a loud *pssshh.* "You and this *fughesi* line 'bout, *I'm old.* You've got—what—four, five years on me? You could be my older sister." He clapped his hands together loud and dipped his head to give Nora the once-over. "More like my blond, white, older sister from another mister. But still fine as fuck and"—he spanned the expansive kitchen again, even spinning around on his heels as if part of an elegant dance to place his eye on its marble countertops, custom cabinetry veneered in stained maple, dazzling pendant lights, and shining stainless-steel details—"in a minute rich as fuck to match."

Although she felt a twinge of the disquiet starting to bubble up in her stomach, she pushed against it, forcing it back down into the dark pit from which it came with just two words, whispered so softly she barely moved her lips: "*Do nothing.*"

"Well, you go do your supportive thing," Nora said, and returned to her station in front of the blender. "And I'll keep working on this, uh, *stale cocktail business*"—she rubbed the base of the machine like a belly and scrunched up her face at Mateo—"sweet baby brother."

"A'ight. I earned that one." Mateo swooped in for another hug and kept moving to the door. "For serious, though. If you change your mind and want to roll, text me. You might want to clear the *fifty-leven* messages you got on there from ol' girl first, though."

"Who?"

Mateo gave Nora a look. "Who else? She's a case, that one."

"Don't start." Nora raised a foot in a playful kick as he turned to leave.

"Check you later," he hollered on the way to the foyer.

Nora was already scrolling through her messages with her head down. She shouted, "Have fun, and don't stay out past curfew!"

There was a string of at least fourteen messages from Jenna, each text getting more clipped as the timestamp rolled on and finally devolving into blaring one-word curses in ALL CAPS. Nora decided to forgo the text reply and called her.

"What the fuck? Are you at the bottom of the Hudson?"

"Sorry, sorry," Nora said, trying in vain to talk over her best friend. "I'm fine. I'm on dry land, at home. No sleeps. No fishes." An easy laugh fell from her lips.

"Seriously? This is funny to you? You've been a complete disaster lately, total bag of nerves. Then you flake on me for dinner and go MIA for hours. I was fixin' to text Fisher and everything, but you want to giggle now?"

"Easy, Callaway. Easy. I apologize for the dinner thing. My phone got fried—drenched in water—and I was wrapped up in all of that. I meant to ask Oli to have someone reach out to you about dinner and—*shit*—the wedding planner. I meant to push the meet-up with her, too, but I forgot about everything. I'm really sorry."

"You were going to have one of your staffers *reach out to me* about dinner instead of, say, showing up as planned?" Jenna sniffed. "Going the Beaumont way already, *ain'tcha?*"

"Jenna. Don't be like that. I said I was sorry, and I am."
Nora eyed the unmixed champagne slush in the blender and
waited for the ice in Jenna's voice to melt as well. She knew her
friend prided herself on being no-nonsense, having a notori-
ously thick outer shell. Nora also knew that it was more of a
cobbled-together version of Jenna, this brassy woman with big
boobs, bigger gumption, and grit along with some true warmth,
a saving grace, glazed over top. She knew that at her heart,
Jenna was as vulnerable and soft and wanting as everyone
else—maybe even more so. And Nora let her friend have these
moments of bluster and theater because she'd learned long ago
that allowing someone their story was easier than rolling out
the truth.

"Okay," Jenna said, her voice smoothed. "Just . . . just don't
do that again. I was actually worried. Last couple of days,
you've been really out of it and with you going ghost like that,
I didn't know what to think."

"Like, maybe I swapped out the champagne bottle for razor
blades on my way to the bathtub this time?"

*Shit.*

The minute the words left her, Nora wanted to claw at them,
drag them back to her mouth, and swallow them. "Oh, I—
listen, Jenna, I'm sorry. That was just—"

"Not very funny."

"I know. I didn't mean to—" Nora dipped her head, clapping a hand over her eyes. "I'm sorry. That was way out . . . I'm
sorry. Mateo was just here and we talked and he said some stuff
that made me shift the angle on all the crap stewing in my head
and I'm finally feeling like myself again and . . . well, I guess
that means being an asshole with absolutely no tact. That was
dumb. Sorry."

The silence that followed was long enough for regret to set
in under Nora's skin. *Why did I listen to anything Mateo said?*

Suicide would always be a barbed subject with Jenna. Two of her five siblings—oldest brothers—had killed themselves within a year of each other. It was the awful thing she and Fisher had in common, but that they never dared discuss. Nora thought up and in turn abandoned a dozen different ways to steer the conversation toward better, rested waters.

Mateo, she thought. Jenna was sweet on him. He had mentioned to Nora earlier in the week what he was planning to wear to the wedding: a slim-fitting jean suit made from raw selvage denim, with a dress sneaker and colorful custom bow tie.

As Nora took a breath, a grin already starting up on her face, Jenna finally spoke. "Do you want to know what's really chapping my ass? It's not all on your disappearing act—although, *don't pull that shit again.* But it's something one of my editors said to me today."

Nora moved the phone away from her mouth and exhaled loudly. "What'd they say? Am I going to have to come choke a bitch?"

Jenna's laugh was back and it sounded honest, relieved, making Nora's grin bend farther up along her face.

"No, it's nothing like that," Jenna said. "This woman, she just came back from maternity leave and, first of all, looks even skinnier than before she left. It's like, *Stop it already. This isn't Hollywood.* But anyway, my real bone with her is—look, I know this stuff is heavy and weird for you, but I just honestly really need to talk about this for a minute. Is that enough of a *trigger warning?*"

Nora's smile snapped like a rubber band. "Actually, I'm sorry, Callaway, but I can't really get into this right, right now. Is that okay? Just let me know you're intact at least and not crafting one of your dragon-fire emails."

"I'm fine. She's not hot-garbage horrible, but it was just something she said about my fucking eggs and how—"

"I'm so sorry to cut you off, honey, but I'm supposed to go over some last-min wedding stuff with Fisher and we're doing a Skype thing. I want to, uh, freshen up, you know?" Nora said, trying to keep her voice as light as Jenna's. Plus, she noticed that a lie seemed to flow easier when she stripped away even the slightest traces of angst from her tone.

"*Riiiight.* I see you. Get the kitty camera ready. Not mad at that. What time is it for him over there anyway?"

"Who knows? I'm not into those facts." Nora moved back over to the blender and grabbed the near-empty bottle of champagne.

"Well, the facts are always friendly," Jenna chirped. "Every bit of evidence one can acquire, in any area, leads one that much closer to what is true. My daddy used to always say that. It's actually from psychologist Carl Rogers, but Kenneth Callaway practically made it his very own brilliance. It's one of those things that never makes sense on its own, you know? *The facts are always friendly.* It's almost fortune cookie-ish, right? I kind of filed it away anyway, for later, when I can attach some kind of meaning to it."

Nora shrugged and pursed her lips, prepping to take a swig from her bottle. In the face of Jenna's psychobabble, "Do nothing" felt like much better advice.

"You're drinking again?"

Startled, Nora pulled up from the bottle just as the fizzy goodness was about to hit her lips. "Wh-what," she said, coughing and wiping the splashed drops from her cheek. "How did you know . . . what are you, a witch?"

"No," Jenna said, chuckling. "I just know you very, very well, friend-o."

A wash of something ugly spread across Nora's face. "Right. You do," she said flatly.

"*Hey,* what happened?" Jenna said. The sound of her voice

was so dulcet it sounded almost foreign, like she was speaking a different language, and it made Nora uneasy. "Look, hon, I'm not passing judgment on you about the drinking thing. This is me; you know I take my coffee highly Irish. I'm just saying, this is a super-stressful time for you, and drinking alone in a bathtub is not the right salve. Because, sweet pea, that dress? The last thing you need is a beer pooch pressing through that stellar garment on your wedding day. If nothing else, do it for the sake of that dress."

"So this is not AA, then?" Nora hissed.

"Sweetie, I'm *not* judging you. It's a suggestion to maybe come at things from a new angle. Like look at my production manager, Angelica. She's always on and on about how running basically saved her life when her starter marriage fell apart," Jenna said, the sweetness in her voice quickly melting away. "Wait. Bad example. Point is, the whole jogging in the open air thing helped her work shit out. It's that or yoga, and frankly," she snorted, "I'd take someone droning on about their pace or shin splints or whatever over those yoga assholes with their sweaty-crotch leggings any day."

"There was a point here?"

"Yes, and it's a valid one: The next time you're feeling stabby and over it with all the wedding crap, go for a run instead of grabbing a bottle. Is that so awful?"

Nora nodded, but said nothing. She could hear that Jenna was rattled by the long silence; her breathing was choppy and getting louder. But she stayed quiet, staring out the window and tracing the frame of the tall building next door between blinks.

"Nora," Jenna said. "Come on."

There was a bass note of desperation in Jenna's few words, a pleading that made Nora's stomach turn. She settled into the quiet even more. Silence. Stony, chilled silence. It was her signature move, a power play from back in the late Montreal days when she was under the exclusive care of the Bourdains after her mother died. It was also the one thing the couple couldn't force Nora to do: talk. When Mrs. Bourdain came to Nora's darkened bedroom—just next door to the one her mother slept in and that had become thick with sorrow—she said she had "good news." That something could ever be good with her mother gone was unimaginable to Nora. Mrs. Bourdain was wearing a butter yellow sundress and a loose, lime-green cape. Her white-blond hair was swept back into a classic chignon, and her makeup was pristine. Nora could still picture the slight shimmer to her light pink lipstick so clear nearly a decade and a half later. Mrs. Bourdain's face looked like the start of spring— sun-kissed and warm—as she stood next to Nora's unmade bed, smiling down at her.

"The adoption, it's been approved," Mrs. Bourdain said, and placed her soft hand on Nora's bare shoulder. "Your mother, may she rest, we did right by her. She would be happy."

Nora barely turned her head to look at the woman. The hand on her shoulder took on the weight of ten bricks, but Nora said nothing. And as Mrs. Bourdain—or Elise, as she insisted Nora call her now—went on, trying to convince her that the adoption was not out of some moral obligation to their maid's hard years of service, but instead her mother's long-held wish fulfilled, Nora remained still, soundless.

"You're a Bourdain now," Elise said, gritting her teeth in place of a smile. "It really is a gift, you know? The name. You'll see that life's kinks will be smoothed out now that you're like us."

Nora said nothing. Not a nod or blink.

She also kept her mouth shut when, not even a full year after her mother's passing, Elise came to her basement room once again with more "good news."

"You've been accepted, dear," she said, practically beaming, "to the renowned Immaculate Heart boarding school, in Vermont. You leave in six weeks. But don't worry; we'll have plenty of help packing you up, and Mr. Noel has kindly offered to drive you there."

And again, her hand went to Nora's shoulder, resting there light at first, turning heavy and pressing shortly after.

Nora said nothing. But inside she wailed as an unmistakable relief coursed through her body. She would be away from the attentions of Dr. Bourdain for months at a time. Maybe there were still good things to be found in a world without her mother.

By the time Elise Bourdain took fourteen-year-old Nora to her personal salon to have the girl's hair chemically straightened and the color lightened (with brows to match), Nora's silence had become another member of the small family. She had also come to the decision that she needed to be a person who could not be chipped away at. Immutable. And so Nora went along with the new hair, the new surname, the new version of herself, never once balking. It was the only way she knew to avoid destroying herself.

"I know you'll wear our name well," Elise said to a blond and blanched Nora two days before she was shipped off to Vermont.

"Nor? What's up here? The silence is killing me," Jenna said. "You know I love you and I'm only doing my part as your maid of honor, best friend, and all-around wise woman of the world." She cracked up, laughing a little too hard and loud for the moment.

Finally, Nora spoke. "It's okay, Callaway." She rolled her eyes and turned her back to the wide window. "I know you do. It's just—I don't like people trying to force shit on me, try to change who I am."

"I get it, Popeye. That's not this. Best interests; it's what I'm dealing in. Always."

"Right," Nora said, bending down to scoop up the champagne bottle at her feet. "I should go, though."

"Of course, of course. Go do your thing, and tell Fisher I

said hey," Jenna said in one fast breath. "Call me later if you want to talk, okay? Be good."

*Do nothing.*

"Always," Nora said sweetly. She pressed the button to hang up, tucked the bottle under her arm, and headed straight to the back guest bathroom.

# CHAPTER 7

A strange chime echoed through the bathroom. Nora un-
furled her body in the tub, groggy and squinting. Even though
the bathtub had long been her safe space, the place she could
truly be alone and untroubled, this one was starting to feel like
a pit. Everything felt dry and irritated: eyes, face, lips. The sound
continued; it was her phone ringing—some default, robot
melody. She sat up and reached for the thing lying faceup by the
drain.

The screen told her BATMAN was trying to connect a video
call.

"Shit!" Nora barked. She jumped out of the tub and bolted
down the hall to her bedroom, flying into the bed and pulling
the covers up to her neck over her rumpled clothes. She didn't
want Fisher to see her waking up in the bathtub, mascara still
rimming her eyes. Nora took a deep breath and pressed the
Voice Only button.

"Hey," Fisher said. "Wait. I can't see you. I want to see you."

She tried to quietly clear the rasp from her throat. "I know.
It's my phone; I spilled a full vase of water on it and it's been
acting weird since. Sorry, baby. It's just my voice for right now.
Good morn—is it still morning? What time is it there?"

"Noon. But it's still a good morning. Darlin', I would trade a hundred sunsets for just one good morning with you."

"Aw, Fish." A sweet, easy smile bloomed. "What am I going to do with you?"

"Marry me."

Nora felt that familiar surge in her chest, as if every chamber of her heart was filling up. She closed her eyes, crossed her legs, clenched her fists, and tightened her muscles, squeezing all the parts of her body like a dense hug that started from inside. Fisher, he made her happy, and she wanted to feel exactly as she did right then—minus the hangover—every day.

"You there?"

"Yeah, I'm here. I'm just . . . I miss you, Beaumont," Nora said. She let the hand that cupped her face drop, sliding it down her front, tracing the smooth skin along her neck, between her breasts, along her stomach, and then off to the side, tucking her fingers beneath the thin band of her panties. "And I want you here." She pushed her hand, fast and rough, down inside her silky underwear, her fingers starting their slow, rhythmic circles. "Not in two days," she whispered. "Right. Now." Nora let out a low, steamy moan. "Right now. Right here," she continued, with more heavy breaths and hot whispers.

"Mack. Babe," he said, sucking in air through his teeth. "Don't do that. You are . . ." Fisher let out a roguish chuckle. "You are so bad. You know I'm sitting in a glass office here, right? Don't you dare start this."

Nora giggled and pulled her hands out from under the covers. "Fine," she said, flatly. "I'll stop. But I still miss you."

"Jesus. You have to stop."

"What do you mean? I did," Nora said, wrapping her voice in innocence.

"Let's just change the subject, okay, Naughty Nora?"

"I'll do whatever you like," she said, whispering again.

"Okay," he laughed. "Let's talk about my mother."

Nora pressed her head back deeper into the high pillow. "You win." She sat up in the bed. "Lady Eleanor as cold shower. *Hmm.* What would Freud say about that?"

"All right, Dr. Armchair, PhD. Let's dial it down. I actually do need to talk to you about my mother."

"Oh." Nora's shoulders tensed up. "Is everything okay?"

"Yeah, of course. It's about the tea."

"The tea?"

"Yes, I knew something like this was coming and I was planning on giving you a heads-up. I know how you are about surprises—"

"Complete and total uncut hate for surprises," Nora said, frowning.

"Correct. But this Geneva pothole happened and look, the gist is, my mother wants to have you up for tea. She's been dropping hints about it for a solid two weeks. It's kind of her thing. She did it for Rock's and Asher's wives. And, frankly, she's been waiting forever to do this for me and my wife-to-be."

"So, she wants me to go up to the house to have tea with her?"

"Well, I don't want to say it's a *tea party,* but . . . it's a tea party. It may come across a bit formal and overwrought, but that's Mother. Essentially, she wants to show you off to her dearest friends."

"Right." Nora rolled her eyes.

"Maybe it's a good thing that I can't see you and your eye-rolling right now."

"Fish, I'm not rolling my eyes," Nora said, moving the phone away from her ear to grimace at it. "I just find it weird, prancing me around like I'm some show pony. Makes me uncomfortable."

"There's no need for you to be uncomfortable. You're not a *pony.* Mother loves you. And you're responsible for making her son incredibly happy. That makes *her* happy. Hence the tea."

Nora swung her legs over the edge of the bed and stared

down at her dangling feet. "Fisher, do I have to say what the real issue is here?" She paused, hoping he'd fill in the rest for her. Nothing came. "You say your mother wants to show me off to all the other grand heiresses and guardians of the family's good name, but we both know that these types of gatherings with these types of women always, always find their way back to being about babies, specifically when *I* will provide you with one." She slumped forward, resting her upper body on her knees. This part never felt good. But like most people hiding beneath a lie, Nora believed she was doing the right thing. She had to believe it.

"Mack." Fisher dropped his voice, and Nora heard what sounded like the quiet click of a door closing. "Babe, my mother knows about you and your . . . well, she knows where we stand on the subject of children. And, more important, she adores you. She would never put you in a position where you would be made to feel ashamed or inadequate about any of it. Please. This isn't even your fault. You know that." Nora's head dropped and she blinked back tears. "The dice turns up this way for some people and they deal with it. That's us. We dealt with it, and we're good." He took a breath. "It's just tea."

Nora could almost see his grin balancing on the words and it only made the tears she held rush in faster. *Fisher didn't deserve any of this,* she thought. But he could never know the truth. It would ruin him, and them, without a trace of redemption. She pulled her body up and wiped her wet face with the back of her fist. Nora angled the phone away from her mouth. *Christ.* "It's just tea," she said into the phone, and shook her head, an attempt to bring herself back into the moment. "Okay. I'll go. When should I pop by?"

"Oh, no. There's no *popping by* for this. Like I said, it's Mother. Her staff will be reaching out to you today—that is, if they haven't already left the box with the doorman—to extend an invitation."

"A box?"

"Again, it's Mother. But don't worry about any of it. You'll be wonderful. All of those—what did you call them?—*keepers of the family name,* they're going to be absolutely smitten with you. Come on. They have no choice."

"What am I going to do with you?"

"I'll show you later tonight, Naughty Nora. Make sure your video is *turned on.*"

"Hmm. Yes, sir," Nora purred. "Until tonight."

"Until tonight. I love you."

"You have no choice."

Nora hung up the call and flopped back on the bed. The surge returned to her body, running down to her fingertips and toes. She lay there staring up at the ceiling smiling, electrified and unruffled. This moment, this is what she needed and she was basking in it. Right up until it came, like a meteor burning through her world's atmosphere, and crashed into her brain, tearing giant holes in everything.

*"The facts are always friendly."*

It blared in her head like an off-key reprise.

*"The facts are always friendly."*

She closed her eyes, squeezed them, as if that could change the track, break the loop playing in her brain. It was no use. Her phone let out its strange ring again and like that, the drone was over. Nora saw Oli's face pop up on the phone's screen and answered.

"Oli," Nora said, sounding relieved. "Say something good."

"Glad Mateo got the phone stuff worked out. That's good, right?"

"Sure. It'll do. What's up? Am I already late for something?"

"Ha. No. Actually, I thought I was going straight to voice mail, given the hour. Then remembered that you're probably up . . . given the hour. But, speaking of being late, your wedding boss-lady sent a guy to the studio to do some paperwork business with you yesterday."

"*Ah.* Yeah, I meant to message you about that. Crap."

"No big deal. I took care of it. I know where you keep your passport," Oli said. "You just have to sign some shit when you get in today and I'll messenger it back to her. Then *boom*— you're a Beaumont, and it's all good in the 'hood."

Nora nodded.

"Oh! On the subject of hoods. We have a new client: Jay Schuyler. That kid with the dating app Facebook just bought? He's come into lots of money-dollars, obvi. Translation: he's ditching the Killer Mike T-shirts, those wretched camo pants, and that frowsy hoodie he lives in for something a little more upgraded and sharp."

Nora chuckled at Oli's use of the word *frowsy*. It's something she heard her mother sometimes say under her breath about certain kinds of white women whom they would encounter at the grocery store, on the bus, or occasionally at church. Those women who looked down their noses at Nora's mother as if their little lives were worth more than hers. Whenever Nora witnessed these moments that rested in between disregard and judgment, it would leave her fuming for weeks. She remembered the looks they gave the two of them, the raised brows, the pushed-up mouths and snickers. *Stay there with your frowsy self,* her mother would hiss as she breezed past them without so much as a bat of her eye. As devoted as Mona Gittens was to her God, she never fully committed to the notion of turning the other cheek.

"He's ready to grow up. Good for him," Nora said to Oli.

"More like *someone*'s ready for him to grow up. I think his lawyers strongly recommended he get sorted," Oli snickered. "There are a lot of jagged edges that need smoothing with this kid. Doesn't give even the thinnest slice of a shit about how he comes across or the right way to deal with people in general life. He's real . . . external. Nuance is a different language to him, you know? Jay Schuyler definitely needs guidance, a template for how to be human in these streets, because right now—this kid is spinning out, hard."

"Right, so, he's one of these hard seeds wrapped in wads of money and set out in the sun, but underneath it all he's—"

"Still a hard seed. Yeah, that's totally it," Oli said. "That's really good, Nor. Like, such a perfect way of describing his whole situation. You're good."

"I just know the type." Nora smiled to herself. A hard seed. That's exactly how her own mother would have described Nora when she first arrived in New York with her "school money" bank account cleaned out and shoved into the bottom hidden pocket of her lumpy backpack and an altered identity—again. Vincent helped her sand down the last of the prickly fringes so she could move through this new beau monde. But most of the Nora Mackenzie transformation work came from Nora Mackenzie herself. She had picked up on the patterns of reinvention—deflection, magnetism, sheer conviction—from watching Mrs. Bourdain's artful rewiring of her.

"So, when I get in you can give me the full rundown on Jay's deal," Nora said.

"Well . . . I'm thinking this time me and Mateo can cover this. You can swoop in at the end for last looks and give us your head nod on what we've pulled."

"Oh," Nora said, narrowing her eyes. "He didn't come to us to work with me?"

"No," Oli said, before blurting out, "I mean, of course he knows who you are."

"Oh-kay . . ."

"Mateo brought him in. They have a mutual friend who's a deejay and . . ." She trailed off, then loudly cleared her throat. "You have the wedding, which is, like, *blink* and it's here. It'll probably be like this anyway, right? Me and Mateo—and, eventually, Kazzy; she's killing it lately—we're all kind of taking the lead on clients more. It just makes sense, with you being married off into—"

Nora bristled. "Into what exactly, Oli?"

Oli cleared her throat again, and Nora could hear the creaking of her chair beneath a shaky exhale. "You're going to be an official *Beaumont of Manhattan*. I hardly think you'll have space in that life for helping these guys pick out suits."

"It's more than that, picking out suits. This is my career. It's what I do, and I'm good at it. Why would I just walk away from that—because I got married?"

"Nora. Jeez. I-I'm talking about how I can help make *your* life easier. That's all. It's not an attack on your feminism. I know this work is important to you. I know who you are. But I'm wondering if you know who you're about to become. Because, real talk? Nora Beaumont means something so totally different from Nora Mackenzie. That name, it's got weight on it. That's just facts."

Nora was long past tired of hearing about *facts,* but she wasn't up for adding yet another person to her bad side today. It wasn't even 9 AM. She moved to swallow the whole thing and right the morning. "This is true. You're not wrong. It *is* different. I'm sorry. My back went up—instinct. It's been me and those clients for so long; they're like my very special projects, all of them." She smiled because that part—the unvarnished joy she felt about her faithful clientele and seeing her polished touch and fine haberdasheries on full display—was accurate. "Guess I should get used to it, right?"

"With the quickness, woman." Oli's tone seemed light again. "Anyway, I'll let you get back to your morning. See you at the studio. This time I'm gonna jangle my keys super loud when I get in."

"Preemptive," Nora said. "I'm into it."

After the call, Nora tossed her new phone on the nightstand

and hopped out of bed before her mind had the chance to drag her back into the dark. She opened the blinds, fixed the pillows, and made the bed. Eager to peel out of the last pieces of stale clothing and wash a fresh day into her skin, Nora hustled to the bathroom. As she reached to turn on both showerheads, she heard the lobby phone ring.

"Good morning, Miss Nora. I'm sorry to disturb."

"Morning, Javie. It's okay. You're not disturbing me at all."

"I said I didn't want to call this early, but this guy, he wouldn't take no, you know?"

"Which guy?"

"Messenger, but official type, you know? He said he needed to make sure that you got this box and wanted verbal confirmation, and his boss *needs* to know you got it in your hands so it's not sitting on a table down here and all this. I told him: Look, it's too early for this kind of thing. But this guy . . . Anyway, you have a box here delivered to you from . . . it says here, The Beaumont House. I can have one of my guys run it up to you later. I would, but I'm gotta wait here for—"

"Javie, it's fine. I'll be heading down shortly, so I'll scoop it on my way out."

"Very good. Again, my apologies. Have a good rest of mornin', Miss Nora."

"That's the plan, Javie."

———❖———

By the time Nora got back home, it was dark and her mood was leaning that way, too. It had been a day filled with various people telling her how different everything would be once she crossed over the line and became an official Beaumont. All of it grated her nerves, so much so that the insides of her mouth started to itch and the incessant yawning began—an ancient, faded tell of Nora's akin to an eye twitch or gnawed-at fingernails. She tried rubbing her tongue along the roof of her mouth a few times when it started to get out of hand, but soon remembered that that was how to stifle a sneeze, not a yawn. Even with the covered mouth, her watering eyes gave it all away.

"You should just bounce early," Mateo had told Nora more than once, while looking at her as one would a decidedly sleepy toddler or lost kitten.

Oli kept pulling Nora aside offering up her own brand of subtle suggestions while practically shoving the woman out the door.

*We'll take care of all this.*

*It's handled.*

*No big deal; don't worry about it.*

When Nora finally took the hint and left, announcing that she had forgotten a meeting scheduled with the wedding planner, no one raised a head or a brow. Although it seemed clear to all that the meeting was likely made-up, the team was in a groove and just let the fib dissolve on its own. And Nora moved through the room toward the door as she always did: nose high, focus fixed, chest open, and breathing easy.

After a drink at a new bar far uptown, Nora walked to Central Park and found her way to the Conservatory Garden. Along with the Flatiron Building, the Conservatory Garden was Nora's favorite place in all of New York City. The Garden in the summer was truly hard to beat. So tucked away, but open and free. To be hidden yet still surrounded by lush greenery and colorful flowers, wrapped in that beauty and fragrance, it felt like the Heaven Nora's mother told her was promised to us, *God's children.*

She discovered the space by chance only days after stepping off the Greyhound at Port Authority a decade ago. Back then—thirty days short of being an official high school graduate—she was still reeling from everything that had sent her running away from Vermont and from her life. The garden and its brilliant offerings are what saved Nora in those first years in the city; she swears by it. She would walk along the many acres, moving through the smaller gardens; going from the French to the English and then the Italian one and back again. As she would stare out at the late spring flowers, blessing them with new names all her own, Nora began to notice that the urgency and anguish that had been vibrating in her fingertips, they were fading, falling away. Instead of thinking about Mrs. Bourdain, the betrayal, Nora would consider which flowers her mother would have enjoyed most. The Lilac Droplet (actual name: Roy Davidson Lungwort).

As she admired each flower, Nora felt the weight of everything lifting from her shoulders. Breathing came easier, the chronic headache subsided, and the frown lines that had taken over her face melted back, letting the glow return to her features.

And Nora soon started visiting the Conservatory Garden to read, flip through fashion magazines, and just *be,* alone in the rare quiet of New York. It's in this same garden that she met Vincent Dunn one windy autumn day, where she signed the lease paperwork on her office space, and also where Fisher arranged a picnic lunch for the two of them on their third date. The garden had become a private happy box for Nora, one that never emptied and that possessed the power to make even the mundane magical.

Now, sitting in it smiling and floating on clouds back through time, Nora reached into her purse for her phone and dialed. Fisher answered, but sounded immediately on edge, hurried, crisp, and she instantly regretted calling. Nora went ahead anyway. "Hey, I was thinking about you. I'm at our garden, in Central Park and I—"

"Listen. Nora." Fisher typically used her first name in moments like this, when he was deep in business mode. "I am—"

"Busy. I get it. Not a big deal."

"What I was *about* to say is, I am going to call you back in thirty-five minutes. But if it's not a big deal, as you just said, then we can pick this up in about three, three and a half hours, if that works on your end."

Nora shook her head, annoyed—at herself more than anything.

"You still there?" Fisher said, his tone flat.

"Yes, I am. Sorry. I was distracted by . . . this bird here." Nora cringed. "We can just talk later tonight or even tomorrow morning when you wake up."

"That works. Oh, and, Nora?" Fisher's voice eased up. Nora started smiling again. "You do need to get back to my mother. Her assistant needs your RSVP for the tea. Can you please look into that at your earliest?"

Nora felt her cheeks warm and the corners of her mouth began twitching. "Oh. Yeah. Of course. I'll . . . do that right now."

"Works. I have to run, but we'll talk tomorrow, yes?"

"Yes, speak to you then," she said, as if talking to her accountant.

"Very good. Tomorrow."

Nora slipped the phone into her bag and walked right back to the bar far uptown, leaving behind her beloved respite and all its vivid memories tucked inside.

Looking at the tea party invitation box, still unopened, Nora took another swig of beer, the last of Fisher's favorite brand. She slammed the bottle down and started moving toward her champagne fridge but stopped short. This invitation yet unseen was literally driving her to drink and she felt ridiculous. "It's just tea," she said, and doubled back to the box sitting on the kitchen counter. She ripped it open and read the note out loud, mockingly imitating Lady Eleanor's trademark through-her-teeth affect:

*Lady Eleanor D. Beaumont*
*Requests the honor of your company*
*For afternoon tea to welcome*
*Miss Nora Mackenzie into our family*

Nora stopped reading and stared at the word *family*. The black calligraphy ink looked shiny and fresh, not all the way dry. She traced the strokes of the lettering with her finger, then checked the tip of it, halfway expecting to find a smudge of ink there. She set the beer bottle down on the counter along with the thick invitation and walked over to the closest mirror in the hall. Nora brushed back the stray wisps of her blond hair and stood taking in her reflection.

"I'm so honored to be accepted—" She stopped, cleared her throat, and started again, but louder and more maudlin. "I'm truly touched by the tremendous warmth the entire Beaumont family continues to show me. I can't remember a time that I've felt so wrapped in unconditional kindness and love. This—an authentic, wonderful, whole family—is what I've dreamed of all my life; it's what I've always wanted. So, thank you. I am ever grateful to you, Lady Eleanor." Nora bowed before the mirror, her hand to her chest. And when she stood up, visions of her mother came crashing through the glass. There she was, looming large in the room, her brown skin wan, her jaw slack, and her hooded eyes resting on Nora. Each phantom version of her mother looked more sorrowful than the next, and Nora knew why. It was the look her mother would give her whenever Nora was skirting the truth.

She moved back from the mirror, keeping her eyes to the floor. It was the one place she didn't see her mother's face. With careful steps, she made her way to the kitchen counter again—never once looking up—and reached for the beer bottle. It was empty.

"Of course," she muttered, and let out a long exhale, tossing her head back. She opened her eyes and was relieved to find nothing before her but the high ceiling. Her mother was gone.

Another long breath.

Then, an idea: Nora decided to follow Jenna's advice and instead of popping open another bottle of something, she would suit up and go for a run.

---

It was sluggish at first. Nora could hear the beer sloshing around in her stomach. But she stuck with it, picking up her pace as she cut through SoHo on her way to Little Italy and hitting her stride as she crossed Broome Street. The night was warm with a kind breeze that kicked up right when Nora needed it most. But her left leg caught a stitch, her arches felt pinched, and she figured she had three more blocks in her, tops. Still, it all felt good, invigorating. Her mind was clear and focused on only one thing: getting to the finish line, which Nora had already decided was going to be at the Bean House Café one block away.

She slowed to an easy trot, pulling out her phone to check her stats on the running app that she had downloaded in the elevator ride to the lobby. Nora, her head down and thumb scrolling the phone, took a tiny leap up the uneven, high sidewalk. She had done it so often, hopped over the sidewalk's quirky edge, that she could do it blindfolded and still glide into the always-busy coffee shop with her usual grace. But this time was not usual. This time she should have been watching her step.

*Crunch. Splash. Goddammit.*

She had smashed right into someone walking out of the café. Light brown liquid dripped down the front of her expensive, white wind jacket. It was iced coffee and it had already soaked right through. Nora barely looked up at the person before she started apologizing.

"I am *so* sorry," she said, slipping her (miraculously) dry phone into the zippered angle pocket. "Please, let me pay for your drinks." Nora wiggled her hands out of the jacket's damp thumbholes and reached for the slim fold of cash stashed in her other pocket—for emergencies. (Nora really was her mother's very own child.)

That's when she finally raised her head and made eyes with the collision victim.

That's when her world stopped spinning. She swallowed hard and her full breath anchored in her belly.

"Holy shit," the woman said. She was standing across from Nora, also wearing spilled coffee, but with more of it sprayed across her brown skin, and she held the scraps of the wreckage: cracked plastic cups, a bent straw, a couple stray ice cubes resting in the crook of her arm. "I can't believe it. It's you! Nora Bourdain. Jesus fucking Christ, it's really you! Finally."

"I-I-I don't—" *Fix your face.* Nora squared her shoulders and stuffed the money back into her pocket. "I have no idea what you're talking about, miss. Like I said, I'm sorry—"

"Sorry? That's you. *I'm* not sorry. This day—right this minute—this is the fucking best! I ran into, like *literally* ran into the fabulous Nora Bourdain. What luck, what luck, call me a duck." The woman chuckled and tossed the clutter of cups and ice into the gutter just past Nora's feet. "You know, for a minute I started to believe that I imagined you, dreamed you up. But no, you're real"—she dusted off her hands, dragging her eyes slowly up Nora's frame—"and lookatcha, still pulling *this* shit. You're about that long game, huh? *Wow.* That's commitment; I'll give you that." She shook her head and gave Nora the once-over again. "Nora muhfuckin' Bourdain, in the flesh. I really should hit a bodega and buy me a lottery ticket."

"Listen. I don't know what you think is happening, but I already offered to pay for your mocha whipped bullshit," Nora said, her hand waving across the dripping mess along the woman's top. "You declined. So, it looks like we're done here."

As Nora moved left to leave, the woman stepped in her path, blocking the way. "Oh, no-no. Not this time," she said, leaning into Nora's face. "It's not going down like that. Not again. I'll definitely be seeing you around, Miss Bourdain. *Definitely*. Hashtag facts only. Now"—she pulled out of Nora's space—"I'm going back in the Bean House and get a redo on my iced-up deliciousness. But thank you, truly, for this *exquisite* evening. Later, buddy!"

Nora walked away, not daring to look back. But once she rounded the corner, her body folded at the middle, as if kicked, and she stumbled back to what she believed was a yellow wall—that is, until the thing started moving. Nora couldn't hear what the cab driver was saying, but from his flailing arms she guessed that he was likely cursing at her. She sputtered some words at him and he nodded. She pulled the cab door open and, still doubled over, Nora slid into the back and stayed curled up on her side like a sick animal, her face pressed against the seat.

The cab bounced and dipped, picked up speed, and stopped hard over and again, jostling Nora around. Her mind had taken leave of her body, so she felt nothing. All Nora could process was that she had just met up with her horrible past—crashed right into it—and its name is Ghetto Dawn.

Her real name is Dawn Brooks, but Nora and her small, enviable circle of friends gave her the mean moniker shortly after the girl arrived at the prestigious boarding school in their junior year. Dawn was a black, self-assured, hard-shelled, scholarship student from starkly humble beginnings in Chicago. Upon meeting Nora, she smirked and nodded, knowing something about the school's golden princess "didn't curl all the way over." She started snooping around, digging into anything Nora touched. Dawn stayed suspicious from the very beginning right up to the moment Nora created the end.

Nora hadn't thought about Ghetto Dawn in forever. Not once since she watched her being escorted from their school flanked by the security guard and a young state trooper. Yet here she was, present day, standing before Nora with her smirk as crooked as a decade ago and refusing to break her classic deep stare.

Nora pulled herself mostly upright in the back of the cab and leaned her head against the cracked-open window. Those last days with Dawn at Immaculate Heart spiraled through her brain with a blistering heat.

"Well, look at you," Dawn had said. She was leaning on the sink closest to the antique half lite door with frosted glass.

Nora swallowed hard. The gulping sound was loud in her ears. She had just gotten out of the showers. She turned her back to Dawn and put her robe on over her towel. "What, did you come in here to hurl or something?"

Dawn chuckled. "No, not my style."

"What is your style, sneaking up on people in the shower?" Nora stepped lightly over to the sink near Dawn. She kept her eyes low on her own reflection in the mirror.

"That's not me either," Dawn said.

"So what, you're just going to stand there, all creepy and staring?" She turned on the faucet and splashed water on her already-wet face.

"You're really doing this, huh?"

"What?" Nora locked the faucet and finally looked at Dawn. "I can use these showers. Emily's doing an ice-bath soak or something in ours."

"Oh, you're going to just stand there and act like you don't know what's up?"

Nora's hands started tingling. She balled them into fists and used them to prop herself up against the edge of the sink. "I don't know what your problem is, but I'd like some privacy. So . . . do you mind?"

"Actually, I don't mind. But I'm sure your white homegirls would."

Nora's heart started its rhythmic punch again. The rise and fall of her chest picked up the tempo. She knew her eyes were shifty, but couldn't summon the calm to stop them from darting around the empty bathroom. From somewhere in the base of her stomach, the words came. "You know what? Fuck you."

"Fuck me?" Dawn tossed her head back and laughed. Her mouth was wide and her nostrils flared. The cackle was loud and hard. "Fuck me? You're the one who's fucked. I mean, how much hate must you have swirling around your gut to do *this?*" She drew a circle around Nora's face with her pointed finger. "Pretending that you're some white bitch with a trust fund? But you know what, they bought it. They all bought that shit."

Nora's elbows buckled, sending her swaying forward into the basin. She put a hand out in time to stop from crashing into the mirror. She pushed against it and slid her other hand along the inside of the sink, trying to regain her balance.

Dawn stepped in, closer, leering.

Nora eyed the door behind Dawn.

"You know what's crazy? I think I almost bought your bullshit, too." Dawn clucked her tongue. "Almost."

Nora looked away and stared down into the sink. The throbbing by her temples slowed. Her heartbeat moved from the middle of her throat and settled back into her chest, but the churning in her stomach remained. She turned toward Dawn again, gazing at her feet, studying the girl's ratty slippers. She slowly shook her head. "You don't know anything about me," Nora said. She paused and licked her lips. She started again, louder, slower, and raising her eyes enough to lock in on Dawn. "You don't know anything about me."

"I know that you're one lying piece of shit," Dawn said with a mix of delight and disgust. "The worst part is, I work *so* hard to get people to like me, to get them to trust me and still, there are no guarantees. But you, you're out here standing on the grandest of lies—*you're* the one they shouldn't trust. You're the one to be afraid of, but you slide on through and they stay giving me the side looks. So fucked up."

Nora wrapped the robe tighter around her and pulled the sash snug. "Just stay out of my way," she said, and gathered her expensive monogrammed cosmetics bag. She wanted to drop everything and tear down the hall, but instead Nora put her full concentration behind walking past Dawn and out of the bathroom with her jaw locked and head high and not even a hint of a glance back. By the time she arrived back in her suite, the door shut tight behind her, Nora dropped everything: the pretense, the cool, and the flimsy theory that no one would ever find out. Dawn was going to unmask her; Nora was convinced of this, so she committed all of her energy and ideas to making sure that that didn't happen.

A recent spate of petty theft on the seniors' dorm floor and burnout tenth-grader Cat Dipalo's near-fatal drug overdose at the school gave Nora all that she needed to put her savage plan in play. Using little else besides her good name, charm, and raw talent of persuasion, Nora dealt her preemptive blow: She discredited Dawn by setting her up to look like the thief and drug dealer that the school had struggled to root out. Dawn was immediately expelled.

The way Ghetto Dawn's eyes burned a hole into Nora tonight, even with the coffee dripping from her chin, it was so menacing.

Nora couldn't shake that look. It was clear: She has never forgotten or forgiven Nora.

*But that was Nora Bourdain,* she thought, once the static lifted from her brain. That version of Nora was long gone, changed for good, along with the blighted surname.

This was going to be a problem. Dawn Brooks was going to be a problem. It was a solid fact and Nora was terrified, because as she discovered many years ago, the facts are not friendly. The evidence is out to get you. And the truth will ruin your life.

# CHAPTER 8

Her phone rang again and Nora pressed Ignore again. It was Fisher calling, as promised, to say good morning. She had been sprawled out in the tub the first time he rang at 6:01 on the dot. She had been awake for hours and was unable to speak more than a few jumbled words at a time. And Nora was in no better shape to handle his second call either. She heard the chime notifying her that there was a new text message but ignored that, too. It was the doorbell chime sounding out twice in full that finally got her to move.

Nora hauled her stiff body out of the empty tub, stepping over the huddle of bottles on the floor beside her. She walked toward the front door, dragging Fisher's open robe that hung from her shoulders behind her like a necrotic limb. She was still wearing the stained windbreaker from last night, zipped up all the way right under her chin, and her tight sport-shorts panties. When Nora reached the door, she opened it wide and slid down the wall next to it in the foyer. She sat there staring out at nothing, waiting almost motionless for over an hour.

The security phone buzzed. Nora, barely blinking, reached up to the panel above her head and yanked the phone down. She placed it by her ear and said nothing.

"Uh, morning, Miss Nora? It's Javie. I . . . sorry to disturb you so early, but I have Miss Jenna down here. She said you're expecting her? Normally, that's okay, but it being so early and everything, I thought it's best I buzz you."

Nora grunted out a sound that was close enough to an affirmation, and Javie let Jenna proceed up to the penthouse.

"Nor?" Jenna said quietly. She pushed the door open farther and crept in on eggshells. "Oh, Jesus," she said, startled by Nora slumped over by the wall, still cradling the lobby phone. "Honey, are you okay?" Jenna slammed the door shut and swooped down to Nora's level. She caught a glimpse of Nora's dirty jacket beneath the open robe. "Oh, my God! What happened? What is this, mud? Puke?" Jenna ripped open the robe and scanned the dried mess on Nora's jacket. "*What the*—Nora, are you physically hurt? Did someone . . . hurt you?"

Nora gave a slight shake of her head and kept a hazy gaze just past Jenna's shoulder. "It's coffee," she said. The words slipped out in a hush through her dry, cracked lips.

"Coffee?" Jenna said, her face red and misted over with sweat. She did a quick scan of the rest of Nora's bunched-up body and slinked closer to her catatonic best friend. " 'I need you please come,' that's it. That's all you texted. I burn it down here, come upstairs, and the door's wide open; you're sitting on the floor like a zombie and covered in old coffee stains. What the *fuck* is going on? Do we need to call Fish, tell him to come back early?"

Nora moved her eyes to meet Jenna's and shook her head again. "I-I can't . . . I don't know what . . ." Her tears came in with a sting, and she crumpled into a sobbing, trembling heap.

Jenna threw her arms around Nora's twitching body and pulled her in close. "Honey, honey, it's okay. Don't force it. Let's just baby-step this," she said, gently rocking Nora. "First, let's clean you up, all right? A hot shower, get you out of these coffee-dirty clothes, and we'll go from there." She helped Nora up and guided her to the master bathroom. "I'll, uh"—she gestured to the guest bathroom down the hall with a tilt of her head—"clean up all the other stuff down there while you're showering." She smiled. It was gentle, kind, and it only made Nora's chest hurt more. "And I'll call Oli. You're not going in today. They can handle it."

A stiff nod was all that Nora had.

Even as Jenna helped Nora out of her grimy clothes, as she put her broken friend to sit on the padded bench by the window while she tested the shower's warmth with her hand, as she tucked Nora's limp hair behind her ears and looked into her clouded eyes with clear empathy and caring, Nora couldn't find the words to tell her *thank you. . . .*

*I'm sorry. . . .*

*This is all a lie.*

Nora skipped the mirror—she knew what she looked like—and went straight into the shower. As the hot water covered her shaking body, she dropped her head back and watched the steam dancing by the lights high above. The shower had always been her special space, a haven from the roughness of regular life, the place where she could recover. And after leaving parts of herself on the floor of Dr. Bourdain's study, in the basements of curious boys' homes, or wedged into a box she had kept hidden under her dorm room bed, the shower stall—no matter how stark or opulent—was where Nora went to glue the remaining pieces of herself back together.

The shower was also where Nora did her thinking, devising ways to survive being demolished by the walls that threatened to crush her. Dawn was a wall. Back in their senior year at boarding school, Dawn was explicit with her intentions: She was going to destroy her. She told Nora this outright as the two were hustling into chemistry class, late. This ran deeper than a simple threat for Nora. Dawn's words sliced into Nora's white, bright, unruffled, self-contained life in Vermont. There, she was *Nora Bourdain:* popular, revered, idolized, and, most important, accepted. Finally she belonged, no longer unclaimed and rejected. And it was all so immediate; she was an instant hit at Immaculate Heart. Nora herself was surprised at how well this deception launched by Mrs. Bourdain had played at the school. Of course she was white. Of course she was wealthy, privileged, held under a special, glowing light. She deserved to be there. She deserved to be in any room that she cared to grace. The thought of Dawn, cheap and malicious, unraveling her handsome life was too much to process.

She knew something had to be done.

And so Nora would spend hours swaying in the shower at school—often three times a day—thinking of ways to stop Ghetto Dawn. With administrators already whispering about the uptick in petty theft and prescription drug abuse at the school, it wasn't hard to cultivate the seeds of suspicion around Dawn. After all, she was new—and black. In fact, Dawn was the only (visible) African-American student in both the junior and senior classes combined.

The ambient *shush* of the running water grew louder as Nora tuned in to the present again. It was soothing, this sound, and she closed her eyes and listened. But her mind refused to stay put. This bad luck encounter with Dawn had her bouncing from one horrible idea to the next, desperately searching for an answer to the question: What now?

Subscribing to *you'll probably never see her again* theories was weak and witless. Nora knew Dawn meant it; she'd see her around. And the "do nothing" refrain was just as useless. She even considered doing the absolute worst possible thing: stepping out from underneath the deception and coming clean to Fisher and her friends, but the real truth was, she didn't want to. The alternative—being an outlier again, being unclaimed and rejected—Nora wanted no parts of it. She took a deep breath and another slow turn under the rain shower, letting the water beat down her back. It stung, but she kept going with it a few minutes more before shutting it off. She had been in there a long while and was sure Jenna would come knocking soon.

Nora slipped Fisher's robe back over her heated body and stood in front of the long marble counter, looking at the tall mirror above, staring through it, past herself. Her face was clean, but still puffy around the eyes. She let her robe drop a little and turned, angling her body in the mirror to get a glimpse at what brought the stinging. She spotted a long, red scratch near the top of her shoulder. Touching it only made it hurt more, but she kept running her finger the length of it. Finally, Nora went to the narrow built-in cabinet for some ointment and a clear bandage and patched herself up. She pulled the robe back up over herself and returned to the mirror. The tears were brimming again. Nora looked down and shook her head.

A light knock at the door.

"Hon, you okay in there?" Jenna said. "You're going to look like a raisin by the time you get out."

Nora let out a deep, slow breath. "I'm almost done," she said, and went back to the mirror, forcing a smile. It was pinched and pained, but it would have to do.

She walked out to the light echo of clinking coming from the kitchen. Nora followed the sound and found Jenna in there shoving the last of the empty champagne bottles into an opaque garbage bag and tying it up. "Oh, God, you don't have to do that," Nora said, embarrassed.

Jenna waved her off. "Please. It's nothing. Plus, you don't want your cleaning ladies thinking there might be a *teeny* problem here. I know they say that they don't snoop or judge—they tell you that, but you know what? They all fucking judge. And they snoop! It's unwritten." She removed the gold polka-dotted apron she'd been wearing and slung it over a chair. The pretty apron was part of a gift from the surprise bridal shower that Nora's staff threw her a month ago. It was from Kazzy, the recent Oberlin grad and classic California girl who joined Nora's team on Oli's recommendation. She had put together a darling basket of "little lady" must-haves that looked fresh from the 1950s. It was a wink to *Mad Men,* a show Kazzy adored and that Nora merely pretended to. Jenna rolled her eyes at the gift basket—*in front of Kazzy*—when Nora opened it. It was an inside joke that Nora thought was sweet, but Jenna considered obsequious. Jenna wasn't a fan of Kazzy in general. From her name (not short for anything) down to how hard she laughed at any of Nora's even marginally funny quips. She's so desperate to be liked, Jenna had told Nora after only briefly interacting with the then new-to-the-team Kazzy. Nora couldn't see it, and didn't want to.

"Thanks, but really, it's fine," Nora said, walking toward Jenna and squeezing her shoulder. "We don't have cleaners." She eased the apron off of the chair and was folding it when she caught herself. "I mean, right now. This week. We don't have the cleaners coming this week. Scheduling thing." Nora fired the cleaners a month after moving into Fisher's penthouse. She didn't think they were doing an adequate job. Her mother would have found a million things wrong with their work. Nora took over the cleaning herself. It's therapeutic, she told Fisher when he balked. And it was in a way. Cleaning, using the rather thorough Mona Gittens method, made her feel like her mother was there in spirit, moving through the rooms with her, giving her head nods with each job well done.

"Well, it's already done. One less thing, right?"

"Right. Thank you, Jenna."

"So, I don't *technically* need to be anywhere until after lunch." Jenna slung her arm around Nora's neck. "I say, cheese, bread, tons of butter, and a dedicated *Teen Mom 2* binge. And before you say another word, you should know that I make a mean grilled cheese—*with* sliced tomato." She started nodding, her eyes closed and grin stretched.

Even though she wanted nothing more than to crawl back into the tub, Nora knew she had no choice but to consent to Jenna's plan. "Okay, Callaway. Sounds good."

"Cool. Now, while I get started"—she grabbed the neatly folded apron from the counter—"you work on finding me one of those lux, baller robes. I want to look like a cloud, too, god-dammit."

Nora smiled. "I'll get one for you. We have a couple by the guest room."

Jenna dragged the apron over herself and started wildly opening drawers, cupboards, the pantry, the fridge, gathering her tools and product. "Perf," she said, without looking up.

Nora felt the knot in between her shoulder blades loosen as she watched the top of her friend's head teeter about, perusing the knife block. They didn't get the chance to do this often enough, just hang out, stowed away, carefree and cheese-ready. They especially didn't do it at the penthouse. Jenna said she didn't like feeling like she was encroaching on Fisher's space, but really she was too concerned about one of Fisher's rich cronies—or worse, his "snotty hottie" younger brothers—popping in and catching her unawares. Nora walked down the hall to the closet just outside her favorite bathroom. She dipped her head in to spy on Jenna's cleanup work. Not bad, she thought, and continued on to the linen closet.

A careless tug at the extra robe caused it to tumble off the hanger and slump down to the floor. Nora bent down to grab it and her eye landed on the box peeking out from beneath its dusty quilt. She glanced behind her before sliding the box out farther from under its cloak and carefully lifted the lid. Her hands went straight to the twin stacks of cards, all of them from her mother. Some wished her Happy Birthday, while others sent Christmas and Easter greetings complete with dramatic script font, crucifixes, bright sunbeams through clouds, and various white, luminous, praying hands. Nora's mother didn't have the means to give her daughter gifts with the desired brands and logos emblazoned upon them. Instead of money, the woman opted to invest her time in searching out the just-right card to give her daughter. She would often start looking for it a month or more before the holiday (and her only child's birthday was long considered one). While out on her weekly market runs, Nora's mother would build in extra time for the Hallmark store in the strip mall by the pharmacy. It was important, she said, to let those you love know it, to get the words out any way you can, even if they rhyme and someone else wrote them for you.

"Give me my flowers while I yet live, so that I can see the beauty that they bring," Nora's mother would sing in a slow, low, sweet hum. It was a line from a gospel tune by Rev. James Cleveland, a favorite, and one that her mother believed in so deeply that she told Nora—in her hoarse voice soaked in sick— to never bring any flowers to the grave awaiting her. "It's in the shadows," her mother had said, in those last days, "but I am not afraid. The Lord, He will comfort me. And He will watch over you, too, sweet girl. He will. That's why I know I can close my eyes now." She had reached up for Nora's wet face, patting it the way she used to when Nora was a child and scared to sleep in her bed alone. "'Trust in Him, with all your heart, and lean not on your own understanding,' Proverbs says, 'in all your ways submit to Him, and he will make your paths straight.'"

This was one of the last things Nora's mother said to her while she was still lucid. It always angered Nora that it was a Bible quote and not something that she could actually hold on to. The Bible, God, prayer, those were her mother's underpinnings, and Nora had no faith in any of it. She believed that people were just people, not blessed or holy or trying to do unto others as they would have done unto themselves. There was no Golden Rule. How you are, how you behave and treat people, how you move through this life rests on one belief: that you're the good guy. It's the guiding principle. Relying on it absolves you from any responsibility for cut corners, deceit, wickedness, or corruption. It's the sponge that cleans everything up.

"I don't believe this horseshit!" Jenna said.

Nora, startled, tossed the cards back into the box and shoved it under the quilt. She hopped up and turned around with the robe dragging by her leg. Jenna sounded a lot closer than she actually was. "Wh-what?"

Jenna held up Nora's iPad, pointing at the screen turned out toward Nora, her mouth ajar. "This is complete and total bullshit."

Nora's mind raced. Had she stupidly left something on the counter from the night before? Were there traces of the past—his obituary onscreen—forgotten out in the open for Jenna to find? It all sounded ludicrous, but the thoughts kept coming. It was Dawn. It was her fault. She reignited Nora's panic, and anything seemed possible. Nora even started looking for ways out, both physical and otherwise. She kept her eyes trained on Jenna and stayed ready to move when she moved.

Jenna shook the thin tablet again, angling it toward Nora. "It's over," she said, incredulous. "The marriage I got ordained for and officiated a couple months back—Abigail and Brandon? They split already! Can you believe that shit?" She turned the iPad back around and looked at the screen and, with a raised brow, added, "Actually, they weren't legit married all the way . . . because of some sorted mish-mosh, I didn't get around to filing the marriage license at town hall." Nora's eyes went wide. "Well, it was Connecticut and I was out of sorts the morning after . . . and also totally boinking the best man. I swear I left that place with a giant, gross hickey and a raging UTI. Awful." She rested Nora's iPad back on the side counter.

"Are you fucking kidding me?"

"What? I was out of my element. I'm a city girl, Nor."

"Jesus, Jenna. I thought something real happened."

"Uh, these two people who professed their amazing love for each other in front of three hundred and fifty of their nearest and dearest, after five years together, split up only ten days after their wedding. That all sounds pretty fucking real to me, friend. And, and, *and*"—Jenna held up both hands in the air as if under arrest—"I'm only finding out about this implosion now, a full *two months* after the wedding." She chuckled and dropped her arms, crossing them over her propped-up chest. "They should really be sending a thank-you note. They probably don't even have to tangle up with annulment headaches because of me."

Nora turned up her lip and frowned. "Why would you even tell me this?"

"Because you're a nosy bitch like me, and you like to see reality TV shit play out in real life?" It was Jenna's turn to have her face streaked with outrage. "Why *wouldn't* I tell you this?"

"Because I'm about to get married. Why tell me about someone's whole life blowing up right after they get married."

Jenna's mouth slid into a grin and her frown lines smoothed out. "Sweetie. There's nothing even remotely the same about those two assholes and you and Fish. Abbie was cheating on that dude for, like, eight months. He was fixin' to have kids right away and she wanted to wait three years. She was hoping to move to Rhode Island closer to her parents and Brandon plans on dying in that townhouse on the Upper West Side." Jenna moved closer to Nora, smiled, and held her head to the side. "They were not made for each other," she chuckled. "Not even a little bit. Honey, you and Fisher have nothing to worry about. It's rock solid with you two. Those are facts. And facts are what?"

Nora shook her head.

"Friendly, sweetie." Jenna grabbed Nora's shoulders and shimmied them. "Facts are friendly. So, lighten up. You are making yourself crazy for nothing."

Jenna smiled at her. Nora sent a strained one back.

"Sorry, I just—"

"Nope, no more sorrys," Jenna said, tugging at the sash on Nora's robe, making it tighter. "It's all about cheese right now, okay? We don't have all day, and I need to see what hot garbage these *Teen Moms* are getting into."

Nora handed her the extra robe. "I think you'll need this."

"Hell, yes. And I'm taking off my bra, too. You've been warned."

"*Brace yourself,* is what you mean."

"Oh, you're so deep in the jealous, blondie. So deep."

Arm in arm, they walked back to the kitchen to gather their lukewarm grilled cheese sandwiches and then trickled over to the soft gray couches parked in front of the flat-screen. Laughter flowed and Nora willed her mind to remain focused and wrapped up in the moment, no matter how hard the outside world poked and taunted her.

# CHAPTER 9

The doctor's head bobbed between Nora's open legs propped up in stirrups. "So, how you feeling about the wedding—hang on. Just scooch your bottom down a smidge more for me, please." Her already high-pitched, baby voice was brighter, more cheerful.

Nora did as told, rolling her eyes at the awkward sounds: the crinkle of the paper under her, the clank of the exam table's metal parts as she shifted, the squish of the doctor's lubed-up glove entering her. *Small price,* she told herself, as she did every time she went to her gynecologist.

As much as she cringed at the experience of being probed under unkind, daytime lighting, Nora liked feeling reassured that everything down there was working according to plan. She had started using an IUD almost on the day she turned twenty-one. It took her a few tries to find a gynecologist who was okay with this, but then she landed in Dr. Fiona Mulligan's tony Upper West Side practice and her wish was granted. Nora had read all the research she could dig up and liked the fact that the IUD was twenty times more effective than the pill. Plus, she always thought the pill was way too risky anyway. If you forgot to take it one day or if you vomited it up along with your ridiculous amounts of alcohol and cheap, undercooked seafood, then you could be staring down the barrel of pregnancy test pee stick. But more than the chance of getting pregnant, it was how the pill left the *maybe-baby* window open that truly rankled her. Nora did not want children. Ever. With the IUD, she felt more in control of making sure she stayed child-free. She didn't have to think about it or, moreover, talk about it.

After her first full-weekend sleepover at Fisher's penthouse, he started buzzing around the subject of birth control over coffee, likely because he didn't spy her popping the pill at any point during their three-day sequestered sex adventure. He continued with condoms until it was clear that they were getting serious. That's when the topics of marriage and kids (and those wretched condoms) were broached, and Fisher asked her plainly if she would consider going on the pill.

"I don't need to," she told him, startled by her own voice. And then, like an unruly belch, more words came tumbling out of her mouth, "Because I can't have children." She didn't pause to take a breath or a beat. She was in it now and made the quick choice to keep going. "It's my ovaries. Something called PC—"

"PCOS. Right," he interrupted. "I'm so sorry, Mack. I'm an idiot for pushing you on this. I'm sorry." Fisher's face had dropped by that point and he looked over at Nora with concern before reaching for her hand. She didn't realize then how much Fisher knew about medicine. Owing to his work with the family's institute, he seemed to know a touch about most everything. This made Nora drill down and arm herself with as much research and information about polycystic ovary syndrome as possible. She never wanted to be caught knowing less about her own body—or feigned syndrome—than he did. That she was outright lying to this man didn't perturb her as much—not then, anyway.

"So, are you excited, nervous, or just ready to be done with the whole thing?" Dr. Mulligan continued.

"Definitely the latter," Nora said with a long sigh.

"That was me, too," Dr. Mulligan said. "Just give me the ring, sign the paper, and let's get on with our lives, right? Granted, that was twenty-one years and three kids ago, but that anxious feeling—Jesus Murphy—that was pretty awful." She kept trying to meet Nora's eyes, make it seem as though the two were just catching up after randomly running into each other at a stoplight in midtown. Her efforts were not appreciated. When it came to bedside manner, Nora preferred something a little more distant and perfunctory from her doctors.

"Pretty much," Nora said, counting down the minutes until it was over.

Finally, the doctor popped up from her rolling stool, peeled off her gloves, and was at the sink vigorously washing her hands, all in one smooth move. "Everything looks great," she said, ripping two stiff-looking paper-towel sheets from the dispenser. "Why don't you get dressed and come chat with me in my office about"—she smiled and winked—"what you want to do next."

Nora didn't scramble to get dressed as usual. She didn't move, and instead sat listening as the hum of the overhead lights grew louder. She looked down at her dangling feet, pointing her toes and relaxing them and over again, taking the moment of relative quiet to gather her thoughts. Nora knew what she wanted to happen when she went into Dr. Mulligan's office to chat, but she also knew what was likely going to happen: nothing. Just more stale quotes from the *This Is a Serious Decision* book served up to her like they're fresh and unfamiliar. It was the wink. It gave it all away.

Nora wanted to stop using the IUD. Although she had only recently stopped worrying about Fisher one day feeling the device's strings during sex, the bigger reason for this change was that she wanted something more permanent: tubal ligation. She'd wanted this since the age of twelve, when her first period came and her mother chirped, "You're *an official woman,* Rah-Rah." As the mother went on to halfheartedly explain the reason for her "monthlies," the idea of pregnancy and children only filled young Nora with more dread. Creating a tiny being and subjecting it to even a thin slice of what Nora knew the world could offer, it all felt cold and cruel. Might as well toss the weak thing into a pack of wolves, she thought back then.

She still does.

But now, there's also more. Nora would have no guarantees about how her baby would come out looking—carved from alabaster or teak? Would it have her light freckles, her good golden hair, her green eyes, or would it strike back to some long-ago generation from her mother's side with skin the color of a nutmeg seed and a nappy head? She could never know those answers. The one thing she did know was: that baby would be the truth. The risk was far too great. No children ever, that was her only assurance. But each gynecologist she went to asking to have her tubes tied only saw this girl in her twenties standing before them clutching a limp belief, a basic know-nothing who *thinks* she doesn't want to experience the joys of being a mother. She was met with an immediate *no* along with one or more of the following reasons:

*You're too young.*

*You may want children down the line.*

*When you get married, you'll change your mind.*

*What if your husband wants kids?*

(The last one came from the only male OB/GYN Nora went to—a referral she received at a cocktail party. She never went back to him.)

Before Nora could settle into the office chair, Dr. Mulligan started up. "All right. So, now, the wedding's just weeks away, right? Do you want to talk about scheduling an early removal of the IUD? It's a very simple procedure, exactly like a regular pelvic exam. I'll insert the speculum so I can locate the IUD strings. Then, I just tug on them"—she held her hand up by her face and pulled slightly, as if holding thread—"which effectively pulls the IUD out of your cervix, and we're done. I'd recommend taking some ibuprofen for any cramping that might occur. But even that's fairly light, not unlike regular menstrual cramps. Nothing to worry about." She smiled and reclined in her chair. "Or maybe you want to continue with it, and you come see me when you're back from your honeymoon." Another wink.

Everything about the doctor annoyed Nora: from the way she was leaning back and her beaming face to her baby voice and chipped nail polish. It was too casual and knowing and wrong. Nora sat up straight and let her eyes rest on the doctor's wide face for a breath past what was comfortable. "Actually, yes, I do want the IUD taken out." She clenched her jaw and narrowed her eyes ever slightly, enough to bring a chill to the cramped room. "And then I want my tubes tied once it's removed."

Dr. Mulligan brought herself to sit upright, shifting in her seat. "Now, Nora, again, I really have to caution you—"

"No, you don't. With all due respect, Dr. Mulligan, you've gone over this with me a few times now and my mind has not changed. I still have no interest in becoming pregnant, giving birth, or being a mother. This was the case when I was single. And it's still how I feel, staunchly so, now that I'm engaged and about to be married. I've always felt this way—never once a doubt."

"It's irreversible, though, Nora."

"If this is a litigious concern, I will sign any and all legal forms saying that I am fully aware of the permanence of the procedure and understand the risks of the surgery."

The doctor let out a deep, loud sigh and kept her head

down, her eyes trained on the open folder atop her desk. "This is what I can do . . . Give me a couple weeks, let me talk to the other doctors here at the practice, and I'll call you myself to let you know where we landed on this."

"That's fair," Nora said, holding her expectations and any hint of fulfillment at bay.

"Again, you have to give me a couple of weeks. There are a few moving parts here, including one of the partners possibly leaving—but that's not public information yet. Please, keep that part under—"

"My hat?" Nora gave her a firm nod, but resisted the urge to follow it with a mocking wink. "I can definitely do that."

"I appreciate it."

"And I appreciate you taking me and my request seriously."

"I don't think I had much of a choice there," the doctor said. Her already watered-down smile was fading as she closed the file folder on her desk.

Nora shook her head. "No, not really."

———✦———

The atelier was full but quiet. Nora walked in, keeping her eyes straight and dark sunglasses on. Oli was on a call; her expression looked attentive, but pleasant. She spotted Nora and nodded in her direction, and Nora dipped her head in reply. While normally she would check in with everyone, go around the space handing out shoulder squeezes, kind pats high on backs, and funny callbacks to inside jokes, this late morning, she did none of it. Nora went directly to her office and closed the door behind her.

With Fisher due home that night, Nora was experiencing a steady mix of anticipation and angst. He had been away less than a week, but it felt more like a month, and she was still rattled by the coffee shop encounter. Dawn's smirking face would jump out at Nora at the least opportune moments: while blow-drying her hair or making coffee in the French press or right now, as she stared down at the large envelope from the wedding planner's office. A soft knock on her door brought Nora back.

"Hey." Oli squeezed into the slim opening and held the door against her. "You okay?"

"Hey, yeah. I'm good. Come on in."

Oli slid in through the door and perched on one of Nora's custom, white bergère chairs. "You okay—for real?"

*Fix your face.* "Yeah, of course. Totally." Nora made sure her smile didn't look too labored. "The other day with Jenna calling in sick for me . . . that was just something I ate."

"Something you *ate?* Next thing you'll tell me is that you were suffering from exhaustion." Oli clucked her tongue. "Nor, it's me. You can say it. What's really going on? Is it wedding stuff? Oh, by the way, I finally asked Michaela to come with me, and she said yes," Oli beamed.

"That's great, Oli. I'm so happy for you."

"Sorry, I highjacked the moment. I just haven't had a second to catch you up on everything."

"It's fine. You didn't highjack anything."

"So you're good?"

"Oli. Please, I'm fine. It's nothing but a bunch of little things that, when all pooled together, don't amount to much. Anyway, back to Michaela. I'm really excited she's coming to the wedding with you. She's beautiful, and so sweet."

"Yeah, she makes me kind of nervous and sometimes she'll bust me, like, gawking at her. Those sharp-as-hell cheekbones . . . I'm just—wow. And I keep telling her that I don't need anything else in my tea with her around. She really is super sweet."

"Shit! *Tea.*" Nora cupped her head in her hands. "I forgot."

"Did you . . . want some?" Oli said, her sculpted brows coming together on her forehead.

"No, it's—I forgot to RSVP for this tea party bullshit that Fisher's mother is hosting *in my honor* or whatever."

"Wow. A classic Lady E jam, huh? Should be *inneresting*," she chuckled. "Do you want me to—"

"Go with me? Yes!"

"Oh, no-no-no. I was about to say, do you want me to call it in for you—the RSVP. That's all. I don't play well at those kinds of parties. I'm not super into being asked where my family is *really* from or giving anthropology lessons on how someone can be both Chinese and Jamaican. Then there are the forty questions about my *interesting* tattoos and the horrified expressions on their faces when they spot my sternum piercing. Hard pass. I honestly can't with these rich white ladies." Oli openly cringed. "You know what I mean. You're cool . . . and not old."

A weird silence billowed up between them. Oli started fluffing her bangs: her telltale sign of discomfort. Nora cleared her throat and flipped through the imaginary cue cards in her mind, searching for a joke, an anecdote, any towline to bring them back to a smoother course. But there was nothing. Instead she turned the whole boat around and steered right toward safer shores: business.

"Hey, is Mateo in?"

Oli nodded, her brows inching closer together.

"Great. Let me call him in to join us." Nora typed a quick message on the internal messenger app. "He'll be right in," she said to Oli with a sniff.

Mateo was at the door before Nora could sit back all the way in her chair. He had his usual yellow notepad and thin Sharpie in hand. "Ready to take dictation, bawse," he said in an exaggerated New Yorker accent, and pretending to aggressively chew gum.

Nora shook her head, smiling. "Just get in here, nutcase."

He sidled up to the chair next to Oli and winked at her as he sat down, but her stern expression remained. Mateo moved his eyes between Oli and Nora. "Are we planning a funeral now? Because I threw down, like, a blanket rule at the top of the year that I'm not attending any funerals. Not a one."

"Oh, good Christ, Mateo," Nora said, waving her hands in his direction. "I think you need to reconsider what blanket rules are. No, there's no funeral. I wanted to pull you in on this powwow about Jay Schuyler. You brought him in, yes?" Through the corner of her eye, Nora saw Oli's face tighten. "And I hear that he's a lot of work, so . . . let's get on it and Eliza Doolittle this bitch."

Mateo laughed and rubbed his hands together. "Oh, you know I'm always here for Nora Mackenzie taking off the gloves and molding muthafuckas like Play-Doh." He turned to look at Oli again, mid-chuckle. His grin dimmed and he leaned over toward her. "Yo, what's with you? This is, like, your shit. You love this part."

Oli smiled the tightest of smiles. "Nothing's wrong. I just . . . I'm just listening."

Nora ignored Oli's obvious sulk. "Cool. Let's get our plan together," she said, and stood up behind her desk, triggering Mateo and Oli (dragging) to do the same. "Matts, why don't you set a time for your boy Schuyler to come in here for a pre-lim meet."

"On it," he said, and turned to leave. He motioned with a tilt of his head for Oli to follow. She shot him an iced glare and sat back down instead. Off her look, Mateo shook his head and left.

"And do you need me to start sketching out a plan for—"

"Actually," Nora interrupted, "if you could handle that tea party RSVP for me and add a large arrangement from Bloom with a nice note"—Nora made air quotes—"*from me* to smooth over my super-late reply, that would be great. Also, give me everything you have on the Schuyler kid." Nora reached for one of her bright blue Sharpie pens from the gold cup on her desk and bent over jotting an illegible, short string of words on the closest notepad. She could feel Oli's big eyes on her, growing Keane-like with each mention of the client. Nora knew exactly what she was doing, and did it anyway. The flipping through her notebook, no longer meeting Oli's gaze, acting as though everything was an afterthought—it was all theater; a way to remind those who were under her that they were under her.

Oli stuttered a few details from Jay's profile. She was clearly taken aback and put off by the territorial dance Nora had introduced. But Nora pressed on, acting as if Oli's bent facial expression and furrowed brow had gone unnoticed. She had seen firsthand how well this passive-aggressive tactic worked. Elise Bourdain had taught the master class on it, and Nora turned out to be her A-plus student.

"This sounds good," Nora said, and closed her notebook with a flourish. "I think you and Mateo have a good start here. Just email everything, plus whatever notes, and I'll get started."

Oli nodded once and shot up from her seat. "Okay, then." Her voice was as tight as her lips. "Thanks for your help. I'll get on that RSVP for you."

"Great. Thanks, lady." She watched Oli's back as it slunk out of her office. "Oh, and, Oli"—Oli turned back to look at Nora with a slim thread of hope in her eyes—"mind closing the door behind you?" Nora said through a firm grin. At the sound of the click, Nora dropped to her chair and spun it around to grab her phone from her bag that was resting on the credenza behind her. She wanted to call Jenna and confess what had just happened. She was the one person Nora could count on not to pass judgment when her inner asshole took the wheel and drove right up to the edge of a cliff. Jenna—well-known for being a demanding, sometimes jerk at work—was also good with offering up suggestions on how to apologize after stomping on toes. ("Everyone appreciates a nice bottle of Pinot Noir and handpicked macarons," Jenna said.)

Nora spotted a notification on the phone. Facebook. She brought the phone closer to her scrunched-up face. *Facebook?* Odd, she thought. She hadn't messed around with this thing, much less received a notification in over two years. Did Mateo fiddle with her settings? She stared down at the red icon as if it alone could soothe her befuddlement. She shook her head and clicked through, mainly to get rid of the now-annoying red mark. It was a Friend Request.

*Click.*

The profile photo was a perfect, shiny golden egg set on a blue pillow.

### Nwad Bea Roo-Kayes
### 1 mutual friend

Maybe a new, international client? But whom would they have in common? Nora made a point not to mix business with social and kept a very small, vetted group of contacts on the app. Nwad Bea Roos-Kayes had a fairly locked-up profile, too: no photos, nothing accessible in the About Me section, just this one mutual friend. It's probably Oli. No, Mateo, she thought. Nwad sounded like a man's name, from Dubai or somewhere similar; Mateo's reach was broad.

*Click.*

The mutual friend's profile popped up. Nora lurched forward and choked on her breath. It was her, Nora, barely smiling in an old photo from the Immaculate Heart yearbook and under it, her former name. *Nora Bourdain.*

She dropped the phone hard on the desk and pushed her chair away with such force it almost toppled over with her in it. Nora swallowed hard, stood up, and stepped toward the desk, slow and cautious, leaning over the phone (still intact, no cracks) like an ill-timed jack-in-the-box. She touched the screen to navigate back to the original friend request. *Nwad.*

"Jesus Christ." It was *Dawn* spelled backward. And the surname was actually a jumble-puzzle version of Brooks.

*Fuck.*

Nora moved back from the desk again and rushed over to the window. *How did she find me?* Her breathing was ragged now. She pressed her forehead on the window, hoping the cold of it would do its work, but nothing changed, she was still agitated and could hear the drum of her heartbeat echoing deep in her ears. Nora dipped her chin into her chest, put her hands to her head—pressing down on her scalp—and started counting breaths between whispers and quiet.

It wasn't working. She wanted to call out to Oli, but couldn't bring herself to do it. The tension from their last exchange was still palpable, floating around in Nora's office. She tried focusing in on one person walking the streets way down below. If she could make out one person—a guy with a bright jacket, a woman with an overbearing hat, even a bike messenger snaking through the toppled dominoes of cabs, then she would be on her way to some sense of calm. This brand of people-watching from on high had worked a few times before. Looking down from eleven stories above and seeing everyone just moving through their lives restored Nora's sense of balance.

She hadn't pinpointed anyone on the street, but could feel an even rhythm returning to her chest anyway.

Dawn can't do this. Not again. The last time left enough of a mark.

Nora looked back at the phone on the desk, then did a sweep of the whole room with her eyes. She had built all of this on her own, without the Bourdain name, without trepidation, and certainly without the threat of some pest slinking up from the sewer trying to take it away from her. She didn't spend the last ten years walking around on her tiptoes looking over her shoulder and had no plans to start now. Nora went back to the desk, snatched up the phone, and deleted Facebook from it and cleared the cache, too, for good measure. She slipped the pen back into the gold cup, straightened the vase and folders, and lined up her chair perfectly to the desk. She nodded. A stiff drink (or three) was in order. Nora pulled out a lip gloss from the top drawer and smoothed it over her lips, then punched out a quick text:

> **not weds but you up for Snack Time today?**
> *bitch, please. do not need to ask 2x.*
> **soosh and sake??**
> *Oh my god yes!!! Morimoto in 30*
> **there/square**
> *btw good timing . . . was fixin to sext w/sports bro*
> **barf. Say nothing more Callaway! I want to keep my appetite kthxbye!**

# CHAPTER 10

"Make sure the doorman helps her in, okay, Mr. Wally?" Jenna said as she eased Nora into the back of the car. "Nora, darlin', I'm not sure when you became such a cheap date, but Jesus, woman, you're tighter'n bark on a log."

"I'm fine. I'm happy and excited, that's all. Fisher's coming home to me!" Nora fell back into the seat and dissolved into a throaty chuckle. "To *me*," she said again, but louder and clapping her free hand against her chest. "And nothing can change that. Nothing. I won't let it."

"Damn straight," Jenna said, grunting as she hoisted Nora's legs into the car. "I don't know who told you that shots would be a good move, but they lied to you, sweetie. Now"—she reached for Nora's bag that was lying partly crushed on her elbow—"let me make sure your phone is on and close by because—"

Nora jolted upright and recoiled, shielding her handbag from Jenna.

"Whoa, whoa," Jenna said, both hands held up by her ears. "I'm not going to steal your shit. I'm trying to help here. Look, I'm even loaning you Mr. Wally and my car."

Nora glanced up at the driver in his rearview. He held her in his gaze long enough to make her stop snickering. Mr. Noel used to look back at her in his rearview, too, but it was different; it was friendly, warm. There was something else at the base of this driver's eyes as he glared at Nora. And it wasn't just about being lumped together with the car, an inanimate thing that can be borrowed. The sentiment behind his look was vague, but Nora definitely felt it now the same way she had the first time that she tagged along with Jenna in the back of his immaculate sedan.

This man, he was no Mr. Noel.

Geoff Noel had been the Bourdain family driver for as long as Nora could remember. Longer. Nora's mother liked to tell her that "Geo" was one of the first names she was able to say clearly as a child. It was a sweet story that Nora knew was embellished; she was six after all, and speaking clearly, using her vast and impressive vocabulary. But she played along especially because of the way he would smile whenever he heard it told. It made the myth worth it. Nora would help Mr. Noel with his English, gently correcting his heavy Creole tongue from the backseat when he drove Nora and her mother to church on Sundays. (Nora's mother insisted on sitting up front with him.) And he would try—unsuccessfully each time—to introduce Nora to *sounds of home*. Zouk music from his Haitian brother living in Martinique often played on low in the car whenever Mr. Noel ran Nora here and there on errands for her sick, then dying mother. He was a good man who cared for Nora. She believed it, trusted it, and wished Geo were here now, with the fast guitar and steel drum ping-pang rhythms of his music growing louder as his smile widened.

Mr. Wally cleared his throat loudly, finally breaking the staredown happening in the rearview. "*Awright*. Good enough. But let me see if I hearin' yuh right," he said. His Bajan accent was dense and prickled Nora's ears. "You want me to come back for you after she get home?" He was clumsily turned around in the driver's seat facing Nora, but with his eyes slanted toward Jenna.

"No, thank you, Mr. Wally. It's probably easier for me to grab a cab."

"I could call in to one of de men in dispatch to come out for you. It ain't a problem *attall*," he said, still talking over Nora's head.

"Aw, you take such good care of me. But no, I'll hop in a cab the minute you guys pull off. I promise," Jenna said.

Mr. Wally fixed his body straight again and put his hand back on the gearshift at his leg. He had quit gawking at Nora through the mirror and kept his eyes on the bustling intersection in front of him.

Jenna leaned into the car farther and pulled the seat belt around Nora.

"I can do it," Nora snapped, and swiped the buckle head from her friend's hand. "I'm not a toddler."

"You sure? 'Cause this feels like a tantrum in the making and it's not the cutest."

"Sorry, I just think all of this"—Nora fanned her hand around the car's interior and the back of Mr. Wally's head—"it's *to'ly,* t-t-to—totally unnecessary."

"Yet you're slurring your words. All right, it's a wrap on Nora Mackenzie, people," Jenna shouted to the buildings behind her.

"Ssh. Keep your voice down," Nora said, her finger wagging near her own lips.

"Okay, it's curtains." Jenna grabbed the buckle back from Nora and snapped the belt in place before slamming the door. She poked her head through the open window, reached in, and stroked Nora's hair. "You'll sleep this off, sweet pea, and by the time Fish gets home you'll be a lot less hot mess and just hot. Ready for him and—"

"Yeah, yeah, and his big dick. Yes, we know, Jenna." Nora flopped back onto the supple seat. "Fisher's got a huge penis. Not news."

Jenna's eyes turned into saucers and she unleashed her belly-cackle, with her head tossed back. "Nora Mackenzie." She craned her neck to the driver. "Oh, Mr. Wally, I'm so sorry about my friend. Excuse her. This girl's drunker'n Cooter Brown."

Nora's grin dropped and she peered at her friend. "Don't say that. Don't apologize about me. I'm not a mistake."

Jenna frowned and pulled back from the window. "Now, hang on a good minute. No one's saying anything about you being a *mistake*. But, honey, you have to admit, you are acting a bit outside of yourself. I mean, you were pounding those shots with those garbage burger frat boys in there; then you just spilled out into the street, and now you're sitting up talking all crude about your guy's nether business in front of"—she darted her eyes in Mr. Wally's direction and whispered— "every-old-anyone. Come on. If the boot was on the other foot, what would you think?"

Nora turned her body to face Jenna and, without breaking her stare, said, "I would think . . . maybe you had a shitty day and this is how you were trying to glue it back together. And I would help you. Not judge you."

Jenna stepped closer to the car window, her voice hushed. "I know you would. I know. And that's what I'm doing for you here, Nora. Just let Mr. Wally get you home. Text—no, *call* me when you're close—and take a cool shower when you get in. By the time Fisher arrives, you'll be cleaned up and as right as rain." She reached in again to push Nora's hair from her eyes. "We'll talk later, okay, sweetie."

Nora nodded and leaned back in the seat. "Okay." She looked over at her friend. "Thank you."

"No Biggie Smalls, hon."

———◆———

Nora looked out the window at the endless row of buildings melding into a massive gray smear with splotches of deep amber, steely blue, and bone white—the lights shimmying in between the blurred structures. The late-evening sky was dim and overcast, but she could still make out the shapes of thin, stretched clouds. Leaned up against the door, her head on the darkened window, looking out calmed her spinning brain. It also helped her avoid catching any wayward glances from Mr. Wally.

She closed her eyes and tried to imagine how it will be when Fisher walks in and sees her there on their bed waiting for him. His favorite nightie or nothing but the sheets draped over her fresh, showered body? Nora bounced back and forth between the choices, unsure of which one he'd love more. He is going to be so happy to see her, just as she is to see him. It really didn't matter what she was wearing, he was going to devour her, and it made her body warm thinking about it.

Nora sat up and scanned her surroundings. They had just passed the Powell Building; they were close to the penthouse. The high squeak of the brakes as the car came to a stop sent Nora's shoulder into her ears again. It was time.

Mr. Wally cleared his throat loudly and reached up to turn on the interior light over the rearview. Nora unfastened her seat belt and slid across the backseat to the passenger side of the car. She paused for another deep inhale, her hand on the silver door handle, and glanced over at Mr. Wally.

"I'm good from here," she said quietly. "No need to walk me in."

"Okay, then," Mr. Wally said, adding a rigid nod.

Nora pulled her phone out of her bag and flopped it about with a limp wrist. "I'll just call her when I get inside, so, um . . . thanks."

"You have a good night, *mistruss*."

*Mistruss*. That's how her mother used to say it, she thought, and smiled at the driver. He looked back at her with his eyes searing. Nora hustled out of the car and he pulled off just as quickly.

She hit Jenna's number as she watched the car's taillights shrink and melt into the night.

"Hey."

"Hey, sweetie. You almost home?"

Nora nodded. "Yeah."

"How's Mr. Wally—has he recovered yet?" Jenna said with a chuckle.

"Yeah, I guess."

"Oh, he's just an ol' boiled peanut. Don't worry about him. He'll be fine. But you . . . let's work on getting you fine, too."

"I'm okay."

"Well, you will be. Just drink tons of water and pop a couple Advil. I would give you my real, tried and true hangover cure, but it involves raw egg, mayonnaise, and eye of newt. Fisher does not want *any* part of that, sugar. Trust."

"Okay. Thanks."

"All right, sweetie, take it easy, okay. Lots of water. And debrief in the morning? I want to hear all about the sexy-lexy reunion. You know I'm a nosy bitch!"

Nora rolled her eyes and a small grin started to slide along her face. "That you are. Good night."

"Texas forever!"

Inside the cool of the marble foyer, her heels clacking in echo, Nora released the breath she didn't realize she had been holding. She gave a quick head nod to the night doorman. He was new, young, and wearing a jacket at least two sizes too large. That was one thing Nora noted about Javie, he was always pristine: his uniform crisp and ironed, his hair sharp and exactly the same every day in a tapered fade with a knife-edge part on the left, and his only accessories were a gold wedding band and a long gold chain with a heavy crucifix that peeked out of the middle buttons on his shirt a handful of times. He was simple and classic with a level of courtesy and professionalism that never faltered. Nora appreciated his overall comportment. There was a sense of majesty to it. He never missed a day of work. Even in the blizzard, he was there, ringing Nora up to check on her with Fisher overseas. Javie was a real part of home base for her.

The late-evening and night staff was a different case. Never consistent or reliable, Nora once counted six new doormen in the span of eight nights.

"Ah, these guys. They're young," Javie told Nora when she mentioned the rotating evening staff. "There's always something better around the corner calling them over, you know?"

When she glanced back at the new guy, making sure she hadn't spotted him there before, he waved her over. "Are you Nora, uh, *Miss* Nora . . . Mackensing?"

"*Mackenzie,* yes." Nora kept her phone in her hand and visible as she walked over to him. Just in case.

"Okay, good. Mackenzie. Mackenzie, got it. There's a package for you, Miss Mackenzie." He held up a lime-green pastry box with a distinct chocolate-brown bow tied large on top.

It was from Angie's, the pastry shop that shared a wall with Bean House Café. Nora knew Angie's packaging well. She and Fisher often stopped by back when their Sundays were still shapeless and fun. Angie's jumbo almond croissant drew the crowds, but Nora coveted her coconut pastries. Sticky, sweet, doughy, and stuffed with finely grated coconut browned and sweetened with sugar and soaked in extracts, they were so close to the Bajan coconut turnovers that Nora's mother baked for her when she was a child, before they moved into the Bourdain house. Sitting on a small bench in a small park eating one of Angie's turnovers, reading the Sunday Styles section with her long leg stretched across Fisher's lap, her sunglasses pushed up through her thick hair and perched atop her head, and thinking only of how good and tasty her life was. Those mornings were Nora's own quiet requiem for her mother. But the trips to Angie's became errands, not amusement, and Fisher stopped tagging along. She didn't buy the turnovers, but instead put in standing orders, selections of her client favorites, gifts, tokens of thanks, and charming introductions. And soon Nora handed over the Angie's run to Oli and then passed it along again to interns.

"I'm not expecting anything," Nora said. She stretched out her hand well before she was at a reasonable distance to actually take the box from the young guard. "I wonder if it was supposed to go to my atelier, maybe."

"I don't know . . . it's just here." He leaned out from behind the desk toward Nora. "They waited for a little bit and then left it."

Nora dropped her phone into the side of her bag and slid both hands under the pretty box. "What do you mean they waited? The delivery guy?"

"Ah, no. It was a woman."

"A woman delivery person?"

"Nah, she was dressed regular. Said she was a friend, so she waited for you."

The box balancing on Nora's hand dipped, pitching forward. The doorman grabbed for it, saving it from the drop, and rested it on the desk again.

"Oh, sorry. I just . . . sorry. Did she leave her name?"

He shook his head. "Just the box, and there's a note tucked in on the side there." The doorman darted his eyes between Nora and the box. "She was real nice, your friend."

Nora understood. "Right . . ." She reached into her bag to the front pocket where she kept a couple singles. "Thanks for your help, Mr. . . . ?"

"Junior. Everybody calls me Junior."

Nora handed him a thin fold of dollars. "Thanks, Junior."

"No, thank you, miss. That's nice of you. Do you want me to—" He looked down at the box again.

"God, no. I can carry it up," she sniffed. "Good night, Junior."

"You too, miss."

She wanted to slice into the box, tear open the note, but somehow kept it together through the elevator ride up. Inside the penthouse, Nora dropped everything—handbag, keys, dollar bills—on the counter and attacked the box, ruining its bow with scissors down the center. She lifted the top, releasing its baked goodness into the air, the fragrance floating up her nose. And under the parchment, stacked artfully, were two dozen black-and-white cookies. The note from the side of the box fell flat onto one of them. Nora ripped into the small envelope.

*Special treats from me to "you."*
*Enjoy it all, friend.*
*xoxo*

She stared down at the note, even bringing it closer up to her eyes, and read the first line three times, breaking down the words.

*From me. To "you."*

She focused in on the quotation marks, squinting, pursing her lips. *Oli,* she thought, and her tight expression smoothed out. But why the quotations? Why so anonymous? And Oli doesn't do desserts. She grabbed her phone and texted Jenna:

> **hey did u send cookies to me by messenger?**
> *wait . . . u still drunk? is this code???*
> **srsly did you have 2 doz b&w cookies sent?**
> *Never. I get the harmony stuff & Seinfeld thing, but theyre gross!*
> **box from Angie's pastry arrived. Note but no name.**
> *Probs client . . . or interns trying to get in good??*
> **maybe. anyway talk tmrw . . . Exhausted.**
> *WATER YOURSELF PLS.*
> **oh god. enough. bye!**

Nora tapped her fingers against the card and read it aloud once more. The crumple in her brow returned and stayed there as she walked over to the security phone by the front door, holding the card tight in one hand. She pressed the Video button and waited the few seconds for Junior's face to show up in the monitor.

"Hey, Miss Mackenzie. Everything all right?" He gripped the corded phone piece of the elaborate intercom system. Nora didn't like the video feature. More than the clear intrusion into her privacy, it was how the doorman (usually Javie) looked like an inmate behind the prison glass partition that really troubled her.

"Yeah . . . actually, just a question: Who'd you say delivered this box again? What did this woman look like?"

"Uh, she looked regular. You know, nice. Friendly."

"No, I mean, what did she *look like* look like? Was she Asian, did she have long hair?"

"Oh, okay. I feel you. Nah, she was black. African-American.

Her hair was kind of medium, I guess." Nora's eyes drifted away from the video monitor as the gears in her brain clicked into motion. She gritted her teeth. "She said she was your friend from, like, back in the day, college or school or something," Junior continued.

*Shit. Dawn.*

Nora took a breath, balanced her tone, brought her focus back to the monitor, and forced a smile. "Did she leave a name? They didn't sign the card"—she flashed it in front of the monitor—"and I can't quite place which friend this is, you know? Just another quick question, I don't want to keep you."

"No doubt, no doubt. Okay, what do you want to know? She came in, like, five or six minutes after I started my shift and—"

"Wait. Do you think Javie saw her before he left?"

"I don't know. But Javie," he chuckled, "he sees everything. I could call him at home and ask."

"No, no. Let's not disturb him. She said she wanted to wait for me?"

"Let me see." Junior tipped his head back, chin to the ceiling. "She came in like a few minutes after I got here and asked for you, said she hadn't seen you in a minute and that she wanted to surprise you and take the box up to your spot." Nora opened her eyes wide, and Junior put his hand up near his face in response. "*But* I know that's against the rules. So I called up, you know, to *announce the visitor* and get your okay to send her up there, but you were out. That's when she said she's cool with waiting for a bit."

"How long did she stay?"

"That, I don't recall. But she kept looking at her phone, so not long. I think she had somewhere else to be."

"All right, thanks, Junior."

"No problem. Oh! One last thing . . . Earlier, you know when you gave me the tip, um, there was a twenty mixed up with the singles. Maybe you didn't realize and—"

Nora shook her head. "It's fine. Honestly. Keep it."

"For real? Thank you, Miss Mackenzie! That's super nice of you."

"Don't mention it," she said, clenching her jaw to keep her smile intact. "But, just one favor, between us? Next time that old college friend stops by tell her I'm not here, even if I am. Then call me on my cell, okay? Number's in the books."

Junior raised a finger near his winking eye and pointed it at the monitor like a toy gun, chuckling. "Right. I got you. It's like *that,* huh?"

Nora nodded. "Yeah, something like that. Thanks." She pressed the Video button again. The minute the screen went black, Nora felt the waves in her stomach turn to flames. Her breath went ragged. She dropped the note card like a lit matchstick and stomped back into the kitchen to the box and swept it off the counter, sending the cookies toppling to the floor with a low thud.

"No," she said with force. "Not again." She wanted to throw something else. Wild, her eyes searched the counter and landed on a vase. Down it went with another sweep of her arm. A mug half filled with stale coffee followed, then her keys, then the jarred candle, then a wide bowl, then some blurred-out square—everything blended into the gray of the marble counter-top and Nora, her arms thrashing, could no longer make out the details of the items she sent flying.

An urgent need to tear at things took over next. Nora, bending and twisting, stripped away her clothes, her dangling neck-laces and jewelry, letting them fall by her feet as she stumbled to the bathroom, unconcerned with the sounds of buttons popping and fabric tearing. It all had to come off at once. The engagement ring—the last article still on her body—scorched her finger. She dragged it off and tossed the heavy rock onto a mirrored tray on her dresser before storming into the open shower with the charge of a fighter entering the ring. She flung the faucet handles to the right and lunged with her already sweaty, wet face into the rainfall. What stung at first soon settled into something soothing. The water slid over her, kneading the stiffness out of her back, neck, legs, shoulders. Nora tilted her head and let the shower massage her scalp, hoping the kind touch would somehow seep into her brain, too. She took deeper breaths and let them out slowly as the fever in her belly relented. Finally she felt steady enough to sit down and dropped her weight onto the boulder rock seat behind her. She looked at herself, tracing the river running down the middle of her chest and pooling between her closed, stretched-out legs. Nora didn't want to think about anything else right then. She just wanted to feel good, and the water trickling down her body felt good. She leaned her head back against the textured tiles and brought a leg up, bending it and tucking her foot behind her knee. Nora tracked the water's path from the base of her neck down over her breast and stomach, moving her hand farther and farther in a smooth line until she could slide two fingers inside of her soft opening. She kept her eyes closed and head back, fingers gliding in and out, rough but rhythmic. As she picked up the tempo of the stroke—her breathing uneven again and her skin prickly—she heard it: Fisher yelling her name.

She opened her eyes and he was standing just outside the frameless shower.

"Nora, are you okay?" His face was flushed and frantic. "Jesus! What happened?" Fisher reached into the shower toward Nora—his jacket drenched—and she leapt out into his arms before he could touch her.

"I'm so glad you're home," she sobbed into his neck, and wrapped herself around him tighter.

He tried to pry her away a little, to get a clearer look. "Nora, what happened? What happened to you?" His voice cracked. He brushed back the wet hair from Nora's face, her mascara smeared, and his eyes went wide. "Did someone hurt you? What happened? There's smashed shit everywhere, your clothes are ripped and tossed on the floor. What—"

Nora shook her head firmly. "It's okay. It's nothing. I'm okay," she said on repeat, and started kissing Fisher—his face, neck, mouth—with each word.

"Nora . . . what . . . Nora—"

"No," she whispered. "Just Mack. Only Mack."

Fisher tried to get more words out, but they only melted in her mouth. And Nora, starved, kissed him deeper. He gave in and pressed his torso into her nakedness. She peeled off his jacket and he helped her remove his shirt, pitching it to the side like a useless husk. Fisher stepped out of his pants, dragged off his shoes and socks, and quickly scooped up Nora. They kissed more—deeper, harder, and untamed—as they staggered over to the running water.

"Mack," Fisher growled as they backed into the shower. "Promise me you're okay."

"Promise," she whispered into his lips.

In the shower Fisher put Nora to stand, leaned up against the glass, and worked his way down the center of her. She grabbed his thick hair and pushed his head down farther, arching into him. He seemed to like Nora guiding his face to just below her waist and positioning it to be exactly where she needed it. Nora rested her hand lightly on the crown of his head as it swayed and she tried to let time collapse on itself as it often did whenever they vanished into each other this way. But it all felt off, unfamiliar. Wrong. The urge to tear away at something returned, more insistent and dire this time, and Nora wanted to break out of her own skin. She yanked Fisher's head up from between her legs, gripping a thicket of his hair as if it were the end of the rope saving her from falling to her death.

"I can't. I'm sorry," she said, unable to fully look him in the eye. She stepped back from him and slicked her drenched hair. "I'm sorry."

Fisher rose to his feet and moved closer to Nora. "What is happening right now?"

*Fucking Ghetto Dawn.* Nora shook her head and stepped back from him again. "It's just work shit. I shouldn't have brought it home." She slipped out of the shower and grabbed a towel, wrapping it tight around herself.

Fisher turned off the water and followed her out of the shower. He grabbed a towel and pulled it around his waist, never breaking his gaze on Nora. "What the hell could be so horrible that you did all of that?"

She turned away from him and faced the mirror, but didn't look up at the reflection. "It's nothing."

"*Nothing?* It looks like a brawl went down. When I came in and saw all of that and you weren't answering me—Jesus—I didn't know what I was going to find in this bathroom." He padded over to his side of the countertop and leaned back on it. Nora could feel his eyes on her, peering, but kept looking down at her sink. "Babe, this is not nothing." He tilted his top half toward her. "Talk to me. Please."

"It's just a lot of small things stacked up on top of each other and . . . they just kind of fell over and spilled all over the kitchen." She glanced his way. "Sorry about that. I'll clean it up now." Nora tightened the tuck of the towel around her chest and started to make her way toward the bathroom door.

"Hey, hey, wait a minute." He grabbed Nora by the waist and pulled her into him. "That can wait. What's up with you? One minute you're trying to eat me alive and now"—he dipped his head to her bowed one—"you're doing everything to get away from me. Can't even look at me."

Nora forced her eyes to angle up and stay locked on his. "I'm embarrassed, okay?" She said it as quickly as it came to her. "I was out with Jenna and we had too many one-toomanys and I came home horny and pissy drunk and you caught me in here masturbating and then—"

"Hang on. What?" He frowned, but there was a slick grin just beneath it. Nora knew that his poker face was the worst.

"Yes, okay, *yes,* I was rubbing one out when you busted in. And now I'm totally mortified." She buried her face in his smooth chest and held her breath, barely blinking, waiting to see if the story floated. It wasn't until she heard the soft rumble of a chuckle stirring in his lungs that she exhaled.

Fisher pulled her into a deep hug. "Mack, I don't know how many times I need to say this for you to start trusting it: You can be yourself with me. I love everything about you; always will. These are facts."

*Facts.*

Nora's eyes shot open at the word. Dawn, the cookies, the smirking note, all of it came crashing into her brain like a trash can on fire.

Ghetto Dawn had risen from the dead, and she was poking Nora in all of her soft spots with a blunt knife. She needed to be stopped and shoved back down into her muddy grave. These were the facts that were staring Nora in the face, and this time she had no plans on running away from them.

# CHAPTER 11

Nora squinted at Oli, narrowing in on her full lips. She couldn't understand the words leaving Oli's mouth and thought staring at it might help.

"Again, I'm just telling you what the customer service lady told me," Oli said. She looked annoyed and exasperated mixed together in one batch of *pissed*. Nora couldn't figure out whether it was because of what happened or because she'd asked her to repeat the story a third time. "She said that a flag was placed on the account. Suspicious activity. I think they think it's possibly identity theft."

"Possibly? You and me—we are the only ones authorized on this card," Nora said, taking a break from peering at Oli's face. "If there are funky charges, then it's absolutely identity theft."

"I know, but there was something weird going on. I tried to chat up the rep on the phone to get the scoop. She sounded young. The young ones always spill tea. But she kept saying, *That's so weird*. Like, repeatedly, with every keystroke." Oli nodded slowly and stretched in her seat, her limbs splayed like a starfish in the spotless white chair. "Wait. *Maybe*"—her body snapping up straight and index finger jutting out—"this is something larger scale. What if someone fucking with our corporate card is only the small potatoes of a much bigger, nastier scandal? Maybe this is only a small part of a major hack to ruin corporate America, like on that show with our boy—*Mr. Robot.*"

Nora was back to squinting at Oli, but with a scowl added, "Could you not?"

"Sorry." Oli shrugged. "I'm reading this thing in the *New Yorker.*"

Nora flipped open her laptop. "Does the client know about the declined charges?"

"No, and Isobel was very cool about everything. She said we could just pick up the order and submit payment later. And, *yes,* I'm taking her and Riko out for dinner next week as a thank-you. They tried to say no, but I made it an offer they couldn't refuse."

"Good." Nora turned her attention back to her computer. "I'll call and thank them anyway."

"Cool . . ."

Nora moved her eyes up from the screen to Oli. "You're lingering. Is there more bullshit to add to this already hot-garbage day?"

"Hot garbage. Well, shit. I was going to ask if you're getting hyped. Wedding is two weeks away, almost exactly today. But"—Oli made a face like a bird and took her voice high into her nose—"*mi naa badda, bwoy. Mi mudduh seh mi too chatty-chatty.*" She swept her hands, dramatically, across the space between them as if wiping a slate clean. Her smile broke through, ruining her serious take. It always quietly tickled Nora when Oli spoke patois and put on a Jamaican accent. The quick impression smoothed away Nora's grimace. "Nora, you are wound extra tight. And for no reason. I mean, the wedding planner is no joke, everything's coast. You should be so Gucci right now—that's what Mateo keeps saying whenever he sees you all tense and bothered. Which is a lot lately, I should add.

I already told you that we've got your back here. You can relax, Nor. We know what we're doing. . . . You just got to let us."

"I know. You're right." Nora gently swatted her laptop closed and looked at Oli with soft eyes and a tilt of her head. "Listen, I need to apologize for the other day. I'm holding on with this tight fist and it's a total waste of energy. I know you have my back."

"Always," Oli said, nodding. "And no need to apologize. The other day is the other day. We've moved on to today, right?"

"Right." Nora smiled. "Thanks, Oli. And we'll sort out this credit card fraud thing. I'll give a call in a sec. I want to do a bit of my own *CSI* on it first."

"Cool. Keep me posted." Oli stood up. "I'm taking Kazzy with me to Botang and Lo to pull shirts in about ten."

"Good move. Botang and Lo always delivers." She re-opened her laptop. "If I head out before you're back, I'll email you"—Nora raised her brow—"*not to check up*. Just to blow kisses and sing sweet, sweet T-Swift songs in your ears."

Oli chuckled. "Why, are you breaking up with me?"

"Never ever that." Nora's grin stretched even more as she began clacking away at her computer with alacrity.

"Open or closed?" Oli asked when she got to Nora's office door.

"Maybe closed," she said. "I may have to put my big-girl voice on for these customer service rep assholes."

As she was about to close it, Oli popped her head back in the door. "Oh, totally forgot: We've got a new client."

"Yeah, I know. The dating app kid. Jay. We went over this, Oli."

"No, it's another 'nother new client. I just had the prelim on the phone with his right-hand man—well, lady; it was a woman—yesterday. She was actually really nice."

Nora's eyes shot up from her screen.

Oli continued. "She seems, like, really on top of the guy's style needs and preferences. Personally"—Oli slipped more of herself through the half-open door and lowered her voice just above a whisper—"I thought it was another one of those gross Manhattan sugar-daddy bullshits, but after talking to her for a good bit, I don't think she gets down like that. She might actually be on Team *Punaani*. Plus, her boss is, like, way old, she said. He's based in Vermont, I think. Retired heart surgeon. Pascal is his name. Dr. Pascal Bourdain."

Nora's breath caught in her chest. "What?" She clenched her jaw and felt a twitch span her entire face. "What did you say?"

"Which part?" Oli said.

"Who did you talk to on the phone yesterday? What was the woman's name?" Nora rose from her chair, leaning into the desk like an animal about to pounce.

"Oh, her name's really pretty, but she had to spell it for me: Nwad. She was really—"

"Nice. Yeah, I know," Nora hissed.

"Everything good?" Oli slid through the door entirely and took steps toward Nora.

*Fix your face.* "Yeah," she said, and sat back down, her lips still pursed. "I was remembering something." She shook her head and smiled, but knew it probably looked more like a sneer or pained wince. "Do you mind emailing me that file and any notes on"—Nora exhaled—"Dr. Bourdain. I just want to check him out and stuff."

"Absolutely." Oli nodded and went back to the door. "You sure you're all right?"

"Totally," she said beneath another strained grin.

"Cool. I'll send it before we head out." Oli closed the door behind her.

Nora stayed still, staring at her computer screen until it went black. "What the fuck?" She leaned back and moved her gaze to the ceiling high above her. Her stomach started churning. Thinking about all of it was beginning to hurt her brain. The *ping* of her email brought her attention and her laptop screen back from dim.

To: Nora Mackenzie
Subject: Bourdain prelim file
From: Olivia Chung

———

Here you go . . .
Pretty standard.
STOP WORRYING.
::OC

Nora didn't bother clicking on the attachment. Pascal Bourdain was dead. She knew that any information about his *style interests* would be pure fiction and the contact information for Nwad fake. Nora scrunched her brows. This was a waste of time, pulling at threads in this counterfeit tapestry. She needed to reach into her computer and squeeze Dawn out. Make contact. Nora opened up Google and searched "Dawn Brooks" again. She tried Facebook again and tried even ridiculous variations on the spelling. She tried Immaculate Heart's alumni website again. Twitter again. Instagram again. And back to Google again. She closed her eyes and tried thinking back to that night they collided again. Tried to see more, find clues: What was Dawn wearing? What was she carrying besides the coffee tray? She tried slowing down the moment again. Everything again, and still nothing. No trace of her.

She looked around her desk for something safe to pitch at the wall, but instead snatched up her office phone and dialed.

"Hey, Callaway, I know you don't do work calls, but this is quick and important."

"Okay. What's up?"

Nora shifted in her seat. "It's a weird question."

"Go for it."

"If you had to find someone, who would you call?"

"Living or dead?"

"Callaway, I'm serious."

"So am I! We're going to press on book five from the Manhattan Medium. Dead is a viable option."

"Alive. If you had to find someone living, who'd you call?"

"You mean, like a private dick?" Jenna chuckled.

"Jesus. Yes, a detective. Do you have a go-to?"

"No, but . . . our receptionist, Kate, she had some crazy catfish horror story and needed to track down this guy. Well, someone we *think* is a guy."

"So, yes, then?" Nora said, clipped and annoyed.

"Yeah. Yes, I know someone who could help. Wait, so, who are we trying to find?"

Nora scanned her email inbox. "This client. He's trying to be funny with the money he owes us, and I need to track him down."

"Hmm. Isn't that something your accounts person can do? I mean, a detective? For some dude trying to stiff you on the invoice—that seems a bit drastic, no?"

"It's more involved than that, *obviously*," Nora said.

"All right. Noted," Jenna said. Nora could practically see her through the phone, her hand raised to her face and eyebrows pulled up to her hairline. "I'll ask Kate for the guy's info and email it to you. Works?"

Nora nodded. "Works. Thanks."

"Is there . . . something else? You sound like there's something else."

"Well." Nora closed her computer and exhaled. "There's one other thing. It's kind of a huge favor."

"If it involves more college boys and piss-water shots, I'm going to pass—shockingly."

"It's a tea party."

"I already don't like where this is going. I'm having flash-backs to back home."

"Just . . . hear me out. It's up at the Beaumont house tomorrow. Lady Eleanor is hosting a gathering for me. In my honor."

"Oh, sweet Jesus. Are you fixin' to ask *me* to go with you?"

"Maybe."

"Nora, honey. You know I love me some big hats, small cups, and ghastly floral prints, but as my grandma Gigi used to say: This is not my blessing, sweetheart. This is all you. Ellie wants to show you off."

"That's what Fish said. She wants to show me off to her friends, like I'm the new show pony they've just acquired. It's insulting."

"Insulting? To be the belle of the ball and have all those blue-haired blue bloods welcome you into their grand fold is far, far from insulting, Nor. And can you blame her for wanting to trot you out? When it comes to show ponies, honey, you are a blue-ribbon thoroughbred. It's goddamn ridiculous how amazing you are."

Nora's face crumpled. She knew the tears were next. "Jenna, I—"

"Don't you dare, Nora. Just accept the truth for once. Plus, I have to run, so this is me getting the last word. And relax. You'll be fab tomorrow. Byeeee."

The agitation in her stomach climbed up her chest and set-tled at the back of Nora's throat with a burn. She slumped down in her seat, spinning it around to face the wallpaper, and let her eyes glide along the stretch of the wisteria. Her mind drifting along with it, remembering the last time Dawn carved a hole in the center of her good life and dragged the guts clean out of it. Nora wrapped her arms around her middle and squeezed, trying to hold it all in, but the pain of the incised wound was too great, too real. She curled over in her chair and tucked her pounding head between her knees. This was what she used to do when she wanted to fade into the walls. Head down, tuck. She did it most nights in the lonely basement room after her mother had gone to sleep. Nora would sit up, ease herself over to the edge of her bed: head down, tuck. After her mother was gone, lowered slow and gentle beneath the earth, it was the only way to stop the ringing in her ears: head down, tuck. At Immaculate, whenever she feared that her golden casing was beginning to tarnish, when Dawn added her toxic imprint to any amity that Nora had enjoyed: head down, tuck. And it worked until it didn't, like on that haunting day, when Elise Bourdain let the insurmountable truth slip out.

"You knew," Nora had said, the air struggling to escape her lungs. "All this time, all these years, you knew." She was in the old-fashioned, wood phone booth at the end of the hall by the boarders' den, the black receiver pressed hard against her ear, trying to hear what she couldn't hear. The silence on the other end of the line was long and harrowing. Then two words, low but piercing: "*I'm sorry.*"

It had never once occurred to Nora that Mrs. Bourdain knew and that she still did nothing to stop her husband's sick habit.

She had buckled at her waist and fell forward all while still gripping the phone. "That's why I'm here," Nora had said, seething. "You sent *me* away, not him." Even with her head tucked between her knees, nothing had changed. Her brain was a brush fire. The next words out of Mrs. Bourdain's mouth registered as a jumble of sounds and Nora slammed the phone down before the string of noise ended. She tried again: head down, tucked. But it was useless, ruined. Nora packed up her few belongings in the small hours of that night and left Vermont for good. It was the only fix.

The *ding* of her email sounded loudly. Startled, Nora spun around in her chair and flung open her laptop. Twenty-eight new messages. She scrolled down to Jenna's—*P.I. info!*—and clicked on it. Nora quickly scratched the man's name and number on a slip of paper from her desk and stuffed it into her bag with her cell phone and left, convinced once again that this was the only fix.

# CHAPTER 12

More than his hair or his luminous blue eyes or the small constellation of flat moles that dotted the left side of his jaw, it was Fisher's back that Nora could stare at forever. Broad, brawny, unwrinkled, his back seemed sculpted from some rare, undiscovered clay. In the mornings, awake long before he was, Nora would often open her eyes hoping that he had turned away from her in the night and his back would be there to greet her. If not, she would gently nudge and roll him over so that she could press her body into it, nestle her face deep into the curves of its muscles and inhale him. She would run her hand smooth along the top of his shoulders, glide down the side of his ribs, and wrap her arms around him and try to sync up to the rhythm of his breath. And she'd stay there until he was finally ready to wake up on his own, reach around and grip her thigh or pull her leg over him like covers.

Like right now.

"Tell the truth," he said, partly into his pillow, "how long have you been awake?"

Nora took another hit of his soapy scent and sighed deeply. "A while."

"If nothing else, babe, it's sleep. You need sleep."

"I'll sleep when I'm eighty . . . or on the honeymoon—"

"*Whichever comes first,*" they said in unison.

"Before you even think it I know it," Fisher said, chuckling. He turned over to face her. "I'm already inside your brain, wife." He tilted his head and kissed Nora's shoulder.

"Isn't that bad luck?"

"Morning kisses?"

"No, using the terms *wife, husband,* before they're legit."

"Never heard that one. And I know everything there is to know about weddings and marriage and luck." He gave her his half smile and his eyes lit up through the sleepiness. "Okay. Now that that's settled, it's the gym for me. What's your plan?"

Nora moved her head slightly from him. "Tea party."

"Of course," he said, and propped up on his elbow, looking down at Nora. "How are you feeling about it?"

"I mean . . . I'm going."

"Mack. Don't be like that. It's just tea. She's done this for Rock's and Asher's wives and they were basically just teenage girls, fresh out of school, these bags of nerves in ridiculously high heels," he said, grinning. Then, as if his brain changed channels on him without warning, Fisher's chin dropped to his neck. He shook his head slowly. "When our father died, we were all too young to really remember much. It was sudden. I remember that; it was so quick. But my mother, she held all the memories for us, you know? And then Garrett"—he shook his head more, faster, and squared his jaw—"I was sixteen when he took his life. That, I remember. Always." Nora reached out and stroked his arm. "Losing him really broke something in her. I mean, she was never going to be making us cookies. But when Garrett . . . there was a vacancy that just grew wider; you could see it behind her eyes. Like she's operating on half a heart. With Asher landing in London and Rock all the way in Geneva, she really leaned on me to be the head of the family, for years. Except now I'm leaving it, I'm leaving her." He glanced over at Nora and frowned. "It's how she sees it. I can't discount that. And she wants to feel like she's giving you her blessing. With everything she's lived through, it's the easiest thing to let her have, you know?" He fell back on his pillow, looking up at the ceiling. "It's just tea for you, but it's important for her."

Fisher turned his head toward Nora and gave her another kiss, this one landing between her brows. He rolled back over to his side of the bed and sat at the edge of it. Nora watched his back as he stretched. She knew the T-shirt would come next and grinned while waiting for it. On gym mornings, Fisher kept his gear on a nearby leather ottoman so that there would be no distractions, no tangents. He would get dressed right there from the edge of the bed—shoes and all—and go straight to the front door, only tossing a "see you in a bit" back at Nora. Turning back to even look at her, they knew from previous experience, would be a clear misstep. But before he left, she got to watch him get dressed. The way he'd put on his T-shirt was her favorite. It was quick and thrusting: arms punched through sleeves one after the other, shirt dragged over his head, just like the sexy thirty-year-old "teen" vampires did it on the television shows Nora refused to admit she enjoyed.

"See you in a bit," Fisher said over his shoulder, and was gone.

Nora shot up from the bed and grabbed her phone on the nightstand. She had memorized the investigator's number after starting to dial and hanging up a dozen times already. She pressed the numbers—all of them—and hit the Send icon. Nora cleared her throat and straightened out of her slump in the bed while it rang. When it stopped and she heard the crackling sound of connection, she leapt out of the bed and hustled into the bathroom, closing the door behind her.

"This is Keith Wittrock." His voice was heavy and dragging, as if opening his mouth to speak was a bridge too far.

"Yes, hello. Good morning. This is . . . I'm calling. I want to—"

"Ma'am. I'm a private investigator. *Private* being the operative word. Speak your piece. I've heard everything before. Do you need me to find someone purposely lost? Track down some proof on an intimate involvement? Defuse a scam? You let me know how I can help, and I'll do my best."

Nora took a deep breath and let it go. "I'm trying to find someone. A woman. From high school. She's popped up again after about ten years and she's trying to . . . stir things up."

"Things that you don't want stirred. Got it," he said, flatly. Nora could hear his chair squeaking through the phone. "Let's start here: What's your name? It doesn't have to be real, just something I can call you as we talk."

Nora panicked. "Hyacinth," she spat out and cringed. It was her middle and she hated it.

"Okay, *Hyacinth*," he said. "That works."

She rolled her eyes. Everything about him—from his disinterested, yawning tone to the mocking way he uttered her name—felt wrong. Regret crawled up her arm and nestled in her ear. This was a mistake. *She can't get to me.*

"She can't get to me," Nora said, surprised that the thought leaked out into the air.

"What's that?"

"I don't think I'm ready to move forward here, Mr.—"

"Keith is fine. And if you want to think it over, that's fine, too."

"Great. Thanks. I'll give it some more thought."

"Right," he said.

Nora hung up without saying good-bye. She had felt simple

enough for even calling him, and now she wanted the silliness to end as quickly as possible. She deleted Keith Wittrock's number from her call list, flung her phone onto the bed, and headed straight to the shower to get ready.

———◆·◆———

She knew she was fussing, but applied a third choice of lipstick anyway. Nora took a look at herself in the mirror once more, turning slowly to inspect everything in the reflection. She fixed the accordion pleats off the side of her summer beige Bottega Veneta dress by pressing the already sharp creases in between her fingers. She smoothed the floating wisp of hair into the rest of the loose side ponytail. She puckered her lips and rolled them together. This shade of rose pink was the right choice, she thought, and gave herself an overall nod. She sat back carefully in her dressing room chair—trying to maintain the integrity of her outfit's crispness—and slipped into her nude-colored heels. Nora stood and took one more one-last-check of her full glow in the mirror before grabbing her flat clutch and turning out the lights.

"Shit. The car." Nora reached into her bag for her phone to call down to Fisher's new driver. Fisher had sent a text while she was in the shower insisting that she take his SUV and not roll the dice with a yellow cab.

She looked at her phone:

*1 Missed Call & Voice Mail*

Nora shook her head and smiled. "My God, Fisher. I'll take the car already," she said out loud, and clicked through to the voice mail.

*Ms. Mackenzie, this is Jennifer calling from
Grace Carter's office. If you could give us a call*

*back when you have a moment today, that would be great. There seems to be a small issue with the seating plan; something's not matching up. I've followed this call with an email. Thanks.*

Nora stared at her phone as the message bounced around her brain. What issue? Did Oli forget something? One glance at the time made her shake off the small worry that was starting to creep in. *Later*, she said to herself, and dialed Fisher's driver. Every fold was straight, every hair in place. She was ready to step into the den of rich, white-haired widows and nothing was going to distract her.

<hr>

The chilly SUV stopped at the last intersection on Fifth Avenue before turning onto the quiet, tree-lined street with the famous Beaumont manse. Nora drifted away thinking back to the first time she stepped foot into the palatial home, one of the most storied in the city. Fisher had taken her there to introduce her to his mother only weeks after they had met.

"It'll seem like a lot at first," he whispered to her as they pulled up to the spectacular seven-story residence, and Nora's mouth sailed open. "But that's just at first. It'll settle in and you'll soon see what I see: just the place where my mother lives." That he never once called her *mom*, always mother (and occasionally, in reference, Lady Eleanor) was Nora's first note-to-self that this prestigious address with its seven stories of neo-Georgian-style architecture—soaring ceilings, countless bathrooms, dormer windows, and steeply sloping roof—would never *settle in* and be anything but grand.

Every piece of furniture, plaster molding, framed artwork, fireplace, chandelier, and artifact—even the air moving through the seventeen rooms—in the Beaumont mansion was stately and perfect. Nora actually found herself trembling and a little breathless as she stood next to Fisher that first time she took in the staggering views of Central Park and the Manhattan skyline from the generous roof. The buildings, even at night, looked like the lined-up trophies of a matchless champion.

"Will I be returning for you this evening, Miss Mackenzie?" the driver asked, bringing Nora's attention back to the brightness of the day. Although she had heard him the first time, the frozen grin on her face seemed to spur the driver to repeat the question.

"Oh, yes. That would be nice," she said, finally. "Thank you, Leonard." Nora looked out her window past the iron fence at the lush forecourt of the Beaumont manor, trying to make out what she could of the secondary entrance on the lower level. A part of her hoped that Fisher would be standing there to surprise her, and she could catch a glimpse of him lurking. He told her that he had some business to attend to after his gym stop. It all sounded so vague, she thought *just maybe,* but ultimately knew it was a flimsy wish. "Actually, could you give me a quick moment, Leonard? I just want to finish a thought here." Nora smiled at him through the rearview.

He raised his eyes in the mirror; they were soft and friendly. He smiled back. "Of course, Miss Mackenzie. We're a little early. You have time."

"Thanks . . . and, honestly, call me Nora. It's really fine."

Leonard gave an awkward nod that let Nora know that *Miss Mackenzie* was staying, that is, until it changed to *Mrs. Beaumont* in thirteen days. She pulled out her phone and sent Jenna a quick text.

> **hey you sure you don't want to be my date for this?**
> *Not for ALL the tea in C H I N A . . . lolz!*
> **hate you more today than yesterday. I swear!**

HAVE YOU MET NORA? / 167

*Lies. #hearteyes*
**get off my phone!**
*call me later. Say wuzzup to Ellie Elle Cool J.*
**you are the worst. complete and total worst**

Nora glanced up at the back of Leonard's head. His hair was very slick and dark and looked hardened like he had only recently been introduced to sculpting pomade. His zealous hairstyling somehow set Nora at ease. It made him seem fallible, regular, instead of sitting in judgment like Mr. Wally. "I'm all good," she said to his stiff hair. "Thanks."

"My pleasure," he said, and started getting out of the car.

"It's okay, it's okay," Nora said quickly. "No need for you to open the door for me. Truly. It's fine."

He turned partway in his seat, a frown pinching his face. "Are you—"

"Yes, totally sure. It's fine. But thank you."

Leonard shimmied himself back into his seat, buckled up his seat belt, and gripped the steering wheel at ten and two. "I will . . . see you later, then? If you would, please have the doorman call over to me twenty minutes before I'm needed here."

Nora nodded and hopped out of the car and stepped over to Leonard's window. He looked confused still and suddenly self-conscious, almost unsure of his next move. She noticed a strip of sweat down the center of his nose. She gestured for him to roll down the window. As he did, Nora leaned in a little, hovering. "You'll get used to me. You'll get used to all of this, too," she said, fanning her hand at the small castle behind her.

Leonard gave Nora a slip of a glance and returned to looking just beyond the steering wheel. "You're all set, ma'am," was all that he could seem to muster.

Nora backed away from the car smiling and waving as it

drove off. The interaction, brief and labored as it was, gave her a boost, a surge that made her actually want to step into the tea party and everything that awaited her inside. She was taking her own advice she had given to Leonard; she was getting used to all of it.

Then, a voice from over her left shoulder: "Took you long enough."

Nora spun around and her hand flew to her chest. Ghetto Dawn was standing off the side of the Beaumonts' gate with her arm stretched out leaning on it. Nora peered at her. She was wearing a light blue summer dress with cap sleeves, cinched waist, and wide flared skirt. She looked pulled together and pleasant. Then she unleashed her smirk.

"So," Dawn said. "We goin' in or . . . nah?"

The words shot up through Nora's chest and throat, scorching. "What the *fuck* are you doing here?"

"*Pssh.* I'm going to the tea party," she said, and moseyed over to Nora. "Right? Isn't that the plan?" Dawn slid her flat clutch under her arm. Nora stared at it in disbelief. The signature angled bottom, the brushed peach suede and distinct orange python across the flap, it was identical to the Narciso Rodriguez bag Nora had at home. The same one she had been obsessed with throughout the spring.

"Oh, you like my pocketbook?" Dawn said, shrugging one shoulder. "I should thank you for this. I saw you rocking it a bit ago—it was a photo of you in *The New York Times*"—she flicked her hand near her face as if fanning away a fly—"and I was, like, *Wow, that is dope as hell.* The real python part tripped me up, though. I kinda wobbled on that point—for PETA, you know—but then I said, *Whatevs. Just get it.* And here we are." She wedged the bag deeper under her arm and said, barely under her breath, "Wasn't my dime anyway."

"What can you—how did . . ." Nora threw a glance over her shoulder and lowered her voice. "Are you fucking stalking me?"

"Hmm. Not really. I just like to make it my business to know your business. And, like Liam Neeson says"—she winked—" 'I have a very particular set of skills' that allow me to do that."

"Are you crazy? What the hell is this? What do you want?"

"Nope, not crazy. This is us standing out here chatting, about to bop into this tea party. Now, are you coming? I don't think the *ladies who lunch* are about that CP time."

Nora moved in closer to Dawn and squinted as she looked right into her eyes. "I don't know what you think you're trying to do, but it's not happening. You can't be here. You can't go in there or anywhere with me. This is not a game," she said, seething. "I got your cookies and your Facebook bullshit, and I'm guessing you're the one who's been fucking around with my credit cards, but that's it. You're done. And you can't be here. I don't even know how you found out about this."

"Oh, thanks go to Olivia Chung on that."

"What . . . Oli told you?"

Dawn made a face. "Yeah, but she doesn't know that she helped me out. Once she emailed that RSVP, it was cake." She shifted in her shoes, rocking from one side to the other. "And that's all I'll say about that. Can't give away all my tricks, right?"

Nora thought for a moment. Her eyes flickered, searching the sidewalk, and her brows were furrowed so deep she could feel the strain across her forehead. Nora dropped back on her heels and looked up at Dawn with a start. "You hacked our email system? Identity theft—that's your play."

"Identity theft? Are you kidding me right now? Do you even have a real identity?" Dawn chuckled. "Girl, please. Now, let's get on with this. We're officially late to the party."

Nora shook her head. "I told you"—she steadied herself and stepped toward Dawn again—"you can't be here. And you're not going in there or anywhere with me." She was close enough now that she could smell the coffee on Dawn's breath. "Do you understand?"

Dawn's face folded. She bowed her head and turned away from Nora; her hand flew up to shield her eyes as her shoulder bounced. Nora exhaled over the sound of Dawn's sniveling and released her clenched jaw. She thought about reaching for her phone and calling Jenna, Fisher, Leonard, the police. But as she moved her hand to the corner of her bag tucked under her arm, too, Dawn spun around. Her face was scrunched up, but she was laughing, not crying.

"You are good, you know that? I mean, you've got this white-woman thing down to the bone; you even flex your privilege like it's regular. I mean, it's masterful—for real." Dawn shook her head as her laughter petered out. She stretched her arm to the gate and went back to leaning on it. Her expression hardened and her eyes narrowed at Nora. "Here's what I understand: We're going into that palace in there together because we're dear old friends from boarding school in Vermont and we just ran into each other recently and now can't bear to be apart because we need to catch up on all the things. I mean, this is kind of the truth, right? Except the dear old friends part is kind of sketch, but, hey, people change. The other version of this?" She tilted her head without breaking her stare. "I run up in there anyway and spill the whole fucking boiling pot of trash all over those sparkling hardwood floors. Choice is yours, coach."

"Why are you doing this?" Nora said. She heard the desperation in her voice and hated it. "What do you want from me?"

"It's not about what I want, Nora. It's about what you deserve."

"Look." Nora softened everything: her eyes, her voice, her back, the muscles in her neck. "I get it, all right? What I did, getting you in trouble like that, it was shitty. No, it was fucked up. And I'm sorry. Really." She took a long breath. "But we were seventeen, Dawn. Ten years ago is ten years ago. We came out of all that okay—for the most part." She giggled and gave Dawn a half smile, the one that set her green eyes to their brightest. It was the sweet, teasing grin that she would set loose on unprepared men and women alike, who would invariably bend her way. Fisher was helpless to this particular beam, transmuted into melted butter before her eyes.

Not with Dawn.

Nora's allure and golden dust fell flat to the uneven sidewalk around Dawn's feet.

"Except it's not *all okay*. And ten years ago feels like ten minutes ago in my book." Dawn released her gate lean and stood up straight. "You don't get it, do you?" She huffed and glanced at the skies. "You ruined. My. Life," she said, punctuating each word with a jabbed finger into the heated air between them. "Destroyed. And then ran away like some weak bitch." She shook her head and huffed again. "I've been looking for you for *years*. Each time I think I've let go for good, moved away from all of it enough that I can start to live a life, it comes back to me, like some fucking boomerang to the face. Start looking all over again. And then, one random, nothing day"—she laughed deep in her throat—"I look up and there you are, in black and white in the goddamn newspaper. One rich white dude was getting sued by some other rich white dude, who turned out to be *your* rich white dude. And watch you: hanging off his arm with your snake bag and your serious face, and I couldn't believe. I found the yeti! Right here in New York City, my new, clean-slate home. What are the chances? *Shiiitt.* And now you want to try to bench me?" A slanted grin went wide across Dawn's face. "I just got in the game."

An ocean of sick roiled in Nora's stomach. She could feel

her heart beating in her ears, her neck throbbing and tongue going mossy. This was it: the house engulfing in flames and she had no choice but to jump from the roof to her death. She didn't want to collapse in front of Dawn, but her knees were soft and her head spinning. Nora carefully scanned the street behind Dawn, tracing an exit strategy. The truth had become too big, too unwieldy and harrowing to leash and walk it through her life. She didn't want to run again, but Ghetto Dawn had left her with no alternative. Standing outside the imposing home of her soon-to-be mother-in-law with a small, but superb team of prominent, exceedingly wealthy women inside waiting to greet her, Nora knew this was the biggest stage on which to trip and fall. Trusting Dawn to play by the rules she herself had set out was asking too much, Nora thought. What if she decided to spill the truth anyway, no matter how closely Nora followed the pretense?

"Don't do this," Nora said, the words scratching their way out of her mouth.

"What? Bitch, it is entirely too late for all of that. You're wasting everybody's time, and we're mad late as it is. Let's get on with it."

"How do I know . . ."

"What are you mumbling?" Dawn said, annoyed.

Nora cleared her throat and finally looked up. "How do I know you're going to hold up your end? How do I know you're not going to fuck me once we clear the door?"

Dawn sighed. "You don't. You're going to have to trust me."

Nora shook her head and took a few steps back. She checked over Dawn's shoulder, scoping out the street again.

"All right, look," Dawn said, and gripped Nora rough by the elbow. "If we go in right now"—she rolled her eyes—"I'll stick to the long-lost BFF bullshit. But I swear to God, if you take even one more step away from me and try to bounce, it's a fucking wrap. Feel me?"

With her words steadily clogging her throat—colluding to choke her to death—Nora could only narrow her eyes at Dawn and nod, stiff and targeted like a headbutt.

"Good," Dawn said, letting loose her grip on Nora, leaving a hand hovering by the elbow. "Now, pull out that smile and get the twinkle poppin' in them green eyes and let's go."

# CHAPTER 13

They walked through the gate and up the first set of steps in a slow-moving procession. Nora kept sneaking looks at Dawn's hand balancing in the air, ready to grab at her if she dared to veer even an inch off course. This is how a hostage must feel, Nora thought, as Dawn nudged her to pick up the pace. All that was missing to make this scene in the thriller complete was Dawn's gun, hidden beneath a draped jacket, pointed directly at Nora's left kidney. She shook her head to try to rid her mind of the movie scenes. Real life was proving horrifying enough. Nora wanted to vomit; she also wanted to let her knees buckle and lay herself down on the cool concrete. The trapped animal feeling returned, and now there was no question about what would happen next: She wouldn't gnaw off the snared tail or paw. Nora knew that she would give in, submit, let the pain from her lesions take over and just wait for death.

When they reached the building's oversize front door, Dawn eased up her fire breathing and gave Nora a bit of space. "Play it right," she said, and motioned with her head for Nora to go in first.

The main doorman greeted them both at the formal entrance and showed them to the private elevator. He pressed the button to the floor they needed to go to and bowed to them ever so slightly, tipping his pretend hat, as the doors closed.

"This is fancy," Dawn said, looking over at Nora leaning on the other side of the cab. "I can see why you want to be up in this mix so bad."

Nora said nothing and kept her eyes trained on the backlit onyx elevator panels behind Dawn. They were pretty, she thought, each panel with its own special veining pattern. The effect—an amber glow throughout the elevator cab—seemed more potent and regenerated to Nora's eyes now than ever before. She noticed how the light of it bounced off of Dawn's deep brown skin, making it radiant and beautiful. Nora found herself staring at Dawn, her coldhearted enemy, and admiring her. The *ding* let her know that the smooth elevator ride was over—and so was her life, as she knew it.

The doors opened to a bright parlor, and a waft of hyacinth filled Nora's nose. She recognized the scent anywhere, because of her middle name and also because of how much her mother loved the way the flower smelled. It was actually the impetus for the one time Nora ever remembered her mother splurging on something for herself. It was one of the last of their annual Mother's Day brunches. After church, as usual, Nora and her mother would go for special breakfast at the lavish Café de Paris at the Ritz Carlton. Her mother had dressed up for the event, beyond her usual Sunday best, donning her thick gold bangles, linked chain, and sparkly clip-on earrings. Her ears had been pierced when she was a child back in Barbados, but she had started wearing clip-ons a few years after immigrating to Canada. She told Nora that she noticed all of the most glamorous women on TV, especially those who played roles in the "stories," wore clip-on earrings, and she liked how they would slip them off when it came time to talk on the phone. "Them is real *finessers,* all of them," Nora's mother would say about the soap stars nearly every time she watched.

This breakfast tradition involved Geo driving them from church to the restaurant (Nora's mother as always sat up front with him.). Her mother considered it the height of luxury— and laziness, if you wanted to hear the truth—to be chauffeured around this way, having someone wait outside in a car for you like it's a horse and carriage. She would always have to be talked into it, assured by Geo himself that it was not an inconvenience. But this one time, this last time, she didn't seem too troubled about having Geo wait on them. After the church service, Nora's mother even lingered around afterward in the rec room with the other congregants sipping coffee, tea, and juice and nibbling homemade butter cookies. She took her time at the restaurant, too. Ordering more than usual, and only taking a few, nothing bites of everything. And though the day was about honoring and celebrating mothers, Mona still insisted on paying for the two of them. "You ain't working nowhere, Ra-Ra," she said when Nora cringed when the check was placed between them. "You are my gift," she told her daughter. "Pay me a compliment, if you want to pay something."

After the breakfast, after the third cup of tea, and it was time to go, Nora's mother asked Geo if he wouldn't mind making one more stop before home. She needed to pick up something at The Bay, she said. It was a small, expensive bottle of perfume that smelled of hyacinth and gardenias.

"It cost more than it should," her mother said, as they got ready for bed in their basement later that evening. "But in life, sometimes you do things to make you happy, no matter the cost, even if it's just for the one day. Always remember I said so."

There were tears brimming in her eyes. Nora figured she was just tired, sleepy—she had been so easily spent those last few months. She didn't give it another thought, not until thirty-eight days later when her mother was dead and in the ground. It clicked then, and it was too late. The night after the funeral,

Nora made sure to wrap the tiny bottle of perfume in a padded envelope and slide it into her box with the other keepsakes from her terrible, truncated, Montreal life.

Lady Beaumont's secondary butler met Nora at the elevator doors; his face registered something that looked like a smile. "Welcome, Miss Mackenzie and Miss . . ." The butler's eyes drifted over to Dawn.

"Nwad," Dawn said, smiling and dipping her head to him.

"Very well, Miss N—"

"First-name basis works fine," she interrupted. "Just Nwad."

Plainly uncomfortable with the informality, the butler furrowed his brows and folded his already thin lips. "Very well, Miss *Nwad*. Welcome." He turned his attention back to Nora. "Lady Beaumont has been eagerly awaiting your arrival."

"Great. Same here," Dawn said, looking between the butler and Nora, amused.

"Oh, this is my friend from school. High school," Nora said, trying to temper the rising awkwardness. "And we just . . . ran into each other recently. It's all very exciting."

"Indeed," the butler said, barely raising his brows and nodding. "If you'd like to leave any personal items with me," he said, gesturing to their purses. Dawn clutched at hers tight and glared at the butler. "Or you may hold on to them on your own and follow me to the ballroom." He spun sharply on his heel and started his stiff-back glide deeper into the house.

"The ballroom? Oh, I'm into this," Dawn whispered into the back of Nora's head. "Could've done without the purse-snatcher routine, though. Better wayfinding system needed, STAT."

"Shut. Up," Nora said through the side of her tight, plastered-on smile.

"He can't hear shit," she said, again into the back of Nora's head, but louder.

Nora shot her an icy stare.

"Oh, relax," Dawn sighed, and rolled her eyes. "That's the only way this is going to be any fun."

There was nothing fun about any of this, Nora thought and shook her head. She checked to see if the butler was paying any mind to the murmuring commotion behind him.

He wasn't.

They entered the ballroom. It was opulent: swathed in a muted green silk, the perfectly balanced satin curtains that honored the right flecks of deep colors knotted into the Savonnerie carpet, and all of it illuminated by the French chandelier hanging in the center of the home's most elaborate room. Nora caught the wide-eyed look on Dawn's face. She remembered having a similar expression sweeping her own face when she first saw the room. She had to actively work at not staring up at the walls and that chandelier and try to appear unruffled, breathing easy through her nose instead of loud through her open mouth.

The butler disappeared into the drapes or into thin air, Nora couldn't tell, and she and Dawn were left standing in the bright glare of all the room's eyes on them. The women, nearly all of them bony and creased with their unnaturally flaxen hair stiff and tall or dark, sleek, and brushed back with streaks of white-gray, were dressed to perfection in limited variations of the same outfit: rich-colored, elaborately patterned, cropped blazers over simply detailed, high-necked shift dresses with sensible shoes that cost more than a cross-country airline ticket. And everywhere, pearls the size of mothballs and shimmering diamonds in gold battled for your attention.

"Nora," Lady Eleanor called out in her light, honeyed voice that she pushed through a clenched jaw. She had her arms already extended and hands reaching for Nora's from clear across the room. "Welcome, welcome." She connected with Nora's hands and squeezed them lightly in hers, then pulled

Nora in for a kiss on both cheeks. Nora liked that the pecks actually landed soft on her face, real contact, not the flighty air
kisses that everyone else in her world relied on. The kisses felt
like home, like the pleasant two-cheeked ones from Montreal
that harmless strangers and friends alike dispensed when they'd
encounter you on the street corner and at front doors for en-
trances and exits. Nora leaned into the embrace and tried to
inhale Lady Eleanor's signature fragrance, but the hyacinth
was still tickling her nose.

"I'm so glad you're here," Lady Eleanor said, smiling. She
pulled back from the hug and her eyes fell on Dawn standing
just behind Nora. "And you brought your work collaborator
with you, then?"

"Oh, no," Nora said, forcing a chuckle. "This is"—she
struggled to say the name, it sounded ridiculous and fake—
"Nwad . . ."

"Roo-Kayes. Nwad Bea Roos-Kayes," Dawn said, and gave
the older woman her hand. "Nora can't seem to remember my
new married name."

"Right," Nora said. "It's all very new to me."

Lady Eleanor's grin went wider as the handshake ended.
"Well, how lovely that you could join us."

"Yes, this is kind of a surprise, and I apologize for not letting your staff know that she would be tagging along. It was
rather last minute. Actually, we just ran into each other a few
days ago after not seeing one another for ten years."

"My, my," Lady Eleanor said, her voice filled with wonder.

"Again, my apologies about this. It's inconsiderate, I know,"
Nora said. "And I'm sorry."

"Nonsense. No apology needed, dear." She touched Nora's
forearm and squeezed it. "Any friend is a friend, isn't that
right?"

"Thanks for having me," Dawn said, looking around at some
of the other faces in the room. "Thank you all. This is . . . nice."

Nora tucked her lips into themselves. It was taking everything not to roll her eyes or scream or punch Dawn in the neck.

"May we get you something to drink?" Lady Eleanor said, moving her thin arm out, a beck to the closest server. "Sparkling water, coffee, tea? There are also delightful cocktails, if you so choose."

Nora tilted her head and opened her mouth to answer the kind offer, but Dawn's voice broke in. "That would be great. A cocktail for lunch sounds like old times, doesn't it, buddy?" Dawn said, and nudged Nora's side. "It's like we got transported back to high school, right?" Nora's eyebrows yanked themselves to her forehead and she felt the flutter in her stomach start to inch up her throat. Dawn busted out in a hollow laugh. "I'm just kidding!" she said, looking around the room of old women. "There was no underaged drinking at our school. We were all very good girls. Right, Nora?"

"Of course," Nora said, and gritted her teeth at Dawn in a tense smile. "But that was then, as they say. And we could probably gossip forever about those old high school days." She noticed the older women hobbling over to them, interested. She had hooked them and continued to pull. "Let's get back to the now, why don't we?" Nora faded the nosy circle to the background and set her glare directly on Dawn. "Why don't you share with all of us a little bit about what you do now? I had asked you before, when we had coffee the other day, but then we got distracted by I don't know what—talking about that geography teacher we all had crushes on, Mr. Jarrett?" Soft, polite laughter ballooned out around her. Nora had been in rooms like this before and knew exactly how to work them. She turned her charm levels up a few more notches. "If I didn't know you better, I'd say it's almost as if you're trying to keep your new life a secret," Nora said, chuckling and smiling more naturally. She turned back to the women. "Dawn was always particularly untalented at keeping secrets."

"That sounds like our Tilly," said one of the ladies with the tallest, whitest hair. "We all know she couldn't hold a secret even if it had handles." The women all laughed, a feathery, sprinkle of a laugh, and nodded.

"May she rest," another woman said, prompting the others to shake their heads, their laughter going listless.

"In the spirit of the late great Tilly Montgomery," Nora said, and opened her hand to Dawn, gesturing for her to take the imaginary stage before them, "do tell." More of the women moved toward them, closing in the sloppy circle. Most of them looked earnest and curious, taking in Dawn from head (especially) to toe. Some looked on with cardboard faces and pursed lips, seemingly unconvinced whether they should place their consideration anywhere near Dawn. "From the little you *did* tell me," Nora continued, "it sounds pretty fascinating." She signaled to one of the servers moving around the room in their artful waltz, and in a stage whisper told him, "I'll have some tea after all. No sugar, no cream, no honey. A bit of lemon. Thank you." She looked over at Dawn—her eyes were slightly narrowed at Nora. "And my good friend here will have . . . *Nwad,* would you like some tea, too, before you get started?"

"Just coffee," Dawn said. Her face was suddenly serious.

It was the meekest Nora had seen Dawn so far. She knew it was a big chance, giving Dawn the floor, but looking at her now, it felt like a big gain. Turning the spotlight back on Dawn was the first sign of leverage, and Nora wanted to play it through. She was also intrigued: Would Dawn let any of her own real story spill out? What happened to her after she got expelled in high school? And how did she find her way underneath Nora's skin again?

"Oh, now we are all here with bated breath, Nwad," Lady Eleanor said to Dawn. "Do share with us about your work and where you've landed after—what was it?—these ten years you and Nora have had apart."

Two servers brought over the chalk-white porcelain cups and saucers, presenting them to Nora and Dawn in a coordinated bow.

Dawn looked into the cup and started, sounding slow and careful. "Let's see . . . I'm married. I got married to my mister two years ago, and we live in Harlem." She paused and took a sip—slurping loudly—from her cup. "He is a teacher, and I work for an internet company. Computer programming. I'm really good with computers." Another pause; another long sip.

Nora flashed a look at Lady Eleanor. Her narrow face looked pleasant, not as severe as it often did, and her eyes were keen, as if waiting for the good part of Dawn's story to kick in. Instead Dawn took to her cup, sipping. And then finally, she flickered awake and looked up from her coffee. "Actually, I have a really funny story to add to all this"—she turned to Nora, her smirk refueled—"and I think Nora would really enjoy this one. But first, I'm going to get a drip more of that cream for my delicious coffee—lighten it up some."

Lady Eleanor raised her chin and eyebrow in the direction of the closest butler, who in turn signaled for the servers to hurry over to Dawn.

"No, no, no," Dawn said, her hand waving off the slim man stepping lively toward her. "I can do this. Besides, I don't think anyone can get the perfect mix of black and white that I'm looking for. I'm so particular about my coffee."

"Oh, I—very well," Lady Eleanor said. "Someone will show you to the station."

"I can do that," Nora interjected.

"Well . . . all right, then . . . that's fine," Lady Eleanor said. She shot a stern look at the server. "Help yourselves." Her face returned to its previous relaxed state.

Nora walked closely behind Dawn. "What are you doing?" she whispered.

"I could ask you the same," Dawn snapped, and set her saucer on the high table.

"Keep your voice down."

Dawn poured more cream into the cup and stirred. She shook her head, not looking up from her caramel-colored brew. "These decaying bitches, they don't even know what to make of me. And clearly, by this stunt you're pulling, neither do you. Thing is"—she raised just her eyes to Nora—"you're going to end up with your feelings hurt. That part is already written."

The words felt like a flaming arrow shot through Nora's gut. Any semblance of upper hand that she had sensed moments ago trickled out of the center of her now.

Without warning, a swell of gasps and murmurs took over the room. Nora turned toward the din. The servers were rushing to one of the old ladies. She was slumped over on the couch, her head dropped to the side and face completely flushed.

"She's having a reaction," someone yelped. "Call an ambulance!"

Men and women dressed in black pants and crisp white shirts came running from all corners hidden and plain, and darted over to the ill woman. The buzz got louder as the woman sunk further into the chair. Nora overheard the butler who had greeted them at the elevator yell "allergic reaction" and "call now" at one of the other workers, everyone with the same worry drawn across their faces. The closer Dawn stepped into the confusion, the farther away Nora moved from it, leaning toward the door.

"I think there's tree nuts of some sort in one of the salads," one woman said, from behind Nora, startling her. "This is dreadful. She's deathly allergic."

Nora stared back at the woman, speechless, and kept sliding toward the exit. She didn't want to know anything about anything if it didn't pertain to her getting out of there this minute. She kept her eyes trained to the floor and her movements discreet. She looked up only once, quickly, to check on Dawn, who was deep in the thick of the commotion. Nora heard herself breathing; it was fast and loud, coming through her mouth. Tears were pooling. She thought back to the one or two occasions where she had an opening to explain how this jumbled mess of fiction started, and how each time she turned away from it and ran. Maybe she would have been okay if she had flouted Mrs. Bourdain's duplicitous plan and instead entered Immaculate as herself: the only daughter of a black saint and a pathetic, vanished white father. Maybe she would have been all right, accepted, and held up as a good person worthy of friends and favor, much like Dawn herself had been when she first arrived at the school. But *maybe* was the cry of the hopeless, she knew, and it served no one, especially not now. This moment was not for *maybe;* it was for certainty, action, and escape. She needed to leave this havoc behind—both the tumult of the poisoned old woman on the couch and what will undoubtedly be left of her life after she is unmasked by Dawn. She needed to start again on an unmarked page. And it would have to be different. She would have to launch her new existence far, far away from everything she had built in New York, and it would need to begin with the truth.

As Nora reached the elevator and moved her hand to press the call button, the doors slid open. Three EMTs—a woman out front and two men behind her—barreled through, wheeling a gurney between them. The butler was there, standing beside Nora in a heartbeat, and directing the ambulance workers to the collapsed woman.

"Thank you for showing them in, Miss Mackenzie," he told Nora, and gently patted her shoulder.

And without another pause or breath, Nora entered the elevator and pressed the button for the lobby floor. Dawn was nowhere in sight, but Nora waited until the doors fully closed before she let herself exhale. Her charm and spirit had long fizzled, and two things made themselves explicitly clear: Dawn was set on destruction, and Nora needed a plan B, because running away was not an option.

# CHAPTER 14

"It was awful," Nora said, pinching the bridge of her nose with her fingers. She was sitting on the side of their tub, her hair drenched and bathrobe tied tight. "I mean, just frightening."

"I know. My mother was pretty shaken up when she called," Fisher said, leaning against the counter. "I knew something was very wrong when she called my cell phone. I didn't even think she personally knew the number. She never calls me on that." He stood and went to the basket under the sink, then grabbed another towel and handed it to Nora. "Are you okay?"

She covered her face with the towel and nodded.

Fisher sat next to her on the tub's edge. "I'm serious, Mack; you all right? That was scary. Thank God Mrs. Newbold is going to be fine, but it was dicey for a brief moment there."

"Yeah, I'm just glad she's all right." Nora wiped the towel over her face again and then applied it to the soaked ends of her hair, gently squeezing out the water. "What else did your mother say about everything?"

"Well, she's mortified. Thinks she will be smeared amongst her friends, and no one will want to attend an event at the house ever again."

"It's not her fault, though."

"True, but she's worried all the same. That woman could have died today all because her body was essentially doing its job. I mean, yes, it's naturally defending itself—albeit going kind of overboard, right? Truly fascinating to see how one body can react so adversely to something that's completely innocuous to another."

Nora continued sponging her hair. Usually, hearing Fisher get deep into talking about the intrigue steeped in the human body and geek out over medical research would be an undeniable turn-on for her. Like earlier in the spring, when he spoke excited and almost giddy for a solid thirty minutes about the study the Institute was conducting on an alternate to polonium-210, the highly radioactive substance so toxic that a dose as small as a speck of dust will become a slow, sure, silent death sentence. Nora couldn't keep track of all the research points, but talk of alpha particles and energy and central nervous systems—all of it landed Fisher with a blow job in the kitchen right where he stood.

"Did your mother mention anything else about the gathering?" Nora said, patting her hair and trying to sound casual. "Like, what happened after the ambulance rescued Mrs. Newbold? I'm sure the remaining guests were kind of freaked out and probably stuck around to talk."

"Yes, freaked out; they were definitely that. Even the waitstaff, my mother said they were flustered as well."

Nora kept her voice even. "Right, but that's it? I mean, nothing else was mentioned about what happened after Mrs. Newbold got sick? Nothing about what everyone did after—or what they said?"

Fisher turned to look at Nora. She noticed a very distinct wrinkle between his brows. She knew this slightly soured look. Fisher would often make that face if he felt someone was being inconsiderate or rude, like when a person interrupted him as he was speaking. It didn't matter if he was talking business or

basketball, don't cut him off. She'd gone a pinch too far in trying to decipher what Dawn said after she ran off and wasn't
sure if there was a way to reel it back.

"Look, Mack," Fisher said, "what do you want me to say?
All of the women were completely horrified. They watched
their friend nearly die because of something she ingested.
What else is there for them to say afterward?"

Nora turned away, pretending to dry the other side of her
hair and positioning the towel so it obscured his full view of
her. "I'm just curious. Was pretty strange—the whole thing."

Fisher gently took the white towel from Nora's hand and
started brushing it through her hair. Nora's shoulders crept up
to her ears while her eyes searched the floor. Tender as the moment was supposed to be, she wanted no part of it. Although
he had often stroked—and sometimes pulled—her hair as they
rolled around the bed or floor, their bodies pressed up against
each other, moving to their own intense cadence, this time felt
wrong, intrusive. Nora had noticed a clump of hair by the
drain when she got out of the shower. The wad of hair was
longer and bigger than what she knew to be normal and only
added to her already jangled nerves. It was happening: horrible history repeating. Ghetto Dawn was dangling the secret
over Nora's head like an anvil on a string and she was falling
apart behind it.

"Mack, what are you not telling me?" He paused on the hair
handling and sighed. "I can't keep asking you this."

Nora slid her long hair out from his grip and moved along
the tub's edge away from Fisher, creating some distance while
staying close enough for the intimacy of the moment to remain
intact. She searched the floor again, hoping to find anything
that resembled *what to say* lying flat on the expensive tiles. The
feeling of bursting into tears surged, but she blinked it all
back. She wanted to tell him something, just not the truth.

Nora had decided as she hustled home on foot from the tea party disaster that telling anyone who she really was—what she really was—as some sort of preemptive strike against Dawn didn't make sense. It would only help Dawn get what she wants: Nora losing everything.

She had skipped the call to Leonard to collect her from the Beaumont mansion and briskly walked by each vacant cab heading downtown. With every stride, Nora became more convinced that she wanted to win—the grand prize being Fisher and the life she deserved—because Dawn would never relent. Nora thought about how she had run away from Montreal and Dr. Bourdain's predatory ways. How she had run away from Immaculate Heart and the threats of exposure. And how she had run away from the Bourdain name and the betrayal behind it. She had made her way out of each of those lives, often broken and bruised, but still breathing. She knew that when it came down to fight or flight, she would choose to take off, without hesitation or even a slim desire to look back. And now again, because of Dawn, she would be forced to choose once more.

But this was different. Nora didn't want to leave anything behind. She didn't want to move on to a new world, this time maybe across the ocean (Paris, Milan). She didn't want to start fresh, this time maybe even walk freely as a mixed-race woman, albeit with a broken heart. And she also didn't want to disarm Dawn's threat by telling Fisher and her friends the truth about her identity, and hang on to hope that their love will prevail over any shame or humiliation the revelation may bring. She wanted the wedding and the family and Fisher. She ran her fingers over the engagement ring as she walked home, rubbing it like a genie's bottle—her three wishes already set to be granted.

There would be no running, she told herself as she neared

the Chrysler Building, thirty-five blocks into her march home. She stopped when she reached the shiny chrome skyscraper, gaping up at its spire aimed at the sky miles above. Nora nodded, and it was settled: She was going to reach out to Dawn and ask to meet with her. She was going to offer up a large sum of money, enough to not only dazzle Dawn, but also derail her. She was going to be adamant, firm, and she was going to be prepared to offer even more cash to buy her silence. And she felt sure of the plan because she knew that, just like her, Dawn didn't come from much of anything. Like her, Dawn was shoved into the margins, desperate to be allowed into the main room. Money is that needed bridge. And Nora was betting everything that Dawn would hop on it and take it to go far, far away.

She felt Fisher move closer before he actually did. He was right next to her on the tub. "Mack, talk to me," Fisher said, his shoulder softly butting up against hers. "Whatever it is, we can deal with it."

"It's nerves," Nora said. "I've told you."

"It's more. Maybe it's my lizard brain or whatever, but I just know it's more. It's what's keeping you up at night and drinking in the empty tub instead and making your shoulders tight and, frankly, it's probably what made you freak out at my mother's house."

Nora snapped a look at him. "What are you talking about?"

He lowered his chin, his eyes softening as he stared into hers. "Nora, I know that you left." She started to shake her head. "Yes, you left. As soon as the ambulance came, you were gone."

"What is this," Nora said, her eyes bulging. She stood up and took a step toward the sink. Fisher reached out and grabbed her wrist.

"Don't run off, Mack."

"I'm not running," she barked.

"Okay, okay," Fisher said, and gently tugged at her to come back to him. "Just take it easy, okay? This isn't anything. It's me and you, talking. That's all." He tried to guide her over to sit on his lap.

She shook her head. "I don't want to sit right now." Nora twisted her wrist free from his light grip. "Let me be, okay?" She went to the sink and rinsed her face with cool water. She could feel the pulse in her temple and knew that her telltale vein was exposed. Nora wiped her face with a fresh hand towel and kept it draped there for a moment longer. She didn't want to look at Fisher; she couldn't. "I just need a minute, Fish," Nora said through the towel. "Give me that, okay?"

"Of course." His voice sounded close behind Nora, though he didn't touch her. "But I think we need to talk about the gorilla in the room: your mother, her passing. It's affecting you. Clearly. The wedding only pulled all of that to the surface."

It could have been the word *gorilla* or the mention of her mother soon after it—either way, something snapped inside. Nora heard it. "Can you just get out of here, Fisher? *Please,*" she cried into the towel still covering her face. "Just, please. Let me be."

A click of the door came next. Then, quiet. Nora didn't move the towel and instead used it to muffle her hollow sobs. She wanted to kick and scream and fight the air. Everything she didn't want to happen was happening. Dawn had infiltrated the inner layer, dragging disquiet and distrust in behind her. And Nora was lashing out at the people she loved most. In their three and a half years together, she had never once raised her voice at Fisher. Their disagreements were brief and would be resolved shortly after they started, with one of them (or both) owning up to the bad choices and behavior that caused the small fire to erupt. And here she was practically shoving him out the bathroom door with a frying pan tossed at his head. This bickering, squirming, sobbing, disconnected, disaster couple was not them. This was all Dawn.

Nora calmed her breath and used the damp towel to dry her face as best she could. She righted herself in the wide mirror and tried to soften the starkness of her red, puffed-up face. *Fish, I'm sorry,* she said to herself. It didn't seem like enough, so she practiced the apology silently, adding and removing words from the line, tweaking her expression and posture each time.

Leaned in, robe parted down to her belly, lips pouting: *Fish, I love you so much and really can't wait to be your wife.*

Hands clasped behind her back, eyes smiling and sweet: *Honey, can you ever forgive me. I'm an official monster bride and totally out of control.*

Nora rehearsed her lines and variations over and again until she stopped and just looked into the mirror, fixed on her washed-out face. She opened her mouth, licked her lips, and let the truth fall freely: "Fish, I have been lying to you about everything. I'm half-black. My mother was a maid. And her boss repeatedly raped and sodomized me when I was nine until I turned thirteen, a month before Mum died from pancreatic cancer. The vicious wolf he called a wife adopted me, gave me her blond hair, her bleached coloring, and their burdened family name, and shipped me off to boarding school. But she knew about everything, she knew what he was doing to me in his study, and she let him continue. He's dead now, and I hope she'll soon follow. And all that's left is the secret of it that I've carried strapped to my back for the last fourteen years. I love you, but I don't deserve you, and you deserve better. I wish it wasn't this way, but it is. I'm sorry."

There were no tears and Nora's shoulders didn't roll into her chest. She was standing straight, unwavering, and looking herself in the eye. That's when she heard it: a crash of glass and Fisher's voice booming. Nora bolted out of the bathroom, grabbing the robe sash and looping it into a quick, tight knot as she ran toward the noise. Her mind moved as quickly as her feet. What if Dawn followed her home and had been lying in wait in the cool shadows of the building for the right moment to pounce? She spotted droplets of blood near the kitchen entryway and now her mind ran ahead of her, envisioning in gross detail what she might find around the corner. She backed away from the kitchen slowly and scanned the immediate area around her.

Nothing.

Nora hadn't noticed it before, but there were no convenient wedges of thick wood or hefty vases or weapons of any sort masquerading as ornaments in Fisher's penthouse. Nora's mother used to keep a short lead pipe hidden under her bed. She told her daughter it was a fallen-off piece from the bed frame. Nora had figured out early on what it was really for, but still couldn't picture her mother actually swinging it at some burglar's head.

Still frozen in place, Nora craned her neck toward the hall that led to the front door and elevator. Nothing looked disturbed. Then she took a breath and charged into the kitchen, her fists balled. More blood drops, a smashed water pitcher, and no one else.

"Fisher?" Nora called out. She shook her head at the horror movie cliché of it and called out again, louder.

"Out here," Fisher yelled back from the terrace.

Nora rushed over. "What are you doing out—"

He was on a call, his left hand wrapped in a bloody tea towel and raised above his head. Fisher looked at the sloppy tourniquet, then back at Nora, and rolled his eyes at her before mouthing the word *fuck* and shaking his head. Though she couldn't figure out the how, Nora was able to interpret the what: Fisher had broken the glass pitcher and cut himself while trying to clean it up with one hand—the other was pressing the phone to his ear.

"Exactly, Colin," he said, turning his attention back to his call. "This is now top priority. Don't worry about the extra hours, just fix it."

Nora hurried back inside and went straight to the hall closet near the guest bathroom. It was where she had put the first-aid kit when she moved into the penthouse. The plain white box was filled with the usual bandages, gauze, dressing pads, and ointments, but also contained bottles of generic prescription painkillers that Fisher sometimes brought home from meetings with pharmaceutical reps and forgot about. Nora had stashed the pills in the box deep in the closet after one particularly reckless night out with Jenna. That they didn't land in a gurney or the back of a patrol car that Sunday remained, for Nora, a testament to the power of blondness, breasts, and privilege. *Out of sight, out of mind,* she told herself when she transferred the drugs from the medicine cabinet in their bathroom to the closet way down the hall. It's also what she told herself when she slid the old, flat box with the last vestiges of home under a low shelf in that same closet. And it worked, too. Nora hadn't thought of Montreal or the items in the box for years. Not until nine days ago when she was reading about a new menswear designer in the *Montreal Gazette* online and spotted his face first, then the name—Dr. Pascal Bourdain—in the obituaries.

She heard Fisher's voice closer now, inside the house. He was still on the phone, but his tone had changed. It wasn't as clipped or stern as a moment ago on the terrace. He was probably talking to his brother, she thought, and pulled out some gauze and adhesive tape from the box and a gray washcloth from the tall stack on the shelf. She met Fisher in the kitchen.

"Rock, it's some kind of worm virus. That's not going to fix it," he said. His face was red and his jaw clenched. It wasn't his typical comportment, especially when talking to one of his brothers. Even if they were going over business issues, there was always a sense of ease around it. "IT says that this thing basically encrypts itself. Finding it is going to take some time. Hackers. Jesus. I don't know why we're getting targeted." Nora sidled over to him with the first-aid tools. She smiled up at him and reached for his wounded hand tucked under his armpit, carefully rolling it out and unspooling the bloody towel. He winced, but tried to cover it with a tight smile and continued talking. "Right. They like to leave signatures. Exactly. Colin said they're often tucked away deep into shit, but this one—" He winced again.

"Sorry," Nora whispered. She didn't realize the grip she had on his hand while trying to disinfect it. The cut wasn't as bad as it looked once the blood was cleaned away. Nora peeled off some of the tape and bandaged up the hand, taking care to be easy with her touch. When she was done, she brought his hand up to her lips and kissed it.

He moved the phone from his mouth. "I love you, babe. Off in two seconds," he said. "Yeah, I'm here, Rock. Thanking Mack for . . . being a saint." Fisher winked at her.

Nora made a gesture wiggling her fingers, flitting about, miming cleaning up the smashed pitcher. Fisher dipped his head at her and put his bandaged hand to his heart; then he moved off to the side to pace.

She looked down at the blood and the shards of glass, unsure of which to tackle first, and glanced back at her man, Fisher. The winks and smiles and softness—she was forgiven for yelling him out of the bathroom. It's like it never even happened. Nora stooped down and dragged the dirty tea towel through the blood, smearing it a little before actively wiping up the mess. She listened to Fisher talking in the background and felt a calm wash over her.

"Colin's looking into it. He said he didn't recognize that name or handle or whatever," Fisher said to his brother. "And it was different than other hacker handles, he said. More basic, like a regular name." Fisher chuckled. "Yeah, exactly, like a John Smith, but this was just a last name: Bourdain."

Nora gasped and dropped the large pieces of glass that she had collected, shattering them into even smaller bits. She hopped up and turned to face Fisher, who was quickly stepping toward her.

"Hey, I gotta call you back," Fisher said in one breath, and was by Nora's side in seconds. "Babe, you all right? Did you cut yourself?"

"No, I . . . I just . . . it slipped."

"Mack, you're trembling." He took her hands in his. "You okay?"

"Yeah." She nodded. "Yeah, totally. I must've nicked or pinched my finger or something, but see"—she fanned her hand by him—"no blood. It's totally fine." She went back to the glass on the kitchen floor mainly to get a few seconds to pull herself together without Fisher staring at her, frowning. She returned to picking up what few large pieces of the broken pitcher she could gather from the floor.

*Fix your face.*

The trembling in her hands was still there, but she was able to steady her voice just enough. After a beat, Fisher bent down to help.

"Sorry about this mess," he said, grabbing the soggy tea towel. "I'm going to toss this." He walked over to the sink and dropped the rag in it. Nora was tempted to say something about it not being the garbage, but swallowed the comment. She needed to focus on how to start this conversation as if everything were regular.

"So, what all happened?" Nora kept her head down, eyes fixed on the glass and the wet floor.

"Other than me not knowing how to work a water pitcher?" he said, sighing. Nora could hear the irritation resting at the base of his voice. "Rock called to tell me about our system getting hacked just as I was reading the red-flag email about it. I was getting some water for you—or at least that was the attempt—and it slipped or, shit, maybe I smashed it on purpose. I'm so annoyed. I mean, Jesus. We're about medical research, helping people get healthy, why hack into us?"

"It's fucked up, for sure. I'm sorry, honey." Nora kept her back turned to Fisher, but could hear his footsteps pacing, coming close to her, then moving away again. "Can your team fix it?"

"Yeah, it's going to mean some late nights for a couple guys, but it's not a complete shit show."

"And did I overhear you say something about the hackers leaving a name or something?" Nora knew she had to make eye contact soon, to stand soon, to actually clean up the floor soon; she needed to act like her heart was not trying to climb up her throat. But her entire brain ached. Dawn was everywhere. She had burrowed into Nora's life and was now scratching her paws at the Beaumonts' door.

"Yeah, there was handle in the code," Fisher said. Nora finally looked over at him. "Colin said it was left behind on purpose. *Bourdain.*" He shrugged. "But who knows what that even means or if it's useful. My only focus is patching things up and securing the walls against something similar happening down the line. These guys can become a total pain in the ass."

"Yeah, they can be," Nora said, her voice trailing off.

"All right, that's it," Fisher said. He walked over to the mess pile on the floor and hovered by Nora's shoulder. "I can't watch this anymore, not in good conscience. You've been picking around the same four pieces of broken glass for the last twenty hours." He held out a hand to help Nora stand up. "I'll take care of this mess; it's my fault anyway. You go get out of that robe, finish getting dressed."

"You sure?" Nora said. "I mean, you only have one hand."

"Sometimes that's all it takes, babe."

She smiled. "And we're good—you and me?"

"We're good, always."

Nora nodded, beaming as she backed away from him and continued out of the kitchen. The minute she cleared the corner, Nora spun around and shuffled to her dressing room, grabbing her phone from the nightstand on her way there. The closed door didn't seem to be enough; Nora poured herself into the deepest corner of the closet beneath the shelf with her color-coordinated, perfectly folded sweaters. She needed to make sure no one could possibly overhear her, even though she didn't yet know who to call or even what she'd say to them. Nora held the phone in both hands for a breath, drumming her fingers along the sleek back of it. She took another deep breath and tried to let it out slowly. It was all weighing heavy on her. She could feel it in the line between her shoulder blades, the very back of her neck, and the arches in her feet. Even her nails suffered; they were peeling and brittle.

She couldn't understand how Dawn was doing it. For as many lines as Nora had drawn in the sand, Ghetto Dawn kept crossing them. The special set of skills that she had mentioned to Nora seemed to run deeper than simply meddling and fooling a credit card customer service rep on the phone. Nora knew this now. Dawn's reach went far and she was capable of digging her dirty claws into anyone.

But it can't be Fisher. It can't be the Beaumonts. Nora needed to make sure Fisher and his family stayed in the bubble, protected.

She opened up her email and started typing a note to Oli, but stopped after a handful of words and stared at the slow-blinking cursor. The gears in Nora's brain picked up speed.

"She's hacking into my email," Nora said in the quietest whisper. "She's hacking into everything."

Nora rested the phone on the floor next to her. It was starting to come together: the Facebook request, finding her home
address, the credit card charges—it all fit. She remembered
reading a tech post years back about how hackers would get
into a person's iCloud and use the Find My iPhone app to
watch folks move around, track where they are and where they
go. Nora swallowed hard and looked over at her phone with
her eyes cut and angry. *That's how Dawn keeps popping up
everywhere.* A new thought crashed into Nora's brain and she
sat up as if shot in the back. "Mateo," she said, and snatched
up her phone again. She dialed his number instead of emailing
or texting.

"Boss-lady! A phone call, though?"

"Hey, yeah, I know. I can't trust email right now. It's kind of
why I'm reaching out."

"Can't trust email? Not dubious at all," he said, snickering.
"What's going on?"

"Remember a couple months ago, you were telling me and
Oli about this girl on Twitter who was, like, reverse-trolling
people by posting their personal information on there."

"Pettysburg Address, yeah, yeah. She is so dope. That woman
has those assholes begging her to stop putting them on blast,
pleading with her to delete the shit she posts about them."
Mateo laughed. "That chick is hilarious."

"Okay, her. What did you call it again, what she's doing?"

"What, *doxing?*"

"Yeah, that. How do you do it? I mean, how does someone
get into your personal stuff like that?"

"Because people in general are dummies and don't know
how to lock their shit up on the interwebs. They use the same
easy-to-crack passwords for, like, everything from their bank
accounts to their wack-ass Instagram. Listen, the most basic of
basic web searches can land you right in the middle of anyone's
private *bidniss*—their cell number, where they live, their email,

their IP address, their SSN, credit card info, all their social media bullshit, even their work internal memos. It's all out there. And if someone's really good, they can dig even deeper. And what's really fucked up is, since all of that information is public, dropping dox is technically legal."

"Shit." The twitch in her brow doubled its intensity and she felt a tingling in her right foot. She flexed and wiggled it around on the floor and spotted three large drops of blood left behind, where her big toe was. Nora pulled the leg up to check. There was a cut on the bottom of the foot from the broken glass. "Goddammit."

"For real. Hold up—someone doxed you?"

Nora let the question linger for a half second, then blurted out an answer, "Yeah." She nodded and a gust of relief settled over her, making the sting of her cut toe fall away. "Yes, someone is definitely doxing me."

"Man, that fucking sucks. Do you know who's trying to come for you?"

She paused again, trying in haste to calculate the risks of speaking too freely. "Might have an idea. Someone from long ago."

"Like Canada long ago? Damn, I thought you guys were basically cold-weather hippies—peace and love and all *sore-ry* everything."

Nora rolled her eyes. "Oh, my God, don't start. Please."

"All right, all right. But, seriously, is this person, like, harassing you, trying to blackmail you or something? I mean, the wedding *is* coming up. You're going to be a target for this kind of shit. I'm surprised it took this long, to be honest with you."

"How about not being honest with me," Nora said, letting her annoyance ooze out. "I don't need to hear that I should just expect this invasion of my privacy all because I'm marrying someone with a name in this fucking city."

"Chill, chill. I hear you. My bad. Not what I meant, okay?"

Mateo said. Nora grunted—a half response to his limp apology. "So, what are you going to do about it?"

Nora chewed at her lips. "Something," she said. "That's all I know right now. Something."

"Well, I know this dude—yo, I shouldn't be saying anything. I don't want NSA adding me to their files, man." Mateo sighed. "But since it's you . . . All right, look, this dude from back in my skate park days, he does this kind of stuff, only he's working for the right side of things, know what I'm sayin'? He's an infosec engineer."

"Infosec?"

"Information security engineer," he said. Nora didn't like how exasperated Mateo sounded, as if he were the kid showing up his obtuse mom for the hundredth time that day.

"I'm sorry that we're not all up on the hacking glossary of terms, Mateo."

"I wasn't—Nora, obviously this has got you on edge. I don't blame you. This shit is ridiculous. But, come on. I might not rock a cape, but I be on the Justice League. I'm with the good guys. Only trying to help you, okay?"

Nora let the silence ride out for a minute and tried to smooth the sharp edge in her voice. "I know. I know you are, Matts."

"All right. So, here's what: You need to go and change up your whole shit. New passwords for everything. Make sure they're long and crazy, because those are the ones that work like a brick wall; trust. Throw in that two-factor authentication for your log-ins, too. Call all the credit cards—anywhere that you used your social or any personal info, call and let them know that there's been a breach."

"Crap. The wedding planner. Her office left a message. Something about the seating plan. I thought it was to confirm for the fifth time that, no, we will *not* be having a separate groom and bride side at the ceremony. But maybe it's about my credit card or a declined charge."

"Exactly. Call that planner back, like, yesterday. I'll talk to Dylan and Ravi about securing the email at work, if that's been affected. For now, you should stay off of email. I'll tell Oli and crew the same. You can still text, but only use iMessage. That's encrypted end to end, so you're pretty safe there. Overall, just watch what you're putting out there. I know you don't get down with the selfies and shit, so that's good. And if you want, I'll send the smoke signals out to my *Mr. Robot* for an assist, if needed."

"Jesus. How do you know all of this? Aren't you a fashion guy?"

"Yeah, I'm that," he snickered, "but you can't just be one thing. Not in this wild world, you know?"

"Right." The sting had returned to Nora's cut foot and brought with it some throbbing. "Thanks for all of this, Matts. I should go."

"Don't mention it. It's how we do. And don't worry about any of this, Nor. Ninety percent of these hacker assholes is just that: assholes. Secure your shit and they'll go away, off to find the next fool with *password123* for a password. Anyway, catch you later, all right?"

"Later."

Nora hung up and folded her legs in close so that the injured toe faced up. The thoughts of what to do next rolled in like a rough tide, leaving her dizzy and nauseated. She pressed her finger into the wound on her foot; she wanted to feel something distinct, recognizable. Pain made sense. Everything else that swirled around inside did not.

There was a light knock. "Mack," Fisher said through the side of the dressing room door. "You all right in there?"

Nora ran the back of her hand under her wet nose and

stretched an intense, fake grin across her face. She took her voice out of her nose, but made sure to keep it as pleasant as possible. "Oh, yeah. Totally, honey," she sang. "Getting ready to meet Jenna. Trying to decide which shoes I want to go with: Ancient Greek Sandals or my Lanvin cap toe sneakers. The gun-metal color of the Lanvins is kind of speaking to me, you know?" Talking to Fisher about fashion beyond the broadest strokes was the surest way to send him racing in the other direction. Though Nora didn't pull out this piece of kryptonite often, it felt necessary right now. She needed more time to get her mind on the right track.

"You be you, Mack. That's always the right choice," he said, his voice getting quieter. Nora could almost envision him slowly backing away.

She peeled herself out of the corner and moved a little closer to the locked door. "Thanks. Lanvins it is!" she said, and tried to smile wider, but her face gave out and crumpled. Tears lined her eyes. Nora covered her mouth with the sleeve of her robe.

"Hey, so, I've got to go into the office. Asher and his team are calling in from London about this whole hacker cluster-fuck. I'm trying to make sure it's not a midnight call for them. Text me if you and Jenna call it quits early and you want to do a late dinner. The Dutch, private room?"

Nora nodded, but couldn't stop her chin from quivering enough to speak. "*Mmm,*" she warbled.

"All right. Love you."

"*Mwah,*" she said, pressing her face to the door, hoping the kissing sound would suffice and that he'd walk away content.

"Have fun," he said.

Nora kept her ear flat against the door listening for his foot-steps to fade. When she could hear nothing but quiet, she scuttled back to her corner under the shelf, leaving a trail of smeared blood behind. She sat there clutching her phone, staring at the uneven red lines on the fluffed white rug like art.

This was it, the watermark on the wall. And an idea, born of hardened scar tissue and exasperation, came into a finer focus for her. Nora knew what needed to happen, and at last she was ready to make sure that it did.

# CHAPTER 15

Nora positioned herself at the small square table so that her back was at the wall. She arrived early enough to get the right table, the one that gave her the cleanest view of the Bean House Café entrance. She ordered hot water with lemon and asked for it in a large to-go cup dressed up to look like a latte. Just because it was the only thing Nora could keep down over the last two days didn't mean she had to relish it. Through some artful delusion and assumed "wedding jitters," she maintained the illusion of enjoying regular things. The to-go cup masquerade was high on her list of tricks.

After thirty minutes had passed, she went back to the counter for a refill on her water. "Make it melting hot, please," she told the barista, and handed over the half-drunk cup. "In about ten minutes, please bring it over to me along with a Good Morning Blondie in a mug for my guest. She should be here by then. We'll be just over there." She turned and pointed out the prime table.

"You bet," the server said, busily tapping the screen of the iPad POS system. "Will that be all, ma'am?" she asked, finally looking up at Nora.

"Yes, that'll be all. Thank you"—she glanced at her name tag—"Gillian."

She snorted. "You're like the first person to get it right the first time around. I usually have to correct people that it's not a soft *G*. It's hard, like *go* or *gum* or . . . *Gillian*."

Nora made a face. "That's annoying."

"Honestly? I don't even bother correcting them anymore and just let the whole soft-*G* thing ride."

"Well, you should keep correcting them." Nora's smile dimmed. "Don't let other people tell you who you are."

The server nodded. "I know. You're totally right. I shouldn't. It's *my* name."

Nora's smile warmed up again and she gave Gillian a crisp $20 bill.

"Okay, out of twenty, that's—"

Nora flashed her palm. "Keep the change."

The young woman's eyes went wide behind her elaborate glasses. "That's *so* nice of you! Thanks a lot. We'll have that order out in"—she looked down at the tablet screen—"about eight minutes or less. Probably less."

"Perfect."

Nora went back to the table and settled in, keeping her shoulders leveled and back straight like the wall, and waited for Dawn to show.

Staring into the blurry cloud of people walking in and out of the café, Nora tried hard not to check the watch that spun loose around her now-thinner wrist. She had a knack for guessing where the hands of the clock pointed without looking. It was her personal parlor game, developed in the wee hours of those restless nights at Immaculate Heart. And, like too many other things, she had recently pulled out the quirky coping mechanism from her dark closet and put it back in rotation. The temptation to touch her hair—gathered in a slack bun at the very top of her head—was also high. But she made a strong effort to resist resting on that old habit, too. She had already collected enough blond clumps in the shower; the last thing she needed now was a parade of helpless strands tumbling from her head to her shoulders and sailing down to the table in front of Dawn.

With each flutter in her chest or the slightest pulsation of the vein by her temple, Nora started counting her breaths. She had stopped relying on running through the old classmates' names. It only made things worse, wrenching her back a decade ago to the very day that her world upended and left her sprawled on her dorm's dingy hallway floor. Everything that happened that terrible day had been playing on Nora's mind nonstop this week from the moment she woke in the early morning until she pretended to fall asleep next to Fisher late at night. She could remember each beat, each wounded expression, each word, and each weighty pause between them. Nora didn't even have to close her eyes to conjure up the pucker-sour look on Dawn's face as she was shown off the school premises, her hands behind her back, her whole body steeped in anger, stomping toward the vestibule with the whisper campaign that Nora had started reaching its natural crescendo behind her. For all concerned, Dawn was a thief, a liar, and the vulgar element that had sullied the school's good name, and everyone was glad to see her gone.

Nora remembered, too, how quickly she made herself forget about Dawn. Before the school's immense front door closed all the way on her back, Nora had already forced the girl and the threat she represented into oblivion. How relieved she felt right then, how unencumbered. It was almost as free as she had felt when she realized Immaculate ensured her an escape from Dr. Bourdain.

But that relief over Dawn being gone withered and rotted to

a stench mere hours later, when Nora returned a call from "home" in Montreal and Mrs. Bourdain dropped a cruel and deliberate comment about the history of happenings in her husband's study.

She knew. She knew for years.

She knew and still chose spite and viciousness over protecting Nora from her husband's savagery.

She knew, and sitting there in the stuffy, old wood phone booth, Nora then knew that Elise Bourdain was sicker than her husband could ever be.

All of this Nora had pushed to the back of her consciousness, so far away that she almost convinced herself that it didn't happen. Dawn was a figment and Mrs. Bourdain, the witch in a very bad dream. She bolted from the school that same night with two suitcases, a backpack, and The Box, and headed for the bus station—thanks to a begged ride from Wyatt, the secondary line cook who was plainly sweet on her. And just before she hopped into the front seat of Wyatt's dented Toyota and slammed the door, Nora spoke a promise to herself out loud: "This will not be my story." She said it twice and set it in stone, vowing never to look back.

And now she was sitting here ten years later, with the wall holding her up, waiting to break that firm bond and confront her ugly, forgotten past.

Dawn arrived at 9:30 AM sharp. They immediately made eye contact and Dawn started over to the table, walking as if time was not yet a thing. Nora's heart began beating a little faster as she got closer.

"Slow, easy," Nora said to herself, hardly parting her lips enough for the words to crawl out. She took a quick in-and-out breath—keeping her movements relaxed—and watched Dawn approaching. She was wearing a sundress that closely resembled the one Nora wore to the Beaumonts' annual Kentucky

Derby brunch. Candid shots of her and Fisher standing on a vast lawn appeared in the Sunday Style section the next week. The closer Dawn got, the more Nora could pick up the details of the dress; it was nearly identical to her own at home, but she made sure none of this registered on her face.

"Well, good morning, sunshine," Dawn said to Nora, and pulled out her chair with added drama. The café server strode by as Dawn sat down.

"Good morning. My name is Gillian. And I have your order right here." She lowered the small, round tray to the table. "Your super-nice friend already ordered for you," the server said, and placed the bowl-sized, foamy mug in front of Dawn. "Here's your Blondie—our most popular latte. I made it myself, actually."

"Oh, lucky me," Dawn said, flatly, staring over at Nora.

"If it's not your cup of tea, so to speak, just let me know and we'll be happy to make you a new order with something you'll like."

"No, no. I'm sure I'll love it. My super-nice friend here has super-good taste." Dawn smiled up at the server.

Gillian smiled back. "Awesome. And here"—she dipped the tray slightly toward Nora—"is your—"

"Thank you, Gillian," Nora said, cutting her short and scooping up her black and red paper cup. "That's all for now. Thanks so much."

Nora gripped her cup and watched Dawn watching Gillian walk away.

"She kind of reminds me of your partner from boarding school, Addison? The red hair, the dope cat-eye glasses—even back then she had that whole cool nerd-girl thing on lock," Dawn said. She cupped her hands around the giant mug and started gently blowing through the curled steam. "Addison O'Brien, right? She was one of your better friends. What's she up to these days—oh, dear," she said, with exaggerated surprise, "how would you know, right? Actually, I think I saw her on Facebook when I was looking for you. She has a different last name, too. But her change was legit. Married. He's a doctor, if I remember correctly. No kids yet, though, but"—Dawn crossed her middle and index fingers near her face and affected a creaky voice—"*fingers crossed for a hashtag blessed baby bump next yearrrr.*"

Nora felt her nostrils beginning to flare, but managed to tame things down with a sip from her to-go cup. "That's good. Glad to hear that she's well," she said, adding a sincere smile. Nora really was happy to hear that Addison was good. She was one of the first people to befriend Nora shortly after she arrived at the school. They had been walking into the same math class, and Addison was a bubble of red hair and white teeth. She wore vintage cat-eye frames and, that day, a dab of glitter blush high on her left cheekbone. She'd asked Nora where she was from, whom she roomed with, and where she was planning to sit for lunch, all in a single breath as they'd settled into their desks.

That afternoon in the cafeteria Addison had introduced Nora to *her* best friend, Emily Beck, who wasn't quite as welcoming. She'd barely given Nora a side glance near the end of her spirited conversation with Addison about their "perv-o religion teacher Mr. Sullivan." Nora could never remember much of what was said that day or whether Emily even spoke to her beyond a crisp "hey," but without effort, she could still bring to mind how she felt in their company—untroubled. The anxiousness about being thrust into another alien environment with a new name, new narrative, and new essence fell away listening to the two girls gripe and gossip. In that moment Nora started to see clearly this new world for what it was (a clean slate) instead of what it wasn't (home).

"Speaking of Facebook, that was pretty sharp of you," Dawn said, dipping her nose into her coffee mug. After each deep sip from her hot brew she would let out a low, contented sigh. "Sending out those flares on FB for me to find, that was a good move. But then I always knew you were brighter than most," she said, and dragged her eyes from the top of Nora's high blond bun down to the slightly chipped blush polish on her hand resting on the table. "I could also mean literally bright, too, huh, Barbie?"

And there it was: that smirk.

Nora squeezed her left fist balled up tight in her lap. It helped her jaw to stay loose and eyebrows unknotted. *Slow, easy,* she reminded herself, and kept her gaze on Dawn light, not focused, not staring. Everything, from her breathing to her blinking, needed to stay slow and easy.

"Thanks for meeting me," Nora said.

"Oh, I didn't have a choice. Curiosity was about to ruin me! Now that you've got all your shit locked up and encrypted—good job, by the way. Looks like you got some high-level assistance for that alley-oop—the ball's back in your court"—she raised the cup and took a sip—"for now. Plus, I feel like it's more fun this way, don't you?"

"Dawn, I asked you to meet me here because I want to formally apologize to you. What I did to you in high school was cruel and horrible and, actually, pretty unforgivable. But I'm hoping that you can find it somewhere in you to forgive my bad, selfish choices and let me at least start to make amends, set things right between us." Nora paused to sip her hot water and assess Dawn's reaction so far. Was she listening and intrigued, or simply indignant, just waiting to snap back? Nora had rehearsed for both scenarios.

"You looking for a truce?" Dawn said. She raised a brow at Nora.

"I wouldn't say that. I mean, let's face it, this isn't exactly a war, Dawn." Nora gave her a small, knowing grin, but got nothing in return. "I'm looking to clean up my mess. Call it restitution." She placed both hands on the table. A move to ensure she didn't clutch her bag that contained two fat envelopes with three hundred and fifty thousand dollars split evenly between them.

"*Restitution?* Oh, what, we're in court now?" Dawn chuckled and shook her head. "Are you trying to compensate me for damages?"

Nora kept her eyes steady on her.

Dawn rested her mug down and pushed back from the table. "Is that what this is? You're trying to buy me, buy your way out of the shit pile?"

"Look, I'm not trying to buy you. Like I said, I want to take responsibility and clean up—"

"Your mess. Right. I heard that part. I heard everything you said. And it all boils down to you doing whatever it takes to skate on out of this whole tangled-up fuckery clean and free, and just golden."

Nora moved both hands to her lap and clenched her fists. She had prepared for this reaction, she told herself, and needed to breathe through and stick with it. "Dawn, listen to me," she started, her face serious, "I'm not throwing money at you. I would never insult you like that. Money isn't the fix here. I came to apologize, ask your forgiveness, and to see if there's any way I can right my wrongs with you. And as a big first step, I'm hoping that you'll let me start fresh with you as friends. Real friends."

"How can you say *real* when everything about you is fake?" Dawn squinted and all the creases on her face bunched together.

Nora bowed her head. She knew her lines, but let the silence play its own role. She closed her eyes and folded her lips tight like a dam holding back a deluge. *Just do it,* she said to herself.

And then, after one last deep sigh, she did.

"I'm sorry. I can't . . ." Nora kept her head down and made sure to amplify the quickening of her breath, the increasing rise and fall of her chest. "This is really hard. I'm sorry."

"The truth isn't hard," Dawn hissed. "It's just the truth; it's easy."

"I know . . . that's not what I mean." Nora raised her head a little and glanced across the table. She knew her eyes were red and rimmed with tears; she could feel it. "I don't want to remember the truth."

"What are you even talking about?"

"I've never really told anyone . . . I can't," Nora said, making her voice small and weak.

Dawn snapped, "Is this a game to you? One email, one anonymous call, and you're done. Do you get that?"

"Yes, yes, I get it. Trust me, okay? I know this is not a game." Nora's voice cracked at the exact moment it should. She took a trembling sip from her cup. "Look"—she raised her head all the way—"my past, the truth, it's really fucked up. And I've never told anyone the whole thing."

Dawn raised her mug to her mouth, but paused before slowly tilting it toward her lips. "What whole thing?" she said, and placed the cup back on the table without taking her sip. She looked intrigued.

Nora squirmed in her chair. "It's just that I've never—" She stopped and looked over her shoulder, returning to their conversation with her voice slightly above a whisper. "I've never talked about this out loud before."

"Well, now you have to speak on it. *Jesus.* The buildup," Dawn said, shaking her head. "Just out with it."

"It's my father . . . he . . . he, um . . ." Nora tented over the bridge of her nose with both hands and sniffled. "He . . ." She swallowed hard, opened and closed her mouth a few times over, trying to form the words. "He raped me." The pooled tears snaked down her face. "He molested me for years, from when I turned nine until I got sent away to Immaculate."

"What the fuck?" Dawn's mouth hung open. She put her elbows on the table, leaning in farther with her face scrunched up as if she were straining to hear the faintest note. "Are you for real?"

"Yes!" Nora barked. "Why would I lie about this shit? He was sick and vile. I was a *child*. And he broke me. I could never figure out how to piece myself back together, patch myself up. It was easier to make like it never happened. I didn't want it to be real. So I erased it, all of it, and just pretended that it didn't happen. I had to become someone else. I couldn't continue moving through a world where a man would do that to a child, and his wife would do nothing to stop it." She turned her mouth down in utter disgust. This was one part of the whole planned performance that Nora didn't have to force. It was the truth, raw and palpable.

"Wait, your mom *knew about it?*" Dawn squawked. Nora shot her a look and she caught herself, doing a quick sweep of the tables nearest to them. She started again with her voice lowered. "What kind of mother . . . She knew and let it go on?" Dawn looked as if she wanted to smash the mug to the floor, but kept her heated stare on Nora like she was waiting for something.

Confirmation. Nora realized she hadn't really answered Dawn's question about her mother knowing. All she would have to do is nod, Nora thought, and they could move on to the next act. But Nora couldn't bring herself to say that, *Yes, my mother knew that I was being molested.*

A vision of Nora's mother, her serene face, appeared just beyond Dawn's shoulder. It was unexpected and jarring and sent a shudder through Nora's entire body. Her real mother didn't know about the abuse. Nora was sure of it. Mona Gittens would never let that sickness stand. And the Bourdains would have certainly met their end by poison cooked into their food before they could harm her girl-child *one more day.* "Let me just go and sit down in the people's jail," Nora could hear her mother saying.

"My mom," Dawn said, "she would never allow some man to mess with me like that. Never. She'd butcher that rank *muhfuckuh* in his sleep. No doubt." Dawn pushed out her chin. "What did your moms do?"

Nora nodded, the image of her mother still hovering. "She sent me away. To Immaculate." Keeping it basic—using hazy terms like, *she, that woman, his wife*—made it easier for her to push away her mother's haunting likeness and continue the story. "And I went along with that wish, her wish for me to be gone. It meant getting away from him. So I went. I never wanted to look back. I didn't want to be that broken, dirty person anymore. I didn't want to carry it around with me; I was ashamed."

Dawn stared at Nora, right into her eyes for a long few seconds. "That's how this started?" she said. Her tone had mellowed, but there was still a thin layer of suspicion pressing through the surface.

Nora gave her a stiff nod.

"But why a white girl? Why not escape all that sick bullshit at home and just be you when you tried to start fresh?"

"Dawn, when I got there, there was no one there like me"—

she gestured at Dawn—"or you. All those girls, they were happy and red cheeks and mascara. They were unbroken. I wanted to be one of them, not this . . . mixed up, other thing. And because I look how I look, people at Immaculate made assumptions about me and I didn't have the nerve to correct them."

Dawn sat back in her seat, cocked her head to the side, and held Nora's gaze. The silence squatted on the table between them for a full minute.

Finally, Dawn pulled herself up and scooted to the edge of her seat. "So this whole thing . . . this"—she fanned her hand around Nora—"all of this is based on, what—some omission?"

"It's not that simple," Nora said.

"It never is."

"Look." Nora moved to the edge of her chair, too. "My wedding is almost a week away, Dawn. One week. And I *really* want to marry this man. He's good and sweet, and he loves me in a way that I didn't even know existed. I can't lose that. I don't want to be broken again."

"The truth's not gonna break you. You've heard it before: The truth will set you free. If he's all that, then tell him the truth. Doesn't he deserve that?"

"It's too late. That's the truth. I'm in too deep. I wouldn't even know where to start."

"So, you're just okay living like this. Just pass—"

"I know it sounds crazy, that I'm living this life," Nora interrupted. She didn't want the word to even be uttered. "But it is my life, and I can't pick it apart. I don't want to destroy it."

"Why don't you say what you really want to say?" Dawn peeled off a new smirk. "You don't want *me* to destroy your life."

"No, I don't."

"Yet here we are."

"Dawn, I meant what I said: I want to start on a clean slate with you, as friends. And I'm asking you, pleading with you as a friend to let this go. Let it go. They, him, his wife—they don't matter anymore."

"What, 'cause you've forgiven them?"

"No, just forgot them. They don't have a hold on me. Not now." Nora looked deep into Dawn's face. Her skin was smooth, and her eyes were strong and piercing. She exhaled and pushed the line out of her mouth with it. "They died."

Dawn unfolded her arms and relaxed her rigid posture. "Both of them?" The honest expression that colored her face— shock or condolence or comfort or all of it mixed together— stirred a twinge of remorse in Nora's gut behind the lie.

Nora nodded.

"Cancer?"

"For her. Him, heart attack. The famous heart surgeon felled by a heart attack," Nora said, a slight shrug to her shoulder. "Guess that's irony."

"Fuck irony. Justice is what was needed. He should've been shoved into a prison box and just rot there."

"My point is, this . . . my way of living, it's not hurting anyone." Nora pulled herself up straight, aligned with the wall behind her. "I'm happy. That's all I've ever wanted."

"Okay," Dawn said, firmly.

Nora's eyes lit up through the remaining tears. "Okay?"

"Yeah. Okay, as in I heard you. You asked me to come meet you to hear you out and I did. I heard you."

The flash of brightness in Nora's face fell away. "You heard me. So, what does that mean?"

"It means my coffee is cold and this little meet-up is over." Dawn's tenor reverted to sour. "And *that* means I'm gonna go." She pushed back her chair with a strident scrape to the floor.

In an instant, before she could even gauge whether it was a smart move or not, Nora reached out and grabbed Dawn's tense arm. "Wait! Please. Just wait a minute." She took a breath and let go of the arm, but her hand remained floating over it. She was teetering on the edge of her seat, holding the corner of the table for balance. "You have to tell me if you're going to say any—I mean, do we have an understanding?"

"I'll think about it. That's as understanding as I'll ever be."

Nora's head sank to her chest and she tried to put a cork on the scream coursing through her body, rising up her throat.

"Don't worry. We have time," Dawn said, and stood up, dusting invisible crumbs from her pretty dress. "I'll know by wedding day."

Nora's head shot up. "Wait, what do you mean?"

"J. F. Christ. You always want to know what people mean when it's right there in front of you." Dawn rolled her eyes. "At the tea party. Before ol' girl got carted off on the gurney, your mother-in-law-to-be, she was looking for you. I should've told her that you did what you do, run away the minute shit gets real." Dawn lifted her chair and pushed it into the table's edge. "Instead, I did you a solid and told her that you just got a call from your wedding planner"—she grinned—"about the seating chart. Anyway, we got to talkin' about your big day, and she asked if she was going to see me there. *Since she so enjoyed talking with me,*" Dawn said, clenching her teeth and turning her nose up in an overdone spoof. "I didn't have an answer. To be real with you, I wasn't sure this wedding was gonna actually happen, because, well, you know. But then, Lady Beaumont says, '*Of course* you're going to be there.' So I said the only thing I could: '*Of course!*'" Dawn's laugh sounded like it had teeth, crunching the air like ice cubes. "Life comes at you fast, right?"

"Dawn . . ." Nora moved to stand.

"I told you I'd think about it," Dawn said, and her chuckle vanished. She pointed a finger at Nora. "You better not push it." She turned on her low heels and left.

Nora dropped back in her seat and watched as her promise of a new world glided out the door.

# CHAPTER 16

"Hon, the only way you're going to truly relax is by giving yourself permission to do so," Jenna said, and stuffed her phone into the generous pocket of the luxury robe perfectly embroidered with the spa's gold logo by the left lapel. "I mean, put *your* oxygen mask on first." She sat down next to Nora on the soft bench and rested her hand at the top of her friend's exposed back. "It's what the universe would do . . ." Jenna's face crumpled into laughter. "Oh, my God. Can you imagine?" Her holler echoed through the quiet changing room. "Did I totally sound like Richelle Simon just now, with her full line of five-digit, woo-woo bullshit?"

Nora smiled and tightened the thick towel wrapped around her chest. "A little bit."

"I wish publishers could work under a pseudonym for some titles. I'm so embarrassed by that Simon book. The whole billionaire housewife gives tips on living your best life—please, such garbage. Just stay home and shoot those perfect babies out your Texas Tunnel, Richelle!" Jenna pursed her lips and swept her thick brown hair to one side, letting it cascade down her shoulder like a waterfall. "But seriously, enough about Richelle Simon; back to you. This whole day is about you releasing all that wedding stress, just leave it and let it melt away into these fucking outstanding Kashwére robes." Jenna slipped hers off and draped it over the door of an open locker.

Being naked in front of other people didn't bother Jenna. She had told Nora on the first of their many regular visits to Mandarin Oriental Spa that nude felt more comfortable than wearing clothes to her, especially after the near decade of work and therapy she had put into feeling comfortable in her own skin. "Nothing more potently toxic to a girl's self-worth than the one-two punch of a Southern mama and an outspoken Gigi," she had said while sprawled out next to Nora in the special, amethyst crystal steam room. "The number of times I've been called fat—in the most colorful ways, too—the word doesn't even sound the same to me anymore."

"I'm okay," Nora said, and shook her head. She could hear how limp and unconvincing she sounded. "I'm getting close to it, anyway."

Jenna smiled and passed her classic *oh, sweetie* condolences look onto Nora. "Well, you know what you need?" She stood and moved her robe to hang inside the locker, pulled out a towel, and wrapped it around her waist. "Remember that ancient episode of *Sex and the City* where Samantha hits the spa and finds out there's a masseur who goes down on some of his women clients? Kevin. I will never forget that dude's name." She bunched her hair up into a floppy mess of a bun. "Ol' Kev provided plenty of source material for *Up in My Room Diddlin' with Teen Jenna.*"

Nora groaned. "Gross, Callaway."

"Gross? It's nature, Nora. It's nature and beautiful and totally what you need right now. We all need a Kevin. The Mandarin needs a Kevin. Unless"—Jenna's face went straight—"there *is* a Kevin here, but we don't qualify for the secret menu. How dare you, Kevin!"

"You need serious help," Nora said, laughing, fully and finally.

"I'm serious, a little head would set you straight. But not from Fish. Like, you need non-husband-related stranger face. It will hotwire your brain and clear out all that shit clouding things up. Set you on to some next-level calm and common sense. Trust me. Why do you think I'm so fucking sharp all the time?"

Nora frowned at her friend. "Please tell me you're not collecting cunnilingus from randoms you meet on that dating app—what's it called again, Winnerz?"

"Spinnerz. And no, that's a whole different audience," she smirked. And for a flash Nora was reminded of Dawn, her face and that leer.

Since their meet-up yesterday, Nora couldn't shake her. Everything reminded her of Dawn. Even as she dozed off in the wee hours, Nora would jolt awake sweating, her jaw and body sore from being clenched so tight, and Dawn—her voice, her smirk, her scowl, her chronic animus—would be there, so real it left Nora trembling and covered in goose flesh.

She had done all that she could, rehearsed her scenes and played them to the letter. And still, Dawn was going to burn her life down.

Or she wasn't.

Nora kept thinking that she saw something in Dawn's eyes, a sliver of something as she turned to leave the café yesterday that looked like compassion. Perhaps it was pity, but it didn't matter, because it was there and it was a seed. From her time spent at the Conservatory Garden, Nora knew what good could come from a seed.

Fisher managed to sleep through her fits in the bed, and when he did wake up, Nora feigned sleep. She felt him brush the hair by her temple with the backs of his fingers, but remained still as stone, silently begging him to leave. Getting out of the bed felt like too much to ask, and pretending to be animated, excited to be awake and breathing seemed unimaginable. She almost muted Jenna's early-morning call; she was not yet ready to be nice to anyone.

"Get ready to put the *ah* in spa, woman. I have us booked for the complete works—Quintessence Body Scrub, Bio-Radiance Facial, Therapeutic Massage, Aroma Stone mani-pedis, *and* a bento box lunch, bitch. I've forgotten nothing. I've even slotted in some time for me to do a bit of the sunless tan—not advisable for brides-to-be. Plus you're the perfect blush of pale for that gorgeous gown of yours. However, I did leave room for you to roll over to Nadia's for a wax. It's next door, she's the best—I told you she does all the porn gals, right? Anyway, I'll get some color on this skin while you get your li'l Susan stripped bare and we can meet up at Blue Meadow for a real lunch right afterward."

"Jenna, I . . . I can't do all that. It's nice and it's sweet of you, but I can't. I just need some rest today."

"Can't."

"Can't what?"

"You can't say no to this, hon. It's coming straight from Fisher. He told me you've been maximum stressed these last couple weeks. And I was, like, and water is wet, bro. Tell me something I *don't* know."

"Wait, wait . . . he told you this how? Did he email you?" The panic in Nora's voice was piercing, but she didn't have it in her to modulate anything. Mateo's secret infosec contact had shored up her emails and her *newer* new iPhone, but Nora was still nervous that Dawn could play Peeping Tom into her life through other channels, namely Fisher.

"I don't even think Fisher knows my email address. No, he called me, which was also a little awkward. He sounded so unsure, as if he dialed the wrong number but just rolled with it to save face. But when he started talking about you and how you're not sleeping or even eating, well, hon, I dropped every-thing. I knew exactly what to do, and so, spa day with your MOH or HBIC, as I prefer to be called for the rest of this week."

"Only this week?" Nora said, a half of a grin edging up.

"You know me too well. So . . . let's get up, slide into our basic white-girl yoga pants, and hit that spa."

"And I can't say no to this, huh?"

"Nope."

Jenna pulled two white towels from the fluffy stack and flung one over her shoulders, barely covering her breasts, and bundled up the second at her waist. "First stop," she said, jab-bing her index finger toward the spa locker room ceiling, "that pool. Swear to God it's comprised of, like, seventy-nine per-cent Taylor Swift's tears. You'll see." Jenna slid her hand into the tight space between Nora's crossed arms and tugged her toward the locker room's exit.

Standing by the spa vitality pool together, Jenna wasted no time and lowered herself into it. "This feels *so* good," she said, her eyes closed and face flushed. "Wouldn't it be awesome to have one of these at home?" She looked over at Nora. "You should totally talk to Fish about that. He'd do it, too, because that is a man in absolute, dumb love with you." She closed her eyes again and dropped her head back, sinking deeper into the calming water. "You know he'd do anything for you, his won-derful, magical creature."

"Don't call me a creature," Nora said under her breath. The tears were moving in.

"What's that?" Jenna's head was still tilted back.

Nora cleared her throat. "Nothing," she said, and splashed water over her face. *It doesn't matter.*

Jenna pulled her chin down and looked at Nora with bright eyes. She was laughing, chuckling. "I literally just put my hand in this pool to reach for my phone in my nonexistent pocket.

I've got phantom vibration syndrome like I'm Sweaty Betty or some tragic millennial. But that's how hooked I am on this goddamn podcast. Have you been listening to *Slay?* It's amazing. The case they're following this season is about this guy, a British spy named Edmund Thackeray and—"

"I know. Oli listens to it," Nora said, tuning back into the moment. "She's obsessed with the show, with the whole story."

"I'm obsessed, too. You kind of have to be obsessed. It's so damn good. They were supposed to upload the new episode yesterday morning, but there was a glitch or whatever and now all of us junkies are strung out waiting on the corner for someone to sling them rocks. Has me so on edge, I can't even tell you. I'm not supposed to be so keyed up; it's Saturday, y'all! All this agita, that's what the weekday is for. And this next episode—it's supposed to come out any minute now today and I'm, like, jonesing. It's right at the crux of this whole fucked-up story. It's all about the poison right now. I mean, radioactive polonium-210? Jesus Christ! Who does that? That shit is crazy."

"It really is. Fisher was talking about it a couple months back. They were doing tests with something just like it at the Institute."

"Oh, my God. Do you force Fish to take *Silkwood* showers when he comes home, because—"

"*Silkwood?*"

Jenna lowered her chin more and gave Nora a frowning, appalled look. "You've never seen *Silkwood?* Starring the goddess Meryl Streep and Goldie's Kurt? And also *Cher,* for all that's good and holy. Plus, those plum awful accents. None of this rings bells for you?"

All Nora could offer was an empty stare and shake of her head.

"*Dagnabbit,*" Jenna squawked, "who raised you?"

Nora cut her eyes at her friend and the hairs at the back of her neck stood tall as she spat the words out. "My mother. My mother raised me."

"Oh, Jesus. Nora, I'm . . . I didn't mean it like," Jenna stuttered. "It's just a thing you say and I didn't mean to say it like that. It came out wrong. That was stupid, and I'm sorry." She pushed through the water, moving over toward Nora, who sat motionless, glaring back at her. "Hon, I'm so sorry." She continued on her pool path to Nora and opened herself up, prepping for a hug as she got closer.

*No.*

Nora threw her arms out, sweeping them in front of her in a block and shaking her head hard. "No!" she said again, this time out loud and with the force of a strike. But Jenna kept coming, making Nora back up with each of her sure steps.

"Hold on." Jenna exposed her palms to Nora and slowed her forward movement. "Honey, I know. I know. Believe me, I know how much you miss her right now. This is the happiest time in your entire life and your mother, she's not here, and it fucking sucks. Cancer fucking sucks. It hurts. I know." She inched over to Nora. "Your mom, she's not here, but you can't push away your support that is, you know? All of us—Fisher, the Beaumonts, Oli, me—we are standing with you, because we love you. We can't help ourselves." She smiled. It was weak and thin, but Nora saw it. "We love you; we're here, behind you. And if we have to carry you down the aisle on our shoulders to make sure you are standing next to Fisher telling the world 'I do,' that's what will happen. That's where you belong, Nora. You deserve to be standing there with him. We all believe that. You need to start believing it, too." Jenna reached out and pulled Nora into a tight grasp. "The truth is the truth, hon. Accept it."

Every measure of Nora's being started folding in on itself. She knew that she couldn't keep the spigot locked tight any longer, and so she let go, burying her face in Jenna's naked shoulder and weeping.

"This is what you needed. Let it all fall into this pool, hon," Jenna said, cradling the back of Nora's head in her hand. "And leave it here. Let these ridiculous *oxygen-intensified* waters handle it."

Nora gave her a half nod between sobs.

"And, look, I apologize about the thing I said before . . . I'm sorry. I put my fucking foot in my mouth—*again*. What else is new, right? But don't give another thought to it. This is your time to be happy. Focus on that."

Nora pulled away and leaned back on the pool's smooth wall, wiping her wet face with her wet hands. "I'm . . . I'm such a mess," she said, trying to regulate her staccato breathing. "I'm sorry."

"No, don't be sorry. Nothing for you to be sorry about. Just be happy."

Nora stared off at the cluster of soft bubbles floating in the farthest corner. She shook her head and said simply: "She won't let me."

"Honey, who won't let you?"

Nora wanted to look over at her friend and call out the bogeyman, say her name into the quiet and let it reverberate through the secluded room. But it would do nothing to make her troubles disappear. Dawn would still be there, ready to strike the match, whether Nora spoke her name or not.

She chose not, and instead splashed more water on her face.

"What has you so tortured, Nora?"

The question only brought back the tears, knitting her brows together again. Jenna swooped in and sat close.

"No, no. Forget it," Jenna said, holding her hands up and waving them in front of Nora. "It doesn't matter who or what. Honestly, none of it matters. Whatever it is, let it fall away into this here pool. No more tears, okay? You're at the spa, darlin'.

There's no crying at the spa," she said, tacking a chuckle on at the end. "That's a Kardashian rule, goddammit!"

Nora wiped her stinging eyes. "They *do* set the rules, that group." Her voice was gravelly and she could feel the snot from her nose about to tap the edge of her lip, but she smiled anyway.

"Exactly. The Kardashians just know shit. Praise hands." Jenna started moving quickly toward the steps in the shallow pool. "Gotta motor. My massage starts, like, now. You're going in for the body scrub with Charlotte, who is divine. I think we meet up for the pedicures." She grabbed a fresh towel and draped it over her shoulders. "But first, I need to check to see if the new pod episode is available." She rolled her eyes. "*Slay* is my dealer. I need to get my hit. Facts, y'all. See you later." Jenna took a few steps over to the pool again. "You good?"

"I will be," Nora said, smiling up at her. "Jenna . . . thank you."

"Of course," she said.

"You're a good friend."

A strong blush took over Jenna's face and she pulled the end of the towel from around her neck to cover it. "No! Don't you dare. Don't start that!" she yelled, as if Nora's warmth might melt her. "I've got to keep my head in the game for the poison, murder, and subterfuge." She turned and trotted out of the steamy room, giggling.

Without her friend's shoulder and kindness to buoy up the heft of her real problems, Nora let her body sink to the bottom of the heated pool. She held her breath, opened her eyes, and forced herself to stay submerged and not float back up to the top. She needed to stay under so the special, infused waters could seep into her brain and instill it with something potent, something worthwhile and convenient that she could use to permanently shake this pall from her bright, right life.

Dawn was the stain that won't leave. And Nora's hands were raw from all of the scrubbing.

The throbbing in her head got louder as her lungs began to sting.

*Don't exhale.*

*Stay under.*

This would be easy, Nora thought, and closed her eyes against the pain building in her chest, fighting the urge to exhale and fill her straining lungs with clean air. But then her heart broke through. She didn't want to give in. Not like this.

Nora's eyes shot open. She wanted life—her life with Fisher and Jenna and all the good things lined up for her taking. She pulled herself to the top of the pool, gasping and gagging, and rested there, hanging off the ledge of it, catching a new breath.

This was not the way.

She hurried out of the water, a fresh plan sprouting in her gut. She had barely wrapped the towel around herself properly before she was pushing the swing door open hard. Nora needed to get to her phone this minute. She needed to find a way to contact Dawn one more time. No skits, no lines, no calculations, and definitely no money. Nora was going to try a different route with Dawn, one that was direct and honest.

As she rounded the corner, bounding toward the changing rooms, Nora ran right into a tall brunette dressed all in black and soft-heeled shoes.

"Hi. You must be Nora," the woman said. "I'm Charlotte, your body treatment specialist."

Nora stood still for a moment, taking the woman in, noticing everything about her from the sleepy sound of her voice to the way she held the clipboard lightly trapped in arms loosely crossed over her chest. Her eyes softened and she smiled warmly.

"Looks like you were really enjoying the vitality pool?" She sent a smooth, but obvious glance over to the wall clock. "I'm sure you're ready to move on to the next level of your care here at Mandarin Spa today." Charlotte didn't wait for Nora to respond, and gestured to one of the wet rooms near where they stood. "After you," she said, and pointed more explicitly to the room.

"I'm sorry, but I think I need to cancel all of this," Nora said matter-of-factly.

Charlotte tilted her head and looked as puzzled as a new puppy. "Excuse me? I . . . I don't think we can do that."

Nora shook her head and started again. "Right. Well, at least let me take a quick break. This is an emergency." It was Nora's turn not to wait for a response as she skirted the woman and darted to the adjacent door for the changing rooms.

And it really was an emergency for Nora. She was about to save a life. Hers.

# CHAPTER 17

Contacting Dawn turned out to be the easy part. Nora had to climb back down into the pit of red herrings and hacking to get a coded message out to her, all without letting Mateo on to anything. But it worked and here she was at the Bean House Café again sitting at their special table, waiting for Dawn to show.

The barista Gillian seemed to have just arrived for her shift and gave Nora an enthusiastic wave from far behind the shiny espresso machine. Nora put in her same order with a different server: a Good Morning Blondie in a large mug for Dawn and hot water with lemon in a to-go cup for herself.

"Actually," she said as the young woman tapped on the iPad, "can I change that?"

"Sure, I guess," the woman said. She already looked too through with the day and it wasn't yet ten o'clock. Nora smiled at her anyway. "What do you want to change?"

"Instead of the hot water and lemon, I'll have the mint verbena tea, please. And in a mug instead of a to-go cup, if you can."

"So, you basically want to add a teabag to the cup."

"Well"—Nora gnashed her teeth but kept the smile activated—"I guess that's right." She wanted to tell the girl *where to get off,* as her mother would say, but kept her focus on what mattered: Dawn would soon be there and she was likely bringing with her a second chance for Nora. "Thanks"—she looked at the server's name tag—"Hannah." Nora lingered. "Did I say that right, *Hannah?*"

"Um, yeah, sure."

"Sorry . . . I just like to get people's names right. It's important, what we call things, you know?"

Hannah had bottomed out on caring and pushed out a tight, uncomfortable grin that looked more like a wince. "A mint tea to go and a Blondie in a mug. That's all, right?" Nora didn't bother correcting her on the to-go part of the order and nodded. "Great. That brings your total to seven—"

"Here," Nora said, thrusting the crisp bill at her. "Keep the change. We'll be over there." She turned sharply and started over to the table. A limp "thanks" floated out and hit Nora's back when she was halfway there. She didn't bother to respond and sat, relaxed, looking at the door. Her mind was clear and her nerves were beginning to steady out. For this meeting, Nora decided to forgo a plan or scheme. She was simply going to speak from the heart and hope, against everything, that Dawn would choose to hear her.

But the minute Dawn blew through the door, Nora sensed that something was off. There was no carbon copy outfit, no smirk, no easiness about her at all this time. She wore black slim jeans and two dark tanks loose and layered on top of each other. Her arms were very toned; Nora could see each muscle carved out. And her normally twisted, curly hair was pulled up into a tight topknot. Dawn marched over, her glare burning a hole in Nora's forehead. When she reached the table, she stood behind her pushed-in chair—flinty, stiff, and peering down at Nora.

Trying to read Dawn was like flipping through a blank notebook.

Nora took her in, standing there taut and sinewy like a

dancer waiting for the orchestra to begin playing. And for the first time, she noticed the tattoos. One ran the length of Dawn's forearm. It was severe and striking and not at all simple: a tall jet-black tree with bare, rawboned branches that reached out to tickle her wrist and at its base, thick, tangled roots that appeared to vanish into the bend of her arm. The other tattoo sat on the left side of her chest just above her heart. It was a word, one word and period after it—**restore.**—all lowercase, but large enough to be imposing and inked in the blackest black.

Nora figured she should start; say something to at least bump the nose of her boat against the giant iceberg wedged between them. "Hey. Thanks for coming to meet me," she said, and gestured with a quick hand toward the chair in front of Dawn. No response, not even a blink. "I ordered you a latte, if that's okay."

Dawn narrowed her eyes at her.

Hannah came by balancing a tray with their order on her hand. "Hey. Here's your stuff," she said, sounding out of breath and hurried. She looked at Nora, then Dawn, and back to Nora. "Who's getting the Blondie?"

After too long of a pause, Nora began to stutter out a reply, but Hannah had already made the decision and placed the mug by Dawn, who was still standing, and placed Nora's tea near her side of the table and left without another word.

The silence brewed further until Nora sliced into it. "Okay, I give," Nora said, forcing a mellow chuckle. "Why are you just standing there? What's wrong?"

Dawn sighed and arched her back, then peeled off her small cross-body bag and took a seat. She leaned over the mug on the table and started blowing the steam off of her coffee, looking around the café as if she were seated alone and content enough to people-watch.

Nora rolled her eyes. "Do I have to guess or something? Why don't you just say what happened?"

Dawn's eyes shifted back to Nora like freshly calibrated lasers. "What happened is, you lied. Again," she said, firmly. "Like I should expect anything different."

"I didn't lie . . . what are you—I didn't lie to you."

"Do you think I'm an idiot?"

"Dawn, no, I—"

"Stop," she said, raising her palm. "The answer is, *yes,* you do think I'm an idiot. You think you have me figured out. And that will always be your problem." Dawn's voice was as sharp and stinging as her stare.

"I don't think any of that. Just . . . calm down."

"What?" Dawn pushed back in her chair so hard it jutted out of place, scraping the floor. "Don't tell me to calm down. See? You've been playing this part for so long, you even sound like them. 'Bout *calm down.* The fuck outta here with that."

"All right, all right. I didn't mean it like that," Nora said, minding her tone and volume. Her heart was already beating faster. "Look, Dawn, I'm trying to understand what you're talking about. That's all. You're throwing out all this shit at me about lying and thinking you're stupid or whatever, and that's not what's going on. Like, at all."

"This one, this is all me." She thumped at her chest with her two fingers—*dud dud.* "I should've known. You, you're just doing what you do: lie. But I sat here, listening to your story, and I felt for you. I really did. That kind of shit, no one de-serves that. But there was something in what you were saying that didn't curl all the way over. And I couldn't pretend like it didn't have no stench. It was like, Bitch, why are you lying—still? And about *this?* Yo, that is so fucked up."

"Dawn, I told you the truth. I've never told anyone every-thing that happened, but I told you. I told you what hap-pened."

"For fuck's sake, enough already, Nora. Just stop. I checked on it. I looked into your people, all right? The Bourdains."

Nora held her breath and kept her face even—no twitch of the brow or lip—and held Dawn's angry glare.

"I know that old dude died a few weeks ago. Heart surgeon falls over from a heart attack—yeah, I know all about it. And his wife, Elise. I know about her, too. Blond. Thin. Glamour and style down to her toenails. Kind of like you, how you modeled yourself. She's what you're supposed to be, right? Just like her, your *adoptive* mother." The smirk returned. "You left that part out, of course."

"No, it's not like that. Just, wait, let me explain," Nora said, her voice cracking and pleading.

"Explain what, exactly? How this white woman, your so-called mom who died of cancer, is actually all the way alive and kicking in Canada? Montreal, specifically. You go'n speak on *that* magic? Cuz I'm all ears." Her eyebrows collided in the middle of her forehead and she dipped her face into the mug for a long sip.

"Everything I told you about them is true. My mother"— Nora closed her eyes as she said it—"she worked for them. She was their maid. And she . . . died, when I was thirteen, from cancer. They adopted me after she passed away. That's the full truth. And that's why I asked you to meet me. I wanted to let you know everything, for once and for all."

"Oh, is *that* why?" Dawn snickered. "Look at you. Trying your hardest not to break. Keep your face quiet and blank. But that's it. That's what sells you out. That's when I know you're lying."

"You have to stop this," Nora snapped. "I said I'm not lying." Her chest heaved and she could feel the heat rolling through her body, taking over. She gripped the cup of tea, consumed by the urge to dash the piping hot full of it in Dawn's smug face.

"At this point, your words, they don't mean shit. Not an ounce of shit. And to keep it really real? I don't even want to hear my own voice on this anymore either. Tired of talking. It's action now." Dawn waved her hand at Hannah standing behind the counter.

Hannah was tableside before Nora drew her next breath. "Did you need something else," she said, flat like a statement instead of a question.

"Yeah, I need this to go. Could you make the switch?" Dawn pointed at Nora's hand wrapped tight around her black cup. "I want one just like that. All black."

"Sure." Hannah scooped up the mug and hustled back behind the counter.

"Now, that is one person who seems absolutely bored by life," Dawn said, her eyes following the server along her path. "You know what? You should invite her to the wedding, because let me tell you—*fireworks*. Especially when I show up with my plus-one." She leaned into the table, whispering loudly. "Should I give you a couple hints, or just spoiler-out that shit altogether?" Dawn bent her arm like an injured wing. "*Aahh*. Fine. You've twisted it out of me, Nora. I give, I give! And I think life already has too many surprises, don't you? We'll go with the hints. She's tall, blond, white, and *not* a zombie, plus"—Hannah swooped in and dropped off the cup, and Dawn held her chin up and mouth ajar watching the young girl walk away as if waiting for her to be out of earshot—"*plus* she's glamour and style right down to her toenails."

The strength of the punch landed square in Nora's gut. "What?"

"*Mm-hmm,*" Dawn hummed, and sipped from her to-go cup.

"Why . . . why would you do that?" Nora felt the tremble in her chin. She could smell the fury on Dawn's breath.

"Why do you keep asking questions that you already know the answer to? I don't have time to play these slow games with you. I've got to get myself ready for the big day. And you should be pleased. Now you'll have some family—someone from home—sitting on your side of the aisle." Dawn hopped up from her seat, clutching her cup. She slung her bag over herself with her free hand and smiled down at Nora. "See you in a week, buddy."

Dawn could have sprouted wings and flown away for all Nora knew, because she was in a tunnel or dropped into a well, wrapped in complete darkness. Everything felt uneven and turned around, her bearings thrown off to the side. She had listened to what Dawn said, but couldn't bring herself to really hear it. All sound melded together into a muffled groan right then.

She had pushed Dawn, her dedicated enemy, over a cliff and it was clearer now like never before that she had every intention of dragging Nora down to the rocky bottom with her. The only choice left for Nora was whether to keep her eyes open or shut as they plummeted.

Hannah buzzed back around the table asking something or another. Nora couldn't hear; it was all a murmur. She stared up at the young girl, studying her face, noting the swath of enlarged pores and faded pockmarks along her cheek, tracing each line, bump, and speck from her brow bone to her chin. Hannah started to look harder, more menacing and apathetic to Nora as each quarter of a second slipped by. Hannah's moving lips soon curled and she waved her hand around. She was holding something and fanned that, too.

The room's sound began to crystalize and Nora's thoughts floated back down to earth. She noticed that Hannah was now stooping by the side of the table and mopping up a small puddle.

It was her tea. She had dropped the cup to the floor. Although, clearly, it must have happened a half moment ago, Nora had no memory of the cup slipping from her hand. "I . . . I'm so sorry," Nora started. "It slipped and . . ." Hannah was not interested. She didn't even bother to acknowledge Nora's bumbling in any way.

Looking around the café, the few sets of weary eyes bobbing between her and Hannah's cleanup, Nora slipped back into her former self and did the only thing she could: grabbed her things, hopped over the bent server, and scrambled out the door.

# CHAPTER 18

The bile seemed never-ending. Nora had been hunched over the toilet since the night moved into the small hours. When Fisher knocked on the door letting her know that he was home, she managed to squeeze out "bad fish" and "food poisoning" from behind the locked bathroom door.

"Aw, Mack. Do you want me to get you something? Ginger tea—your favorite?"

"Un-uh."

She heard him try the door.

"Babe, at least unlock this in case you faint again. I want to know that I can get to you this time, okay?"

"Okay," she said beneath a belch.

"Jesus. You poor thing. I'm going to camp out here."

"No, I'm fine."

"No, you're not. I'm grabbing the quilt and the pillows. End of story."

A tiny smile had started to creep up. She wanted to tell him thank you, to tell him he was the sweetest, to tell him she loved him more now than even yesterday. But all that came out was more vomit and sick.

From the light sliding through the bathroom windows, Nora could tell it was proper morning. She had survived. Her insides were long flushed away, and her lips were so cracked and peeling she winced each time she ran her wooly tongue along them, but she was alive. Nora uncurled her body and crept over to the sink, pulling herself up with the counter. She used the little energy remaining to lift her head and look in the mirror. Her eyes were bloodshot, her face sallow, and parts of her hair were dry and crunchy, while other spots were damp and stringy. More than death, she looked like misery and torture warmed over a grease fire.

She pumped out a wide circle of soap into her hand and lathered it over her face. She needed to scrub off whatever she could from the horrible last twenty-four hours, if only just the thin first layer.

"Mack?" Fisher called out, his voice morning-raspy.

The sound of the water must have stirred Fisher awake, Nora thought. Her mind clicked on fully and she remembered that he had promised to sleep on the floor just outside the bathroom door. She wanted to smile, but it hurt.

"Nora, you okay in there?"

She could smell the worry through the door. "Yeah." She cleared her raw throat and grimaced. "I'll be right out, hon." Nora smoothed her hair back, but it made little difference. She stripped out of her gamy clothes, brushed her teeth, wrapped her hair in a towel and her body in a robe, and stepped lightly toward the door. *He loves you,* she whispered to herself, and opened the door with all her might. She needed to see him and feel him; it was urgent.

Fisher was sitting cross-legged, leaned back and propped

up on a fat, square pillow. He looked tired, worn. Next to him: the first-aid kit from the hallway closet. The picture of him cracked Nora's hollowed-out core into pieces. She started taking three of the six steps to reach him, but couldn't keep it together and crumpled where she stood. She landed in his arms. He kissed the top of her forehead and said nothing more; or he did, but she couldn't hear anything above her own wailing. And they stayed there, Nora draped over him like a sheet, only moving to breathe and sink deeper into each other. She cried until the tears refused to come anymore; then it was just her low whimper lulling her into a dream where, at last, she slept.

---

Nora woke up in a sweat not on the floor with Fisher, but tucked into their king bed alone. She pulled herself to sit up. Her eyes darted around the room. The robe was gone and Fisher's shirt—one of her favorites—was hanging off her shoulders, held together at her middle by a couple of done-up buttons. The room was dim, but light still leaked through a part in the drapes. *Is this a new day? Did the last one really happen?* She reached for her phone. There was a note stuck to the top of it.

> *Mack—*
> *Ginger tea in kitchen. Had to leave.*
> *Prep for last board meeting before it breaks*
> *for summer. Call when you get up.*
> *Sleep more.*
> *FCB*

As sweet and charming as Fisher is, his missives were dearly lacking. Nora never enjoyed receiving notes from him and, in the beginning, would always make fun of them with Jenna.

They were typically cold and stiff, not unlike the average business memo. He regularly signed off his emails to her with *Regards*. And she would regularly roll her eyes reading it. But this time, this note, she cupped it in her hand like a rare bird and stared at it, rereading the three lines over and again.

This time, this note, took her back to the ones her mother often left for her on top of whatever book Nora had fallen asleep reading. They were mostly instructive—*Daughter, do this, make sure that, mind you don't whatever, and I'll be back soon, Your mother*—but Nora treasured the notes all the same. They were almost like small, thin pieces of her mother captured and recorded on paper for posterity. Nora also loved the woman's penmanship. It was beautiful.

When she first moved to New York to the lonely apartment with windows that looked out at a dingy brick wall, Nora would often pull out The Box from way under the bed and fish around for some of the stacked notes. Once out, she would sniff the backs of the papers and note cards, hoping for the even slightest hint of Mona Gittens. Nora would run her fingers along the lettering, tracing each line and curve of the ink against the still-white paper. It was her version of prayer, her way to sing a hymn to what used to be, when she had a mother who was alive and never failed to love her. But as she moved further into her newest life, the more obvious it became that The Box should stay hidden. It got pushed under beds, then into locked-up chests, and finally to the unseen underbelly of a deep closet, camouflaged by quilts and fabric and other boxes. As it stood, Nora hadn't looked at one of her mother's notes in over four years.

She slipped Fisher's note into the breast pocket of his shirt that she wore and, as if a starting pistol had sounded, Nora grabbed her phone and bounded out of bed, down to the hallway closet near the guest bathroom.

Things were not how she left them. Boxes were shifted, silk scarves were bunched up, and end pieces of suiting fabric hung off shelves.

*First-aid kit,* she remembered. Fisher had rummaged through the closet last night to find it.

She dropped to her knees to check on the state of The Box. It was undisturbed beneath its layers of disguise. She let out a long, stale breath. But Nora knew it was still too close for comfort. One curious poke around and it would be over. Questions she couldn't answer quickly enough would follow, and the shroud would fall away soon after. It would be the destruction that her enemy had guaranteed, but this way the detonator would be in her own hand instead of Ghetto Dawn's.

Nora pulled the box all the way out, and the mix of scarves and swatches landed wherever they wanted. She didn't care about any of that. Keeping things tidy and organized didn't have even a quarter of the urgency that dealing with the contents of this box did. She ripped off the top and looked into it with the same sense of foreboding she would staring down a dark well in the middle of the secluded woods at the pitch-black of night. Nora reached in and dragged out the first handful. There were notes and scraps of papers and cards, plus a few stray puzzle pieces and even fewer pictures. She let the bulk of it drop to the floor and across her lap, and focused on the three photographs left behind: one with Nora grinning, missing her two front teeth, and holding up an enormous cupcake with a thick number-six candle jutting out the middle; another had Nora and her mother, one arm wrapped around each other, standing outside their junky old apartment building. Nora was giving a thumbs-up. And the third photo was the Christmas one with the black thumbprint splotch covering Dr. Bourdain's face.

She had thought about destroying these pictures—and everything else in the box—back when she first moved to the boarding school. Burn it all; that was the plan. Even the scarves that had belonged to her mother, the bright ones she wore over her bald head during those last weeks. Nora was going to put a flame to it and dust the remains into the large garbage bins behind the school by the kitchen's rear doors. But each time, back in those early days at Immaculate, something would distract her, sidetrack her, or make her think twice about scrapping the remaining bits of her mother for good.

But now these weren't sentimental keepsakes. They were evidence.

Nora felt a familiar wave of flutters in her stomach and a flickering in her chest. The thoughts that came next were quick, but clear. She stuffed everything back into the box and got to her feet in a rush. The latex gloves were there next to the first-aid kit's empty space. She slipped a pair of them on, snatched up the box, and bolted to the small pantry off the kitchen where Fisher kept the lighter fluid for his backup grill, and minutes later was out on the terrace setting her former self on fire. Nora didn't want to watch, so she stepped back and let the flames devour each letter and card and strip of her mother and Montreal.

This was a good first step, she told herself, and leaned back on the table waiting for the right moment to cover over the grill and smother everything. It was a good first step and it was also the easiest one in her new—and final—plan that was both intricate and severe.

When it was over—the lukewarm ashes swept into a large trash bag—Nora took off the gloves and the shirt and crammed them into a separate garbage bag and poured some old wine in after them, followed by that empty bottle. Standing on the private terrace in the nude was oddly refreshing. Nora paused to breathe in the smoky air and feel the soft breeze that started to pick up; it tickled her bare nipples.

Her phone rang out. She hustled inside to get it.

"Hey, Nora. Sorry to bother you so early, but we're still doing calls over emails, yes? And sorry to bother you on the weekend," Oli said. "The last weekend before the big—"

"What's up, Oli?" Nora wasn't in for the chitchat. She kept the call on speakerphone and walked with it over to the bathroom.

"Oh, yeah . . . um, so, Jay Schuyler. Small problem: the tailor jacked up his Prada suit, like majorly, and he's doing a TED Talk today."

Nora pulled a towel around her and sat on the side of the tub. A stringy strand of hair fell over her face; it reeked of smoke. "How did Niccolo jack things up? That doesn't even sound possible. He was basically born on Savile Row."

"I know, I know, but"—she exhaled loudly through the phone—"um, this mistake is on us. We didn't go to Niccolo. We were trying to get time on our side with this and skipped the custom clothier treatment. This other guy we went to, he was supposed to be a master tailor, too. Comes highly recommended."

"Who did the recommending?"

Another pause and long sigh.

"Mateo knew this guy and—you know what? It's a totally useless story. Doesn't matter. We fucked up. That's the basic scoop. So sorry."

"What happened to the suit? Can it be saved?" Nora sat up out of the slouch.

"The pant is fine enough—I can fix that, no problem. It's the jacket. Jay's got short arms—"

"Yeah, yeah, and a long torso. Did this other guy try to alter the sleeve?"

"*Alter* is generous," Oli said. "It looks like Jay's wearing a toddler suit jacket. Completely fucked."

"Did he open it up from the shoulder?"

"You already know the answer there," Oli said, exasperated. "Just tell me what to do and I'll fix it."

Nora walked over to the mirror and rested the phone down on the counter. She looked at her reflection, doing a full sweep of everything—the dark circles under her eyes, the straw-like hair, the pallid and homely state of her face. Despite the general unpleasantness of her overall appearance, Nora felt useful right then, she felt needed and essential. There was a purpose for her, and she was proud about it. "Okay. First, did you guys get a chance to pull the Botang and Lo shirts?"

"Yes, of course," Oli said. "We have more than we need."

"Good. Grab the brightest, busiest one you have and the most basic one of the bunch. Put the shirts and Kazzy in a cab and send her to J. Crew Liquor Store and—what is it, Saturday?—tell her to ask for Gavin. Tell her to say that it's me, calling in a personal. Get the Ludlow suit in the cobalt in his size. Make sure she asks Gavin to set it up. He'll take care of everything." Nora raised her chin in the mirror and brought her shoulders back. "And when you present to Jay, show him both shirts, but angle him toward the busy one. Make it seem as though it was all his choice, though—the change of suit, the color of the shirt—all of it. It's got to seem like his idea."

"Right, right. I know. Thank you so much, Nora. Sorry about all of this. For real."

"It's okay. I'll deal with Mateo and his toddler tailor later."

"Jesus, Nora. You don't need to. I'm mad I even had to call you with this. You've done enough already. Just focus on the wedding. There's enough to worry about there, right?" Oli said, with a light giggle.

Nora scooped up the phone, taking it off speaker and lining it up next to her ear. She wanted to be clear, to be heard, to convince Oli—and herself—of the words that were about to leave her lips. "There is nothing to worry about. I've got it all covered, and it's all going to work out perfectly," she said, slow and mellow. "If nothing else pops up, I guess I'll just see you next Saturday."

"For sure. I can't wait! And thanks again. You're amazing, Nor. I can only aspire to be just like you whenever my big day rolls around."

"Honestly, Oli? Just be you. It'll be enough." Her phone beeped. "Hey, listen. Another call coming through."

"Shit. Not Mateo, right?"

"No, no. Don't worry. It's the maid of honor. I gotta go."

"Cool. Talk to you later."

"Actually, let's hope not."

Oli laughed. "Exactly!"

Nora clicked over to the new call. "Hey, Callaway."

"What's happening, hon?

"About to hop into the shower now and—"

"No, I mean in the overall sense: What is happening with you?"

"Jeez. I had a bit of food poisoning last night. Bad fish. That's all."

"Oh, honey, nuh-uh. That can't be all. Fisher called me again, bright and early this morning. That's twice in as many days, for the scorekeepers in the back. He made it sound like you've completely come undone. Just wrecked. And I've gotta say, I kind of see what he's talking about."

"Ah. Nice. Thanks *a lot,* Jenna."

"Come on now. This isn't like you, with the smudged makeup under the eyes and the ratty bird's nest hair—none of it intentional, by the way. You're riding the Mess Express, sweetie, and I'm gonna need you to step off that thing. Plus, the breakdowns. I still don't know how to explain what I walked in on the other day with you covered in coffee stains—"

"Wait, is that what he said? That my hair looks like a ratty bird's nest?"

"All my words, sugar. I'm not blind. Quite the opposite."

"Yeah, just call you Sharp-Eyed Watson."

"Sharp-eyed what now?"

"Nothing. Something my mother used to say." It wasn't often that she would bring up her mother in regular conversation like this, but with all traces of the woman burned to tossed-out ashes, Nora felt more exceptions could be made.

"Ah, okay," Jenna said.

Nora could almost see her friend grinning through the phone. "She never meant it as a compliment."

"Oh."

"Yeah, *oh*. Doesn't feel great, huh? Well, neither does this shit you're telling me right now."

"Aw, Nora. It's all love, honey. I'm worried about you and so is Fisher. Clearly. The man called me—twice—just to make it all better for you. He'll do whatever it takes to keep joy in your heart. You know that's the for-real real. 'Happy wife, happy life' is a legit mantra for that guy. No one is trying to drag you down. We want you back to you, so we can hit this wedding and shoot out the lights!"

Nora nodded at herself in the mirror. The rising heat coloring her face subsided as quick as it came and her shoulders eased back down from her ears. She smiled. "Is that a Texas thing, shooting out lights for a good time?"

"You know it! Now, bright and too fucking early this morning, my phone starts pinging and dinging. I was, like, what fresh hell is this? Turns out there are notifications set on my phone to remind Bride Nearly-Beaumont to write her vows. It's what you need to be doing one week out, it says."

"Ah . . . right." Nora clapped her hand over her forehead. "I think I set those reminders on your phone months ago."

"But fourteen different alarms and chimes, though? Did I really need that level of irritation? I didn't sign up for this shit," Jenna said, taking on a higher register with her laugh. "Watch, this maid of honor's fixin' to turn into Bitch of Honor in a minute."

"As long as the honor part is there, I'm good."

"Did you even start your vows?"

Nora sighed. "I can't put my brain there. Not yet." It was a lie. The vows had already been written years ago, and she knew her friend would think it weird and possibly desperate had she found out that Nora wrote them the night after Fisher proposed. What started as a doodle stretched across the full page of her notebook turned into something bigger and deeper than even she could process. She folded the paper into the smallest square her fingers could manage and it has lived, tucked it in a corner of her lingerie drawer, ever since.

"Ma'am, you have a week."

"I'll get it done. Maybe next time you and Fisher have your little coffee klatch you should ask him if he's written *his* yet."

"Here you go with this again . . . Nora, the man simply wants to make sure you're all right. That's it. He plans on seeing you walk down that aisle in one piece."

"Sans ratty bird's nest, though, right?"

"*Ugh.* You and that fresh mouth—quit it!"

Nora laughed. It was real and hearty and felt good. "Listen, I do need to take a shower. Have a few things to attack on my list."

"Wait. Before you go," Jenna said, her words sounding measured, her chuckling fading fast. "Seriously, hon. You okay?"

"I will be," Nora said. And for the first time in weeks, she believed this was true. "It's been a little rough, but I'm turning the corner on all of it."

"So I can stop worrying about you?"

"Yeah," Nora said. "You can stop worrying. You know, last night or this morning, really, after we fell asleep on the floor, I woke up in our bed alone. And I don't know, there was something changed when I woke up, something wholly different the minute my eyes flicked open. It was totally okay that Fisher wasn't there; I wasn't scared or confused. I felt . . . good, like the sleep was this hard reset for me. Still feel it now. It makes me know that I'm going to be fine—for real this time."

"Good, because—well, I don't want to be the fluffer on set here—but you're my best girl, Nora. You're one of the real ones, and you know I only root for the real ones."

In the bathroom mirror, Nora could see her emotions pooling at the edge of her eyes. But she couldn't afford tears. Not now. What she needed was conviction, a steel rod run down the center of her back to help her carry out the next step. Dawn had poured hot lava over her life for more than two weeks, and Nora was done, she was tired of feeling desperate and ruined. All she needed to do was hold steady, hold her nerve, and see this thing through. Patient, determined, sure: that's where her focus needed to be. Somewhere between collapsing into sleep on the floor and waking up in their bed feeling rebuilt, Nora had come to her most critical, final decision: Whatever it takes, she was going to disarm Ghetto Dawn—for good.

"I totally sound like the fluffer, don't I?" Jenna said, giggling again.

"Yeah, lady. You're definitely the fluffer in this movie. Also? Gross. Never thought the day would ever come that I would say *fluffer* this much and not be talking about a sandwich." Nora made sure to smile through her words. "Anyway, enough with the marshmallow cream stuff, Callaway. I've got to go take a shower, but . . . I love you, too."

"All right. Same page. Let me know if you need anything—wait, no. My phone and your eight hundred alarms will probably do that for you."

"Bye, Thelma," Nora said, grinning.

"Later, Louise."

# CHAPTER 19

Nora spotted Fisher first. He was sitting on the edge of a square black leather seat in the Institute lobby talking and laughing with the guard. She peered at him from around the corner, watching as he unleashed that laugh with his usual raised-chin-rolled-into-a-mellow-nod. He was wearing light gray suit pants, a slim-cut dark denim shirt with the sleeves rolled, and military-style desert boots, no socks. Nora loved how, even on a Saturday morning, he always looked pulled together. And that he was so dapper—the essence of dashing and good looks—long before she ever came along made his brand of cool all the more that.

She walked out into the open and Fisher shot up from his seat, beaming. Nora smiled back, a true openmouthed kind of grin. Her heart picked up its beat as she walked the long, echoing path to him. She wanted to stop, just for a moment, and wait for this new pounding rhythm to calm down and level off. But she didn't want to delay the feeling of his arms sliding around the low part of her back and his warm, soft mouth connected with her primed lips any more than she had already. She kept marching toward him, her high heels clacking along like the kick drum to the high-hat meter of her pulse. She needed to get there, standing in the middle of his breath, staring up at him, Fisher Beaumont, this man who made her heart leap out of her chest.

He waved a hand at the guard and started his classic long-legged stride to meet Nora. He reached out for her two or three steps before they actually connected and as Fisher brought his face into hers, he said her name—*Mack*. It sounded like melted butter. The kiss was sweet and hungry and Nora felt it through the backs of her knees.

"This is a nice surprise," he said, and squeezed her waist softly. "You look good."

Nora had put a grand effort into every aspect of her appearance for the day. Her hair—washed and shiny and tousled—smelled fresh of vanilla and flowers. The rest of her brought in hints of ylang-ylang and lavender. She wore her Jason Wu floral fields jacquard day dress. She knew how much Fisher liked her in it. The way it hit her high on her upper thigh, "setting those legs free," was the best part, he said. That, and the hidden back zipper; he had the most fun discovering it the first time she wore the puckered dress. Her makeup was detailed and flawless, leaving her face revived and radiant. This glow seemed to emanate from inside, right in the middle of her gut; it started just as Nora stepped out of her long shower. She could feel it, an energy fanning out, down her arms and legs out to her toes and fingertips as she rubbed in her lotion, brushed color over her cheekbones, lined her eyes, and slipped into her clothes. Even as she stood now, basking in Fisher's doting gaze, it was there, smoldering inside.

"I feel good," she said.

"I'm glad you're here." He broke the embrace and took her hand, lacing his fingers in hers as they walked back toward the guard. "I told Rowan I'd clear you through security. You're good for entrance and exit."

Nora waved at the guard from the distance and tried to act

like this wasn't the very linchpin to everything that would happen next. Bypassing security would mean Nora could sidestep the unimaginable indignities she had already sketched out for herself and she'd walk right out of the Institute relatively unscathed. "How is Rowan anyway?" she asked, keeping her elation muffled and her wide eyes trained on her fiancé. Nora smiled and nodded as Fisher spoke, but she heard nothing beyond a few stray words about the guard's nephew or his vacation or his commute from Queens or all of it jumbled together. She was only thinking about her next move and how to maintain an easy, golden smile throughout.

Arm in arm, the two sauntered down the long hall of doors, some open and others locked by keyless card entry. Nora dropped mental crumbs behind every tread. "Am I pulling you away from anything, babe?" she said, as they rounded the bend by the research storage lab. She slowed their walk to a pause just outside its door and turned to face Fisher, cupping her hand around his jaw and smoothing her thumb along the fine edge of it. She looked up at him and slid both arms over his shoulders, a loose wrap of her hands clasped at the back of his neck, and gently pulled him down into her. "I don't want to get in the way," she purred, dropping a hand and slipping it deep into his front pocket. Then she locked in on Fisher's eyes and pressed her body into his, lightly running the tips of her fingers against the firmness beginning to throb in his pants.

"*Mmm,* never," Fisher said, husky and low, and buried his face in Nora's neck.

She used her other hand to guide his up the high hem of her dress, barely lifting it, and parted her legs slightly—enough for Fisher to feel that she wasn't wearing any panties. Nora rocked her hip forward against his leg, back and forth, easy like an old, worn groove. She giggled and moaned and encouraged him to go on kissing her neck all while tilting her head, stealing glances at the lab door behind him. "I think we either need to stop right now," Nora whispered, "or find a cold, slab table in one of these rooms." She drew her face back to look at him, her brow raised.

"You're right. We should stop," Fisher said. He stepped back from Nora, but stayed linked, holding her hand. "You really do look good, Mack. You look like you."

"Thanks, babe. I feel really good," she said, and shoved the card key she had swiped from his pant pocket into a side slot on her purse.

"Agree," he said. The sly bite to his bottom lip faded into a sultry grin.

"Now, now. Don't start," she said, swinging their hand bridge. "Seriously, I don't want to keep you. I know you're prepping for the board meeting Tuesday."

"Actually, it shouldn't take me long to wrap up here. Did you want to stick around, grab some lunch?"

"No, no. Like I said, I was just close by and wanted to stop in and hug you and kiss you and tell you that I *cannot* wait for Saturday." They smiled at each other, giddy like middle schoolers at their first dance. "Plus, I'm on my way to wrap up some other client biz downtown and then it's all wedding everything. Gotta do those vows. *Right?*"

"Don't worry, I've got it covered."

"Don't worry, I believe you."

"Smart move," he said with a nod. "I'm an honest guy. So, you sure you don't want to just hang back and then we can go out or . . . find that cold slab table."

Nora laughed. "Like I've always said, it's a little too clean in here for that kind of smut, sir."

"Fair." He leaned in and rested his still-heated mouth on her forehead. "All right. Thanks for this treat, then. I'll see you tonight?"

"You know it."

"Do you need me to walk you out?"

"Oh, God, no. I'm good." *Stay cool.* "I'll just make my own way. I know where to go," she said with a wink.

He kissed the tips of his fingers and wiggled them at her as he slowly backed away. She returned the tickle-wave. "Okay, you leave first," Nora said. "My turn to watch *you* walk away."

And she did exactly that, staring at his back, silently apologizing over and over for what she was about to do.

Once Fisher cleared the corner at the end of the long hallway, Nora waited another beat to be sure he was gone. Rummaging through her large purse came next. As she rolled the contents of the bag, searching for nothing, Nora took measured steps to the side. She even emptied her cosmetics case into the bottom of the bag to give her more time to casually root around and shuffle over to the left. With each toss of her Chanel lipsticks, her NARS compact, her Tracie Martyn cream, her La Mer mist, and her notebook and her pens and wallet and mints and sunglass case, Nora took a step closer to the lab's locked door. She reached into her bag and pulled out her compact to check her undisturbed hair, as well as the view behind her through the tiny circle's reflection.

She was still alone.

Nora reached into her bag again and took out Fisher's lifted card. His key was one of just ten in the whole organization that was all-access. Over the years she had seen him press the steel gray card up to nearly every door in the Institute. She had even borrowed it a handful of times to move through the building—mainly in and out of his office—while waiting for him to finally go to dinner.

She ruffled her hair, fluffing it out from the roots, and gave the quiet hallway another scan as she flipped her blond length from one side to the next.

All quiet.

She pushed out a hot, short breath that came from her

tummy. *Just do it. Do it.* Nora swished the card over the small black panel with a swift flick of her wrist.

*Bong-bong. Click.*

It was open.

Inside, the door shut behind her with a loud slam. The room was freezing, with dim lights that got brighter the farther Nora stepped into the space. She didn't know how much time she had before someone who actually worked in the lab buzzed by on official business or whether Fisher would soon realize his key card is lost and start scrolling back through the digital security log on his computer to see where he last used it and maybe "misplaced it."

Nora sprang into action, first dragging the hair tie off her wrist and using it to gather her hair back and out of the way. Next, she pulled out a pair of latex gloves from the front pocket of her bag and slipped them on, then reached for the small, sealable medical waste pouch that she had stashed in the hidden compartment of her purse. In it was a pre-sterilized, amber glass vial with glass dropper. Both the container and the vial were pinched from the other first-aid box, the forgotten one at the bottom of Fisher's wardrobe, near his old rugby cleats, half-full of leave-behinds from craving medical supply reps eager to land the Beaumont account.

She had read before, back when Fisher first mentioned polonium, that it can leave a residue on anything with which it comes in contact. She couldn't be sure if the lab's less radioactive substitute would also leave a trail, so she took precautions and packed them in her purse.

Everything in the lab, from the white cabinets to the chrome sink and fixtures, was spotless. Even the epoxy resin countertops had an impeccable shine. Nora didn't know which of the three extra-wide aisles to turn down. She took a half-minute to do a visual sweep of each corner of the room and spotted a row of tall, narrow, stainless-steel refrigerators to the far right; she went there first. The two fridges closest to her opened as one would at home. But the third one in the lineup had a key card panel affixed to the front of it.

"Of course," Nora sneered. "This is probably the one. *Fuck.*" She shook her head, angry at her own carelessness, her stupidity. She had not planned for additional locks.

Nora reached around to the side pocket of her bag for Fisher's keycard. *What if there's a silent alarm? What if there's a different key to get in?* She wanted to drive a heel into the face of this fridge. Instead she pounded her latex-covered fist into her leg. The vein by her temple started throbbing, and the top of her back was damp under her pretty dress. She could hear her breath getting ragged. She looked down the lab's aisle at the door. There was no going back, she knew this, but the urge to run was filling up her lungs. To bolt out of this cold room and keep going until her legs stopped working felt like the only logical thing to do. But she also knew that there was no time or place for logic. Desperation had made sure of that. All she had left was this, and seeing it through was the only way.

She glanced at the key in her hand and back at the door in the distance.

And then, *swipe.*

*Buzz.*

*Clunk.*

It worked. The fridge door popped open. But she couldn't afford even a wafer of relief and kept moving forward. Locating the compound was easy; everything was alphabetical. A change instituted by Rock Beaumont when he took over all R&D operations thirteen months back. Nora overheard most of the conference call about this decision while lying in the bed as Fisher sat on the very edge of it, talking to both of his brothers and the soon-to-be former head of R&D. She and Fisher were supposed to be vacationing, taking in Kalymnos and maybe one or two of the other Greek Islands, but ended up cutting the trip short because of an emergency board meeting that sent them jetting over to Geneva. Fisher tried to tell Nora that the alphabetization of the lab was the most minor of points on the list of topics to be addressed in the meeting, but she didn't buy it. And she would often make jokes with Fisher behind Rock's back about nearly causing a coup over the alphabet. "Today's revolt is brought to you by the letter *R*."

As careful-quick as possible, Nora added twenty drops—then a few more on top—of the lethal mixture to her vial and sealed it up in the pouch before gently sliding it back into the hidden compartment of her roomy handbag. The next steps spun out in a blur. Fridge closed. Gloves off. Door open. Hair down. Hasty steps down the hall.

The main exit was in her view, like the finish line of a grueling marathon. The sweat pooled at the base of her bra. Her knees trembled and she feared her legs would soon start wobbling. Nora was panting, but tried to keep her gait natural, smooth, unremarkable.

And like a gunshot, she heard it ring out behind her: "*Mack?*"

She spun on her heels and almost toppled over. "Oh, hey, hi," she said, sounding breathy and startled. Nora put a hand up against the nearest wall to catch her balance.

Fisher rushed over to her. "You all right there?" he said, still on his way to her.

"Yeah, yeah." Nora gripped her handbag strap. "I just . . . I was . . . my head was in the clouds. You caught me by surprise."

"I caught *you* by surprise? I'm the surprised one. What are you still doing here?"

He was standing right in front of her now. Nora fixed her face and took a breath. "I actually . . . changed my mind, about lunch. I could eat a little something with my fiancé—you won't ever be that again, right?" She smiled, unsure of what she even looked like: sweaty and panicked, or calm and convincing? She moved in to Fisher and hugged him tight. They were in too common of an area to do anything more advanced.

*The keycard. Shit.*

Nora squeezed him harder, extending the hug until a quick thought took shape in her mind. "Let's go back to your office first," she said, letting the quiet words tickle his ear.

Fisher leaned back and looked at her, grinning. "You sure? Thought it was too clean in here."

"Yes, but we're talking about your office now. And I'm pretty sure we already marked our territory in there—a few times."

Fisher, with a slight blush to his face, held out his hand in Nora's path. "Well . . . after you."

# CHAPTER 20

When Oli called first thing Sunday morning, Nora saw her name and answered the phone bracing for bad news. She launched right into a babbling brook-style screed so giddy and giggling that Nora struggled to find an entry point.

"Oli, Oli, hang on. Just pause," Nora said, and rolled out of bed easy. She didn't want to wake Fisher. They had only fallen asleep a few hours earlier, although they had been in bed rolling around together since after dinner. Nora made her way to the guest bathroom and climbed into the tub. "Okay, now first off, are we about to lose a client?"

"No, we're actually okay there." Oli had taken her voice out of the high notes and sounded regular again. "The Liquor Store suit worked out perfectly. Jay was pleased, and he looked smooth and cool and confident, plus his TED Talk was pure flames. The audience wanted to eat him up hot. The whole room was stuck halfway between mesmerized and clamoring to give him a blow job after his whole bit about love and choice. He had them cheering. Swear it sounded like it was a fucking Drake show."

"Glad to hear this, but . . . uh—"

"Right, right. Not why I called," Oli said in a rush. "It's your dress, your wedding gown. It's ready."

Nora shot up straight. "Wait. What are you talking about? My dress has *been* ready. Like, weeks ago. And *you* told me it was stored safe and sound at the very back of our shoe closet, ready to be messengered over, basically, in the next day or so. Do you remember telling me that?"

"I know, but, if I can keep it real with you . . . Nora, your dress was ready for the body you had weeks ago. Not the one now, six days out."

"Excuse me?"

"Hear me out."

Nora rolled her eyes and nestled into the empty tub once more. "Listening," she said, gritting her teeth.

"Okay, well, over the last couple of weeks, you've been dropping weight like crazy. And I know that dress. The nineteen forties nipped waist, the dare-you-to-test-me, strong shoulder, that deep décolleté—the fit needs to be precise or it will be dead wrong. And you know this. It won't matter about the double-faced chiffon or the silk or gossamer. It'll all just look like some random drapes you snatched from the hotel walls and fashioned into a dress like you're Scarlett O'Hara. You don't want that."

"Oh, and you telling me that I'll look like a fucking rake in a shower curtain on my wedding day, that's what I want?"

"You said you'd hear me out, Nor."

"I'm hearing you and you're basically telling me I look like shit."

"Why do you always go there?" Oli said. She sounded wounded, which only annoyed Nora more since she was the one on the receiving end of undercover insults.

"Why do you always think you know what's better for me than I do?"

Oli sighed. "I think I've said this a million times in the last two weeks: I'm trying to help, trying to be a friend. Trying to do whatever will help you do."

"All right," Nora said. "I apologize, okay? It's the stress." She scrunched up her face as if tasting bitter greens. She had long grown tired of defaulting to stress, wedding jitters, prenup pangs, or whatever everyone was quick to tell her was *all that's wrong* with her. "So, did you make the alterations yourself?"

"Jesus, no! Those gilded butterflies make my palms sweaty. I wouldn't want that pressure. Plus, I haven't mastered silk charmeuse all the way yet. No, I called the boutique. All I had to say was: shrinking stressed-out bride-to-be. They were all, *Say no more.* I took the dress there myself and handed it right over to Iris."

"How did you even—"

"Know your, uh, adjusted measurements? I just do." She chuckled and seemed to be waiting for Nora to say something to smooth out the obvious kinks lingering between them.

"You don't have to do that, Oli," Nora said, after a long silence. "It's not your job to worry about me or my measurements or weight loss or whatever."

"I know it's not my *job,* but it's part of being friends, right? You look out for one another. You do things to help each other out. That's how you do for me, from Night One."

Nora shook her head and looked to the window at the gray gauze covering everything in her slanted view. She didn't want to be dragged back into the past, back to that first night when she met Oli. Her focus needed to be on the future. She needed to think about the man asleep in her bed and about the happiest day of their life just around the corner. She needed to concentrate on the day, down to the finest details—the vows she had already written the night after he proposed, the wedding band she had made for him, the flowers she handpicked, even the dress that was likely two sizes too large for her now. Nora stayed fixed on all of it because it helped her to not think about the deadly vial she had hidden in the back of the fridge buried in a half-empty tin of tahini.

"Anyway, the dress is ready. And the even better news is," Oli said, with renewed energy, "Iris can open the shop early today or, if you can't make that work, she said she'll open up on Monday just for you to come in and fit the dress. I think it'll be perfect. I know measurements and I know Iris—neither thing is ever wrong. But it makes sense to fit it today, so there's time. In case. Do you want me to come with you? Check everything?"

"Oh, Oli. That's nice of you to do all of this, but it's really not necess—" Nora's words got caught in her throat. She sat up again and this time continued on out of the tub, heading for the window. "Actually, that would be really cool. I keep thinking I can do everything myself, but having your sharp eye there—that would be nice."

"Of course. What's a good time to tell Iris we'll be there?"

Nora started walking back to her room, passing through the kitchen first. "That I will have to get back to you on. Not today. Definitely tomorrow." She turned on the coffee. "Can I call you back in a couple hours?"

"Sure, but . . . Jesus, can we just go back to emails already? At least Slack or something so we can chat quicker and I don't have to keep calling and waking you up?"

Nora leaned against the counter, listening to the gurgling and whirling of the elaborate machine beside her, and looked over at the fridge. "Soon."

———

Nora skipped the dark internet back roads and instead went directly to Dawn, begging her to meet at the café *one last time.*

Shortly after hanging up from Oli, Nora sent herself an email on the company's internal system.

> I'm ready to own it. I'm ready to be myself.
> Ready to face whatever comes with it.
> And I'm sorry.
> Café :: 11:30 a.m.

She had held on to her suspicion that Dawn was still lurking there. She was right. A reply—set to look like a bounced-back error message—came no more than ninety seconds after Nora sent the note. Buried in the jumble of characters were two clear words: *'bout time.*

To get ready for the meet, Nora needed space. She lied to Fisher, telling him she had to write her vows. "I can't pour my heart out on the paper with you in the same room," she said, starting to climb on top of him in bed. "You're a distraction."

Because it's Nora, he fell for it. They showered together, and tried in vain to keep it brief and about business. Then he left, off to run his own "wedding errands," he said, and she hustled off to the back of her closet.

She pulled out her black rag & bone jeans. Nora hadn't worn them in several seasons and was a little surprised that they were still in there. She ran her hands through short stacks of neatly folded white T-shirts next, searching for something plain and basic. She was going for modest and bare. In all of the years that she had been dressing men, translating their vague aspirations and narrow desires into concrete style and sophistication, Nora knew that the clothes people wear communicate messages about their mood, intentions, and sincerity. It was also something she saw in practice every day watching Mrs. Bourdain manipulate the temper of an entire room by the color of her dress, the specificity behind her hairdo, or the gleam of the pearls she chose to wear.

266 / NICOLE BLADES

Nora needed to exude contrition for this meeting. Showing up to meet Dawn in the Zac Posen pomona skirt she bought last month would only derail her plan. She managed to find an unfussy white tank at the bottom of the pile. It was by Alexander Wang, wispy with an extra-deep V-neck, so she covered it up with an off-the-rack waterfall cardigan that was also forgotten and pushed to the outskirts of her lavish dressing room. She pulled her hair up into a messy bun high on the top of her head and skipped all makeup and facial care save her moisturizer. Nora layered it on thick so as to appear less dewy, more sweaty.

She removed the David Yurman double-drop gold and diamond earrings that she had forgotten to take out last night before she and Fisher fell into bed, greedy and grabbing at each other. And she was sure to leave her engagement ring where it was: on an antique vintage mirror tray atop her vanity along with the Baume & Mercier watch, the Juste un Clou bracelet, the Buccellati Hawaii long necklace, and the staggering Cartier pendant that, like the earrings, were all *just because* gifts from Fisher. And there were more like this in her jewelry drawer. Nora looked at the tray, at her engagement ring, everything glimmering and beautiful, and she shook her head. This—all the sparkling gifts and the man who bestowed them—this was her life, and she loved it.

And she was more than ready to fight for it.

A final glance in the full-length mirror; Nora felt sufficiently stripped-back and muted. Although she didn't like wearing shoes in the house—a Canadian habit she could never seem to shake and one that Fisher playfully mocked—Nora put on black leather slip-on sneakers in the room before walking briskly to the kitchen. She had to do it this way, be completely ready, so that there would be no space for doubt or delays once she was standing in front of the fridge with the vial of deadly potion sitting in her handbag.

She grabbed the sealed pouch from the tahini tin and wrapped it in the palm of a single latex glove, which she then placed carefully in the cell phone slot of her bag. And without a second thought, Nora went straight toward the front door, ready to face her past and future at once.

# CHAPTER 21

Dawn was seated at the table when Nora arrived. She was early, backing the door, sitting at a different table across the room. It appeared she'd already ordered for herself; she had a to-go cup off to the side. All of this sent Nora's heart racing, and she eased back out of the café to gather a new breath; the old one was just snatched.

"Walk away," Nora whispered to herself, as she tried to shuffle out of the path of an old couple entering Bean House arm in arm. She found the closest wall, warm brick, and pressed her back up against it as her head began to thump.

*Just walk away. Fast.*

She squeezed her eyes shut. A vision of her as a little girl popped into her brain; she's sprinting across the crisp green of the Bourdains' backyard, running without any thought of a destination or outcome. She could see her young face—a mix of exhilaration and fright painted over it—and she imagined what it might look like if she were to try that now. Her heart beat louder; she was sure everyone standing nearby could hear it.

Nora shook away the withering reverie and tried to steel her nerves. She was going in there. No matter what, she was going in there.

She clenched her fists and pounded one into the palm of the other. She inhaled and exhaled slowly. She ran her hand along the knuckles and fingers, where her engagement ring would be, should be, and was instantly sure.

She was going in there. Now.

Nora fixed her face, forcing down the pitch in her brows, and let some slack into her tight jaw. She gripped the strap of her bag, slung across her body, and barged through the café doors.

As she approached the table, she sent her shoulders down, back, and took another long breath. *In and out.* She walked right over to the empty chair facing Dawn and stood there, looking down at her for a beat. She knew her face looked sweaty and washed out—she could feel it—and it had nothing to do with the layers of moisturizer she had put on. It was real, and it may have been just the unexpected accessory she needed.

Dawn glanced up and her eyes went wide. "*Daaaamn, Gina!* You look a hot mess. What do you call this look—Deathbed Dorothy? *Gahtdamn.* Is there a vaccine for you?"

Nora pulled out the chair and sat down. "Thanks for coming." Her eyes fell on Dawn's to-go cup and before she could fully realize, she was staring at it. She caught herself and covered her face with both hands.

"Oh, hell no," Dawn spat. "We are *not* doing this. You're not gonna be sitting over there bawling like we're breaking up. Pull it together and speak on why you brought me here."

"Sorry," Nora said. There were no tears, but she wiped her eyes anyway. If nothing, it would make them look more irritated and red. "I . . . just . . . it's hard. It took a lot for me to walk through there." She motioned with her chin at the doors behind Dawn, who turned her head to glance over that way. This gave Nora another chance to look at the cup. "I almost ran off. But that's done with. There's nowhere for me to go. No more running, right?"

Dawn folded over in laughter. A cruel, loud-for-no-good-reason cackle that made their closest neighbors shoot glances at them. "You know what you remind me of? You ever hear about the boiled frog experiment?" She didn't wait for Nora's reply. "It's the story that some politician supposedly told about how if you put a frog in a pot of boiling water, it will hop on out of there. Because, *hello:* boiling water. But, if you put that frog in, like, room-temp water at first and slowly turn the flame up underneath it, the dumb thing will sit there content and clueless to the fact that it's getting boiled alive until it's too late to scramble out of there." Her laugh returned, but it was quieter, gritty, and sounded like it was bouncing between her lungs. "You remind me of the frog."

Nora made a face. "Look, Dawn, I didn't ask you here to insult me and—"

"Hold up. There's more to it. I mean, seriously, please, if you try to boil a frog—no matter if it's scalding or a slow simmer—that frog is going to jump out that pot. See, that story, the politician shit, it's a myth. A lie. And *that's* why you remind me of the frog."

Nora clutched the strap of her bag against her stomach. "Like I said, I'm done with all of that. I'm done."

Dawn tilted her head. "I'm go'n play your role for a minute and ask, *What does that mean?*"

"It means I'm done, okay? I'm going to come clean and tell people the truth about who I am."

Dawn brought her cup to her smirking mouth for a sip and tipped it back. It was the sign Nora was hoping for.

"I'm tired of carrying all of it. I want to set it down now."

"So what does that look like?" Dawn said, swirling her cup around near her face. "What does setting it down look like? Hell, you're getting married on Saturday."

"I'm not . . . I'm not getting married. I told Fisher this morning, just before coming here, I told him that I couldn't marry him."

"Just like that? *Boom:* Yeah, about that wedding, fam . . . Nah."

"No, it wasn't just like anything. It really destroyed him. I destroyed him."

Dawn got serious, her face hardening like clay. "Am I supposed to feel a way about that? Poor him?"

"No, I'm not saying that."

"Do you even know what happened to me after you decided to make up stories about me?"

"Dawn, I've apologized to you, and I meant it. I'm truly sorry. If I could, I would take it all back in a snap. But that was ten years ago. There's nothing I can do now."

"That shit went on my permanent record. I lost the scholarship. My father had to pay back all this money that he didn't have. And I couldn't even get a job to help out because you branded me. No one was hiring me. This little ghetto-ass drug dealer and thief. No school would take me. Not for over a year. And when I did get into a school, it was to some junkyard, international bullshit with all these ESL kids."

"Jesus. I'm . . . I'm really sorry, Dawn."

"But wanna know what the worst part was? Not the ESL kids or the black mark that went everywhere I did or living at the shelter after we lost every fucking thing to that school payback and the legal fees. The really worst, worst part was that even my own father didn't believe me. He believed *you.* They all did. That muhfuckuh said he thought I was capable. Capable. His own daughter, capable of stealing and dealing. Can you believe that shit?" She shook and swished her cup around more. "That hurt. It really wrecked me. My dad, he was one of the last people I would ever expect to jump ship and let me sink by myself. But he did, and I did—I sank right to the bottom."

"Dawn, I don't know what to say besides I'm sorry. And I'm trying to make things right however I can. Trying to fix it."

"It took me a damn near lifetime to fix it. And it's still not fixed," Dawn said, shaking her head and looking off at people straggling by their table. "I'm not fixed. My father went to his grave thinking that about me, that I'm just messy and wrong. So I'm *real* curious to see your plans for fixing it."

"I told you I'm not getting married Saturday."

"So you called off the wedding. So fucking what. How's that fix anything? You'll be still outchea living your white so-right life even if you don't marry ol' dude. Shit. You'll probably line yourself up another Billionaire Brad in a couple months. Still rocking with that lie."

Nora leaned in closer to the table. "What if"—she lowered her voice and started again—"what if you let me tell people the truth on my own, without a ticking clock behind my ear? You don't have to do anything except . . . not bring her here."

"Who, your wacko stepmom?"

Nora nodded.

"What if I don't care about your what-ifs? What if I want to see you suffer, humiliated, smashed to pieces? What if that's what's going to fix it? I've waited my entire adult life for this moment. Why would I short myself like that? So that it's easier for you?"

"Dawn, please. I'm literally begging you."

"See, all of this"—she waved her hand across Nora's face—"it doesn't mean shit. You messed up and fucked with the wrong bitch. I'm the coldest cube in the tray. Thought you figured that out by now."

Dawn started to stretch around her chair for her purse that hung off the back.

"Please, don't leave yet." Nora reached across the table to touch Dawn's hand and purposely knocked over the to-go cup.

The caramel-colored liquid rushed across the table like a current. Dawn scooted back from the table trying to dodge the liquid coming for her. "*Aw, shit!*"

Nora jumped up. "I'm so sorry! I . . . I was trying to . . . Dawn, I'm sorry."

Gillian was bounding over to the table with a drenched rag. She attacked the spill with it. "It's okay," she said to both Nora and Dawn. "This happens all the time."

"No, no. This," Dawn said, switching her finger between her and Nora, "this doesn't happen ever. This is rare."

Gillian looked confused and just turned her attention back to the wet table.

"I'm so sorry," Nora said again. "Let me replace it for you. Blondie, right?"

Dawn settled back down in her seat. "Yeah, a Blondie," she sighed.

Nora nodded, quick and jittery like a puppy. She could tell that Dawn was enjoying this, at least partway, seeing her being so obsequious, the drippy apologies and the "yes, ma'am" attention, the way she was practically groveling, it all seemed so delicious to her. Nora could see a spark in Dawn's eye; it was growing almost as big as her smirk.

Nora hustled to the counter to put in the new order. Hannah was there and she looked as irritated as days before.

"What can I get started for you?" she said, barely making eye contact.

"Um, I . . . I . . . uh," Nora stumbled over her words. She knew that she had to act like nothing were different, like she was not about to drop venom right down her unsuspecting enemy's throat. She blinked back her trepidation and forced a smile. "Yeah, I would like a large Good Morning Blondie and—"

"Hot water in a cup?" She finally looked up from the iPad screen, smirking.

Nora cut her eyes at Hannah basking in smugness, but talked herself down from addressing it. She didn't want to do anything that would flag her or make the morning or this interaction memorable. "Actually, yes. Thanks. Make that a to-go cup for the hot water only, please."

"Okay." She tapped on the iPad system. "We'll bring that right out."

"Oh, actually, I'm just going to wait and take them over myself . . . if that's okay."

"I don't care. Up to you. That will be five dollars even," Hannah said.

Nora gave her a ten-dollar bill and waited for the change that Hannah seemed slow to hand over. "Uh, could I get five singles," Nora said, stalling. She desperately wanted to turn and check whether Dawn was still there, waiting.

Hannah gave Nora the crumply bills and she stuffed them all into the tips jar on the counter, looking dead into Hannah's eyes. "Thanks," she said, with a pinched, folded-lip smile. It was her sliver of a moment to be petty and stoop to Hannah's level, and she enjoyed it for as long as it lasted.

*Unmarly.* That's how Nora's mother would describe someone like Hannah. Unmarly. It's unmannerly in Bajan speak and it perfectly describes the greasy girl whipping up Dawn's caramel treat.

Hannah thrust the two cups at Nora—first the to-go, then the mug.

"On second thought, I'm going to do a coffee," Nora said, and handed the hot water cup back to the server. "Let me just get this over to my friend and I'll be back to order something for myself in a bit."

"That's fine," she said, flatly, and moved on to the next customer in line before Nora had a chance to say another word.

"Thanks," Nora said anyway, and headed over to the straws/napkins/sugar station off to the side. But there was a tall, lanky man posted up, spread over most of the counter space. She couldn't wait for him to clear out. Nora knew that she had four, maybe five seconds—tops—to add the compound to the coffee and be so smooth about it no one even looked at her twice.

Nora's eyes batted around the floor, moving between her sneakers and the wet spots on the ground. She knew the clock had run out; there was no time for hesitation or deliberation. *Act. Act now.*

She turned her shoulder away from the bulk of the room, drew in her breath, held it, and—in one swift but smooth move—pulled out the vial dropper nestled in the latex glove inside her open purse and splashed five drips into the coffee mug. When she spun back around, she still was not breathing. There was a twinge of something that pushed against the walls of her lungs. But with her first sure step back toward the table, Nora finally exhaled. She kept her face even, not allowing for even a shiver along her spine, and stepped quickly over to Dawn. She gently rested the mug down in front of her.

"Thanks for the coffee," Dawn said, sounding as if it caused her pain to do so.

"Don't mention it." Nora sat down on the literal edge of the seat.

Dawn raised the mug to her lips and paused. "What . . . you're not having anything?"

Nora shook her head. "My nerves are shot. Can't eat." She fixed her stare on the cup, unable to bring herself to look beyond it at Dawn's face or eyes.

"Always precious."

Nora dug her fingernails into her bouncing leg under the table, watching for Dawn to sip the spiked coffee.

She blew through the steam coming off the mug. "Tell you what," Dawn said, moving the cup back a space from right under her lips, "I'll let you have your big reveal moment. I'll call off the stepmom, and you can tell your people that you're not really their people or whatever. You do it on your own this week. But just this week. After that, it's my turn to hit the stage."

"I . . . I don't know what to say . . ."

"Me either," Dawn said, and drank from the cup. "I guess I'm feeling generous . . . or maybe it's this fancy coffee."

Nora nodded, trying to stifle the curl of a smile scratching at her cheek. "Thank you, Dawn. I can't tell you how much I appreciate this. Thank you." She stood up and nodded again. "I'll be in touch, I guess."

Dawn's smirk spread along the side of her smooth face. "Or I will," she said, dipping her nose back into the mug.

Nora looked at her this time, studying her features for a beat. "Good-bye, Dawn," she said, with a grit to her voice. And she walked away, never once looking back at the dying woman she left in her wake.

# Chapter 22

Jenna stepped into the low buzz of the room and floated a look at Nora. "Uh, he wants to talk to you."

Nora turned to the stylist touching up her hair. "Can you give us a minute?" she asked him sweetly.

"Of course," he said, and nudged his hovering assistant. "Let's step out," he said in hushed tones to the young woman dressed in all black.

Once they cleared the room, Nora turned her body in the seat, angling as best she could, without disturbing her gown, toward her best friend. "Why?"

Jenna stepped in closer. "Why what, hon?"

"Did he tell you why he wants to talk to me?"

"Yeah, totally. He stood there and told me everything he plans to say to you down to the last syllable." Jenna rolled her eyes with full drama. "Jesus, I don't know why. He came looking for me and said he needs to talk to you. *Needs* to."

The old churn that Nora thought she had lost for good returned to her stomach with a vengeance. She swallowed hard, but more saliva filled in after each gulp. She turned to look at herself in the lit mirror of the dressing table. Her face was perfect, right down to the nude color on her lips. She glanced down at the cluster of gilded butterflies gathered at her waist beneath the plunging décolleté—the ones handcrafted in the atelier of Maison Lemarié, makers of the famous Chanel camellias. The spectacular, golden flit of wings and shimmer caught the light of the warm bulbs around the mirror and launched an array of twinkles. She looked back over at Jenna and let out a heavy sigh. "But what does he want to say to me? I mean, now—twenty minutes before I walk down the aisle?" Nora couldn't mask the uneasiness. She simply didn't know how.

"Hey, hey," Jenna said, shaking her head and taking a few more steps toward Nora. "That whole bad luck thing is a myth. No facts at all. So what if he sees you before you say 'I do'? Whatever. You look beautiful. And that dress—sweet Jesus. God himself dreamed this one up just for you. And Oli and Iris made it fit like"—she kissed her fingertips and threw it away—"*perfezione.* That means 'perfect' in Italian. Learned that from my date, who's probably sitting out there wondering if he's going to get a taste of my cannoli tonight." Jenna pursed her lips and narrowed her eyes. "It's not looking good."

Nora blew air hard through her nose—the best laugh she could muster—and then went back to concentrated worry. She didn't want to cry, and so she pressed down on the bones in her left thumb to stave off the tears.

"Sweetie, all jokes aside," Jenna said, finally stepping up right next to Nora. "Whatever Fisher has to say to you, he'll say to you. But it doesn't matter. The thing is, you're gorgeous and amazing and brilliant as fuck, and all of that will still be true tomorrow regardless of what he says when I step out of this room and he steps in. Facts."

Nora nodded quickly. "Thanks." She reached out for Jenna, grabbing her wrist and giving it a light squeeze. "Thank you. And . . ." She nodded some more, but even quicker, like a bobblehead doll.

Jenna cocked her head to the side. "Send him in?"

"Yeah."

"Okay." Jenna started toward the door, but turned back and added a broad grin. "By the way, all jokes back to the center? Thinking Italian Date out there might just get a little taste of the cannoli tonight. Just the tip."

Nora shook her head but cracked a smile. "Just get Fisher in here, please."

Jenna left, closing the door slightly as she did. Nora glanced up at her reflection and at the champagne silk brocade cape suspended from a hook and wide satin hanger on the armoire just behind her. She thought the 1940s-inspired cape would be too much for her wedding look, but was convinced otherwise by both Jenna and Oli in separate sittings.

"These white gold embellishments are spare but so striking," Oli said, her eyes brimming with amazement, when she first saw it on a distant rack at the boutique. "You have to have this, Nora. Seriously. These paillettes have been applied by hand with a Lunéville hook. I mean, a fucking Lunéville hook. Painstaking ain't the word. And this shit is so old Hollywood Glamour with just a splash of Khaleesi herself—Daenerys Stormborn of the House Targaryen, First of her name."

"Is that *Game of Thrones* again?" Nora had said, tossing her head back on the boutique's snow-white couch. "I told you, I'm never gonna watch that show. Give up, already, Oli!"

"But she's the Mother of Dragons, though."

"Nope."

"Fine. Don't watch. Miss out on the greatest show ever. But do not, I repeat, do not miss out on this cape, Nora. This, plus that dress? Come on. Pure fire."

———◦◦◦———

Fisher stepped in. He was wearing his custom white tie, Tom Ford black three-piece tuxedo, and a cream ranunculus boutonniere, selected by Mateo, positioned perfectly by his heart. He was dazzling, and Nora stood up, breathless, as he moved deeper into the room and came into full view.

"Hi," he said, and smiled.

"Hi," she said, a quiver starting in her chin.

"Nora, you look . . . beautiful," Fisher said, taking her in.

She was too struck by the fact that he called her Nora, and not Mack, to respond in kind. She looked at him, trying to see through his meek grin to find a hint of what he had to say before he said it.

*What if he knows?* She had kept watch of the local news on TV and scoured the internet and police blotters over the last six days, making sure that there were no reports of a suspicious death of a young black woman. What if Dawn had an in-the-event-of-my-death plan and now it's over, she thought. Now he knows. Nora felt a tremble in her knees and flowing up her legs to the center of her body. "Uh, thank you," she said, finally, several beats too late. "You look beautiful, too. I mean, handsome—but beautiful, too."

He started to titter, and it put her tremble at ease, but the roiling in her tummy remained. "Thanks," he said, and stepped toward her. "Let's—" He gestured with his head at the padded chairs beside them.

"I'm good," Nora said, trying to smile. "I've been sitting practically all day with hair and makeup and stuff."

He sat down and gestured again at her seat. "Please, sit. For me."

She did as told and braced herself for complete and utter heartbreak. Fisher sat back in his chair and stared down at his hands folded in his lap.

"Fisher, I—"

He held up a hand. "Let me just . . . let me just start, okay?"

Nora nodded.

"You know that I'm a public man. It's what makes my pri-

vate life that much more important. And I value trust and loy-
alty above everything."

"I know that."

"The circle around me, it's small, tight, loyal. I trust them."
Nora looked down at his shiny shoes, wishing he would drop
the hammer on her already, tell her that he knows that she's a
fraud. Walking her through the how and why he wants nothing
to do with her felt unnecessary and heartless. "As you should.
You should trust them, your circle—one hundred percent."

"Please . . . let me finish."

"You don't have to do this."

"No, I do."

"No, you don't. I get it, Fisher. I know that you—"

"Nora, I saw you at the lab. I saw the tapes."

Her stomach dropped to her feet. "What . . . ?"

"There are cameras *everywhere* at the Institute, Nora, but
especially hidden in the lab. The other day, when you came by,
when you said you were just stopping in to say hello and then
we . . . we had sex in my office and went to lunch. I saw you on
the security footage sneaking into the lab before all of that."

"No, no, no." Nora's vein was pounding at her temple. Her
throat was getting smaller and she was sure vomit would come
seeping through the corners of her mouth.

Fisher sliced the thickness between them with the side of his
hand. "Nora, you lied. You said you were there for me, but we
both know that's not true. Your whole reason for coming to
the Institute was to get into that lab. I saw you moving around,
looking over your shoulder at the door—you were clearly
doing something you shouldn't be—and I watched you hustle
out of there. I *saw* you."

"Oh, God," her voiced quivered. "I . . . I can explain."

"No, please, just listen. I said I saw the recorded footage
from the lab. I saw it and then I deleted it. No one else has seen
it. And no one will. Only me."

282 / NICOLE BLADES

"I don't understand."

Fisher leaned toward Nora, his eyes locked in on hers. "When I gave you that ring and asked you to be my wife, I gave you my trust, too. When I gave you that ring, it came with the promise of the Beaumont name."

Nora closed her eyes. It was over. She opened her mouth to speak, to apologize, beg for forgiveness, or maybe confess—to all of it—but stopped short when she felt the warmth of Fisher's hand on hers. She looked at him. His face was bright, beaming, and tears gathering.

"I know that this, right now, minutes before our wedding . . . I know it's ridiculous; coming to you like this is absolutely wrong, but"—he looked down at their clasped hands and squeezed hers harder—"I cannot stand up at that altar without telling you this: I don't know what you were doing in there. I don't want to know the details of why either," he said. "My father would always say to us, 'Make your choice and stand next to it.' And right now I'm choosing you. I'm choosing to trust you, trust that the lab was the last of it. No more lies, about anything." He moved to the edge of his chair and pulled her hand to his chest. "Mack, you're it for me. You are what matters most. And I will always protect you, but I have to know if this is what you want, too: me, this life, us together as a solid team, nothing in the closet."

Nora flashed right back to Mrs. Bourdain—patient zero of her sick secret—telling her to do the name proud, to be white and right, just before sending her away to boarding school. Back then she didn't have a chance to say good-bye to her old, original life before being hustled up to the front row of her new one. Back then she went along with the lie because the alternative—being discounted and dismissed—was no real choice. Walking into the promise of the Bourdain name was all she could do. Back then.

But now, faced with a new commitment to a name, a new burden, and new, thick, messy layers to the lie, Nora did have a choice this time.

And she made it, and stood next to it.

She unfolded her brows, relaxed her stiff carriage, and softened her eyes. "Fisher," she said, taking her hand back from covering part of his thumping breast. "I do. I want you, our life. There are no more secrets, no closets. I do want this, us." Nora's face melted into a toothy smile and she lunged into Fisher, wrapping her arms tight around his neck. He pulled Nora to him, pressing some of the gilded butterflies into his white waistcoat and open, black fishtail jacket.

"I love you," he said, muffled and talking into her neck.

"I love you, too," she said right into his ear.

They pulled apart at almost the exact same time.

"So, you ready to do this?" Fisher stood up and buttoned his jacket; his face still winking and delighted, his eyes wet.

"You know it," Nora said. "I'll need a few more minutes to freshen up and then I'll be basically running down that aisle to you."

"My beautiful, beautiful bride," he said, and bent over, planting a kiss on Nora's forehead. "Minutes away, can you believe it?"

"No! That's why I need Antonio back in here to finish fixing this hair."

"You look perfect," Fisher said, heading toward the door. "But I'll let Jenna sort out the hairdresser part for you." He spun around to get one more glimpse of Nora in her golden moment. "Next time I see you, you'll be a Beaumont. My Beaumont."

———◆———

Sitting alone in her elegant dressing suite, Nora turns to the mirror, peering at her full reflection. She reaches for a small pot of gloss from the vast makeup kit on the table and, using her fingers, dabs more color to the center of her lips. And without as much as a twitch in her brow, she says it out loud for herself and anyone else who dares to listen: "Hi, I'm Nora Beaumont."

# Acknowledgments

This story has circled the sun with me many times, and to have it finally out in the world on its own fills me with absolute joy. There are so many people to thank for getting me here, I could never list them all. But please know that even if your name doesn't pop up on these pages, it's written on my heart and I'm forever grateful for your support.

I must start with my outstanding parents, Maureen and Tony Blades, who have shown me so clearly what unconditional love is all about. They believe in me and in every one of my dreams so much that I have no choice but to do the same. I love you.

Thank you to my sisters, Yvette and Nailah. You are stellar. I don't think I'm lucky, I *know* that I am. To have you as friends as well as family, always cheering, makes me believe that no matter how high or far the star, I can reach out and grab it. Also sending much love to my brother and the rest of my family.

To the Burtons, your unyielding love and support over these years have kept me full and afloat. It means the world to be a part of such a wonderful family.

Many thanks to my agent, Sharon Pelletier, for being my calm, wise advocate. I'm honored to be on the Dystel, Goderich & Bourret team.

To my editor, Selena James, I'm fortunate to have a talent like you in my corner. Thank you to Lulu Martinez and the Kensington Publishing Corp. for working so hard for this book. And special thanks goes to Tanya Farrell of Wunderkind PR.

I am grateful to Brit McGinnis. You are sharp, wise, and ever patient. Thank you for swooping in, always with an offer to help.

Special salute to Ravi Howard: You saved the day, homie. Your expert notes on my pages helped reset my coordinates and launch me off in the right direction. I owe you (at least a cold drink or something, right?).

More immense thanks to my people: Saada Branker; Robert Edison Sandiford; Nella Cramer; Sharon Pendana; Charles Bennett; Phillip Moithuk Shung; Todd Wilson; Barney Bishop; Craig Carter; Lloyd Boston; Colleen Oakley; Cheryl Della Pietra; A'driane Nieves; Karen Walrond; Kristin Wald; Susan Harrison; Carrie Firestone; the Sacred Heart crew; my band of supporters on Facebook, Twitter, and Instagram; and my fantastic designer/magician, Wendy Avery; plus so many others.

To my delightful boy, QB: Thank you for filling my heart every single day. That you are so proud of your mom the writer just about melts me to a puddle. (I will write a book that you can read—soon, my sweetheart.)

And to Scott, the remarkable star in this love story we've been writing for thirteen-plus years, thank you for showing me that happiness is real and ours for the taking. I love you.

# HAVE YOU MET NORA?

## Nicole Blades

## ABOUT THIS GUIDE

The suggested questions are included to
enhance your group's reading of
Nicole Blades's *Have You Met Nora?*

# Discussion Questions

1. Mrs. Bourdain sets the lie about Nora's identity in motion before shipping her off to boarding school in Vermont. Why does Nora continue with this fraud long after she runs away and starts a new life in New York?

2. As an adult, is Nora's passing more a lie by omission (she never corrects the assumptions of others)? Does this change how you view her and her deception?

3. Is Nora more afraid of her race or her true socioeconomic background being exposed?

4. Why is Nora so vehemently against having children?

5. Had Jenna ever found out about Nora's identity, do you think she would have forgiven her? Would Oli or Mateo?

6. Did you think there was a point where Nora might actually tell the truth—either to Fisher, Jenna, or Oli?

7. Fisher is a righteous man who is also protective of his family's name. If Nora's truth were revealed—including her infertility lie—would he be able to maintain his principles and his love for Nora? Did you think he was going to leave Nora at the altar?

8. When did you realize that Dawn was behind all of the mischief erupting in Nora's golden life?

9. At the tea party hosted at Lady Eleanor's, Dawn—as "Nwad"—told the women that she was married and lived in Harlem. Do you think that was the truth? Why or why not?

10. Did you think that Nora was capable of getting rid of Dawn—permanently?

DON'T MISS

*THE THUNDER BENEATH US*

**By Nicole Blades**


To the world, Best Lightburn is a talented writer rising up the masthead at an international style magazine. Then there's the other Best, the one who has chosen to recast herself as an only child rather than confront the truth. And after years of covering up the past, her guilt is detonating through every facet of her seemingly charmed life. . . .


Enjoy the following excerpt from

*The Thunder Beneath Us.* . . .

# Prologue

*Montreal*
*December, Ten Years Ago.*

I'm still looking up at the constellation when I hear the thunder. Only it's not clapping through the blue night skies. It's under our feet.

Bryant goes in first. He was carrying the bag. Swallowed up almost silently, he's gone before the sounds can sync up with the pictures. It takes another set of seconds for me to recognize that the fingers pinching my body, attempting to pierce me, drag at me from the inside, aren't fingers at all. It's the cold in the water, the ice, and it's trying to steal my breath.

There's this hollow, haunting, barking sound just behind my left ear. It's Benjamin. Thick slush and jagged, cracked plates try to flood his gasping mouth, but he's still calling for me. The cruel stars conspire to shine their brightest now as I catch a full view of what is happening. I see Ben's face, his eyes. All the familiar of him is wiped clean away; only fear is left. I want to tell him to stop thrashing, stop panicking, to save his energy for crawling out of the hole, and that we'll be all right, but there's a rattling noise and it's building; I can't even hear my thoughts. It's the bones in my jaw; they're clanging together. It's happening to Benjamin too. Somehow he's pulled me close enough that I can see his mouth—still above water—shaking. But I can also see the terror streaked across his face.

I need to get out. We need to get out. Everything's heavy. Everything's slow.

He's pulling me again with that one free arm, this time with the secret strength he had tucked in his thick leather jacket. That goddamn jacket. I didn't want to hear another word about his prized jacket just a moment ago, before the world cracked and we fell in. Now I'm hoping somehow it saves us.

———◆———

"You need to get fly, Bestba," Benjamin said as we approached the lake. "Feel the butter *smoothism* of this jacket, though. Now check your wooly-mammoth styles and tell me, honestly, who's got dopeness on lock?"

I swatted his proud hand away from my face. "Jesus. The worst thing they did was buy you that jacket."

"Seriously, is Mum punishing you for something?" Benjamin said. "Is that why she's forcing you to wear that shaggy shit the whole winter?"

"How much more material do you have on my winter coat, Ben? Four, five more jokes? Because the whole bit is well and old now. Time for something new."

"Exactly. Time for something new—for real. Maybe a little leather might help you out of this whole Wookiee situation you're rocking. But, then again, Chewie could be a cute nickname for you this year. You could work with that." He tossed his head back, forcing that choppy laugh into the cold air above us.

"Shut up, fool."

We walked arm in arm anyway. Bryant took his usual posi-

tion—the quiet apex of our sloppy triangle—and started leading us back to the house.

It really was a beautiful leather jacket. I wasn't going to tell
Benjamin that, though. Benjamin had enough hype men in his
day-to-day. He didn't need his sister gassing up his head too.

"I have a shortcut," Bryant yelled back.

"Is it a real one, as in cutting the time it takes us to get back
to Aunt Esther's," Benjamin starts, and I finish—

"Right, or is it one of your shortcuts that really means a
ridiculous, winding detour so you can check out some random
nerd crap?"

"It's a star," Bryant said. He stopped walking and turned
back to us. He put some bass in his voice. "It's stars. It's not
random, and it's not nerd crap either. It's Orion, the Hunter. If
we head through that area there, closer to the lake's edge,
you'll see it. You won't believe how cool it is, but you'll see it."

"I knew you were up to some shit when you brought that
bag with you," I said, rolling my eyes. "It was a fair, as in games
and cotton candy and gold-coin winnings, not a science fair.
Leave the lab coat at home."

Bryant's shoulders and voice dipped. "Whatever. I don't
have a lab coat in here." He shook his head and kept walking.

"Fine, Bryant. We'll do this shortcut, Hunter-watching business," Benjamin yelled ahead to him. "But when—not if—
when we get back mad late, you've got to man up and take the
hit." Benjamin nudged my ribs. "No mouse in the house bullshit this time. They never suspect you anyway."

I nudged Benjamin back. "Yeah, but somehow it'll come
back to be about me, my fault," I said, growling. "You know
I'm the reason for all the bad things, like some permanent jinx.
I'm the only girl in this entire family, but they act like I'm the
absolute worst. I should be walking on silky leaves or carried
on your backs. Where's the princess treatment? Do I need to
add more pink in my life—is that where I went wrong?"

"Pink won't change the truth: You are the worst. Nothing to do with you being the only girl, either. Don't get the facts jumbled, chief." Benjamin let his laugh loose again, then cupped his mouth, hollering ahead. "Yo, Bryant, we're taking your share of sweetbread when we get there. And your ham too. You've been warned."

———

Benjamin's writhing has slowed to a few, weak flutters, but the weight of him, on my back, my arms, my shoulders—it's drawing me in. My brain shorts out and I'm acting on reflex, instincts. I've gone animal and I wiggle out of my swamped coat. I know my legs and arms are moving wildly, only because I can see them pushing the frozen chunks of water around. I feel nothing. I hear nothing. It's all clogged. When I find that solid piece, I dig in and claw at it. Dragging my entire body along the smooth ice, I hear screeching. The noise fills my head, and I realize it's coming from me. I'm howling, afraid to move, afraid not to. Something from low inside, from the pit of my stomach, forces me to roll halfway over, nearly to my back. Again, the sky's lights seem to jump in wattage and I see Benjamin's head gleaming, bobbing, bobbing, nodding and then under.

My eyes open again. I keep them like that longer this time, open, moving around, waiting for awareness to seep in through the corners. There are more lights, but they're not beaming from above the earth. Bright and harsh one moment, warm and flickering the next, these lights have smeared colors: red, blue, maybe soft white. Sounds stay muffled. A clear thought finally arrives: If I close my eyes, I might hear better, filter through the muddy mix of noises and notes, and figure out why and how and what. A new thought crashes in, sabotaging the first one: If I close my eyes, they won't open ever again. I can feel something in my chest; a tightening that works its way in a rough spiral down to my stomach and up along my throat at once. It's my voice, or something like it—I'm scream-ing. Pain and panic and crushing fright press up against me, and I'm roaring now. I call out to Bryant, to Benjamin and I reach for my brothers. The muscles in my arms are activated— I think—but nothing's moving.

———➤◦◄———

"You're okay. You're okay, honey. You're fine. I'm Sandra Bishop; this is Dr. Delaney. You're in the emergency room at Montreal General. Squeeze my hand if you understand."

I don't squeeze. I don't understand. Instead I reach out again, with more of me. It's not fine here. I need to get out. We need to get out.

# CHAPTER 1

*New York City*
*October, Ten Years Later.*

Coochie. *Vajayjay.* Box. Beaver. Taco. Vadge. *Bajingo.* Lady Garden. Call it whatever you want; the goddamn thing just killed
my career.

When I get to Trinity's desk, she's squeezed into a corner
looking serious, uncomfortable, cagey. This doesn't help. She
had a similar cramped-up pose the last time I was called in to
meet with JK like this, all vague and abrupt. If I walk in there
and see anyone from legal, I'm not going to bother taking a
seat. I already figured out which books in my office I'll pack
and which ones to leave on the shelf for my replacement.

I'm supposed to be lightning in a bottle. That's what *Chalk
Board* magazine called me in that "Media's Top 25 Under 25"
piece last week. Mind you, I'm twenty-seven, but I keep popping up on these industry lists anyway. Honestly, it's just code
for *Yes, we let the right one in. Check off the diversity box*. I'm
totally cute, though, so that helps. *Mediagenic*. That's another
word they like pushing up next to my name. Morning-TV pro-
ducers think I'm hilarious, even when I'm feeding them

warmed-over quips I thought up in the shower. *You're great. You're so great.* I'm not. I'm not great. I'm the opposite. Heinous and horrible, a feral beast capable of atrocious things like that night. Like that night with Benjamin. He didn't deserve that, and had those merciless tables been turned, he would have never done that to me. Benjamin, he would have found a different way, because he was good. I'm not. But people are drawn to me, never wanting to let me go (more from *Chalk Board*). They don't know any better. None of them. Fools. They've bought into it, this story of me being golden, blessed, lucky. They haven't clued into what I figured out long ago: that luck is nothing more than a burden.

It's that ignorance, blissful and simple, that makes people want me around, want me close in their circle. All of this should ease the choppy pulse behind my eye right now, send my shoulders down. It doesn't. Because I know I don't deserve good things. Getting fired from a fluffed-out women's magazine job: that sounds more up my alley.

I squeeze my hand into the shallow, front pocket of my jeans. They're extra tight, pencil-cut, and the stiff edge of the denim scratches my knuckles. I don't care about that; I need to feel the smoothness of my tokens.

For the last ten years, I've carried these two gold coins, clicking them together—sometimes loudly—like ruby slippers. They're not worth anything; cheap tokens from the winter fair. They were my brother's. You would think, after everything, I would remember which brother. But I don't. I just know that I need them. They're part of my story.

"You good, T?"

She shrugs, then nods and finally shakes her head.

Crap. I'm done. How am I going to look my dad in the face?

None of this is a surprise, though. As soon as I went from writing legitimate women's health stories to becoming the vagina reporter, that was the signpost and I ignored it—on purpose. Giddy at being special, held up to the light for my merit, not some unfair fluke, I pretended that I was worthy, that I deserved this goodness. And now look at me: mowed down by the vagina. At least I know how to get a bump-free bikini line. There's that. There's also:

**28 Sex Moves to Wow Your Guy**
**9 Sexy Steps to Orgasm—Every Time**
**54 Sex Tips to Blow His Mind**
**101 BEST SEX TIPS EVER**
**32 Dirty-Girl Sex Tricks to Drive Him Crazy**
**The 7 Secrets to Bigger, Bolder Orgasms**

All of this is intel that will help me after I get fired today. Clearly.

Fuck this. The vagina will not do me in. It can't. I need to play this thing arrogant, like there's no possible way I could have made another misstep in print.

I pull my posture up, drop the befuddlement, and add some certainty to my voice. "So, it's two o'clock," I say to Trinity. "Just go on in?"

She's moving her head in an almost circular nod. Trinity doesn't want to answer me and she definitely doesn't want to look at me. I try to read her jerky movements anyway. Trinity Windsong Cohen (yes, real) is the worst with secrets. All three of my promotions were spoiled by her; the good news blurted out while she was latched to my forearm, in a red-knuckled grip. I move closer to her, lean in, open my clenched torso for any impromptu choke holds and last-minute reveals, but I hear nothing, just the muffled swish of the year-round space heater at her feet.

"Um. Let me just check with James," she says, finally. Her words are run together, her voice barely above a whisper.

The churn in my stomach returns, and I brace for what's coming. Maybe they'll skip the meeting; have Trinity walk me to the kitchen for cupcakes and put me down with one bullet to the back of the head, Mafioso-style. I really wasn't supposed to be here this long anyway.

Trinity slams the phone down and looks right at me. "They're ready for you."

"No cupcakes?" It falls out of my mouth before I have a chance to tuck the thing deep under my tongue.

Her face wrinkles.

"Sorry. I'm—I should go in."

JK meets me a few paces outside of her doorway, smiling, her eyes squinting. That's exactly what she did last time too. It's only been three months since I was here, walking toward JK's tight grin and stepping into a roomful of dead-eyed, dark suits. It was my first transgression, but nothing about it feels truly forgiven. I know they're all waiting for me to put my other pump square in the middle of the shit pile once more, and their collective doubt will be realized. No more waiting, suits, because here we go again—me being summoned to the office, again, for some mysterious reason. Again.

All right. So that this doesn't become Chekhov's gun, here are the three things you need to know about what we'll call The Mistake:

1. Wrote a big cover story about a famous yoga instructor with A-list celeb clients, who occasionally taught classes for the Rest of Us out of her impossibly fabulous SoHo loft.
2. The impossibly fabulous SoHo loft, I found out, actually belonged to her married beau. The married beau is

also the publisher of your favorite celebrity-gossip mag
and blog.
3. I slipped this slimy piece of info into the story. Cut to a
threatened defamation suit, a horrifying deposition with
legal, and a retraction and apology. The PR girls still
spit when they hear my name.

I want to pray or vomit. I can't figure out which will actually
help. Instead, I clear my mind and step lively toward JK's giant
snow-globe office (seriously, everything is dusted in white).
She opens her arms, waving me in like a banking jetliner. As I
clear the corner, I see that no one from legal is there. I let my
deep breath out, slow and quiet. However, the stranger seated
by the window—this gives me pause. Shit. Maybe they found
out about the honor-killing story. I've been working on it in
ultra-stealth mode for months. It's going to be my golden
ticket, my way out of here. Of course, now it will be *literally*
my way out of here. Not golden at all. More like gray, or whatever color goes with insubordination. I'm not technically supposed to be doing this story. But how did they find me out?
These people here are barely journalists; there's not a news-
hound in the bunch. Unless the mailroom guys—*my guys*—
fucked up, and this is what it looks like right before the bus
rolls over you.

"Hey, superstar. Glad you could join us," Susie says, as if I
had a choice. Her voice is a little shaky, odd. All curly, auburn
hair and outsized Clark Kent glasses, Susie is always steady.
This right now is the opposite of steady, the opposite of Susie.
She's practically warbling. I plant my feet and slide into ready
mode. I just decided, this minute, I'm choosing fight over
flight. The only thing I don't like is that my back is to the door,
not the wall.

I hear JK's voice coming up alongside me. "Yes, come on in,
Best. Very excited to have you here."

Stranger Woman, her skin like tempered dark chocolate, barely moves. Only her eyes angle toward me. Already, she's not impressed. She remains seated, even though JK and Susie are standing.

"Make yourself at home," JK says. She gestures to the chair next to the woman. I want to say something strong, unfazed: *No, thanks, I'm good here.* But it's tense enough. I walk over to the white leather seat to the woman's right, leaving enough space between us for our mutual disapproval to rest. "Best Lightburn, meet Joan Marx," JK says. Her grin is a little too wide, eyes glassy, like she just took a toke.

Finally the woman moves. She stands up, her slim pigeon's body bends at the middle, a smooth, shallow bow toward me. Her hair is in micro-braids and her makeup is too much. She's dressed like the plainclothes detectives I see at the all-hours diner near my brownstone, but instead of a wrinkled silk tie to finish the look, she sports a large broach on her left lapel. It's silver and shiny with raised, colored jewels. The control panel, I presume.

I float my hand out to shake hers. The grip is fine, but her hands are clammy.

Strike one.

JK sidles up next to me and touches my arm, gives it a light squeeze—more a soft pulsing—call it whatever, it's her trademark nurture move, something she perfected in twenty-eight years of running magazines filled with disparate, desperate (and often disordered) personalities. It works; my heart rate is slowing. Her moves always work on me: the arm pulsing, the wink, the random clothing compliment in the hallway, and the masterful combo of all three. It makes Janice "James" Kessler seem approachable (but she's not) and makes you feel considered (but you're not).

Susie, still skittish, interrupts the tired magic trick and I get my arm back. "I'm actually a little nervous," she says. "Maybe we should start. Sooner we do, sooner I can get that martini." We all chuckle and mutter things, light, easy, like it's being recorded for background noise on a movie. Stranger Woman is back in her seat, waxen and stiff. Before anyone has a chance to wipe the tight, cheap smirks from our faces, Susie takes a dramatic breath. "Okay. So, here's the quick and dirty on our wonderful friend Joan here: She is the former deputy editor at *Sports World Magazine* and before that she was at *New York News*. And before that, she put in a tour of duty in local network news for a few years. And now here she is, ready to join our team, and we are absolutely thrilled to have her."

I nod in her general direction. JK catches me and her smile dims.

Susie moves through a series of quick, weird tics, the last of which is rubbing the top of her pen. It's annoying and awkward, like everything else about this meeting. If she removes her glasses next and buries them on top of her head, I might as well lean back, expose my neck, give them full access to my carotid artery. Maybe they'll let their New Black One do the honors and have the first cut, although I can't imagine JK being down with bloodstain patterns all over this whiteness. Master move, getting another black woman to do me, though. Who knew JK was so artful?

Another deep breath. "As you know, Best, I love this magazine. It's the child I never had." Susie pauses, looking down at her bouncing knee. "I'm immensely proud of it, and this experience—that's the best word for it, really—it's one for which I remain eternally grateful."

Wait. This is a resignation letter. She's leaving. Susie's leaving and Robot Joan is taking her place. I didn't realize it at first, but I'm shaking my head now as it clicks together. Talk about being clueless. Ten minutes ago, I was positive this meeting was going to be my last day at *James*. I was sure that The Mistake had somehow resurrected itself and was going to finally bite me in the ass. I had every detail planned too: whom I'd call first (Kendra, then my dad), where we'd go to drink right after (Seeks Same bar, the cornerest booth), and what my parting words would be to the entire edit floor of *James* magazine (something from either Jay Z or Biggie—this part was totally game time, but it involved the word *fuck*).

But this time, this whole thing, it isn't even about me. Actually, now I'm pissed. I almost shit my pants, and for what? An intro to Robot Joan? At this point, either tell me how this changes my world here or break out those martinis you mentioned. Make a move, because I'm on deadline. The vagina waits for no one.

"Oh, Susie," JK blurts out. "This is so bittersweet, I know." She turns her head toward me. JK looks legitimately sad. "As you may have already guessed, Susie is leaving us, leaving the company; back to the world of transformative long reads and spellbinding stories in hardcover. We'll be making the official announcement later, but we wanted to let some senior staff in on the news first. And I know you and Susie have such a wonderful relationship, Best, but I'm sure you'd agree that we're *all* going to miss her."

I should say something. That was my cue.

"Well, I am really surprised and also really excited for you, Suze." I turn my chair away from Robot Joan. Of course, it squeaks. "You've been my mama bird here for so long. JK's right: We're all going to really miss you, miss your spirit, miss your New York crazy anecdotes, and all that warm wisdom you share with us every day. And I'm going to miss our talks—I'll treasure them."

I hit all the right notes. Tears are pooling at the base of Susie's eyes. And JK's face is flushed. They exchange warm looks. The sincerity of it all curbs the weirdness that has been muscling through the room since I stepped in. I steal a glance at Joan. She's still in greetings-people-of-Earth mode.

*Oh shit.* She looked right at me. I must be smiling because she is trying to do the same now, but hers is crooked.

Clearly, this android is last year's model.

# Connect with Us

Visit us online at
**KensingtonBooks.com**
to read more from your favorite authors, see books
by series, view reading group guides, and more.

for sneak peeks, chances to win books and prize packs,
and to share your thoughts with other readers.

facebook.com/kensingtonpublishing
twitter.com/kensingtonbooks

## Tell us what you think!

To share your thoughts, submit a review,
or sign up for our eNewsletters, please visit:
**KensingtonBooks.com/TellUs.**